BOUND BY THE UNSPEAKABLE

Unspeakable #2

EMILY A. MYERS

Bound by the Unspeakable

Copyright © 2022 by Emily A. Myers

All rights reserved. This book or any portion thereof may not be reproduced or used in any manner whatsoever without the express written permission of the publisher, except for the use of brief quotations in an article or book review.

This is a work of fiction. Any references to historical events, real people, or real places are used fictitiously. Other names, characters, places, and events are the products of the author's imagination or used in a fictitious manner, and any resemblance to actual persons, living or dead, or actual events and locales is entirely coincidental.

Cover Design by Michelle Fairbanks

Paperback ISBN 979-8-9850282-1-8

eBook ISBN 979-8-9850282-2-5

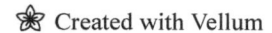

❀ Created with Vellum

This book was written during a difficult time in my life. I dedicate Bound by the Unspeakable to those who helped me make it through — Ashley, Megan, my mom and my grandmother.

CHAPTER 1

I breathe in the sour New Orleans air and sidestep a cigarette-filled puddle as Kat and I make our way to our old stomping grounds just outside the French Quarter. The sweltering June heat ripens the natural musk of the city as the Frenchmen Street musicians play. The sun begins to sink beneath the clouds, prompting tourists to spill out of the brightly colored shops with arms full of souvenirs. They laugh loudly as they make their way back to their hotels to ready themselves for a night filled with dancing and expensive drinks. For me and my girl, though, we prefer something a little off the beaten path. And, considering we haven't seen each other in a year, we have a lot of missed girls' nights to make up for.

Julian and I returned to New Orleans a month and a half ago, after being away for a year. That's what we call it—being away. We were away in Ireland, Scotland, the United Kingdom, some smaller regions of Southern Europe, and even Paris. Thinking of it as a vacation has made explaining our disappearance easier to those who do not know the full truth, which is something I'm working to put behind me since returning to the city I love. It isn't easy, but nights like tonight help distract me from the permanent scars my past has left me with.

"It's just up here," Kat says, pointing toward a lantern-lit alleyway nearly hidden by neon sign after neon sign. I smile, reveling in the familiar surroundings.

Since we returned to New Orleans, my life is very different from the life I previously had in the Marigny. I now live in a century-old double-gallery home in the city's safest and most prestigious neighborhood. Instead of street musicians and colorful cottages lining the streets, I sip my coffee on my second-story balcony as housewives power walk up the oak-tree-lined sidewalk and children play in neighboring parks.

In the two minutes and thirty seconds we gave ourselves before fleeing the city, Julian packed his favorite black jeans and T-shirt, a few family photos, and some of his favorite records into a duffel bag. He managed to grab his violin on the way out the door, but the rest of his things, including the painting that first brought us together, were auctioned off by the landlord when his rent payments stopped coming. The same can be said for most of my things and Kat's less a few items of clothing, a couple books, and photographs.

In truth, it was a sobering experience leaving New Orleans in such a rush. In a matter of two minutes and thirty seconds, I had to determine the items that meant the most to me. When it came down to it, none of it really mattered. I would've given the clothes off my back to know that Kat, Julian, and sweet little Grey were safe. With not much more than that, Julian and I left the only city I've ever truly known as home. And we weren't sure if we'd ever be able to return. Yet now that we have, I long for the items that made it feel like home—Julian's blue velvet couch, his artwork, my bracelets and fedora, even my ten-dollar box fan.

After a year on the run and a month holed up in the decrepit speakeasy, I couldn't wait to move to our new home. And yet it's been the most challenging move of all. I've spent the past two weeks conforming to my new normal, filling our new Garden District home with furniture I don't recognize, antiques, paintings, books, expensive rugs, and even a piano. I've stocked our pantry with food I'll never cook and filled our armoires with essential clothes and shoes. I've created a schedule for home maintenance and even said hello to our nosy neighbors, the DeClairmonts. On the surface, I've become my mother, a happy and hopeful picture of perfection. Inside, I'm still running, running from shadows and secrets I shouldn't know.

Kat and I hook a left and ease down the dark, trash-laden alley. "*Jeez*—I'm not going to lie and say I missed that smell." I pinch my nose closed as a rat the size of a football scurries past Kat.

"*Ah!*" she squeals, nearly falling in her mint-green dress and matching heels.

"I told you not to wear those shoes."

"They go with my outfit."

"How about vomit? Does that go with your outfit too? Because it almost became your main accessory."

"*Almost*, being key," she says, stretching her arms out for extra balance as she tiptoes past human waste to the entrance. I roll my eyes, following behind her in my all-black ensemble with matching black boots.

Inside Midnight Moon, our favorite karaoke bar, the space glows with blue and purple mood lighting and electric wall art. It's less crowded than your typical New Orleans hotspot on a Saturday night, which is exactly why Kat and I started coming here sophomore year. Well, that and the strong beverages and lenient bartenders.

"Hasn't changed a bit," I say with a smile. Kat returns my look of glee as we take a moment to treasure our secret spot.

From what she tells me, she and Demetri enjoyed their time away. They went to New York City for a bit and then to visit Kat's mom in Alabama. He proposed there, and she said yes. Her oval-cut diamond ring glitters on her dainty finger, despite the dim lighting surrounding us. That—that is exactly why Julian and I decided to return to New Orleans, to live life surrounded by friends and family.

Kat's engagement ring is a shining symbol of hope. Each time I look at it, my hope is renewed, hope that things really will be better this time. Hope that we can all live free from the brotherhood's wrath. Hope that Julian and I can take the next step in our own relationship. And yet...

"I'm going to get us a table close to the stage. Do you want to grab the first round?"

"Um, yeah," I say, coming to.

I've been doing that a lot lately, zoning out. I suppose because there is more on my mind than ever. My role in the investigation against the brotherhood was kept private. Only the few policemen and agents I worked with directly know my identity. Still, that accompanied with my father's testimony has been enough to keep me awake at night for fear of the brotherhood's retaliation for the past year.

I thought it would get better when we returned. I thought being surrounded by familiar places and the people I love would help quiet my fears. But, like I said, my life is nothing like the one I once had before my assault, before the brotherhood. I lie awake at night afraid to fall asleep. Behind closed eyes, I see my greatest fears play out like a movie. Not knowing who your enemies are is the hardest part. It could be anyone. The very people you're supposed to trust to protect you could be plotting your death. Kat knows my past has forever changed me. But she doesn't know how deep my struggles are. Perhaps her ignorance is what's made the past few days such a great distraction. But even distractions run their course.

At times, being away felt like an escape. For the first time since graduating high school, I wasn't working. I didn't set an alarm. I had zero bills or responsibilities. Well, my only responsibility was to stay alive. In some ways, the simplicity felt nice. And then, I was reminded that being away wasn't a choice. It wasn't an escape. Rather, it was a race. From one city to the next, we would erase any trace of our existence to avoid being followed. And we managed to stay one step ahead.

Not once in our full year abroad did we encounter the brotherhood. A few pickpockets and drunkards looking for a fight, sure. But nothing we couldn't handle. Still, every day I live in fear of a possible attack. That is why I wear boots. That is why I keep a knife in my purse. That is why I scan every room I enter, noting the entrances and places for a possible attack. Like the bathrooms up ahead located just behind the black velvet stage curtains. Or the lounge zones to my left and right. Couches and upholstered chairs in dark corners conveniently located next to the exit.

My cheeks turn cold as I realize my vulnerable position. Quickly, I move from the landing to the crowded bar, squeezing between two women wearing sparkly dresses. They smell of sharp perfume and whiskey. It makes me long for Julian's simple, clean scent.

Mason contacted us shortly after our return to New Orleans. I was sure to omit Mason from the Club Gent video coverage and our statement to the police after Beaux's death. I wanted to give him and Julian a chance at a proper goodbye before Mason turned himself in for his crimes against women. My efforts, along with the virus that erased all digital evidence against the brotherhood, has kept Mason's involvement with the organization a secret. And after my father was murdered in prison for agreeing to testify against the brotherhood, we know that if Mason turns himself in, he'll be signing his own death warrant. Still, it isn't safe for us to have a relationship. His access to the brotherhood and ability to alert us to any plots against us is what gave us the confidence we needed to return home. Yet, it's also the thing that makes having a relationship with him a risk for both me and Julian. I don't trust that the brotherhood doesn't know of my involvement in the investigation against them, despite the efforts taken by the FBI to keep my name private. But if there is even the slightest chance that the brotherhood isn't aware of me and Julian, we can't make it easier for them to find out by being in Mason's life. Mason made it clear—there is no escaping the brotherhood, even though he wants nothing to do with them. And so, Julian is in LA saying goodbye to the only family he has left.

"Two Midnight Moonshines," I call over the cackles of my fellow patrons.

"Just a second," the bartender says. I nod, ignoring the elbow I just took to the abdomen from Sparkle Queen number two.

I try my best not to blame myself. I tell myself Julian is a grown man capable of making his own choices. And, despite every reason not to, he's chosen to be with me. But I'd be lying if I said it was easy, watching the man you love light up when he hears his brother's voice for the first time in a year. And then, watch that light leave him the second he clicks *End Call*.

I suppose neither one of us is getting the fresh start we wanted. Still—I turn to find Kat sitting front and center. Her strawberry curls are teased to perfection. Her ring finger glistens in the dark club as she texts Demetri. It's almost as bright as her smile. Maybe things are changing, but maybe not all change is bad. And maybe, just maybe, Julian and I will find that sparkle too.

I turn back to the bar to see two Midnight Moonshines sitting before me. I bite my lip, scanning the bar for watchful eyes. I know I'm being paranoid but...

"Excuse me, sir?"

"Yes?" The bartender approaches.

"Would you mind remaking these?"

His dark brows crinkle. "Is there something wrong?" he asks, leaning forward to inspect the drinks.

"No. It's just, I like to be handed my drink. It only takes a couple seconds for certain powders to dissolve, if you know what I mean."

He looks confused for a moment. Of course, men don't have to take the same precautions as women. But brotherhood or not, date rape is real and not something I need to add to my résumé.

"Oh! Of course," he says, my concern finally dawning on him. "Just a second." I nod, watching him closely as he reprepares Kat's and my drinks.

"You didn't."

"I did." Kat sashays back to our table, fresh from the DJ booth. She's just signed us up for the next spot on the karaoke roster. Against my wishes, I might add.

"I told you I didn't want to."

"And I told you too bad." Kat smiles as she sips on her third

Midnight Moonshine. "Besides, who goes to a karaoke bar and doesn't sing karaoke?"

"*We do*," I say, motioning between us. "In all the years we've come here, we've only sung twice. Once on a dare and once—"

"When you were trying to impress that guy from your communications class," Kat blurts out.

"Yes, well, I rest my case," I mumble, taking another sip of my drink.

"Oh, come on. It's been ages since we've had a night like this. And, since we only mark special occasions with a song, tonight fits the bill."

"Your wedding, of course." Kat's demeanor shifts from giggly to quiet. I squint my eyes. "*Kat?*" Kat shifts in her seat and sets her drink down for the first time tonight. My heart feels heavy in my chest as the surrounding air thickens. What isn't she telling me?

"My wedding *is* a special occasion, but not the one I was referring to," Kat admits.

"Okay…so, what were you referring to?" I lean in so I can hear her over the brunette belting "*My Heart Will Go On.*"

Kat drops her eyes to the table. "I've been meaning to tell you, but we were having so much fun. This past week with me staying with you while Julian has been away, it felt like old times."

She's right. Her company this week has been the only thing about New Orleans that's felt like home since my return. As much as I've missed Julian, I've enjoyed every second with Kat. I don't want it to come to an end. But something tells me it's about to.

"Emma." Her blue eyes meet mine. "After the wedding, Demetri and I are moving to Alabama to be near my mom. With Julian returning tomorrow and the wedding just two weeks away, this really is our last hurrah, at least in this sense. I…I'm sorry to tell you like this. I just…I just wanted us to enjoy our time and—"

"We did," I say, sitting up straight as if my posture will help me better process this news. No such luck. Separate houses, sure. But separate states? I don't know if I'm ready for that, not again.

"Emma?" Kat looks at me. Worry contorts her features. It's then that I realize I've been processing a bit too long.

"It's…it's okay," I say then. "It's more than okay. It's amazing that you and Demetri have decided where you'll put down roots." I nod, more to myself than to her. "I just…I feel like I just got you back. I don't want to lose you again."

Kat smiles and reaches her hand out across the table. I take it and cherish her touch. "You never lost me, Emma. And you never will." She squeezes, and we let go to wipe the tears from our eyes. "And Alabama is only a couple hours away. You and Julian will visit all the time and so will we. I know it's sad and hard, but I feel like after this past year, we were never going to be able to go back to how things were. The bond that you and Julian developed while away, that's the bond that's going to carry you through the hard times. Just like the bond I have with Demetri is what carries me. I mean, you must know what I mean."

"No, you're right," I say, taking a deep breath. "I know what you mean, it's just… When we decided to come back, I had this dream that things would be like they used to, with slightly different living arrangements. But so much has changed, Kat. Not just this. It's everything. Living in the Garden District in that big house—I don't fit in there. I went from having Mr. Turnip and Julian as neighbors to now this forty-five-year-old couple who nitpicks over every little thing. I mean, when our furniture was delivered, the woman sat on her front porch all day just to make sure no one nicked her rosebush. And all those rooms, am I supposed to fill them with babies? Because I barely know how to take care of myself." I shake my head, pressing my lips together as I feel on the verge of saying too much. Kat's face shifts with understanding. "I just... I thought things were going to be different."

Kat takes a deep breath and appears to consider her next words carefully. "You don't know how to take care of yourself or...you don't know how to protect yourself?" Kat's question twists my insides as she sees straight through my tantrum. "You thought things were going to be different, as in you thought coming back here would mean you weren't afraid anymore. That you've taken back control. They can no longer hurt you. But that's not true, is it?"

I cross my arms over my chest, not wanting to have this conversation. This is why I haven't told her about—

"I know you've been having nightmares again. I hear you, every night."

"Okay, Kat, stop."

"I'm sorry, it's just... I didn't say anything this week because I thought you would. But now it's obvious you were never planning to."

"Say what exactly?"

"That you're struggling. You blame it on the house and the neighborhood and Hell, after tonight, you'll probably blame it on me leaving. Anything to keep you from accepting the truth that you're afraid."

"Of course I'm afraid." I lean forward in my chair, and shift my eyes into slits. "How could I not be? Even if by some miracle the brotherhood doesn't know of my involvement in the investigation against them, my father outed them. That alone puts a target on my back, even though he did it to save me. And then there's Beaux. Just because he's dead doesn't mean I don't…"

"Don't what?" I shake my head. "Don't what? Emma, talk to me."

"*Why?*" I yell, though thankfully the music is loud enough I don't draw any unwanted attention.

"Because I'm your best friend, Emma. And I'm leaving. And I want to make sure you're going to be okay. And I want you to know that even though we aren't living together anymore, it doesn't mean you can't talk to me. It doesn't mean I don't want to know every little thing that goes through your mind. And I've seen you lying to yourself and to everyone else since you've been back. And I don't get it. And it hurts me because I feel like…"

Kat pauses to compose herself. I can practically feel the burn of her throat as she fights back tears. Seeing her like this pulls my arms from my chest and softens my heart as the reality of her leaving sinks in. She won't be here anymore. She won't help me get ready. We won't stay up all night watching *Gilmore Girls*. She won't annoy the Hell out of me, like she's doing now. The thought draws my lips up into a smile, a genuine smile. The movement feels foreign on my face and that's when I say,

"It's not you, Kat. I'm not intentionally keeping things from you. Well, okay, I am. But it's not because I don't trust you or love you or for a second that you're not my best friend," I assure her. She nods.

"Then why? Why have you been pretending to be okay? I thought you were past that. You made so much progress before you left. And when you told me you were happy, I believed you. But…"

I take a deep breath and get lost in my own mind as Kat continues, the facade I've built over the last few days crumbling.

I did say I was happy. As we sat on the porch swing, finally reunited for the first time in a year, everything I said was the honest truth. I was honest when I said I was happy, happy to be home after all the time that's passed, happy to have a second chance at life with Julian. And when I said Beaux didn't break me, I meant that. He didn't. But... Sometimes, it feels like I am broken, like the happiness I crave will only come in small waves, dancing away in the night right before I fall asleep. Sometimes it feels like I'm never going to escape him and the brotherhood and the psychological scars they've left me with. And as I said before, things have only gotten worse since we've been back.

Nothing around me is familiar, and yet everything is familiar in the worst possible way. Not only is my home foreign to me, I can't walk past Jackson Square without seeing Beaux press me against the oak tree, touching me and threatening me. I cry for help, and no one comes. And Lucid—I can't visit the place that was once my haven without replaying the morning of Beaux's death over and over in my head. The feeling of his arms around me, pulling me away from Julian as he slept. The sharp smell of gasoline. It gives me a headache just thinking about it. The gun aimed at my head. The bullet hole in the ceiling. The broken records as Julian and Beaux wrestled. And the blood. So much blood.

"Emma!" Kat reaches out, steadying my body as I rock back and forth in my chair. This is why I don't talk about it. I can't think about it without it consuming me. And I can't go there, not here, not now. As I focus on Kat, the glossiness leaving my eyes, she removes her hand from mine. We're both quiet for a moment, giving me a chance to collect myself. I finish off my drink, relax in my chair, and... "Emma, talk to me."

I shake my head and look around the club, taking in the smiling faces and the simple moments of drunken joy surrounding me. I wish I could be like that, living in ignorant bliss. But I've been enlightened all too well to the horrors of the world and monstrous men. The truth is, I've been desperate to be reunited with my past life because it's the only life I've known without this enlightenment, without PTSD and anxiety and paranoia and the crippling fear of the brotherhood's retaliation. But what the past six weeks have shown me is, I can never go back. I can never truly escape the scars of my past.

As Kat watches me in anticipation, I know I can't keep the truth in any longer. I part my lips and—

"Up next, Emma and Kat!" the DJ announces. The crowd cheers. Kat slumps in her seat. I can't help but smile.

"I told you you shouldn't have signed us up." I stand, never more thankful to sing karaoke.

CHAPTER 2

We couldn't have picked a more perfect song than "Last Hurrah" by Bebe Rexha to mark the end of one chapter and the beginning of a new one. I know it hasn't hit me yet, what life will be like with Kat no longer living in the same city. I know there will come a day where I'll need her, and she won't be there, not in the way I need her to be. And so, in true Emma fashion, I shove my demons to the darkest corners of my mind, and I do my best to enjoy the moment. The old Emma and Kat deserve it, a last hurrah.

As we sing and dance around the stage, Kat's worry leaves her, and she too gets lost. Lost in the memories of us. I know she isn't dying. And she's right, the drive to her new place in Alabama will probably be easier than going to my hometown of Presley. But it'll be different and I'm not sure how much more different I can take.

When Julian and I were away, each day was different. Different hotels, different names. Julian even covered his most visible tattoos with makeup. Anything repetitive or trackable was dangerous, but we made the best of it. Whether it be a homemade breakfast, a long, romantic walk, or an intimate excursion like visiting a French piano bar, we made time for pockets of happiness in each place we visited. It was the only way to survive. But as I've said a million times before, surviving isn't living.

Julian and I were as happy as we could be, given the circumstances, but I wanted more. I wanted memories, not just of me and Julian, but with my mom, Kat, and my sister. I wanted us to get married and run the business we both love. I wanted a full life, not one controlled by the brotherhood or my past trauma. But, now that we're back, it's clear—the brotherhood's hold over me is stronger than ever. The dreams I have seem so fragile, like at any moment the brotherhood can swoop in and take me away from Julian. Or worse, they can take him away from me.

So much for keeping my demons at bay. I stumble over my words as the song comes to an end. Worry returns to Kat's face, and I know I can't put off telling her the truth much longer. I give her a half smile and place the microphone back on the stand. As my eyes drift to the crowd, my heart stops, and I feel my legs turn to Jell-O.

"Emma, are you coming?" Kat calls as she exits the stage. I hear her but I can't move. I squint, certain my eyes are betraying me what with the blinding stage lights. And yet, I can feel it in my bones as my skin turns cold to the touch. "Emma?" My lips part. I lean on the mic stand for support though I know it's not strong enough to hold me. And then, dizziness takes over and I feel my legs give out beneath me.

"I DON'T KNOW. She just fainted. Wait. Wait. I think she's waking up."

I wince, bringing my hand to my head. It feels as if it's about to split open. Maybe it already has. "Ah…" I moan.

"Emma! Emma, I'm here. You're okay," I hear Kat assure me.

"I don't feel okay." Finally, I open my eyes and push myself to a sitting position. "Where am I?" I look around. In the dim lighting, only one thing is visible—the neon e*xit* sign straight ahead.

"Backstage at Midnight Moon. We were singing and everything was fine. And then you just…you collapsed." I nod and instantly regret it. I let out another moan, burying my head between my hands as I pull my knees to my chest. "You hit your head when you fell. I have ice."

Kat places the Ziploc filled with bar ice next to me. I take a few deep breaths as memories of the collapse flash behind my eyelids. The bright lights. The man I've only ever seen once before. The girl who is far too young to be his date. My stomach twists as I wonder if they're still here. What do I do if they are? What *can* I do? A million scenarios run through my mind, and the only option I'm remotely comfortable with is running straight out that door and not looking back.

"Emma, Julian wants to talk to you." I look up to see Kat's phone in my face with a call running time of ten minutes.

"Ten minutes? I was out that long?"

"Longer. It took us a minute to get you from the stage to back here. They wanted to take you to the bathroom, but I wouldn't let them. No way is my best friend lying on a public bathroom floor. God only knows—"

"Okay, I get it," I cut her off. Again, nausea runs through me as images of things I'd rather not remember flood my mind. "Thank you." I know my tone is clipped, but I'm in too much pain to be nice, even to Kat. I take the phone and lift it to my ear while pressing the ice to my head with my other hand.

"Hey, babe." Julian exhales at the sound of my voice. God only knows what Kat told him. She tends to exaggerate.

"Emma, thank God! Are you okay?"

"I…I don't know. I guess." *Am I?* My head hurts worse than it ever has before. Of course, some of that could be caused by the insane amount of alcohol I've drunk tonight. "My head hurts, but I probably just need rest and water to cleanse my system."

"Maybe you should go to the hospital. Make sure you don't have a concussion."

"More bright lights, loud noises, and people asking me questions—no, thank you. We'll just go home and if I don't feel better tomorrow, then I'll go to the doctor." Kat raises her brow at the mention of the word *doctor,* letting me know she agrees with Julian. I would roll my eyes at her, but I imagine that would make me change my mind.

"What…what triggered it?" I can hear the hesitation in Julian's voice. He doesn't want to ask, but he can't help it. "It's been months since your last spell. I thought things were getting better."

Things were getting better, sort of. But then I saw him, the man who approached me the night I infiltrated Club Gent. What was only a brief interaction was enough for his face to be forever seared into my memory. I imagine he was questioned by the police, maybe even the FBI. But because my body camera only caught him grabbing a drink from a serving tray, they couldn't arrest him, as is evident by his presence here tonight.

I hear myself exhale in frustration as my anxiety becomes more prominent than my pain. "Let's talk when you get home. It's loud here and I really want to get to somewhere quiet." I move the ice from my head to the floor. Julian is quiet for a moment, clearly not happy with my reluctance to share the details of my fainting spell.

"Okay," he finally agrees. "Stay safe. Text me when you make it home. I love you, Emma. And I can't wait to see you tomorrow. Remind me to never leave again."

His words draw a small laugh from me. "I will. I've missed you. And I love you too." Julian and I say our goodbyes, and I draw a calming breath from my lungs. Though from the look on Kat's face, I may have just dodged the easier of the two conversations.

"Emma. What's going on?" Her eyes beg me for answers, answers I can't give her in my current state. I push myself to a standing position, bringing the ice to my head once more.

"Tomorrow. We will talk tomorrow. I just…I need to get out of here." I stand and look around the space. Kat already has our purses, but I imagine our bar tab still needs to be paid. And we'll need a cab. My legs wobble as I try to mentally prepare myself to walk through the club, past the man who, no doubt, plans to drug and assault the poor girl accompanying him. My body is telling me to run, to get the Hell out as fast as I can. My mind tells me to send Kat to the bar to pay the tab while I walk through the alley to grab us a cab. Okay, that option doesn't sound very safe either. Regardless, in matters such as this, my heart usually wins, and my heart tells me to send Kat out of the club while I pay the tab and find a way to warn the young woman that her date is a predator, and she is his prey.

I WATCH as Kat exits the club, silently praying I didn't just put her in even more danger by sending her out into the alley alone. This will have to be quick. From my spot at the bar, which is far less crowded than it was earlier in the night, I glance over my shoulder to check on the young blonde woman who hardly looks old enough to gain entry to the club. The man next to her appears to be in his late thirties to early forties. He has dark hair and eyes and perfectly groomed facial hair. I can see why a woman would fall for him. He's got the tall, dark, and handsome thing going on and is, undoubtedly, rich and well connected. But I've learned the hard way that all that shines isn't gold. Men like him play by different rules created only with the intention of protecting their sins and their reputations.

I turn back to the bar and call the bartender to me as I pull out my wallet. My voice is shaky as I speak, as are my hands. "I need to close out my tab. But before you do, can you add one more drink to it? I also need a napkin and a pen." While the bartender prepares a lifesaving margarita, I use the bar napkin and pen to write a simple message to be delivered to the girl in the Devil's grasp after I leave.

He's dangerous. Get away while you still can.

My insides clench as I stare at the words. I'm not sure if it's the alcohol, the head injury, or the fact that I'm mere feet away from one of the most dangerous men in New Orleans, but I feel like I'm going to vomit.

The bartender sets the drink down in front of me. I instantly pull the napkin to my chest, not wanting him or anyone to see what I've written. I'm not wearing a disguise tonight. If the note were to fall into the wrong hands… I can't risk the brotherhood knowing it came from me. I hand the bartender cash to cover our tab as I stare into the pale-yellow liquid. I was sure to spy what she was drinking before ordering. That way, it'll just look like a refill coming from an attentive bartender. Still, my shoulders ache with the amount of pressure placed on this single cocktail, on this single moment.

I close my eyes, take a deep breath, and, once again, look at the note. My fingers grow cold around the thin, white paper as Samantha Carson's testimony comes to mind.

> *We'd ridden in his car and even though I insisted on getting myself a cab, he assured me it was okay and that he would drive me home. He raped me inside his car, right outside of my house.*

I gulp down the saliva filling my mouth and bring my shaky fingers to my pen once more.

> *Don't tell him you're leaving. Don't let him drive you home.*
> *Just run.*

The pen is loud as it slaps against the wooden bar. As the club nears closing, the music shifts to softer, sadder songs that drunken patrons struggle to sing. The air in the room shifts. It feels more tense as snippets of conversations become audible. The veil of privacy created by chatter and loud music now gone. The bartender approaches me, my change in his hand. This is it. My heart races in my chest as I pray he will go along with my plan, keeping my identity secret. If he doesn't, what will happen? Will the man follow me and Kat home? Will he attack us? How can I do this? I can't put Kat in danger, especially not so close to her wedding. As heartbroken as I am about her leaving, it's the best thing for her. Which is why I haven't told her about my struggles and why I can't tell her about this moment right now. She has to leave. She has to get out of this city before something terrible happens to her. And yet—I think of Beaux, of me, of all the women who came before me. Beaux may be dead, but the pain he inflicted on his victims lives on. Like a flickering ember of a dying fire, there will always be a place inside me that burns with the horror he put me through. I can't let this poor girl be added to the list of victims that is already far too long.

As the bartender finally reaches me, I manage to get the words out with strength and clarity. I tell him to bring the drink to the girl after I've left along with the note, which I've folded neatly to conceal the message I hope saves her life. The bartender looks at me hesitantly, clearly exhausted from a long night of supplying loud, obnoxious customers with beverages that only make them more difficult. Considering how much I've drunk, I'm surprised I'm this sober. Perhaps fear does that to you.

"Please," I beg. I'm not sure if it's the desperate ache in my voice or the fact that my fingers are ice cold as I hand him the note, but something changes in him. He gives me a quiet nod, letting me know I can breathe again. I exhale, thanking him before turning and—

There is a ringing in my ears as my body goes into shock. Coins from my wallet fall to the ground. Instead of their sharp chime, all I hear are the weak yet rapid breaths that escape me as a man with dark hair and golden-brown eyes stares back me. He places his hands on my forearms to steady me as my heart beats so quickly I feel as if it may rip out of my chest. I'm frozen in place despite the fact that his touch is searing hot. Unable to speak, unable to run, I take in his features, determined to memorize every detail of him. And that's when I realize this isn't the same man who's had my heart racing ever since I spotted him in the crowd. His lips move, though the words are still inaudible in my stunned state. I squint as I focus on them, trying to make out what he's saying. Slowly, my hearing returns to me and I hear him ask, "Are you okay?"

I exhale, though relaxed is the last thing I feel as his hands still hold me firmly in place. It's then that I notice his muscles and the fact that he towers over me by at least a foot. I wouldn't stand a chance against him. Mentally, I pray I won't have to.

He then shakes me, dislodging the last of my shock and replacing it with frustration as my head begins to hurt once more. "You in there?"

"Yes," I finally say. "I'm fine. Thank you." I lift my hands to brush my hair behind my ears, forcing him to break his hold on me. He nods and takes a step back before his eyes drift to the ground. Kneeling, he picks up the coins I dropped. My stomach aches at his proximity and the fact that I've overstayed my welcome. The drink I ordered for the innocent blonde will be delivered any moment now.

"Euros," the man at my feet comments. "Have you traveled abroad recently?"

"No," I lie. "They're a gift from a friend who has. Just a souvenir." He nods. Standing, he hands me the coins with an open palm. Rather than pluck them from his hand, prolonging the moment, I flip my hand open for a quick transaction. It's then I notice his ring. It's not a wedding ring. Rather, it's big, bulky, ornamental even, like a family crest. If he turns out to be anything less than the rough-around-the-edges gentleman before me, it'll be a good identifier.

"Can I get you anything to drink, sir?" the bartender asks from behind me.

"No. I won't be here long," the man says all without taking his eyes off me. *Then why did you come? And right before closing?* It's then that my stomach begins to betray me again.

I shift my weight from one leg to the next, making sure I

have the strength to walk up the steps and out of the club, and say, "Excuse me."

The man with the golden eyes takes a step back, letting me pass without any further conversation. *Thank God.* I expected him to be more of a pest.

"Have a good night," he says, though I do not return the pleasantry.

I walk quickly up the steps of Midnight Moon, only turning back once I've got my hand on the door. The bartender comes around the bar with the margarita and napkin on a tray. My heartbeat quickens with each step he takes. I shift my eyes to the back of the man—no, the monster—at the table and I pray the girl next to him has it in her to escape before it's too late. As the bartender reaches their table, drawing the attention of the blonde, my heart quickens but not for the reason you may think. Taking a seat next to the known brotherhood member is the man who bumped into me at the bar, the man who touched me, the man who spoke to me, the man whose eyes are still locked on me. My mouth falls open as my eyes grow wide. He's one of them and I've caught his interest.

CHAPTER 3

I didn't stay to see if the blonde got away. The longer I stared into the golden-brown eyes of the man memorizing every inch of me, the weaker I felt. My hand shook as it pulled the door of the club open. Like Kat earlier in the day, I nearly fell into chunky vomit as I wobbled down the alleyway. We left the club almost an hour ago. Only now has the tension in my bones started to ease as the safety of home surrounds me.

    The soothing smell of lavender and mint fills the air as scalding-hot water pours into our clawfoot tub. I close my eyes and inhale as I rest my hands against the marble vanity before me. The mint is cool against the back of my throat. I breathe in once more, hoping the lavender lives up to its claims of relaxation. And yet, it does nothing to rid my mind of worry—worry for the girl whose innocence was just moments away from being destroyed, worry for the ones I love and what will happen to them if the brotherhood really does figure out who I am. The way the man with the golden eyes looked at me, I couldn't tell if he knew who I was. But the brothers handpick their victims, at least they used to. And if he chooses me, it's only a matter of time until the brotherhood puts the pieces together. And, if they do, one man will be the least of my worries.

I flinch at the thought and force my eyes open as haunting visions play behind them. Standing still won't help anything. I have to get my mind busy on something else. I toss my black skinny jeans to the side and pull my matching tank top over my head. Grabbing a makeup wipe, I remove the remnants of the day. Or at least I try to. I quickly brush my teeth and remove the few pieces of jewelry I've become accustomed to wearing. I do my best to avoid the mirror. I fail. My reflection stares back at me, exhausted and red-faced. My golden-blond hair cascades down my chest, nearly reaching my naval. My thin arms and legs are foreign to me. I suppose all that running took more than just a mental toll. My eyes, green and bright, are the same. It's ironic, really. The things that let you see both the horrible and the great remain the least changed by it all. It's like they have some resiliency that the rest of my being doesn't.

Unable to look into them any longer, I finish undressing and sink into the bubble-filled tub. "Ah…" I moan. My queasy stomach and aching head thank me as the warm water soothes them.

It's quiet save for the occasional gust of wind just outside the surrounding windows. I often wonder about the previous owners of our home. In over one hundred years, I can't imagine the lives these walls must have witnessed. Perhaps a teacher or a doctor. Perhaps someone with even bigger problems than me. I guess it doesn't matter. In one hundred years, no matter our walk, we'll all be gone. And what's left will be nothing but an echo in the breeze, like the one rattling the branches of the oak tree just outside the windowpane. There's simplicity in that, in the promise that one day this torment will end. I just hope I don't have to die to find the peace I so desperately crave. At that, I close my eyes and let the water consume me.

"And I won't pretend to kill you," Beaux says, closing the distance between us. "I'll just do it."

Beaux points the gun at me. I say a silent prayer for my soul and close my eyes. I scream as the gun fires. I drop to the floor and cover my ringing ears with my hands. I hold my breath, waiting to feel the pain of the entry point. It never comes.

I open my eyes and find a bullet hole in the ceiling above me, and Julian and Beaux wrestling on the floor among hundreds of broken records. The gun is loose.

I lift my head above the water, refilling my lungs with air. Aside from when Beaux attacked me the very first time, that was the first time I blacked out. As Beaux pointed the gun at me, I closed my eyes and lost myself in daydreams of Julian, Kat, and my mom. I imagined everything I'd miss. As I walked down the aisle in a white dress, the gunshot meant to take my life echoed through my mind, like church bells ringing, announcing me and Julian as husband and wife. I closed my eyes and waited. I waited for bright lights to blast through the stained-glass windows. I waited for an angel to come down from Heaven and take me home. The angel I was waiting for never came. But another angel did. Julian raced down the aisle with a smile on his face. He took my hands in his and asked, *"Are you ready?"*

"Ready for what?"

"To start our life together."

In that moment, I didn't know if I was alive or if the altar before us would open wide, transporting me into the next realm. Still, I walked. I walked hand in hand with Julian because I knew no matter where I was headed, I wanted him by my side. And then—I woke up.

I'm not sure what the correct term is—a fainting spell or a panic attack—but the same thing happened tonight. Only what played out behind my closed eyes wasn't so pleasant. I was inside Club Gent. Or rather, the abandoned space that used to be Club Gent. The walls were stripped bare of their grandeur, leaving behind only brick. The fountain that anchored the room had been removed. It was quiet, eerily so. And I was alone, until I wasn't.

Laughter echoed through the hollow space. It danced across my skin like the edge of a knife. As the men came into view, my body felt heavy, so heavy I couldn't move. They came closer and closer until the man with the dark hair was just inches from my face. Like the night I first saw him, my fear excited him. And—

I force the visions from me, unable to endure the rest.

No one came to save me. Not Julian. Not Mason, like when he tricked Mistress into letting me and Marissa escape. Nor when he showed up just in time as Beaux approached me from behind. He did what I couldn't, what Julian couldn't. He killed Beaux. He tended to Julian's wound when my efforts failed. He waited, risking his own freedom, until help arrived. I am haunted by that morning—haunted by Julian's blood that covered the record shop floor and by the echo of the gunshot that almost took my life. But most of all, I am haunted by the fact that we couldn't save each other. Kat was right. I am afraid because I know I'm not strong enough to protect myself, to protect Julian. And I wonder, if we ever do come face-to-face with the men responsible for this psychological torment, will we survive? Will we save each other?

If tonight's encounter with the golden-eyed Mr. Mystery is any hint, our move to New Orleans truly will be our last. The question is, will we have the chance to build the life we desire here or will the Devil and his demons catch up, taking what's left of our fragile souls?

I wince, shielding my eyes with my hand as bright lights shine through the thin curtains surrounding me. I sit still, allowing the water to settle. The low hum of a car engine rumbles from the road. I lean forward, listening for voices and footsteps over its purr. We live in a walkable neighborhood. And it's not unusual for our neighbors to have late-night company. Still, after tonight, I'd be foolish to ignore the fact that it's after one a.m. and the DeClairmonts never have company past eleven.

At that, I push myself out of the tub and cover myself with a towel. If the car lights were bullets, I'd be dead in an instant with the way they stream through our entire master bathroom. I flip the light off to obscure the view of any prying eyes and make my way through our bedroom, past the guest room where Kat sleeps, and down the stairs. It's dark, save for the lantern that illuminates our front porch and the car lights that fill our sunroom.

There are three entrances to our home. The front door, straight ahead. The entrance off the sunroom, to my left. And the back door, off the back porch. I press my towel tighter against me and retreat from all three of them toward the kitchen. Grabbing a knife from the cutlery stand, I take a deep breath as adrenaline overcomes me.

I step forward as sweat muddles with the water droplets still covering my body. My long, damp hair lies heavily against my back as water drips from my skin to the hardwood beneath me. I move to check the back entrance. In the silent dark, the drip of water is the only sound save for the low hum of the engine that's been sitting still far longer than even a Southern goodbye. As I move around my home, nausea swirls inside me once more as my nightmares become reality. The last time I had to fight for my life, I almost died. I would've died had Julian not shown up. And even the two of us were no match for Beaux's bullets. It's then that I look at the knife in my hand, and fear shudders through me, reminding me once again, it will offer me no defense against the end of a gun's barrel.

With the back entrance secure, I move slowly to the sunroom. The way the car lights fill the space, I know my body will cast a shadow and whoever is in the vehicle just outside our property line will see me. Still, I won't sleep until I know Kat and I are the only ones within these ancient walls. Just as I reach the wooden columns framing the sunroom, the car engine roars to life. I gasp, nearly falling backward onto the sofa. Just as quickly as my home was filled with light, it is left in darkness. The muffler cracks and pops as it rolls by. I stand still, listening for screeching tires or another idling engine. Nothing. The driver continues and soon the low hum of the engine turns to wind and the only light shining through my windows is that of the moon.

I exhale, taking another step back and— *"Oh shit!"* Grey hisses as I nearly trample her. The knife falls from my hand, clanking against the wooden floor as Grey flings herself from her place next to my foot onto the nearby piano bench. I exhale, lifting my hand to my racing heart. After today, I think I should schedule an appointment with a cardiologist. I've felt on the verge of a heart attack more times than I can count. I kneel to the ground to pick up the knife, doing my best to ignore the fact that my own cat disarmed me in a matter of seconds.

Julian and I considered getting a state-of-the-art security system. Paranoia will do that do to you. But, considering the brotherhood escaped prosecution on the back of a hacker, we decided the cameras may be more of an invasion of privacy than a protection of privacy. Hence my knife-wielding, sopping-wet state.

"I'm sorry, sweetie. Mommy will be more careful next time. Assuming there is a next time."

Grey is hesitant, but finally comes to me. I know her hair will stick to my damp, exposed skin, but I don't care. Her soft purr calms me. And I'd rather not trip over her as I finish checking the house. With a little more ease and Grey in my arms, I check the front door and all the first-floor windows along with the pantry and first-floor bathroom. No one would've made it upstairs without me hearing. And since all the locks and windowsills are intact, there's no reason for me to—

"*Emma?*"

"Jesus, Kat!" I jump, startling Grey so badly she flees from my grasp, leaving behind tiny claw-shaped incisions in my arms. I suppose she thinks she'll be better off fending for herself. She's probably right.

"What are you doing?" Kat asks.

"Just doing my nightly security check. What about you?"

"In a towel? You do your nightly security check in a towel with sopping-wet, unconditioned hair?" Kat cocks her brow and places her hand on her hip.

I manage a half smile, knowing all my efforts to hide my crazy from her have officially failed. "Looks like it."

NESTLED among fuzzy blankets and the soft glow of the crystal chandelier hanging above me, I sit on our sofa and sip my chamomile tea. Grey curls up next to me and within seconds she falls asleep. I'm tempted to join her as a yawn escapes me. But just as I feel my eyelids drifting closed, Kat enters the family room with her own cup of tea and a scowl like the ones my mother used to give me.

"Oh, no you don't," Kat snaps, verbally and physically. "You've been dodging me all night. No, make that all week. No more."

Kat sits across from me in one of the armchairs, her damp hair wrapped in a towel. Knowing my hair will be dry as Hell tomorrow pulls a groan from me. I set my tea on the table next to me and lean against the plush armrest of the sofa. Maybe it's better this way. I'm so exhausted I won't have time to overthink what I tell Kat.

"Lay it on me," I tell her.

Kat purses her lips. She takes a few sips of her tea before setting her cup down on the coffee table between us. "Emma, I don't know the right questions to ask, because I don't know what's going on. But it's obvious something is. So, please, stop playing these games and be honest with me. I'm your best friend. I deserve your honesty."

Her words land heavily on me. Knowing I can't let her leave New Orleans thinking we're in a fight, I flick my eyes to the walnut-stained secretary across the room. My lip quivers as emotion swells inside of me. I should've known I couldn't fool her, but it was nice pretending for a while.

I shove the blankets off me, waking Grey for the second time tonight. She gives me a glare, letting me know only copious amounts of milk will earn back her affection. "We've all had a rough night," I tell her. She does what I imagine is a cat rolling their eyes before making her way across the room to where Kat sits. "Traitor." I exhale and walk slowly from the sofa past Julian's piano to the secretary. Kat watches me quietly, her body tense.

Julian moves his hand up my exposed thigh, grazing the silky fabric of my black dress. As the pianist plays, his song seems to move in the air around us, pulling us together. I inch closer to Julian, nestling my head in the crook of his neck. He's wearing cologne. I inhale it, enjoying his scent.

Tonight is our last night in Paris and we've chosen to spend it at a piano bar that reminds us of home. We sit at a wooden bistro table surrounded by well-dressed patrons, all just as entranced by the musician as we are. Brick walls, glittering chandeliers, and flickering candles create the romantic hideaway for those willing to hunt for it. Just up ahead, framed with velvet curtains the color of plums, is the stage. A man with graying hair moves his fingers across the keys with ease. It's second nature to him, just as the violin is an extension of Julian.

Julian shifts beside me, moving my hair to expose my neck. I turn to him, brows furrowed. "When in Paris, do as the Parisians do," he whispers. His breath is hot against my sensitive skin. He leans in, leaving a trail of wet kisses from my collarbone to my ear. I gasp as his kiss makes my insides tingle. His dark hair brushes against me, tickling the parts of me his mouth doesn't envelop. As Julian's lips meet mine, the pianist finishes his set. It's all the better. I think it's time we return to—

I pull away from Julian as a bright flash draws my attention. Sitting across the room is a man with salt-and-pepper hair dressed in a suit more expensive than the sum of my and Julian's belongings combined. His icy blue eyes stare back at me as he pulls his phone down into his lap. Julian senses the tension in my body and spots the man. His legs are spread as wide as his grin as his fingers move quickly over his phone.

"He took a picture of us," I whisper. Julian's muscles clench beneath the fabric of his white button-down. My heartbeat quickens in my chest as Julian downs the rest of his drink.

"If he's one of them, we'll have to take him out before he can report our location," Julian says softly, turning toward me. My eyes search Julian's for answers to questions I can't bring myself to ask.

"But what if he's innocent? What if—?"

I hand Kat a stack of sketch pads, all filled with charcoal images of suspicious men I've encountered over the last year. I say *suspicious*, but the truth is, they were just men. Men who walked a little too close. Men who looked at me a little too long. Men who, through my eyes, were threats. But the painful reality is, many of them, perhaps all of them, are innocent. And I'll never be able to tell the difference until it's too late.

"Emma, what is this?" Kat asks as I return to my spot on the couch. I pull the blankets over my legs once more and take another sip of my tea.

"Those are the faces of men I've encountered over the last year. Men who I thought were members of the brotherhood."

Kat's eyes move between me and the sketches. There's over one hundred of them. None of them have names. Just basic details jotted on the side like where I saw them and identifiers that may help me spot them again. I call them all Mr. Mystery, just like the man I encountered tonight.

"Jesus, Emma." Kat's eyes widen in horror as she realizes the depths of my paranoia and the scars Beaux and the brotherhood have left me with.

"I didn't lie to you, Kat. When I told you how happy I was to be back, how hopeful I was for the future, that Beaux didn't break me—all of that was the truth. After a month in the speakeasy, I couldn't have been happier to move here, to embrace this new life." I wave my hand, gesturing toward the home we sit in now. "It was traumatizing being there, in the same place that Beaux…in the same place that he nearly killed me *and* Julian. Julian's blood still stains the concrete floor of the record shop. I did my best to ignore it, to push through, pretend that everything was okay, but it wasn't."

Tears fill my eyes as I speak, but I don't bother wiping them away. I'd rather not see Kat's face when she learns the truth.

"I invested myself in this life, keeping busy, buying antiques, doing everything I could to make this house feel like a home. I was running, Kat. Running from the demons that have finally caught up to me since Julian has been gone."

"But why, Emma? Why run from your pain? Why are you pretending everything is okay when it clearly isn't?" I can't hold it in any longer. I choke on the words, unable to force them out. I lean forward, wrapping my arms around my stomach as the pain of the truth roars through me. "Emma." Kat shoves the sketch pads aside and crosses the room to sit next to me. She places her hands on my back, rubbing back and forth.

"Because—" I gasp. "My paranoia almost cost someone their life." I break in her arms as the truth finally finds its way out.

I tell her about the man in Paris and that Julian confronted him outside the bar. He beat him within an inch of his life as he questioned him about the brotherhood. As the man lay unconscious in the alleyway outside the bar, Julian used his thumb to open his cell phone to see if he sent our photo to anyone. Turns out, he owned the club. And his phone was filled with images of patrons enjoying their time. He planned to use the pictures for social media marketing. As the man lay dying, all I could think about was Mr. Turnip. Granted, he wasn't quite as old as Mr. Turnip. But he was an innocent man beaten to death or there about. And this time, it wasn't Beaux who did the beating. It was Julian. And it was all because of me.

That was the night I finally broke. I told Julian I couldn't do it anymore. I couldn't run. Running meant they controlled us. Running meant living in fear. And I couldn't live like that anymore. We thought it through and yes, Mason's ability to warn us of an attack from the brotherhood was the deciding factor when it came to our return to New Orleans. But that wasn't the reason we came back.

We came back because we were becoming the monsters we were running from.

"Since we've been back, I've been hiding my struggles from Julian, from everyone really. In part because I hoped I'd get over them. But mostly because I don't want to put Julian in that position again. I don't want him to become a monster because of me," I cry. Kat shakes her head.

"He was protecting you. And as much as you are on edge, I'm sure he is too."

"I know. But it doesn't matter anymore, because they found me, Kat. They found me and it's only a matter of time until they come for me, until they come for us all."

CHAPTER 4

I told Kat everything, even about the man at Midnight Moon and the girl I hope made it to safety. Neither one of us got much sleep after that. She said she never thought there might be members of the brotherhood still in New Orleans living life like normal. She thought they'd all disappeared to places without extradition in case the investigation into the organization was ever picked up again. And, if I'm being honest, so did I. I never allowed myself to believe the threat was evaded, that I was safe. But, after so much time on the run without an issue from the brotherhood, it didn't occur to me I'd be bumping into them just a few miles from home. And, like all the faces covering the pages of my sketch pads, I'll never know who is innocent and who is out to get me. In a way, I got lucky last night. I was able to recognize the one man, and, from their interaction, I'm almost positive the man with the golden eyes is a member as well. That means I have two faces I can watch out for. But how many others are there?

I shake my head as a pit of warning builds in my gut. We

never should've come back here. But after what Julian did in Paris, what he did because of me, I couldn't go on like that. I just couldn't. If we can't make New Orleans work, I don't know where we'll go or if I even have it in me to run anymore.

At that, a soft breeze lifts my hair and the hem of my white blouse. I welcome it and the small patches of shade the trees above me provide. I'm up early to try to beat the midday heat, despite feeling like a total zombie. I don't leave the house unless it's absolutely necessary. But as I revealed the horror that is my life to Kat, there was one thing I couldn't bring myself to say. One thing I try not to admit, even to myself.

There are several famous cemeteries in New Orleans, each drawing attention for different reasons. From the mass graves of Confederate soldiers in Greenwood, to the resting rich in Metairie, to the oldest and most haunted St. Louis No 1., there is a place for every type of deceased New Orleanian, including the prominent Thomas family. Located in the Garden District, not far from my new home, is a city block surrounded by oak trees draped with Spanish moss. Within the eerie confines of the stone-walled square lie the souls of thousands within sun-bleached tombs. But I'm only here for one.

Sweat beads on my forehead and my throat tightens as I push through the squeaky wrought-iron gate into the cemetery. Past the crumbling tombs of people long forgotten, there is a garden where New Orleans' modern-day royalty rests. Beaux and I once attended a funeral at the ornate Thomas mausoleum. Surrounded by crape myrtles covered in white blooms, flanked by equally as extravagant stone buildings bearing the names of other well-to-do New Orleans families, we laid Marko Thomas, Beaux's adoptive father, to rest.

I can see the white blossoms just up ahead. They dance in the summer breeze, bringing life to the otherwise quiet and lonely place. I stop, as the thick air gusts through my long waves, giving rise to the thin hairs covering my arms. It's as if the souls who take up residence here, or perhaps God himself, are warning me not to continue. I told myself I wouldn't—I wouldn't visit his grave. And yet, I must see it for myself—his name carved in stone. I need to replace the visions I have of him with ones that remind me he's dead. And I'm not.

I continue through Lafayette No. 1 slowly inspecting deformed shadows as I walk. It's no secret the cemeteries are hunting grounds for those up to no good. Thankfully, my inspections find nothing more than broken crosses and rusted wrought-iron fences as the culprits. *Breathe, Emma.* I clench my purse tight against my stomach and pick up my pace. The gravel is slippery beneath the soles of my sandals. I should've worn my boots. But the thought of them reminded me of last night and how close the man with the golden eyes came to me, the way his hands gripped my arms so strong and hard. I was so stunned that I'm not sure I was as disgusted in the moment as I am now. How dare that monster touch me!

By the time I reach the Thomases' mausoleum, I'm angry. Which, I suppose, is better than panicked. But the sight of the two stone angels guarding the entrance in quiet honor makes me take a deep breath and push my anger somewhere deep inside me. I remember the first time I saw them. I thought them so beautiful, so humble as their expressions share in the pain of the families who've suffered a loss. One holds a Bible. The other holds an olive branch. They remind me of the last conversation Beaux and I had. Fittingly, it was about forgiveness. I never gave him mine. He didn't earn it. Could he have? I haven't been to church in a while. Still, I know enough about forgiveness to know that it isn't earned. It's given freely, without condition. I told myself he had to take responsibility for what he'd done. He had to change. He never did. Now that he's gone, he never will. Is that what's holding me back? Is that why visions of him still haunt me? Because even in death, he is a monster? Or is it the realization that me forgiving him has nothing to do with him and everything to do with me? If forgiveness is what it will take to rid myself of Beaux Thomas, I worry I'll never be free of him or, rather, his ghost.

I take a deep breath and climb the stone steps slowly until I reach the door separating the private resting place from the rest of the world. I pull the door open, surprised by how heavy it is, and slip inside. I close it behind me as if leaving it open would allow the souls to escape. I move my eyes immediately to the two lit candles sitting atop a stone table in the middle of the space. They are the only source of movement in the room and the only source of light, aside from the muddled beams of sunshine working their way through the few stained-glass windowpanes. Each lit candle represents a prayer for the dead, and they do not light themselves.

My hands grow clammy as I realize someone has recently visited. Rather than risk bumping into them or any other visitors, I lift my eyes to the wall of internment chambers, searching for only one name. Just to the left of Marko's grave is Beaux's. Surrounded by white marble, a copper placard reads—

Beauregard A. Thomas, June 15th, 1988–May 31st, 2020,
Beloved son.

It's then that a breath escapes me I wasn't aware I'd been holding. I inch forward until my palm rests on the copper placard. I rub my fingers over each letter of Beaux's name, memorizing the feel. The images of us live so vividly in my mind. Maybe now, this image, this reality will be more permanent than any of the others. He's dead. By now, his corpse has probably decomposed. There is nothing recognizable left of Beauregard Thomas. He can't hurt me anymore. He didn't win. I tell myself all the things I need to hear, hoping that one day my mind will listen. As I back away from the placard, a small ember of hope ignites inside me. That is, until memories of last night return.

This war is far from over, both the war inside me and the war lurking around me. Beaux's face will be replaced by another and another until either they're all dead or I am. Perhaps it already has. Images of the man with golden eyes flash through my mind. His dark hair and broad face. His bulky arms larger than I've ever seen on a man. His towering height and undeniable strength. Beaux hid well behind his clean shave, slicked-back hair, and expensive suits. He looked like the perfect gentleman, until he wasn't. But this man—he doesn't hide. He seems like a man who takes what he wants. And, based on our interaction last night, he seems to like the chase as much as the kill. The way he looked at me, it was like he wanted to devour me, slowly, painfully. I shudder, taking another step back from Beaux's grave.

Memories of last night nearly smother my ember of hope. Still, I cling to the last bit of its warmth, giving myself this assurance. I survived Beaux Thomas. I am still standing. I am still breathing. I still have a chance at a better life. And I don't care if I have to go up against one thousand men just like him, I won't give up this chance at happiness with Julian. Until my last breath, I will fight. My anger from before roils through me. I ball my hands into fists, holding on to it for dear life. Then I let the words burning my tongue slip. "I won't pray for you. I won't cry for you. I won't die because of you. I will—"

"Now, is that any way to speak to the dead?" My skin is ice cold as the sound of the unfamiliar voice echoes against the stone walls surrounding us. It's then that my eyes register the light pouring into the small space. I didn't even hear the door open. I close my eyes tightly, moving my fingers into the pocket of my purse. I pull my knife into my hand and slowly turn. Adrenaline courses through me, preparing my body to defend itself.

I work overtime to keep my breaths under control as the man with golden eyes comes into view. He's leaning against the doorframe of the mausoleum with his legs crossed at the ankle. I gulp down the bile in my mouth as I realize I'm cornered.

"Sorry to disturb you. I just came to pay my respects."

I take a step back as the nameless man moves quickly from his place near the door to the candles in front of me. The door to the mausoleum swings shut behind him. Again, I gulp. He takes one candle and uses the flame to light two more.

"One for me and one for you. I wouldn't want you cursed for cursing the dead." His eyes glow even brighter than the night before as he looks at me. I still can't bring myself to speak. Yet, I do put a few more steps between us, inching toward the back of the mausoleum.

What the Hell is this? His words aren't exactly threatening. Neither were his words last night. It's his eyes. Everything about them screams *Run!* And it isn't lost on me that he hasn't acknowledged we've met. Probably because he knows his face is etched permanently into my mind, which is exactly what he hoped to accomplish last night.

"I assume you were addressing Beaux," he says then, turning to face the grave with Beaux's name on it. Of course he would assume I was talking to Beaux. Marko was a saint and Beaux was anything but. I take the opportunity to move behind the table with the candles. It will serve as a barrier between us until I feel strong enough to run.

"Did you know him?" The words scrape through me with fear. Today, he resembles someone Beaux would surround himself with. He's swapped his black jeans and smokey-gray T-shirt for navy blue slacks and a white button-down tucked neatly into his pants. His expensive leather belt and shoes let me know he probably runs in the same social circles as Beaux did. The question is, which ones?

"There was a time when he was like a brother to me." The word *brother* stops me dead in my tracks. I've taken the time his back has been turned to inch closer to the door. But now I'm frozen and I'm directly behind him. All that separates us is the table and four flickering candles. As if sensing my fear, the man before me turns to revel in it. The flames of the candles flicker against his white shirt, making him look like the Devil I suspect him to be. "It's okay. You can go ahead and finish. It's not like he can punish you for what you say."

But you look like you'd like to.

Fear and panic bubble through me. Images of the Parisian man's bloody face race through my mind. Is it happening again? Am I overreacting? Could this man be innocent? He's intimidating as Hell. And the way his eyes linger on me makes my skin crawl. But if he was going to force himself on me, this would be the perfect place, wouldn't it? It's private, quiet, secluded. And how ironic would it be for me to be raped just inches from where my rapist's corpse rots? And yet, he doesn't lunge for me. He doesn't threaten me. He does nothing but make small talk laced with innuendo that could be completely of my own imagination. *The chase, Emma. He likes the chase.* A thick vein in his neck throbs as he waits for my next words. It trails from the edge of his facial hair down his neck, disappearing behind the fabric of his shirt. Another identifier.

I finally find the strength to pull my eyes from his, shifting them to Beaux's grave behind him. I bite the inside of my cheek. Every nerve in my body is on fire as he doesn't remove his eyes from me. He's right. Beaux can't punish me. So, why bother defending myself against a dead man when a real, flesh and blood predator could be standing before me? A fiery ember returns to me, embedding itself in my bones at the sight of Beaux's grave. I get my fill of its warmth and then I shift my gaze back to the man watching me with far too much curiosity to be innocent. I direct the words meant for Beaux at him.

"I will live—despite you."

His lips twitch into a half grin that somehow makes his eyes turn dark. My resistance pleases him. It makes him want to torture me more. But torture isn't death. It's prolonged agony. And with that, I know I've bought myself another day of existence.

At that, I turn on my heel in pursuit of the exit. "Careful out there alone. I know plenty of men who would kill to sink themselves into a pretty little thing like you."

I can't keep the gasp from escaping my lips as his words invade every part of me. There it is—the threat I've been waiting for. He really is one of them. My stomach tightens and I feel as if I may vomit as realization washes over me just as it did last night. I may have been wrong in Paris, but I'm not wrong this time. If I weren't about to rip apart at the seams, I'd be pleased with my intuition. Nevertheless, the sour taste of war fills my mouth. It tastes like blood. I don't spare him a final glance, but I do leave him with words I'm surprised I'm strong enough to say aloud.

"Maybe you should surround yourself with different men." At that, I exit the mausoleum and take off into a sprint, not stopping until I see home.

CHAPTER 5

My breaths are ragged by the time I spot the white columns of my two-story home. I place my hands on my knees, finally allowing myself a moment of reprieve. My entire body aches with exhaustion. Though it is nothing compared to the ache I feel in my heart. How will I tell Julian? How will he respond? I push myself upright, glance over my shoulder to make sure no one has followed me, and then continue down the crumbled sidewalk.

I *know* how he will respond. He'll have us on the first flight out of New Orleans. And this time we won't be coming back. The thought of leaving again, even though this place has never felt less like home, turns my stomach. We can't run forever. With my body aches crawling from my legs to my shoulders, I can't run another inch.

I reach the wrought-iron gate that offers my home a bit of security, push through it, and make my way up the porch steps to my front door. Black shutters rattle against the white walls of the house. As a sudden summer breeze rips past, the gas lantern hanging above me squeaks, as does the porch swing to my left. It won't be long now, and Julian will be back from his trip. I'll have to figure out what I'm going to tell him before he gets here.

When he left New Orleans to say goodbye to Mason, things were so different. We had our whole lives ahead of us. Or so it seemed. In less than twenty-four hours everything has changed. I'm still haunted by an invisible enemy. But now, not all my enemies are faceless. And I get the eerie feeling the man with the golden eyes knows more about me than he's letting on. Last night may have been a coincidence. But visiting Beaux's grave after he's been gone a year? Some family members don't even do that. So, why was he there? Was it really to pay his respects? Or was he following me? The car—was that him last night? Does he know where I live?

I pull my key from my purse as anxiety begins to take over me once more. I unlock the door and— My heart shrivels in my chest at the sound. I open the door to what should be a quiet, untouched home. Instead, my ears ring with sounds of disruption coming from the kitchen. A lump forms in my throat. Cold sweat covers my body. I have half a mind to turn around, close the door, and leave. I don't have it in me to face off with a petty thief. But, even more so, I don't have it in me to face the man with the golden eyes or any friends he may have sent to do his dirty work. And yet, I can't leave. I can't let Julian be the one to walk in on this, whatever *this* is.

I close the front door quietly behind me and pull my phone from my purse. The sound of footsteps makes my legs shake. Without thinking, I cross the foyer to the staircase, tiptoeing to the second-floor landing. After many nights of checking the downstairs for prowlers, I've learned where the squeaky spots are and manage to avoid them with deft skill. Still, as I reach the top, I wish I had a second more to think. The master bedroom is to my right, and the door is wide open.

I cross the landing and enter the guest room to my left. It's empty, save for the four-poster bed I just had delivered and the far too expensive rug it sits on. Hopefully, the invaders have already checked this room, seen it's empty, and won't be back. Just in case they haven't hit it yet, I move across the room to the Jack and Jill bath it shares with the next room over. I lock both doors and immediately dial 911, which should've been the first thing I did when I realized I wasn't alone. I suppose more than my body is exhausted. I can hardly think. Yet, I have enough of my wits to know that of all the times I've imagined this moment, I've chosen the worst possible course of action.

Whether it's the brotherhood or just someone hoping to steal something expensive, the master bedroom is the first place they'll look. And I find myself conveniently located next door with nowhere left to turn. If they haven't checked this room yet and find the bathroom door locked from the other side, it'll be a dead giveaway there's someone in here. If only shower curtains functioned like bullet-proof vests.

I take a deep breath as my adrenaline begins to ease my exhaustion and give way to heart-pounding anxiety. The kitchen threw me off. It would take two seconds for a brotherhood member to see I wasn't there. And what would a burglar want from a kitchen? Almost any piece of jewelry or pair of shoes would be worth more than my most expensive small appliance. Let alone the paintings covering our walls downstairs. My normal plan in this circumstance is to go straight for the kitchen, grab a knife, and slip out the back door to hide in the garage. But…

"Nine-one-one, what's your emergency?" Footsteps accompany the sound of the operator's voice. I instantly turn the volume on my phone down to its lowest register and wait for what will happen next. I don't have it in me to speak, to give away my location to the intruder. But something tells me I've already been found. The doorknob jiggles as my worst fear presents itself. I have no choice. I hope they get here in time.

"This is Emma Marshall." My eyes burn as they watch the brass doorknob, refusing to close even for a second. "I'm at 2603 St. Charles Ave. Please…please hur—"

"Emma? Emma, is that you?" I'm cut off by the familiar voice, though I can't quite place it. Perhaps I'm hearing things, wishful thinking in my dark hour. "Emma, it's me, Mason. Didn't you see Julian downstairs?"

"Mason?" I whisper.

"Hello? Ma'am? If you can hear me, I've dispatched officers to your home. They're about five minutes out. Just listen to my voice. Remain calm. Everything will be fine."

Julian isn't supposed to be home for a few more hours, and there's no way he'd bring Mason back with him when the whole point of his trip was to say goodbye. Still, I…I wonder.

"Ma'am, are you there?"

I set my phone down on the marble vanity and inch closer to the door. I don't hear him anymore, and the brass knob no longer jiggles. The operator said five minutes. By now, it's closer to three. If I'm wrong, I just have to fight him off for three minutes before… Before I talk myself out of it, I move my hand to the doorknob and open the door with all the force I have left.

Mason stands before me, confused, dressed in black mesh shorts and a matching Dri-FIT T-shirt. Relief floods through me like dopamine in an IV. It numbs my nerves so much so I relax into the doorframe, sliding down it to rest on the floor.

"*Jesus!* Emma!" Mason rushes toward me with wild brown eyes, dropping to his knees. He wears the same expression he did the last time I saw him, what I thought would truly be the last time. Mason moves his hands to my face, trying to keep me upright. Everything is fuzzy. I feel myself drifting in and out of consciousness, overwhelmed by the sucker punch of a day I've just had, all of which I endured on a diet of Midnight Moonshine and no sleep. It was only a matter of time until I lost it—both my mind and consciousness. But then I remember.

"Oh no!"

"What? What is it?" Mason asks. I fight through the overwhelming sensation pulsing through my body, realizing that if the police show up and I'm unconscious, both Julian and Mason will go to jail.

"Help me up." I reach my arms above me, and Mason pulls me to a standing position. It's a challenge getting down the stairs, even with Mason's help. But then Julian's tall, tattooed figure comes into view, awaking every fiber of my being. "Julian!" I break free from Mason's grasp and wobble the rest of the way down the stairs, far faster than I should. I nearly trip over my own feet.

Julian, dressed in black jeans and a matching T-shirt, turns sharply at the sound of my voice. At the sight of me, his eyes light up and he reaches me in mere nanoseconds. Despite the plane ride, his black hair is moussed to perfection, adding to his already six foot four inches. My lips tremble as his icy green eyes lock with mine. I'm not sure whether I should cry or laugh. I've missed him beyond words. So beyond, I hardly know what to say. I stand on my tiptoes, leaning into his embrace, and bring my lips to his.

He's been gone only eight days and yet, I feel like it's been an eternity since he's held me, since I've felt safe. If it weren't for Mason, I'd do a lot more than kiss him. But, for now, this will have to do. Our lips move together as if we have one soul, as if the very blood that runs through our veins is of the same source. Call it codependency, call it obsession, call it love—it's all the same, really. The same indescribable feeling that allows two people to tie themselves together in a way that is so permanent, distance is like a death sentence.

"I missed you," I whisper, my lungs finally running out of air. Julian nods, taking my face between his palms. He runs his finger over my raw, red lips. His sweet touch sets my insides on fire. I yearn for more of him.

"I've missed you too, baby, beyond words." I pull my eyes from his and rest my head against his chest. Julian leans forward, nestling his chin in my hair. Intertwining his fingers, he pulls me tighter against him. There it is—the scent I crave on my pillows, sheets, and skin. I inhale his minty rain aroma, allowing it to invade my every pore. He's really home. And then—the front door blasts open, breaking loose from its hinges, as three men dressed in police uniforms enter our home.

"I THOUGHT THEY'D NEVER LEAVE."

"Can you blame them?"

"No."

The police took down my mortifying statement while Julian sat, handcuffed, and Mason hid in the garage. I'm not sure why he felt the need to hide. I suppose Julian will tell me when he explains why he brought him here in the first place. It's not that I mind. I'm just confused. But right now, I can hardly think of Mason, or the police, and how I let my anxiety get the best of me. If it wasn't obvious, Julian and Mason arrived early from LA. When Julian realized I wasn't home, he planned to surprise me with a home-cooked meal. His sweet gesture only makes my mistake even more embarrassing. But, like I said, I can't think of any of that right now. All I can think of is Julian and how I crave his touch.

Julian closes the door to the master bathroom behind us and turns the faucets on in the shower. I can't help but feel a pang of annoyance as I realize Mason being here will mean far less alone time for Julian and me. We'll have to make these small moments count, just like we did when we were away. Julian stalks toward me where I rest against the edge of the vanity. His eyes are dark with lust as they graze my body. But as he gets closer, the lust fades and concern washes over him. "How does your head feel?"

"Oh, right." After everything that's happened since last night, I forgot all about my on-stage collapse, which only makes Julian more concerned. "It's fine. I slept off the headache." Julian nods before crashing his lips into mine. God, he tastes good. It took me a while to get comfortable with sex again. Even after our first time, we took it slow. But now, it's second nature between us and one of my only escapes from the war roaring inside me. When I'm with him, everything fades away. The voices in my head quiet. And it's just the two of us and it's perfect. Julian pulls away then. My forehead wrinkles.

"We have a lot to talk about," he says, taking a step back. The steam from the shower has fogged over the mirrors and made the air in the room thick. My hair sticks to the back of my neck. My clothes stick to my skin.

"I know, but not now." I close the distance between us. "This past week has been Hell without you. And I know there are things we need to discuss. For one, why your brother is our new houseguest." Julian's lips press into a flat line. Oh no. I'm not looking forward to that conversation. "But, for right now…" I take his hands in mine and press my lips to his knuckles. "I want you and only you."

Julian nods. Pulling his hands away, he moves one to my

neck, steadying me for the kind of kiss only he can give. He moves the other to the button on my blue jean shorts and within seconds they fall to my ankles. Julian moves his hands to my bottom, picking me up. My legs wrap around him with a possessive hold as he walks me back to the vanity, his lips never leaving mine. The marble is cool against my exposed skin as he sets me on the countertop. But the sensation is soon replaced by radiating heat and need coiling through me as Julian moves his hands to the buttons on my blouse. Slowly, torturously, he unbuttons them, allowing the tension to build between us. All my sensitive parts yearn for him so much I feel as if I may rip out of the remaining bits of clothing I have. But he knows how I like it, how I like to savor every second of our intimacy, every touch, every glance, every inch.

As Julian undoes the last button, his eyes leave mine for the first time. But only so he can take in the rest of me. He looks me up and down. My toes curl and my spine sits straight. "You are so beautiful," he whispers. And then he places a soft kiss to my forehead, which is now damp in anticipation. This is what I love about being with Julian. He makes love to me and ravages me all at the same time. He protects me and possesses me. He stands both behind me and in front of me. He respects me and loves me like no other ever can, like no other ever will. He is mine. And I, I am happily his.

Julian removes the blouse from my body, sure to graze the sides of my breasts as he does. I push out my chest, wanting more of his touch. But, instead, he takes a step back, letting me know it's my turn to undress him. A smile spreads across my lips and I savor the task, removing his shirt first. His scent fills the air as I pull it from his body. It's intoxicating. Almost as intoxicating as the feel of him. I move my hands up his chest, taking in all his indentations. His black hair is damp with the steam in the room. I brush my fingers through it as I bring my lips to his.

"Thank you for choosing me, especially when you had every reason not to." I mumble the words against his lips. They're so soft, so— Julian brings his finger to my chin, lifting me so that our eyes meet.

"My heart was yours long before we ever met. Neither one of us had a choice in the matter. We were made for each other, truly and imperfectly."

CHAPTER 6

Time with Julian goes by so quickly. After making love in the shower, we ventured to the bedroom. We held each other for hours until Mason came knocking to see if we were still alive. That's going to take some getting used to. I watch Julian as he makes his famous spaghetti. We haven't talked about anything serious yet. We've been savoring the moment. Though I'd be lying if I said our looming conversation isn't on my mind. The fact that Julian is willing to prolong our conversation just as much as I am means that whatever news he and Mason returned with from LA is going to be intense.

As he sautés onions, bell peppers, and jalapeños, I wonder what it could be. We agreed having a relationship with Mason is dangerous. And the way Mason hid while the police were here, it gives me the impression his being here is supposed to be a secret. That or he found himself in trouble in LA for reasons that may or may not be related to the events of last year. I know Julian wouldn't do anything that puts me at risk, which only makes Mason's presence more nerve-racking. And yet, I'm not sure anything they have to say will rival my recount of events from the past few days. As much as I would like to, I can't lie to Julian. When we finally found our way back to each other after the Beaux debacle, we promised no more secrets. But that doesn't make telling him the truth easy, especially after what happened in Paris.

"Can I help with anything?" I ask from my bar stool. Julian's lips draw into an instant smile.

"There are other ways to poison Mason. You don't have to ruin our dinner in the process." I blush. He's right. I'm about as good in the kitchen as my mother is subtle.

"Well, he did interrupt our cuddle time. In this house, that's a punishable offense." I move from my place at the island to pour us both a glass of wine. It's not lost on me that we're joking about Mason rather than discussing his real reason for being here. I cross the room and set Julian's wine next to where he works over the stove. I run my hand up his arm and plant a kiss on his shoulder.

"I'm sorry I didn't talk to you first about him coming. I just…I didn't know how to explain it over the phone. Not to mention, we agreed to only share important details face-to-face. Even the best tech experts haven't figured out how the brotherhood managed to plant that virus. Who knows what their hacking capabilities are?"

My brows crinkle as I see the worry in Julian's eyes. "So, him being here does have something to do with the brotherhood?" Julian nods. The only thing keeping my skin from turning to ice is the steam wafting from the boiling pot of noodles. I turn and make my way back to my bar stool. I have a feeling I'll need to be seated for what comes next. I sit and down the rest of my Moscato while Julian finishes up the pasta sauce and turns off the burners. When he finally looks at me, every muscle in his body is tense. "Just tell me," I whisper.

Julian comes around the island to sit across from me. He takes my hands in his and—

"Three months after we all left New Orleans, two members of the brotherhood approached Mason in LA. They were asking questions about Beaux's death."

"Questions? What…what kind of questions?"

Julian's jaw clenches. He rubs his finger over my palm to try to keep me calm.

"Apparently, some details weren't making sense to them. They wanted to know why he was at Lucid that morning. The fact that a brotherhood member would die in a place of business owned by another brotherhood member seemed suspect. They wanted to make sure there was no foul play among the members."

"Okay, but that doesn't make sense. We told the police everything. That he came there to kill me. That he had a history of abuse. Everything minus the fact that Mason was there and was the one who actually killed Beaux. I mean, Beaux was a top corporate attorney and New Orleans royalty by all modern definitions. The truth of what happened would've been all over the news."

"But that's the thing, Emma. It wasn't. At least, the truth wasn't. We made our official statements in the hospital after I woke from surgery. But…somehow the official police report regarding Beaux's death was altered significantly."

"How significantly?" Both the police and the FBI redacted my name from all records to protect me. But that wasn't permission to completely overlook the horror Beaux put me through.

Julian exhales. "The official story is, Beauregard Thomas was a casualty of a robbery gone wrong at Lucid Records. We all left New Orleans so quickly, the last thing on our minds was making sure the police did their job." Julian leans forward, wiping a tear from my cheek I hadn't even realized had fallen. "I'm so sorry, baby. I know you wanted justice. You fought so hard to get the truth out there—"

"Wha…what does any of this have to do with Mason?" My words are curt. I can't allow myself to feel this pain right now. Once I let it in, I won't be able to focus on anything else. Julian searches my eyes to see if he should continue. Thankfully, he does.

"Whoever changed the official report regarding Beaux's death didn't change the time of death, which just so happened to be before the shop was even open that morning. Because of the speakeasy grand opening party the night before, we pushed back our store opening. Obviously, someone could've still broken in. But that doesn't explain why Beaux would be there at that time. It's a small thing, something someone could easily overlook. But not the brotherhood."

I nod, doing my best to stay focused on Julian rather than the thoughts gnawing at the back of my brain. "I'm sorry. I still don't understand. Why does any of this matter?"

"We've always known that if the brotherhood found out the truth of what happened that morning, why Beaux was there, and ultimately, why your father turned himself in, they'd come for us. But we never thought they'd go after Mason. After all, we've seen the lengths they go to protect their own." Julian's jaw clenches then. It hurts him to think of his brother's involvement with this terrible organization. But I imagine it's even scarier knowing that he's a target. Wait? A target? Because Beaux died at Lucid Records? Things are starting to make sense now in the most horrible way.

"Mason was never our eyes and ears into the brotherhood,

was he?" The words cross my lips as realization hits. If the brotherhood suspects Mason of having something to do with Beaux's death, then they won't trust him. And if they can't trust him, or rather, control him, they'll kill him. Julian shakes his head as tears well in his eyes. "Which means our reason for coming back here was a total lie. We have no way of knowing what the brotherhood has planned, or if they know the truth." I'm monotone as I speak, not giving myself an inch of emotion or I'll surely break.

"He's been in hiding this whole time, Emma. I...I suspected something was wrong when I was able to execute the sale of Cole Creative without his permission. He transferred all of his ownership interest to me after they approached him."

"Wait, you did? Why didn't you say anything?" I furrow my brows in confusion.

"Because..." Julian's voice cracks. "Because I thought he was dead, Emma. And I didn't want to believe it could be true. He's the only family I have left." At that, Julian breaks and I pull him into my arms. Wet tears seep through my T-shirt as I rub my hand up and down Julian's back and into his black, tousled hair. I had no idea Julian was worried for Mason's safety. I mean, of course he'd be worried. I just never thought of Mason as being vulnerable, especially after the police had no reason to go after him.

"It's okay. Shh, shh. It's okay," I console him. "I'm here. I'm your family and I'm not going anywhere."

Julian pulls me in even tighter, so tight I can feel his heart beating against my chest. I close my eyes and allow the rhythmic beat to calm the storm brewing inside of me.

"Emma—" Julian begins but is cut off by Mason as he enters the kitchen.

"I take it you told her."

Julian stands tall, wiping the tears from his face. "Yeah," he breathes. Mason nods, dropping his eyes to the floor. It's then that my heart squeezes in my chest. The past year has been beyond difficult. But having Julian by my side made it bearable, even enjoyable at times. And all that time, Mason was alone. "Mason will be staying with us for a while, until we figure out our next move. It's best no one knows he's here. That way, if the brotherhood attacks, we'll have a secret weapon."

My eyes meet Julian's as he squeezes my shoulder. He wants to assure me that I'll be okay, that they'll protect me. But certainty is the last thing I see on either of their faces. At that, I swallow my fear and cross the room to where Mason stands. "I'm glad you're here. And I'm sorry you had to go through that alone." Mason's brown eyes meet mine and I pull him in for a hug that I hope conveys all the words I cannot.

The last time I saw Mason I was half-naked, racked with anxiety from nearly being raped and shot by Beaux, and covered in Julian's blood. In that moment, he switched into a level of calm that kept me sane when all I wanted to do was break. His actions can and have made him the bad guy on more than one occasion. But I'd be lying if I said his presence doesn't give me strength.

"Thanks, Emma. I'm glad to be here." He gives me a warm smile and I return to Julian's side. "So, can we eat yet? Just because we may be going to war doesn't mean I've lost my appetite."

Julian and I laugh, though it feels strange coming out of me. There's still so much I have to process, so much I have to tell him.

WITH JULIAN and Mason busy getting unpacked, I find a reprieve in the courtyard just off the sunroom. Dark, star-lit sky hangs above me. While thick, humid air with the faintest hint of magnolia blossoms surrounds me. I breathe it in, allowing it to focus my mind as I inch farther into the night. Colorful flowers with names I don't know and perfectly pruned boxwoods surround the square space. They anchor the white wood garage and the wrought-iron fence, helping to protect me from the outside world that's proven so dangerous. This place makes me think of Mr. Turnip and how he always longed for something beautiful to look at. Beauty is in no short supply here in the Garden District. He would've liked it here, which makes me think I could like it here too, if given the chance. And yet, in all their beauty, the flowers and boxwoods are not the things I admire most in this small garden.

In the center of the courtyard is an oak tree with twisted, moss-covered branches that seem to dance in the moonlight. In places, they crash into the ground before jutting up, redirecting their path. I find myself among the lowest branches. Their bark is rough to the touch where the moss doesn't grow. Surrounded by their strength, I feel safe, as if I've entered an enchanted world different from my own.

The oak's limbs are a symbol of resilience that I'm not sure exists anymore. With each obstacle they face, they adapt and move toward the path of least resistance. And they survive hundreds of years, becoming more beautiful with age. Envious, I lean back against the bark of the trunk, blinking away the memories of the night Beaux pressed me into an oak just outside of Jackson Square. It's strange how memories work. They sneak up on you when you least expect them. Things you think you've forgotten instantly bring you to your knees. But not this time. This time my present is more frightening than my past.

I didn't say much during dinner. Julian and Mason discussed Lucid and the speakeasy and if it would be safe to reopen given that it's at the center of the brotherhood's investigation into Beaux's death. A small peace came to me as they talked. Julian and I lived in the speakeasy for a full month while waiting to close on our new home. Of course, we kept our return to New Orleans secret. We didn't even tell Kat or my mom we were back until we'd officially moved into our house. But still, if the brotherhood was keeping tabs on the place, waiting for our return, then they would know we're back and would've come after us by now. Still, I said none of this to Julian or Mason, because I can't think about Lucid and the speakeasy without thinking about Beaux and the fact that after everything he did to me and to so many others, after everything I went through to gather evidence against him, his crimes remain a secret. No doubt his family had something to do with the coverup. They're nice people, but more obsessed with reputation than anyone I've ever known.

I can only imagine the extravagance of his funeral. Just the thought makes me sick to my stomach. Yet, I'm more disturbed by what was left unsaid between the three of us. The brotherhood may be more interested in Mason because of his sworn loyalty to the organization, but Julian's name is also associated with Lucid. If the brotherhood believes for a second that the truth of Beaux's death has been buried, which it has, then they'll come for Julian just like they did Mason, regardless of if they know who I am and the role I played in the investigation against them. This is the reality that brings me to my knees.

I rest my back against the rough bark of the tree and pull my knees to my chest. No tears fall, despite the sharp ache of emotion pulsing through me. Even in death, Beaux threatens to take away my only happiness in this life, my one true love. It's only a matter of time until the brotherhood puts the pieces of that day together. And us being back in New Orleans only makes it easier for them to do so. Still, I'm not ready to give up on this chance at life with Julian. Even if it means putting myself at risk, once again, I will fight for our life together and the love we share.

At that, I push myself up from the ground, inhaling the sweet floral scent once more. I've put off telling Julian the truth for long enough. We speak of the brotherhood as if it's this one being with one head that can be chopped off. But it's anything but. It's a vast organization with more members and intricacies than I will ever know. But the man with the golden eyes, he is one person, one beating heart, one vessel of information. He can be tracked, interrogated, and dealt with. We've been in New Orleans for almost two months and have had no issues until now, until him. Discovering his true motives for following me must be my top priority. Julian won't like what I'm thinking, but I didn't promise I'd ask for his permission. I promised only honesty. And the sooner I'm honest, the sooner I can find that bastard and begin putting the pieces together of my own perilous puzzle. Is he a scout for the brotherhood and part of some larger attack against me? Or does he simply want me for himself?

CHAPTER 7

Just as I escape the safety of the oak's branches, bright lights illuminate my silhouette, casting an Emma-like shadow against the white paint of my home's exterior. The familiar hum of the car that stalked me the night before fills my ears, bringing me to a sudden stop. My heart squeezes tight in my chest as a scream works its way into my lungs. But my body won't release the sound. If I call for help, Julian and Mason will face off with the driver blindly, putting themselves at risk. *Breathe, Emma. Breathe. Focus on identifying the driver.*

I turn, facing the shining globes of light head-on. I feel my body tremble under their gaze, but I work to stand strong. The sports car with the rumbling engine sits on the opposite side of the street across from the DeClairmonts'. It's the perfect vantage point of our home, as last night proved. I manage to take two steps forward to get a better look at the car. I half expect the driver, whose face I cannot see, to race away, knowing they've been detected. But they aren't the one who's scared, and they know it.

"Oh, Emma, dear! Emma! Good, I've been meaning to talk to you." I gasp at the sudden noise, pressing my palm against my chest to steady my racing heart. Mrs. DeClairmont waves as she spots me from her front porch, the beaming light from the car that does not belong giving away my location. Ignoring the strange vehicle across the street, she shimmies down her porch steps, sweet tea in hand, and across the slender alley. She's hardly tall enough to see over the fence, yet she makes her presence known with the clanking of her jewelry and heels as she eases across the brick path.

"H-hi, Mrs. DeClairmont," I stammer, looking between her and the car that's yet to move.

"Hi, sweetie. Listen, I've been meaning to talk to you about your garbage can."

"Mm-hmm." I inch closer to her without removing my eyes from the car. It's so dark I can hardly make out the color. Perhaps a red? A maroon?

"Well, you see, trash day is on Thursday. Which means the only day that it is acceptable to have trash cans visible from the street is on…?"

I brush a mosquito from my arm just as Mrs. DeClairmont snaps her fingers inches from my face. "Excuse me?" She raises her brow, demanding my attention. "It's rude, you know, not to make eye contact when someone is speaking to you." *Great.* I've moved next door to Anne Marshall 2.0.

"I'm sorry," I say through my teeth. "How can I help you?"

"Well, I was just…" Just as I give the brunette Mrs. DeClairmont my attention, the light leaves us, as does the car and its mysterious driver.

"Shit." I exhale, both in relief and frustration.

"Oh, honey. You know if I said that word in front of my

mother, she'd wash my mouth out with soap after whipping me with a switch."

"Well, how unfortunate for you. Anyway, you were saying?" I cross my arms over my chest as I wait to be berated once more by the woman who knows no boundaries. Her burgundy lips press into a flat line as her brow rises in fury. She takes a deep breath as if to preserve her nonexistent manners and—

"I was simply asking that you start bringing your trash can in between trash pickups. We may not have an HOA in this community, but it's an unspoken rule. We don't want our beautiful oak-lined streets smelling of hot garbage, do we?"

Really? Trash cans? That's what this is about? I lost out on the opportunity to see my stalker for *this*? I bite my lip to keep a few more choice words from escaping. Finally, I say, "Sure. I'll make sure the can is taken care of."

"Praise Heaven!" Mrs. DeClairmont lifts her hands to the sky as if I've just granted her her greatest wish. Poor thing. I'm not sure if she should have higher expectations or lower ones. "Anyway, I didn't mean to bother you. Have a good evening."

"You too." I nod and turn toward the house, hardly able to escape her fast enough.

"Um, Emma." I turn at her voice to find her head angled in the direction of the single black trash can sitting just at the edge of my property. Her eyes flick back and forth, and I know I won't be free of her until the street is clear of my can.

"I'll do it now," I say, slapping my hands against my thighs.

"Perfect. Good night, dear." Mrs. DeClairmont retreats to her front porch where she finishes off her sweet tea. Despite the singing crickets and the occasional groan of a frog, I swear I can hear her slurping.

"*Oh, gosh.*" I pinch my nose closed as I shuttle the empty trash can up the brick alleyway and inside Julian and my garage, the residue from last week's garbage remaining ripe. Mrs. DeClairmont was right, though I'll never admit it. "What the…?" Forgetting Julian purchased a car so he and Mason could avoid being tracked through the airports on their way back to New Orleans, I take a few steps back to make sure I'm in the right place. In the middle of what used to be a space with nothing but a few gardening tools hanging on the walls sits a shiny black Dodge Challenger with even shinier rims. The word *Hellcat* brands the back bumper, making it the perfect getaway car—strong and fast with a deep trunk for stowing one's life at a moment's notice.

"Wow." I've never been much of a car person. Back in Presley, it was nothing but big trucks and even bigger SUVs. Here in New Orleans, it's next to impossible to drive anywhere what with the narrow roads and nonexistent parking. But this car? It's beautiful and so Julian.

"Admiring the latest addition to our family?"

"Jesus!" For the second time tonight, I've almost peed my pants and I'm a twenty-six-year-old woman. "Okay, you and everyone else need to learn how to announce yourselves." I look up to find Julian laughing as he leans against the doorframe of the garage. I let out an exasperated huff while enjoying the sight of him. His laugh brightens everything around him and everything inside me.

"Sorry. What's with the trash can?" he asks, pressing the button to close the overhead door behind me.

"Mrs. DeClairmont."

"Of course. I'm not sure whether I should be impressed with her or completely horrified," Julian says, pulling me into his arms.

"I know, right?" I drop my eyes, choosing to focus on a piece of lint stuck to his black T-shirt. He presses a soft kiss to my hair. I try to manage a smile but fail.

"Hey, talk to me." He brings his hand to my chin, forcing me to meet his gaze. I exhale, leaning into his touch.

"It's just...it's a lot." He nods. "Being back here has brought up a lot of things for me. Nightmares, panic attacks, blackouts. And my anxiety is through the roof. I haven't said anything because I know I'm the one who wanted this. I pushed us to come back. And I still want this, Julian. I do. I want this life, this chance to be normal. But...we're not normal, are we?"

Julian watches me intensely as I ramble, working myself up to let out my biggest worries. "We have these scars that no one can see, these enemies that no one knows how to defeat." I lift my hand to his abdomen. Moving my fingers under the hem of his shirt, I caress the place where Beaux's bullet blasted through him. I can never come that close to losing him again. I won't survive it. And yet, if I tell him the truth, or at least, what I suspect, that's exactly what will happen. He won't let me face my enemies alone. Hell, he probably won't let me face them at all.

"I see you," he says then, pulling me from my thoughts. "I see your pain, your worry. How much it hurts you to know that Beaux got away with all the pain he caused you. How scared you are with our new, uncertain reality. And how hard you're working to make this house perfect for us, like we're a normal couple starting out together with a clean slate." He runs his fingers through my hair, draping it over my chest. "But you're right. We're not normal, and nothing about our life is clean and perfect. But, Emma, I will stand by you through anything. It doesn't matter if there's a million men coming after you, I will stand in front of every attack that comes your way, because you are my life, Emma. You are absolutely everything to me."

Tears fill my eyes. Every word he says is genuine. But the way he speaks tonight, it's different than any time before. Perhaps because he knows the time of hypothetical war is coming to an end and with each day that passes, we come closer to a real one where he has to make good on his vow. Julian wipes the tears from my cheeks, his face tight with emotion of his own. "I can't lose you," he whispers.

"I can't lose you either. And I'm scared, Julian. I'm scared that that's exactly what's going to happen. Somehow, someway, whether it's because of me and how I exposed the brotherhood, or because of Beaux and the fact that he had to die at Lucid of all places, I'm terrified that they are going to take you away from me. And I won't survive it, Julian. I just won't." It's then that I break, coming apart at every seam. There is nothing left to hold me together except Julian's arms as he pulls me against him so tightly it feels as if we are one person. We're quiet for a while. There's no space for words when so much love and fear radiate through us.

As my breathing slows and my body stops shaking, Julian releases his hold on me just enough for his eyes to meet mine. I look up at him to find a wrinkle spread across his forehead. His eyes narrow and move between me and the car beside us. "Julian? What is it?" He takes a deep breath, letting his arms fall to his sides. I instantly miss his touch and the safety I feel when he holds me. "*Julian?*"

"Ever since Mason told me about the brotherhood coming after him, I've been running through various scenarios in my head." He shakes his head, his jaw tight. "There's no perfect way for this to play out. There's no reality in which we are normal, no matter how much we both want it." My throat burns with budding emotion. He's saying all the things I know to be true. Yet, all the truths I refuse to give in to. "If the past year has taught us anything, it's that there is only one way to stay safe and that is—"

"No," I blurt out. He reaches for my hand, intertwining our fingers. "Please don't say it," I beg. He presses his lips tightly together. The words do not escape him, yet I hear them all the same. His bright eyes plead with me to listen, listen to reason. But if we were reasonable, we never would've come back. And even though this place haunts me, visions of my past torture me, and the brotherhood is probably mere moments away from tearing every wall we've built down in a tumble of dust, the moments I've had with Kat, with my mom, with shopping, with buying groceries, with Julian, it's the most alive I've felt since Julian and I made love for the first time. After that, when Beaux attacked, everything changed.

"I know we'll never be normal. I know we'll never be safe, especially not here now that we know of the brotherhood's investigation into Beaux's death. But I'm not ready to give in to our reality yet. I want to try to find a way—"

"To what? Take down the brotherhood?" The sharpness in his tone startles me. "Because that will never happen, Emma. The FBI couldn't do it a year ago. What makes you think things will be different now? When the brotherhood has had a year to change their operation, to find new ways to skirt the system?"

I take a step back and turn away from him. He's right. I know he's right. But hearing it, especially from him, doesn't make it any easier to accept. And so I don't. I turn back to him. "It's been a year, Julian. And the brotherhood hasn't come after us once. Maybe they don't know about me, about us. Maybe they've got bigger problems."

"Like Mason and investigating Beaux's death? Which we both know will lead right back to us." His logic silences me once more. "And who's to say they haven't been looking for us this entire time? We stayed on the move. We were smart. Let's say we were one step ahead for a year. We lost all of that ground the second we came back here."

"So then why did you agree? Why did you give me hope by bringing me back here and promising me a life that I so desperately wanted, just to take it away?" Julian flinches and I know I've hit a nerve. The look on his face cleanses me of all my pain and anger. He's the last person on this earth I want to hurt. "I'm sorry. I didn't—"

"Don't apologize," he says, cutting me off. Julian massages his temples before running his fingers through his hair. He takes a moment to calm himself and then— "Emma, I want two things out of this life. First, I want you safe. Second, I want you happy. We came back to New Orleans because not only were you not happy abroad, you were…hopeless. That night in Paris, I saw the hope leave your eyes and that broke me. I knew no amount of safety would give you back your hope, and so, we made a plan to come back. But that plan was based on a certain level of security that we no longer have."

"Mason," I whisper as tears fill my eyes. Julian nods. He crosses the room in two steps, pulling me into his arms once more. He presses his lips into my hair. I pinch my eyes closed, memorizing the feel.

"I don't want to take anything away from you, Emma. But I'm scared too," he admits, lifting my chin so that our eyes meet. "I'm scared that if we stay here, knowing what we know now, I won't be able to protect you." His final words are tainted with emotion, raspy and barely audible. I nod, pressing kisses to his chest all the way up his neck. He moans as my lips draw some of the tension from his shoulders.

"You say you wouldn't survive losing me, Emma. But the truth is, you would." I furrow my brows and open my mouth to tell him he's wrong, but his words stop me. "You would survive because they wouldn't kill you. What they would do to you after I'm gone, that's what haunts me. That's what makes me want to shove you in that car right now, leave this place, and never come back."

His words turn my skin to ice. I know what he's implying. It's something I've done my best not to think about. I drop my eyes as his fear weighs heavily on me. I was ready to risk myself to protect Julian. But, if he loses me, he'll forever be haunted with thoughts of me and what the brotherhood is doing to— I gulp, swallowing bile produced by my own mental images of torture. Collecting myself, I return my gaze to his.

"I hear you. I see you. I understand your fear and that things have changed for us." I drop my eyes then as I search my mind for the best words. "I...I *do* want to stay here, to give life another chance, even though it's been hard on me." Julian tenses beneath my touch. "But...the life that I want isn't just about me. It's with you. And I don't want you on edge, unable to live because you're so worried about protecting me. Nor do I want either of us to be sitting ducks, waiting for the brotherhood to strike. I know it would kill both of us if something happened to the other." I exhale, allowing reason and my love for Julian to guide my words, despite the growing ache inside of me.

"After Kat's wedding, if you still feel the same way as you do now, we can leave New Orleans and never come back. I won't fight you on it. Because, Julian, you are my home, my heart, my strength, my love. You are my hope. And the reason I felt hopeless in Paris wasn't because of where we were physically. It's because I felt myself losing you." I brush my fingers through his hair, reveling in its soft texture.

"I don't understand," Julian whispers. I nod. I know he doesn't. He was protecting me. He doesn't see anything wrong with what he did. And maybe he's right to think that. But what he did, what *we* did, wasn't right. In that moment, we weren't innocent. We weren't victims. We were guilty. And we were the monsters. Second to losing him to the brotherhood, my greatest fear is losing him to me, allowing my fear, my anxiety, my paranoia, my demons to turn him into a monster.

"What happened in Paris can never happen again. I don't want you to beat people for me or kill for me unless my death is imminent. I won't let this world turn you into a monster, like it did—" Julian pulls me into his chest before I say his name. And I'm relieved when the syllables don't cross my lips. Julian is nothing like him, like Beaux. And I would rather die than watch my angel forced into being a devil.

CHAPTER 8

I sip my coffee on my second-story balcony as the morning sun rises. I'm up earlier than I should be, considering I hardly slept the night before. But every time I dozed off, I woke minutes later from nightmares I'd rather not recount. Julian seemed to ease after our conversation last night. I know he won't change his mind about leaving, which only makes my mission to discover the true motives of the man with the golden eyes more pressing. I have two weeks to learn his identity, why he's been following me, and destroy him. If he knows who I am, even if his motives are for his own personal pleasure rather than part of an elaborate brotherhood plot, it won't matter that Julian and I are fleeing once again. He'll be able to track us, which will defeat our entire reason for leaving.

    I exhale and gulp down the last of my hazelnut-flavored beverage. Sounds of children playing drift through the wind. A soft breeze lifts the lacy edge of my silky shorts. It hurts to know I have to leave this place, yet again, out of fear. Sure, I haven't exactly received the fond welcome I'd hoped for. But it still doesn't make leaving any easier. Because this time, not only am I leaving out of fear, I'm leaving with the knowledge that we will never be back. And our chances of settling anywhere to make a life for ourselves are slim. Julian all but said the reason we stayed safe while abroad was because we stayed on the move. I'm not sure I'm built for this nomadic existence. It's certainly not what I want. But I want him. And if I'm willing to die to keep him safe, and I am, then I'm willing to sacrifice the life I want so that we can have a life together, no matter what that journey looks like.

I set my coffee cup to the side and pull my laptop onto my lap. I didn't tell Julian about my Mr. Mystery because I knew he'd have me in that car and three hundred miles away from New Orleans by sunrise. I can't miss Kat's wedding. Of all the things the brotherhood has taken from me—my sense of safety, and at times my sanity—I won't let them take this. My efforts over the next two weeks will have to be careful so that Julian doesn't catch on. But something tells me he'll be too focused on preparing for our departure to notice. At least, I hope.

I open my web browser and immediately go to The Hub's website. When I worked for The Hub, I covered cultural events, which often lent itself to charity galas that members of New Orleans high society attended. But, for today's research, I go to the society section, which would have even more information on the New Orleans elite. The man with the golden eyes mentioned he was good friends with Beaux. And, from the looks of his expensive clothing, I'd say he probably runs in the same circles as the Thomases. So, I start my search through the society pages, looking through images of over-the-top parties.

The Thomases are all over the site, hosting one charity event after the other. Bile rises in my throat as I spot an article praising the Thomas family for triumphing over tragedy. Apparently, in remembrance of their son, they've created a new charity that supports the families who've lost a loved one to gun violence. It's a worthy cause, don't get me wrong, but it still turns my stomach. If anything, they should start a charity for the survivors and victims of sexual assault. But they wouldn't know anything about that, now, would they? My cheeks blush burning red.

"Good morning, beautiful."

I jump as Julian makes his presence known.

"Ah! Again, with the announcing yourself thing." I set my laptop to the side, turning the screen away. I face him, and his lips instantly crash into mine, and I moan. If my mouth wasn't laced with the tinge of coffee and morning breath, I'd be tempted to let my tongue slip into his mouth. "Good morning to you too." Julian pulls away but not before leaving one final kiss on my forehead. I love his forehead kisses.

"I figured you could use a refill." He hands me another cup of coffee. My eyes light up as I take the hot mug.

"One of the many reasons why I love you." He laughs, placing his hand on my shoulder. "You're not having any?"

"I did downstairs. I just wanted to let you know I'm running out for a bit. There's a lot to do between now and—" He stops himself before saying *our departure*. "There are a lot of arrangements to be made for the house, Lucid, and we'll need new identities, if we do end up leaving." I give him a pained grin. I know he's just saying *if* to make me feel better. I appreciate it, but I'm not falling for it.

"I understand," I say. I sip my coffee so the silence between us isn't so obvious. Julian exhales and kneels in front of my rocking chair. My eyes meet his as he sits just inches away. There's pain mixed with the bright green of his irises. I know it hurts him just as much to leave as it does me. Not because he's as attached to the Crescent City, but because he knows I am. The last thing he wants to do is cause me pain. And the last thing I want is to make him feel guilty for doing it. At that, I set my coffee to the side and rub my palm over his cheek. He closes his eyes, letting out another deep breath.

"I'm sorry I'm not strong enough to protect you, to give you the life you deserve." His words catch me off guard and feel like a sucker punch to the stomach.

"*What?* No, no, don't say that." I move my other hand to his face, taking him between my palms. He opens his eyes. His cheeks go taut against me as he holds in his emotion. My throat aches at the sight of him. "Julian, you are protecting me. Leaving is…it's the right thing to do. History has shown my self-preservation skills aren't exactly the best. You insisting we leave *is* you protecting me, in a way that I honestly can't. I'm the one who isn't strong enough."

I shake my head. Everything I say is the truth. I'm not strong enough to leave this place. A year ago, I was, but not now. I'm no longer strong enough to run or defend myself. I'm exhausted, teetering on the brink of hopelessness. And, if it wasn't for Julian and Kat and everyone I fear will be hurt if the brotherhood does come after me, I wouldn't leave. I wouldn't seek them out, like I'm doing now. I would live my life until they came and took it away from me.

"Please believe me when I say these things. It's not easy. And yes, it hurts to leave. It physically hurts. But not because of you." I brush my thumb over his cheekbone. "It's because of them. It's because I can't find a way to break free of them, or at least, the fear they've cast upon me."

Julian leans forward. He rests his face on my thighs and brings his arms around me. I do the same, planting small kisses in his perfectly tousled hair. "And it's not your responsibility to give me the life I deserve." I shake my head. "When do any of us actually get what we deserve to begin with? No, I will be happy with you wherever we are. And the happiness that you bring into my life is worth every sacrifice." I lean down and whisper in his ear, "No amount of time with you will ever be enough."

I plant a single kiss to his temple. He rises, dragging his hands down my thighs. As his eyes meet mine, the silence between us isn't tense. It isn't deafening. It's soft, our love for one another tangible in the air between us.

"What did I do to deserve you?" he whispers, his fingers digging into my thighs as if I may disappear. "Nothing," he says then. "Because we don't get what we deserve."

"I feel the same way," I whisper.

"Emma, I know you may not feel strong right now. You may feel like running is giving up. But you are the strongest person I know. And I don't view us leaving as giving up. In fact, to me, it's the exact opposite. Us leaving is us doing everything we can to be together, to stay alive. Leaving isn't an act of submission. It's an act of courage and desire and hope, hope for a life together that if we stay, would be undoubtedly too short."

I drop his gaze then, contemplating what he's said. "I've never thought of it that way," I admit. He nods, his lips drawing up into a soft smile.

"I know. But maybe changing your perspective will make it a little easier to stomach. And then, one day, our reality will become normal to us. Second nature, like my love for you."

I match his smile. "I'll try."

I PULL my laptop back onto my lap after I'm sure Julian has left and after I've finished my second cup of coffee. His words stick with me, replaying through my mind. In time, I'll come to accept my new reality, just as he has. But right now, I have to protect it or else we won't even have the chance to run. I clear my mind of all thoughts unrelated to the man with the golden eyes and get back to researching. Two hours later, my eyes burn as they finally scan over a face eerily similar to the one plastered across every inch of my mind.

In an article from a year ago, just a month before news of the brotherhood broke and Julian and I fled, the Amato family is pictured outside their family mausoleum in Lafayette No 1. The article is titled *"New Orleans Tycoon, Domenico Amato, Dead at 57."*

I click the article, enlarging the photograph of three women with black veils covering their faces and a man dressed in a black suit standing between them. If his golden eyes weren't recognizable enough, the ring on his finger sure is. He presses his hand to his chest as one of the women takes his arm. His ring on full display sends a chill down my spine. This is what I was looking for. And yet, now that I've found him, I'm overwhelmed with what to do next. For a year now, I've drawn the faces of suspicious men I've felt were following me. But I've never identified them. I've never learned their names, their stories. In many ways, viewing them as nothing more than sketches and threats made it easier. Now, I have to get to know this man, put myself in his shoes, in his life to understand why he's coming after me. It takes a moment for me to compose myself. And then, I begin reading.

> *Businessman and patriarch of the long-standing Amato family, Domenico Amato, has passed away peacefully after a short battle with an aggressive form of pancreatic cancer. Amato leaves behind his wife of thirty-seven years, Rosa, their son, Alister, and their two daughters, Sophia and Cara.*

I open my notepad on my computer and type up my initial findings, noting his name, Alister Amato, and brief details about his family and his father's death. It seems last spring was a hard-hitting season for the city. With this man's death and Beaux's, and all the news surrounding the brotherhood, it's a wonder the New Orleans social scene didn't completely crumble. But from the number of articles I had to scroll through to find this one, I'd say the opposite happened. Clicking back to the article, I continue reading and taking notes as needed.

> *The family laid their loved one to rest in the Amato mausoleum in the garden at Lafayette No. 1. They've requested any love offerings be sent to the Pancreatic Cancer Action Network. In a rare moment following the funeral, Amato's son made a brief statement.*
>
> *"My family and I are overwhelmed with the love and support from my father's friends, business associates, and the patrons of our family's holdings. While we will take our time to mourn this tremendous loss, rest assured, the Amato family remains dedicated to the city of New Orleans and all its citizens."*
>
> *The Amatos, known for maintaining a quiet public image, despite owning over one hundred businesses in New Orleans alone, will now be under new leadership as son, Alister, steps into his father's shoes. Time will tell what this new leadership will mean for the citizens of New Orleans and the many people Amato Family Holdings employees. But, with a statement like that, it seems evident the young Amato wishes to put those who depend on him at ease, despite his own personal tragedy of losing his father.*

I look from my computer to the street in front of my house as

I think through what I've discovered. Okay, first things first. His father passed away just over a year ago, which, in addition to seeing Beaux, could've been why he was at the cemetery the other day. But that still doesn't explain his creepy comments. The article says *rare* statement, and it isn't lying. I remember attending society events with Beaux and his family. If the Amatos really own over one hundred businesses in New Orleans, they would've definitely been there. Yet, I can't remember ever meeting an Amato or even hearing their name in passing. Not to mention, there's nothing in the society pages postdating Domenico's death announcement. If they are heavily involved in the New Orleans social scene, they know how to keep a low profile. Or, at a minimum, they know how to keep their name out of the press, which makes them even more concerning. Most socialites thrive off being mentioned in the press. It's what makes them relevant. If the Amatos are intent on keeping their public image—what was it the article said? Oh right—*quiet*, then it must be for a reason. Perhaps they're hiding something. Or rather, Alister is hiding something, and maybe his father was before him.

Okay, enough assumptions, Emma. Let's deal in facts.

"Okay," I say aloud. I jot down the name *Amato Family Holdings* and make a mental note to review the business section. But first, I scroll through more articles to see if there's anything else related to the Amatos in the society section. Nothing, at least in the six months preceding Domenico's death. Perhaps that's when he was sick. A small pang of sympathy flits through my heart at the thought of his family having to watch him die a slow and disabling death. I quickly replace it with the words Alister said to me yesterday.

I know plenty of men who would kill to sink themselves into a pretty little thing like you.

Yep, there it is, the perfect amount of anger I need to finish my hunt for information.

I search through The Hub's business section and am overwhelmed with what I find. They may keep a low profile socially, but their business dealings are highly publicized. The latest of which involves the creation of a luxury cruise line that will set sail from the Port of New Orleans next summer.

"*Geez*. These people are like mega rich." Cool sweat dampens my back as I consider what one has to do to become that wealthy. Sure, their businesses could bring in the money. And, if I didn't know how blurred the line is between secrets and success, I'd have no doubt their business holdings are on the up-and-up. But... *Assumptions, Emma, assumptions.*

I gulp down my thoughts along with my nerves that have me jittery. My stomach grumbles, and I realize I've been doing this for far too long without any food. Not to mention, Mason will have worked through his jet lag and be awake soon. If I'm going to do this, I have to get out of the house before he wakes and Julian returns.

I go to Instagram on my computer and search for Alister. Nothing. *Shocker.* Even Julian didn't have much of a social media presence when I cyberstalked him. And he didn't have anything to hide. Next, I cross-reference a map of New Orleans with my list of businesses under the Amato Family Holding's umbrella. It in no way encompasses all of them. But that would take more time than I have right now. And I just need a crumb to get me pointed in the right direction. Finally, I find a bar owned by the Amatos that, one, isn't too far away, and two, Alister has been photographed at in the past two weeks. With over one hundred businesses, there is no way he frequents all of them. But, if he's been photographed there, maybe this is one he pays extra attention to. Here's hoping, despite the numb fear crawling up my arms.

I clear my search history and close my laptop. Exhaling, I do my best to mentally prepare myself for a visit to Eve's Garden. The irony of the name isn't lost on me. Either someone in his family loved a woman named Eve or someone in his family has a God complex. Regardless, here's hoping my visit more closely resembles the biblical paradise before the fall of man rather than after.

CHAPTER 9

Okay, so I'm not sure *bar* is the right term to describe Eve's Garden. String lights hang from the black awning, framing the glass-paned entrance and surrounding windows. Dark green vines and white roses crawl up the sides of the weathered brick building. They create an enchanting appeal, practically consuming the simple sign that lets me know I'm in the right place. I glance down, taking in my outfit of choice. Thankfully, I scrolled through enough Instagram photos to pick something appropriate for the upscale eatery.

Pastel pink shorts covered in red and blue florals hit just above my knee. I've paired them with a matching blazer, nude camisole, and tan espadrilles that function much like tennis shoes. Pretty and practical, and the perfect complement to my brown wig and matching contact lenses.

Disguises and aliases aren't new to me. And yet, as I stand across the street, working up the courage to enter the lion's den, I feel more tense than I did even when I infiltrated Club Gent.

Perhaps because now I have more to lose if this investigation goes sideways. I exhale and place my hand over my grumbling, yet queasy stomach. *It's okay, Emma. Breathe.* I close my eyes and take another deep breath. I'm not sure if it's my determination to discover the truth or my body's desperate need for nourishment, but somehow, I put one foot in front of the other until my brown-haired reflection stares back at me in the reflective glass of Eve's front entrance. Another deep breath and—

The smell of crisp apples and magnolia blossoms fills the air of the small shotgun-style space that is Eve's Garden. Inside, it's much darker than I would've thought given the midday sunshine outside. A long bar with wicker and wood bar stools lines the length of the space. Black birdcage chandeliers covered in green vines hang from the ceiling along the length of the bar. The walls are made of dark wood, the same as the floor beneath me. Bottles and bottles of high-end liquor fit nicely in arches carved into the wood behind the bar. I find myself overcome by the beauty of the place. That is, until I'm forced to remember why I'm here.

Sitting toward the back of the space at one of the bistro tables is the man with the golden eyes. He glances up at me quickly, forcing me to lock my legs to keep myself upright. Just as quickly as his eyes find me, he returns his attention to the plate in front of him. I fight the urge to lift my hand to my chest to quell my aching heart. Instead, I force my feet to move, finding an open bar stool within earshot of his table. I slide onto the stool, set my purse on the cream-colored bar in front of me, and exhale.

There are only a few other patrons, despite the popular lunch time. A couple groups of women toward the front of the space and a few men scattered down the length of the bar. I find a little reprieve in knowing that I'm not alone. Unlike my man of interest. He sits alone at his table. The only sounds coming from his direction are the clank of his fork against his plate. I'm not sure how I'll gather the information I need if he isn't speaking to anyone. And yet, the thought of asking to join him keeps me firmly planted in my seat.

"Hi! I'm Fiona. I'll be taking care of you today. Can I get you started with something to drink?" A girl with brown hair approaches me so quickly, I hardly have enough time to process her simple request.

"Um...um, I'm sorry. I've never been here before. Can I see a menu?"

"Sure thing!" Fiona reaches underneath the bar and places an elegant cream-colored menu in front of me. "I'll give you a second and swing back around."

"Thanks," I mumble. I give the menu a once-over, mostly to give myself a moment to calm my nerves. It's then that the two groups of women pay their checks and begin loading their leftovers into to-go boxes. *Crap.* This plan of mine is becoming stupider by the minute. Fiona whips around the counter, closing out the women's checks before topping off the drinks of the men to my right. I have half a mind to come up with an excuse and make a not-so-graceful exit. And then, a warm hand finds its way onto my back, leaving me frozen in place.

"Sorry, I didn't mean to startle you." I turn to find the man with the golden eyes and perfectly chiseled jaw sitting to my left. He waits for me to speak. When I don't, he continues. "I'm Alister Amato, the owner of Eve's Garden. I heard you mention it's your first time in and I wanted to know if I could be of any assistance."

Everything inside me begs me to run. My heart races in my chest. I flit my eyes back and forth, taking in every tiny movement he makes. He motions for Fiona to join us and says something to her I'm too dazed to understand. She nods and darts away to complete whatever task he asked of her. As his eyes meet mine once more, the tension in my body subsides enough for a few words to crawl out of my mouth.

"Thank you. What would you recommend?" His eyes scan my face and I pray with every ounce of my being that he doesn't recognize me. Finally, he moves his attention from me to the menu between us, allowing the muscles in my belly to finally release. He begins explaining their tapas menu, allowing the rest of my nerves to settle.

"The duck quesadilla is really good. Spicy wonton shrimp. Of course, we also offer various sides to round out your meal."

"What's your favorite?" I ask, keeping my words to a minimum. He may not recognize my face, but, after yesterday, it's possible he could recognize my voice. He looks at me then. His lips draw up into a little smile that he quickly forces from his face in favor of professionalism.

"Uh, I like the blackened redfish tacos with a side of grits. It's the perfect combination of spicy and creamy. And it will go perfectly with the cocktail I ordered you." *Hmm?* I frown. When did he order me a cocktail? Oh, that must've been why he called Fiona over. Just as I put two and two together, Fiona returns with two cocktails the color of dried red rose petals or blood, depending on your frame of reference.

"Ma'am, I will have to ask to see your ID. I'm sorry. I didn't think about it before." The poor girl who can't be older than nineteen looks at me apologetically. Of course she didn't think about it. Her boss asked and she delivered without hesitation. Perhaps he's testing her, to see if she follows the rules of the establishment. Though, as I pull my wallet from my purse, I wonder if his test is more for me. My ID will pass the most basic security tests. But if he suspects I'm not who I say I am, an in-depth background check will reveal the truth behind my brunette alias, Lila Hayden. The truth being, beyond a PO box, falsified education records, and a fake Instagram profile, she doesn't exist.

I'm sure to keep certain details on my ID covered as I hand it to Fiona. Out of the corner of my eye, I watch him, the man named Alister. His eyes glance at my hand as I hand the girl my license but for no longer than a second. Fiona inspects the card and hands it back to me. "Thank you," she says, smiling. "Have you had enough time to look over the menu?"

"Yes," I say, slipping my ID back into my wallet. "I'll have the blackened redfish tacos with a side of grits."

"Yes, ma'am." Fiona collects my menu and I return my attention to Alister, somehow finding comfort in Fiona's presence. He lifts his drink, directing me to do the same.

"Cheers," he says. "To new acquaintances."

"To new acquaintances," I repeat, bringing my lips to the bloodred cocktail. *Oh, wow!* The liquid is sweet and warm on my tongue. It tastes like berries and bourbon. If I'd had more than two cups of coffee today, I'd down half of it right now. But considering the emptiness of my stomach and my proximity to a man who'd love nothing more than to have me without my inhibitions, I set the drink to the side. "It's delicious. I'll have more after I get some food in me."

Alister laughs. "It's called the Blood Prince. The sweetness makes it easy to drink. But the more you do, the more you feel the burn of the bourbon. It's sneaky that way."

"Hmm. Interesting. Sounds like whoever named it has a love of metaphors." Alister tilts his head as his eyes narrow. *Is he the Blood Prince?* "The sweetness draws you in, like a pretty face or a kind word, until you're so consumed you don't even realize you're in the Devil's clutches, until it's too late." Alister looks away from me then and takes another sip of his drink. I struck a nerve, which lets me know I've found my in. "So, are you the Blood Prince? The one I should watch out for?" My questions are blunt but posed with an edge of flirtation to throw any suspicions he may have to the back burner. He sits in silence for a moment, thinking over his next words. Then, a small smile lifts his lips. Only this time, he doesn't force the smile away.

"You know, I don't think I caught your name," he says, turning to me. *That's because I didn't mention it.*

"It's Lila." I shift in my seat, watching him closely as he rubs his fingers over the stubble on his face. It's a bit thicker than the day before, which only adds to the sharpness of his jawline.

"Lila." He says my name as if he can taste it, taste the lie that is Lila. "Are you from New Orleans, Lila?"

I exhale and turn to take another sip of my drink. This isn't about me. I have to get the conversation back on him. "No," I say. Which is the truth. I have an entire backstory memorized for all my aliases. None of them are from New Orleans. It's best he thinks I'm just visiting or here on business, so he can't expect to meet up with me at another time. Though, depending on how much information I can get from this encounter, Lila may have to find a way to bump into him yet again.

"That's it? No other details?"

"Do you want more details? Because I'm not exactly in the habit of giving out personal information to strangers. Nor am I sure why you're still sitting here. You asked if you could be of any assistance. Was that with the menu or with something else?" Again, flirtation laces my words. His smile grows as he mistakes the panic in my eyes for glossy-eyed lust. The air is thick between us as I wait for Alister to make a move. More accurately, as I wait to see his response when I deny him his request. Yet, as I remember the strength of his touch from our encounter at Midnight Moon, my insides twist with anxiety. "It doesn't matter anyway," I blurt out, turning away from him so he can't see the fear crawling up my body. "I have a boyfriend."

"That's not surprising." I look straight ahead, refusing to meet his gaze, which lingers on me. "I imagine you had him wrapped around your finger in a matter of minutes. You pulled him in with that pretty face of yours, the soft touch of your skin." I wrap my arms around myself, tugging my blazer to cover my chest. The only skin left for him to see is that of my legs and yet I feel naked as his eyes trace my body. "Tell me, will you burn him in the end? I may be the Blood Prince. But you, Lila, seem like you may be a Blood Princess in your own right."

I swallow his accusation. He's baiting me. Instead of defending myself, or rather, my alias, I ask him the question he thinks he's smart enough to avoid. "Maybe we all have a side of ourselves we like to pretend isn't there. Until the darkness comes oozing out and we can't pretend anymore. You sit here with your gold watch, expensive clothes, and fancy ring. You act like the perfect businessman, overcompensating for the parts of yourself you can't stand." I turn on my stool, bringing myself face-to-face with the man who wants to use me in unspeakable ways. "It's okay to be honest, Mr. Amato. What darkness is lurking inside you? What makes you the Blood Prince?"

My words are soft, allowing our conversation to stay between the two of us. I know that's the only way he'll even consider opening up. He's quiet, yet his eyes do not leave mine. As I watch him, anger bubbles through me, overtaking my fear. He reminds me of Beaux and how he was so good at making you believe he was perfect. I believed him. My family believed him. Well, my father knew the truth of his horror. What's worse, he played right along, allowing all of us to exist naively in their world of lies. Does Alister think he can fool me too? Of course he does. He thinks he can fool everyone. He's just *that good*. Well, guess what? I'm better.

"If I'd known a simple cocktail order was going to lead us here, I would've ordered you a glass of wine."

"And why's that?"

"It's simple, easy, unimposing."

I nod. "Right. Something tells me you're not interested in easy or simple," I say, continuing my game of disinterest and flirtation. It's then that Alister leans forward. He brushes his lips against my cheek as he makes his way to my ear. A gasp escapes me as I freeze, losing all the bravado my alias Lila allows me to have.

His breath is hot against my skin as he whispers, "Something tells me you're a little too interested in me, especially considering you have a boyfriend."

Obviously, I suck at this game. As Alister pulls away, I search my mind for what to say next. Thankfully, a chime from his pocket draws his attention to his phone, giving me a moment more to collect myself.

"As much as I would love to continue this conversation, I have to step away for a business meeting." He doesn't look at me as he rises from his chair, slipping his phone back into the pocket of his trousers. "Fiona," he calls. The young brunette stands in front of us in mere seconds. "Please put Ms. Lila's meal on my tab. Her company was payment enough." Despite the pure detest I feel for this man, I blush as Fiona's eyes dart between us. I would tell him that isn't necessary, but why should I? I'm sure he has many things he needs to pay for. I'll let my meal be the first, but not the last.

"Lila." His voice draws my eyes to him. "It was a true pleasure. Please join us again at Eve's Garden. We'd love to have you." There's a twinkle in his eyes as he takes my hand in his, planting a soft kiss to my knuckles. My stomach burns as his lips meet my flesh, and not because of the bourbon.

CHAPTER 10

Alister disappears through a door at the back of the building as Fiona places a plate of scrumptious-smelling food in front of me. "Can I get you anything else?" Fiona asks, though I can't bring myself to pull my eyes from the last place I saw Alister. "Ma'am?"

"Yes, no. No, I don't need anything else," I say, turning back to her. She nods. Though, unlike before, she doesn't hurry away at her dismissal. She watches me closely, studying me. Her chipper nature gone. "This looks great. Thank you," I say, hoping she'll get the hint and leave me to my thoughts. After that encounter, my brain aches just as much as my stomach does.

"You should be careful." Her words cause a lump to form in my throat and my spine to straighten under her gaze.

"Excuse me?"

"With Mr. Amato," she says, lowering her voice. She glances to her right, making sure no one is listening. I do the same. The two men at the opposite end of the bar are too consumed with their shop talk to worry about us. She turns back to me then. "The people close to him have a tendency to disappear."

"What? What do you mean disappear? Like girlfriends of his?" The words come out of me in a rush. Fiona takes a step back, her lip quivering with emotion. She knows more than she's letting on, more than a girl her age should. But then I remember —the girls the brotherhood preyed on at Club Gent were all young college girls. My stomach twists at the memories of that night.

The men to our right begin to move in their seats, drawing Fiona to the opposite end of the bar. *The people close to him have a tendency to disappear.* A million thoughts race through my head, things even more disturbing than what I already know to be true regarding the brotherhood's operation. I know I don't have proof yet that Alister is one of them. But with every fiber of my being, I believe he is. And, if what Fiona says is true, then they aren't just raping young women, they're—

I lift my hand to my mouth to keep from spewing vomit across the counter in front of me. I stumble from my seat. Leaving my belongings behind, I rush through the back door in search of a bathroom. Hell, at this point, a trash-laden alley will suffice. *Oh, God!* It burns. I make it to the bathroom just in time to empty myself over a toilet. As the last gush of bile leaves me, I fall to my knees, too weak to hold myself up under the weight of this assumption. I told myself I wouldn't allow assumptions to consume me. After everything I've been through, my mind is a dark place of boundless imaginings. But this one—it makes sense. At least, it seems likely. After the events of last year, the brotherhood would've been forced to change the way they operate. What if instead of blackmail, they've found a more permanent way of keeping their evil acts secret?

My stomach churns once more as I think of the girl my father had Beaux dispose of, the girl left half-dead on the bathroom floor of Club Gent, and all the countless others whose stories will never be told. I gag but there is nothing left in me to purge, except memories that have embedded themselves in my essence. I feel weak, weak with the reality unfolding before me. Still, I need proof. I need to know with one hundred percent certainty that he is a member. And then, I need to know every one of his sinister secrets, every girl he's made disappear. It's a path I don't want to venture. And yet, it may just be the thing I need to ensure he never has a chance to come after me or Julian.

I push up from the floor, wash my hands, and rinse my mouth with water. Thankfully, my wig is still intact, and my contacts stay put despite my watering eyes. Fiona was brave to warn me about Alister. I hope with it just being the two of us, she'll be inclined to open up more. But as I make my way through the bathroom door into the short hallway between the main dining space and what I assume is the back exit, my eyes spot the door just down the hall. There's a sign on it that says *Private*. It's probably the manager's office. Yet, considering how often Alister stops by, maybe he uses it for himself. He did say he had to step away for a business meeting. Does that mean he left or is he in there?

I wrap my arms around myself, using my blazer to hide my body despite the sweat beading on my chest. I reach the door in a matter of seconds and press my ear to the cool surface, listening for what may be being said on the other side. Nothing. I hear nothing. For once, I'm relieved to be met with a dead end. Though perhaps my end isn't as dead as I'd like it to be. I take a step back and contemplate my next move. I don't want to, but I know what I have to do. Fiona may be brave enough to warn me of the man she suspects is a monster just as much as I do, but she couldn't possibly know the level of intel I'm in need of. His office, on the other hand, just might be the keeper of all his secrets.

Before I can talk myself out of it, I take a step forward and knock on the door. If he's inside, I don't want to be caught breaking in. After a solid minute of silence, I take a deep breath and reach for the doorknob. To my surprise, it's unlocked, which tells me one thing—I have to hurry because he's coming back.

THE OFFICE IS IMMACULATELY CLEAN, which makes snooping even more difficult. Alister strikes me as the kind of guy who would notice if a pen went missing. On the plus side, there are only a few items on his desk. I flip through the few folders quickly. Everything looks related to the restaurant, supply orders, income reports. Nothing out of the ordinary. Of course, it wouldn't be. If he has the balls to leave his office unlocked, then he must have any incriminating documents hidden out of sight. *Or there aren't any here.* I push the thought from my mind, refusing to give up on my hunch. I know it's a long shot. With over one hundred businesses under his family's umbrella, there's one hundred places he could hide the evidence of his crimes, whether they're crimes against women, financial crimes, or corporate espionage. I wouldn't put any of it past him, and I only need enough to make sure he'll leave me and Julian alone.

A small pang of guilt works its way into my heart as Fiona's quivering lip replays in my mind. I know there's more to this than Alister, more women suffering, and more men getting away with causing them pain, or worse. But Julian is right. The FBI couldn't take the brotherhood down, so what makes me think I can? No. I can't get sidetracked. I have to stay focused on Alister, the man I may actually have a chance to destroy before he destroys me.

After searching through the documents on his desk, I begin pulling open all of his desk drawers until I find the one that's locked. *Gotcha.* Knowing that I can't have much time left before he returns from his meeting, I search his desk frantically for anything that can be used to pick the lock. Settling for a paper clip, I maneuver it with my fingers until it's the right shape to work the lock. Within two minutes, I've got the drawer open. And exhale.

There are only two things in the drawer that was once locked —a gun and a laptop that is no doubt password protected. *Shit.* My heartbeat quickens at the sight of the gun. I grew up around guns, but I never took the time to learn much about them. And ever since Beaux… I take a deep breath and shake my arms out as if the movement will dislodge my nerves. Carefully, I pick the weapon up with both hands and place it on the chair I'd previously pushed to the side. It's heavy, too heavy to be empty. Cool sweat dampens my skin at the realization. Why would a restaurant owner need a gun? Perhaps in case of robberies? Somehow, I doubt that's why he has it.

Shoving all thoughts of the gun from my mind, I return my attention to the laptop. I pull it from its hiding place and into my lap, resting my back against the wooden frame of his desk. If only I had the hacking capabilities of the brotherhood, I wouldn't be discouraged by a simple password. The thought reminds me of the jump drive my father kept. I flip the laptop on its sides, looking for a memory card or a jump drive I could easily swipe. Nothing. I make a mental note to check his desk one last time before saying a quick prayer and opening the laptop to see if it was answered. Sure enough, the laptop requires a password for access. And yet, maybe my prayer was answered after all.

Sticking to the silver keyboard of the device is a lime-green sticky note with an inscription I'm sure I'm not meant to see. *6.16 — AFH 021163 [8] — 22A1* What the...? Is this a password? Coordinates to his dungeon? My hand instantly reaches to the floor in search of my phone before I remember I left my purse on the bar in my quick retreat to the bathroom. Speaking of, it wouldn't surprise me if Fiona comes to check on me with the way I bolted out of there. Though, of course, if she's as wary of Alister as she seems to be, I doubt she'd venture this far down the hallway. I stand and pull the center drawer of his desk open in search of something I can transfer the inscription to. Finding a pad of lime-green sticky notes, I quickly jot down the senseless letters and numbers, while racking my brain as to what they could possibly mean.

"Yeah, we're all set for Wednesday. The boss will be there to inspect the shipment. Hey! Who *the fuck* are you?"

The pen nestled between my fingers falls to the wooden desk. The sound echoes throughout every inch of my body, as does the bellowing voice of the man before me. He has dark hair and eyes that are anchored by scrunched eyebrows. "I...I..." I begin to take a step forward, to explain my presence even though I have no good explanation. But my legs give way beneath me, and I fall to the floor. The man before me slides his phone into his pants pocket and then pulls a gun from behind his back. My limbs feel numb. My vision begins to blur. My inner self screams for me to get up, grab the gun to my left, and shoot, shove, run— do something! But I sit frozen as the man with tanned skin wields the butt of the gun against the side of my face, sending me into the dark haven of unconsciousness.

I KNOW I've begun to wake even before my eyes open. Pain radiates through my cheek and into my jaw. I taste coppery blood before I sense it dripping from my mouth down my chin. A small droplet lands on my breast. The simple sensation shocks all grogginess from me as the hairs on my exposed arms and legs rise. My eyes dart open and my head stands straight, despite the terrible pain wishing me back into oblivion. My clothes have been removed. I sit restrained to a metal chair in nothing but my bra and panties. They even took my shoes. *They.*

You say you wouldn't survive losing me, Emma. But the truth is, you would. You would survive because they wouldn't kill you.

Julian's words rush through me, sending me into panic mode. "No! No!" I scream. I yank my wrists and ankles, trying to wiggle to freedom, but the ropes they've restrained me with only dig deeper into my skin. "Ah!" I wince. My wrists burn under their rough texture. Realizing breaking free isn't an option, I lose control of my breathing. Oxygen escapes me in rapid waves. I consider the size of the room and know I should conserve my air, so I don't suffocate. But knowing and doing are two different things. Every muscle in my body is on high alert, as if I may be stabbed or groped at any second. But it's only me. Aside from the spotlight shining down, the room I'm held in is dark, so dark I can't see ten feet in front of me. A new wave of fear rushes over me as I realize I won't be able to see them coming. With my ragged breathing, I won't be able to hear them either.

After what feels like forever, I gain control of myself enough to realize how badly I screwed up. *Why?* Why did I have to put myself in this position? Why couldn't I just sit at home, wait things out until Kat's wedding, and then run? At least I'd have Julian. At least I'd have a chance at happiness. I understand now more than ever what Julian meant when he said running isn't an act of submission. It's an act of hope. Now, I've ruined everything. I've shredded that glimmer of hope into a million pieces just like they are going to shred me from the inside out. And the worst part is, Julian will never know what happened to me. He'll waste his life looking for me, but he'll never find me. Like Fiona said, people are disappearing. And I'll be one of the many. At that, sobs rip through me, sharper than even my rapid breaths. My body shakes in hopelessness. There's nothing left for me to do except pray for a quick end to this Hell that has been my life. But something tells me the sticky note was the last prayer request God will grant me.

I jump in my seat as a sharp squeak of metal lets me know I'm no longer alone. My chest burns as I try to slow my breathing enough to listen. Finally, the sound of footsteps makes its way to my ears. I open my mouth to scream but nothing comes out. I'm too hoarse. As a figure comes into view, just on the edge of darkness, I pinch my eyes closed. If I see his face, he'll have no choice but to kill me. If his identity remains safe, maybe he'll let me live. I'm hopeless, but my mind won't give in to death, not yet.

"We can do this the easy way or the hard way," a man's voice says. "Personally, I prefer it when women cooperate. It's a shame when their sweet, soft skin breaks beneath my knuckles." As he speaks, I sense him kneel in front of me. He moves his rough hand to my hair and twirls the strands of my wig between his fingers. *Oh no!* If he realizes who I am, I'm even more dead. "But I'll do what I have to to get the truth out of you." At that, he stands, and I hear him walk away. I want to open my eyes so that I can see the blows coming. But I know if I do his wicked face will be the last thing I see. What was it he said? The truth? What truth?

A gasp escapes me as I hear metal chains drag across the concrete floor. My body tingles as every inch of me goes numb, so numb I barely feel it when warm urine drenches my underwear. The man chuckles.

"You must be new if you're already wetting yourself. I haven't even touched you yet." *Yet.* The word repeats over and over again in my mind as I sense him move closer.

"Ah!" I yelp as he drops the metal chains at my feet. A single link hits my toe. It's enough to make my entire body shake. The ropes dig deeper into me as I move.

"Shh, shh, shh," he whispers, kneeling once more. "I don't want to do this. I really don't. Do you understand?" His lips brush against my swollen cheek as he speaks. "Do you understand?" he repeats, this time with more grit. I nod, unable to reply. "Good. Now, all you have to do is answer one question and this will all be over." Again, I nod.

What question? What could he possibly want to know? Somehow my mind still functions enough that I'm reminded of the blackmail videos the brotherhood took of all their members and the women they victimized. Maybe he wants information from me so he can blackmail me into silence. But what can I say? If I tell him my darkest secret, he'll never let me go. And if I lie… My body begins to shake once more as I imagine what he plans to do to me with those chains.

It's then that he presses both of his palms to my thighs. I know he's looking at me head-on. The temptation to open my eyes is overbearing. Still, I fight through. Finally, the words I've been waiting for cross his lips. "Who sent you?"

My forehead wrinkles as the words flow through me. *Who sent you?* Who sent *me*? Does he think I work for the police or the FBI? Does he think the investigation into the brotherhood has been reopened? "No…no one," I blurt out. I'm surprised I'm even able to get the words past the sharp burn of my esophagus. But soon enough, I realize the relief I feel at my simple statement is the dumbest thing I've felt all day, followed by the most painful.

I scream as he wraps the thick metal chains around my neck. The sharp sound is quickly strangled as he pulls the chains taut. He moves as if he means to make a knot in a shoelace. *"Aaaahha!"* The sounds I make aren't human because, in this moment, I'm not being treated like a human. I'm unable to keep my eyes closed through the brutal assault, the bright light searing them, giving me an instant headache and forcing them closed once more. I yank at my arms as my instincts to pull the chains from my throat kick in. But I can't. I can't move. I have to take it until he finds it in his cold, black heart to release me or until I die.

CHAPTER 11

The man stands across the room, caressing the chains with his fingers. I've allowed myself to open my eyes during this moment of reprieve, because I know, after what he's done to me, he has no plans to let me go. The acidic taste of urine lingers on my tongue as I try to fill my lungs with air. My chest burns as the oxygen does not come to me quick enough. My head lolls as my strength wanes. Despite the way the darkness distorts his features, I can see his impatience brewing with the way his mouth presses hard into a flat line. He's running out of time to get the answer he wants. But I don't know what to tell him. I don't know how to make this torture stop. My breathing slows as my body finally starts to recover from his force. Words race through me, daring to escape my lips. And yet, I sit in silence, afraid that my words will tempt him to cause me more pain.

At that, he drops the chains to his feet. My insides clench as I watch him disappear into the darkness. He moves in silence, yet I still sense his presence. Perhaps the room is bigger than I thought. My stomach twists with nausea and I know if I hadn't emptied myself at the restaurant, urine wouldn't be the only inner matter to escape me. As quickly as he departed, he returns. Before I even have a moment to close my eyes, he stands before me, glaring at me with the darkest of expressions. I gasp, both at the man who will be my end and at the object he now holds in his hand.

"I underestimated you," he says then, kneeling once more so his face is mere inches from my flesh. "You've held out longer than some of my own men." I jump in my seat, doing everything I can to shrink away from his touch as he moves toward me. It's no use. He drags his fingers up one of my thighs while he rests the foreign object on the other. "But, of course, they know what I'm capable of. And you clearly do not."

At that, his fingers dig into my gut as he pushes me backward. The legs of the chair give way, sending me crashing into the hard concrete floor. "Ah!" I cry as pain radiates through the back of my head. It is quickly replaced with earth-shattering fear as my end towers over me. He's got the device in his hand. And with a click of a button, a burst of fire spouts from it. "No! No! *Please!*" I beg as he scans my body, assessing the parts of me that would burn the quickest. Or perhaps the slowest. "I don't know what you want from me. If I did, I would tell you. I would do whatever you wanted. *Please!* I'm not the police. I'm not FBI. I'm just a regular girl." My words don't stop him from moving closer. I scream, knowing I can't reason with him. Still, I try again. "I'm just a girl. Please! I don't want to die."

As the words cross my lips, tears fill my eyes, erasing the man from my vision as he drops to his knees above me. He's so close, I can taste his sweat. I've contemplated death many times before. At times, I think I'd welcome it. But, in the end, when I've come face-to-face with it, the truth prevails. I don't want to die. I'm not ready. I've barely done anything worth doing. I've barely had a chance to love, to live.

"Oh, I'm not going to kill you. You'll just wish you were dead. That is, unless you answer my question." He strokes the inside of my thigh with the device. Though the flame is retracted, my insides still burn at his touch. "Last chance," he whispers. "Who sent you? Why were you snooping around my boss's office?"

My breath hitches in my throat as a glimmer of hope comes to me. He never asked me why I was in the office before. I'm not sure my answer will help me. But at least I can give him something. Maybe he'll reward my honesty by putting the torch away.

"I...I'm not sure who your boss is. But, if it's the man I think it is, Alister, I was in his office because I think he's been following me. And I..." Emotion scorches me from the inside out as I know my admission won't save me. If anything, it makes me guilty of the kind of crime this man seems charged with punishing. "I wanted to find something, anything, so that I could ensure my safety from him. I didn't know what I'd find. Even now, I still don't know what the numbers on the sticky note mean. I just wanted my freedom, a chance to disappear from this godforsaken city without the fear of him coming after me."

Something I say makes the man pull away from me, though not far enough for my comfort. Confusion washes over him. "So, you were planning to blackmail him or turn over whatever you found to the police?" I close my eyes, savoring my last moment without pain. All my admission did was buy me time, not my freedom.

"Yes."

The man nods. "And why would my boss be following you? What makes you so special?"

I open my eyes then. If these are my last words, my last *real* words, not cries of agony, I want to say them with grit and look him in the eyes as I call him out as the monster he is. "I'm not special," I say. "I'm just a pretty face and a hole for him to fuck. That's all that matters to men like him, like you. Isn't it?"

I watch as my words settle on him. I expect him to slap me, burn me, screw me. Anything! But he doesn't. He just stares at me before pushing himself up from the ground and moving out of view. As he speaks, he sounds farther away than I expected him to. "What's your name?" he asks.

I hesitate. Do I dare lie to him? It won't take him long to run my story by his boss, by Alister. Alister only just met Lila Hayden. He'll shred through my story quicker than I can come up with a new one. But if I tell him the truth, then the torch will be the last of my worries. My hesitation pays off, at least for a moment longer, as the sharp squeak of metal lets me know someone else has entered the room.

"Thank you, Gio. I'll take it from here." His voice washes over me like ice water. Even with our few encounters, I'll never forget the low, warm sound of the man known as the boss, the Blood Prince—Alister. Has he come to kill me? Or perhaps he wants to feel the pleasure of torturing me for himself.

From where I lie, I can't see Gio as he leaves or Alister as he approaches, but I hear him. His footsteps echo in the otherwise empty space. I close my eyes and take a deep breath. I allow my mind to find Julian's face and then Kat's and then my mom's. I imagine us all sitting at the dining room table. Hot food surrounds us as conversation and laughter fill the room. I don't know what we say to each other. It doesn't matter. What's important are the smiles spread across our faces and the way our cheeks shine bright with love. Eva and Bill join us along with the nephew or niece I'll never get to meet. My lip quivers, the thought bringing me back to my reality just as Alister swoops down. His fingers brush my shoulder as he pulls the chair up and me along with it. Before my mind can anticipate what will happen next, Alister pulls at the chair, yanking me farther and farther away from the spotlight I've grown accustomed to. Darkness consumes me as does the piercing sound of metal against stone.

"BEFORE I CUT you out of these ropes, I need you to promise you won't run. Clearly, we have things to discuss." *What the…?* My eyes dart around the room as Alister positions me in front of a large wooden desk, similar to the one at Eve's Garden. Only this one looks less like a decoy. It's covered in various papers and folders. A laptop, like the one I'd previously discovered, sits in the middle. Behind the desk is a wall of video monitors that cover every inch of the warehouse we must be in. There are guards posted all throughout the property. If I were to run, I wouldn't get very far. Reluctantly, I nod and stare blankly ahead as Alister cuts the ropes from my ankles and wrists. I wince and instantly pull my hands into my lap. The ropes have left my skin red and raw. In places, small speckles of blood shine bright against my otherwise pale skin, much like the drops of blood that have fallen from my mouth down to my breasts.

My attention is pulled from my aching body as Alister crosses the room and opens one of his desk drawers. I'm not sure what's happening or what he plans to do with me. But, in this moment, he seems a nicer devil than the one who just got done torturing me. So, I keep quiet and do as he says. It's then that he pulls a large, white button-down shirt from the drawer. He returns to my side of the desk and hands it to me. I take it, though my eyes do not leave his as I do. Once I have the shirt firmly in my grasp, he backs away once more. I'm thankful for the distance. Gingerly, I slip my arms into the shirt and button it. It's long enough to drape over my knees, which I'm thankful for, though it does nothing to calm my nerves or quell the pain coursing through me.

Alister takes a seat on the opposite side of the desk. He doesn't look at me. Instead, his golden gaze focuses on a random sheet of paper on his desk. He's either deep in thought or his specialty is psychological torture. As I sit, waiting for his next words, a million thoughts race through me, just like I suspect he wants. He wants me to believe there's a chance I walk out of here. He wants to give me a moment to find some hope, a will to live, a will to fight. It'll make it all the more enjoyable when he strips it from me yet again.

I jump as he moves without warning, again reaching for a drawer. From it he retrieves a glass decanter filled with the kind of alcohol that makes your belly warm. He pours himself a glass and then looks at me to see if I'd like any. My insides are raw. Bourbon will only add to my pain. Still, I nod and accept a glass from him. Perhaps it will numb more pain than it will cause. I let him take a sip of his drink first. Once I'm sure it isn't poisoned, I do the same. As the liquid crosses my lips, it stings, and I realize they are chapped from all my screaming. I lift my fingers to them before letting them drift to my neck. I don't have to look in a mirror to know bruises cover my skin. If I thought I would be walking out of here, I'd worry about how I will hide them from Julian and Mason. Alas, I don't think I'll have that problem. I wasn't sure if Alister was a member of the brotherhood or not. But with men like Gio working for him and all the guards lurking around the corners, he either is or he's into something far worse. Either way, I'm screwed.

"I didn't see it," he says then, downing the rest of his drink.

His eyes shift to me, tracing the edges of my face and hair. "You've clearly mastered the art of disguise." *Oh no!* "Emma." My name sounds strange coming off his lips. I can't tell if he's pleased by my presence or disappointed in it. "Remove the wig and contacts. Enough pretending." It's a command, not a request. And I'm in no position to argue.

My hand shakes as I lift my glass to my lips once more, gulping down the sweet, sharp liquid as if it will give me strength. And then, I do as he says. I set my wig and contacts on the chair next to me. Then I remove the cap concealing my blond locks and let them fall over my shoulders. Numbness shudders through me as I know I've been caught. He knows my name. Which means, if he is a member of the brotherhood, I'm more than a random pretty face for his own personal pleasure. I'm his revenge. I'm his captive.

There's another moment of silence between us as he takes me in. Finally, he says, "Can I get you anything for your pain? Some water? Food?" I furrow my brows.

Unable to take it anymore, I say, "Please, just…just get it over with." Tears fill my eyes as I know that's the last thing he'll do. He'll savor every second of his time with me before passing me off to his men and then any member of the brotherhood he can find.

"Get what over with?" I can't bring myself to look at him, to say it. Instead, I pull my knees into my chest and rest my head against them as tears fall, drenching the white fabric of my shirt. "Emma, I'm not…I'm not one of them." His words settle heavily on me, ripping a sharp cry from my chest. He's lying! He has to be. And if he isn't, then what the Hell else have I gotten myself into? "I'm not a member of the brotherhood. And I'm not going to hurt you. Nor will I let any of my men hurt you."

Slowly, I lift my head and rub the tears from my eyes so I can see him clearly. "You already have." He nods, clenching his jaw.

"We didn't know it was you." *Then who did he think I was?* If he's not a member of the brotherhood, then what is worth torturing someone over to keep hidden?

"That would've changed things? You've been following me for days, and you haven't exactly been a gentleman. How am I supposed to believe anything you say now?" I'm surprised by my candor. This man holds my life in his hands. You'd think I'd watch my tongue. But what does it matter? If he is who I think he is, he's going to destroy me no matter what I do or don't say.

"You're right," he concedes with a gentle nod. "I have been following you. But not for the reason your past has you thinking." A lump forms in my throat at his mention of my past. As far as the general public is concerned, evidence against the brotherhood was provided by an anonymous source. The only way he could know about the past he's referring to is if he went looking for it, for me specifically. Even still, he'd have to have friends in high places to pull the search off *or* the brotherhood's hacking capabilities. None of these possibilities make me feel relieved or confident in what he says.

"Then why?" I ask, playing along. He takes a deep breath and rests his elbows on his desk. If I didn't know any better, I'd say he wasn't planning on having this conversation with me. Let's say, hypothetically, I believe him. He's not a member of the brotherhood. He still has some sort of weird obsession with me. And whatever his plan is or was, my showing up wasn't part of it. He's caught off guard, or at least, he seems to be. In the spirit of the hypothetical, what the Hell is going on?

CHAPTER 12

Alister exhales and clenches his jaw once more. Then his golden eyes meet mine. "I had a plan to take down the brotherhood. You were part of it. You just didn't know it." There's a moment of silence between us as his words sink in. As if sensing my disbelief, he pours himself another glass of bourbon and finishes it off while I process this revelation. After news broke of the brotherhood last year, the concept of the organization was no longer a secret. Plenty of people believed in its existence. There just wasn't enough proof to do much about it. Realistically, he could know about the brotherhood without being part of it. But with all his guns and trained killers, why on earth would he think he needs my help going after them? And then there's the bone-chilling thought that if he isn't one of them, what is he? Because he's certainly not innocent.

"I don't understand," I admit. I drop my legs to the floor and sit up straight. "And I'm not saying I believe you. But if I did, why do you need me? You have enough men, guns. And if you truly know about my past, you have connections and the ability to gather intel."

Alister nods. "Yes. I have all those things. But I'm not the one who exposed the largest sex trafficking syndicate in North America. You are." My blood runs cold at the mention of *sex trafficking*.

"*What?* No. No. The brotherhood is an organization of elite men who prey on young women. It's not… They operate out of a nondescript club. They send invitations to college girls of their choosing. Gold calligraphy. Purple drinks. It's all a scheme to lure girls to them. It's not…" As I speak, fear settles in my bones. In all honesty, I don't know much about the brotherhood. All I know are the bits of information I discovered when investigating Beaux. I found the club and a way to get hired to work the party. But that was just one night in one city. If Mason is proof of anything it's that this organization stretches far beyond New Orleans. And with the way they evaded the police and the FBI, the brotherhood is more than just narcissistic, deranged men who feel entitled to women's bodies. They are smart, calculated, skilled. They are criminals.

"The clubs are just one facet of their operation. And it's the easiest part to crack since people talk, even when they're being threatened with exposure. Which is why they can't afford to only prey on local girls. Too many start talking and the walls around the truth begin to crumble. Which, I take it, is how you found your way in."

"So… They traffic girls from other states to these…parties." I can barely say the word. It's not a party these men treat these girls to. It's a taste of Hell. And yet, that's not the most disturbing part of what he's said. "If they're so concerned with keeping their secrets, I assume the girls they traffic never make it home."

Alister looks away from me then. He spins in his chair to assess his video monitors. "That's correct. The local girls they victimize are just a distraction from their real crimes. As the FBI investigated last year, they focused on the universities where the local girls were targeted. They approached the brotherhood as if they are a grounded organization despite being widespread. They never considered the possibility it was all just part of a bigger plan, one that is airborne, seaborne. Who knows?"

His words send shivers down my spine. I was there among all of them. Marissa was a local girl. If Beaux had targeted someone else, a girl not from around here, I could've had this information a year ago. Maybe the FBI would've approached their investigation differently. Maybe, maybe they would've actually gotten them. And yet, I was there, and I didn't even realize. I was so focused on Beaux, I didn't stop to help anyone else, to get more video coverage that could've put more men behind bars. Even Marissa, I almost let Beaux rape her just to catch him in the act. I move my hand to my stomach as guilt, sadness, and anger course through me.

"How do you know all this?" I finally ask, drawing his attention back to me.

"As you said before, I have ways of gathering intel. And I've been keeping an eye on you since your return to the city." He speaks so nonchalantly. As if his actions are the most normal thing in the world. "I assumed you were back to continue investigating the brotherhood after the police made a royal mess of things last year. But it quickly became obvious that was the last thing on your mind. You're still running—from the man that rounds the street corner a little too fast, from your own shadow."

I blush. He's been following me for more than a few days. And if he can find me, so can they. Assuming he's telling the truth about not being one of them.

"If that's true, then what changed? Why did you suddenly make your presence known? At the bar the other night, you didn't even order a drink. You went out of your way to bump into me before..."

"Before meeting with my contact," he finishes. His contact? So, he provides him information on the brotherhood. Or is that just a convenient story to cover up his real involvement with the organization? And besides, why would a member help an outsider try to take down the organization? I can't imagine the brothers would repay that kindness with anything less than death. "When I realized you weren't investigating the brotherhood, I felt you needed a little push."

"A push? So, you want me to investigate them? Why? And what kind of push were you trying to give me?"

"You have a lot of questions. I suppose that's normal."

"*Normal?* If you think any of this is normal, then you are severely disturbed. Though given our location and the fact that you're on a first-name basis with the King of Torment, that should've already been obvious to me."

Alister smiles then, leaning back in his chair. "Gio is not the King of Torment. Though perhaps I should start calling him that. It would be fitting, considering I am who they call the Blood Prince. Make that the Blood King since my father died."

I gulp at his admission. Just as I suspected earlier, there's a history of crime brewing in his blood. The question is, what kind of crime?

"Who's *they*? If you're not a member of the brotherhood, then what are you?"

Alister sits up straight and pours himself another glass of bourbon. That's his third, if I'm counting correctly. He's a large man. But any more than this and perhaps his inhibitions will be low enough for me to make a run for it. Though his consumption won't help me get past his guards. After taking a few sips of his drink, he finally says, "I'm a different kind of monster, Emma. I don't hurt women, unless they come after me."

"And why would a woman come after you?"

"That is not important. What's important is, you and I have the same enemy. My plan to scare you into investigating the brotherhood didn't exactly work. It pointed you in my direction instead. But—"

"Wait. You were hoping to scare me into investigating them?" I shake my head. "If you truly know what I've been through, then you must realize how cruel that is." He sets his glass to the side. The movement is so quick, every muscle in my body tenses.

"Emma, I am not a good man. I do unspeakable things to maintain my control. And when I have an enemy, there is no line I won't cross to destroy them. Perhaps what I did was cruel. But I'd do it again. That's the world I live in."

"And it's the one I fear will consume me," I admit. He doesn't have to remind me he isn't a good man. I never once thought he was. But the way he says there isn't a line he won't cross, it reaffirms my fear of him. He may not be a member of the brotherhood, but he's just as evil and just as capable of using and abusing me.

"I understand that fear. But, Emma, you must know, you're already in it. And once you're in, there is no escaping it." I don't argue with him. A year ago, I would have. I tried to get Beaux to see there was a way out, that he could own up to his wrongdoings and turn himself in. He'd never be free, but I thought at least he could be free of the brotherhood's control. I've since learned, both physically and mentally, their control is inescapable.

Alister drops my gaze then, appearing to consider his next words carefully. The bit of frustration that had enveloped him is now gone. Something tells me he doesn't lose control often. Which means if he ever does, the consequences will be deadly.

"As I was saying, we have a common enemy. I have the manpower, the weapons, and the connections. I can make sure when they go down, they stay down, and not just the New Orleans group. But there are some things even I can't achieve on my own. I have intel that I think you can help piece together. You may have stumbled into this mess by accident, but your stumble allowed the world a glimpse into an organization that had been operating in the shadows for decades. Imagine what you could accomplish if you actually focused on destroying them. With my help, I think we could. And before you put up a front, be honest with yourself. That panicked call to the police yesterday that turned out to be a false alarm. You're scared out of your mind, and you have every reason to be. If they haven't figured out who you are by now, it's only a matter of time until they do. And when they do, they'll come for you. And what Gio did will be nothing more than a welcome memory."

"Is this your way of convincing me to work with you? Convince me to destroy one devil by working with another who's just as intimidating and manipulative?"

Alister exhales. Again, he leans back in his chair. Only this time, he closes his eyes. Is that desperation I sense or just impatience? Does he actually want me to work with him? Does he really think I'm of value to his investigation? I'm not sure how the idea makes me feel. In his presence all I can focus on is my undying need to flee. Regardless of the new information he's shared with me, I don't trust him, not for a second. And if that isn't enough, there are a million other reasons why I will never find myself in his presence again. That is, if he even lets me leave.

"I have one question." It's a lie. I have too many questions for me to process, let alone ask him. So, instead, I ask him the one that's been playing repeatedly in my head ever since he revealed what the brotherhood was. He opens his eyes and motions for me to ask him. I take a deep breath. "If you know all of this, that the brotherhood is a sex trafficking syndicate, that it's been around for decades, then why haven't you done anything about it until now?"

Alister's eyes glaze over as my question hits him. He disappears inside his dark mind, and I wonder what he must be thinking about. For a moment, I have a flash of sympathy for him. If what he says is true, he inherited his evil world from his father. Like Beaux, he was dealt an unfair hand. And, like Beaux, he sees no way out. My sympathy for him leaves me as quickly as it came. His past doesn't excuse the actions of his present, no matter how deep the claws of darkness sink into him. I'm done having sympathy for men who can't understand that. Finally, Alister returns to his body.

"I only recently discovered the extent of the brotherhood's operation." It's a short, simple answer given the amount of time it took him to come up with it. I'm not sure I believe him. And even if I do, he said *the extent* of their operation. So, what? Is he okay with them preying on local girls but not trafficking others? Or vice versa? If he was aware of their heinous actions, no matter the capacity, he should've worked to stop them. If he has the resources he claims to, it's within his power to do so. So, why didn't he? Why has he just sat on the sidelines and let these horrible things happen until now? Why am I even asking myself this? He's a monster. A different kind, sure. But he's still a monster. I can't expect decency or chivalry of him.

With nothing left to say to him, I offer him a nod as my response and sit quietly. He wants something from me. That gives me leverage. If given the opportunity, I'll use it to get him to let me walk out of here in one piece.

Alister stands then and walks to one of the cabinets to our left. My heartbeat quickens in my chest as I watch him. Perhaps it was wrong of me to end our conversation, especially without agreeing to his request. Now he has no reason not to kill me. I tense as his hand grasps something in the cabinet. I glance toward the door and then to the video monitors. I don't see any guards posted outside. Maybe— That's when I see it, the first aid kit in his hand.

Alister approaches me with the kit, a bottle of water, and Advil. I shrivel in my chair at his proximity. "I am sorry for the treatment you've suffered today and in your past." He sits next to me, handing me the water and the Advil. I take it, only because I can use the bottle as a weapon if he tries anything. "The medicine will help with the swelling in your face and the pain. The water will help sooth your throat and allow your muscles to uncoil."

"I'm not sure that's possible in your presence." He smiles to himself. It's not an arrogant smile. Rather, it's a sad one.

"I know you don't trust me. You have no reason to. But I'm not sure what else I can say to change that." At that, he opens the first aid kit and begins pulling out supplies. I watch his hands like a hawk, noting the medical scissors just within reach—both his *and* mine.

"Words mean nothing to me. If you want to prove to me that I can trust you…" I start, but stop, knowing I can only use this leverage once.

"Yes?" he asks, stopping his task to focus on me. My face aches as the words come to me. I'm not sure whether I should bring them into this or not. But he's already admitted to following me. He knows about my past, about Beaux, about why

I was at Club Gent that night. Which means he's got connections in the police department. Which would explain how he knew about the 911 call I made yesterday. And if he knows that, then he knows where I live. He knows about Julian.

My lip quivers as I realize I have no choice. I thought I could use my leverage to make him let me go. But he knows far more about me than I will ever know about him. Within a matter of minutes, he could have men at my house. Seconds more and he could have Julian killed. I can't demand my freedom when I must bargain for the safety of the ones I love. If I do what he asks, maybe he'll grant me this one decency.

I bite back my emotion and force the words across my lips. "If you want to prove to me that I can trust you, if you want my help, you have to promise me one thing."

"Name it." Life brightens his cheeks, and I realize how dim he was before.

"My friends, my family, my love," I choke out. "They will remain untouched. No matter what happens between us, no matter whether we succeed or fail in taking down the brotherhood, you won't harm them. And..." Sensing his delight at my submission, I push for one more thing. "If the brotherhood comes after them, you and your men will protect them."

"What about you?" he asks, his dark brows crinkling. Once more, my lip quivers. And this time, tears fill my eyes.

"Even if we survive going up against the brotherhood, I'm not stupid enough to think you'll let me live. You may be a different kind of monster than they are, but you're still a monster with secrets. My guess is, maintaining your secrets is key to maintaining your control. And you've already admitted you do unspeakable things to maintain your control."

CHAPTER 13

Water trickles from the faucet hanging over the edge of my clawfoot tub. The simple sound keeps me grounded in the present despite the urge to slip into the darkness of my mind. I can still smell the faint hint of urine lingering on my skin. I can taste the copper of the blood that filled my mouth. With all my makeup removed, the oval-shaped purple bruises spread across my throat are on full display. There is a small, stinging cut on my cheek where one of Alister's henchmen slammed his gun into me. The balm Alister applied over it has been wiped away.

Today has been a shocking day. From being kidnapped and tortured, to learning the brotherhood is more complex and more dangerous than I ever could've imagined, to Alister requesting my help in destroying them. I'm still not sure if I believe he isn't one of them. But, no matter what I believe, none of those things were more shocking to me than the moment he tended to my injuries, had his men retrieve my purse from the restaurant, gave me back my clothes, and had Gio drive me home.

He let me go. I didn't have to beg. I didn't even have to ask.

I'm not sure what kind of game he's playing. Perhaps he feels he's demonstrated his power so well I won't dare run or speak out about what I know. And he'd be right.

Gio opens the car door. I sling my legs out of the vehicle and push myself to a standing position. I'm unable to get away from him fast enough, both figuratively and physically. Gio sidesteps in front of me, blocking my path to the front door of my home. My body brushes against his. The brief touch twists my insides. His dark eyes burn my skin as he gazes upon me. I do not meet his gaze. Instead, I keep my eyes focused on the door, the door behind which is safety, behind which is Mason. God! Please don't let him see us. If he does, he'll get himself killed. It's then that Gio says, "Mr. Amato informed me of your request for protection for your loved ones. As his head of security, I'll personally see to their safety."

"Somehow that isn't very comforting," I say. My honesty surprises me. His presence makes me weak, light-headed. Knowing that at any moment he could— I stop myself. Thoughts of chains, torches, and rough hands make me want to vomit. It wasn't long ago he tortured me within an inch of consciousness and now he's responsible for Julian's safety and Kat's. If he uses his talents for good, then maybe they're in good hands. But if he—

"Remember the terms of your deal. No one can know of our plans, of Mr. Amato, of anything you saw or heard today. The Amato family values nothing more than loyalty. And they punish those who betray them with the most ferocity." Gio's warning forces me to meet his eyes. They are cold and certain. Gio said he didn't want to hurt me, and then he proceeded to do just that. His loyalty to the Amato family, to Alister, is undeniable and unwavering. Which means he won't hesitate to make sure I uphold my end of our bargain. Just as I part my lips to tell him I will, he turns, directing his gaze toward my home. "You should get inside and get cleaned up before your boyfriend gets home. I'm told he won't be long."

At Gio's mention of Julian, my breath catches in my throat. He has eyes on him. He knows where he is at this very moment. As easily as Alister and Gio can protect the people I love, they can take them away. With this realization, I put one foot in front of the other and do as Gio says. What choice do I have?

Choice. The only choice I had in all of this was choosing to pursue Alister, alone no less. I made the wrong choice. And now, I'm deeper into this world of despair than I ever planned to be. Alister was right. There is no escape.

I lock the door behind me and press my ear against the wooden frame to listen as the car accelerates, taking Gio far away. Though I suspect not far enough for my comfort—something I'm not sure I'll ever feel again. Behind closed eyes, I'm haunted by the brotherhood. But now, my time awake is haunted by a new kind of terror, a new kind of monster.

"Emma, you're back." I jump at Mason's voice, pulling my purse tight against my chest. Turning to face him, I find him dressed in swim trunks and nothing else. The ripe smell of chlorine and sunscreen fills the air between us. It hides the stench of urine and sweat oozing from me. At least, I hope it does. His brows crinkle as he takes me in. Oh no!

"Yeah," I say, shielding my still swollen cheek with my hair. "I had some errands to run what with our upcoming move." I move past him toward the stairs, avoiding his gaze.

"Move?" Shit! He was asleep when Julian left, which means Julian likely hasn't told him of our plans to leave New Orleans. It's not a big deal for me to mention it to him. But, the longer I stand here, the more likely he is to notice my face and the uncommon odor that seared my nose hairs on the way home.

"Yeah." I take a deep breath, refusing to turn back to him. "Listen, I would explain but I'm exhausted. Can we talk later?"

Mason hesitates. "Sure. You can tell me about your day and what kind of errands bring you home empty-handed." I pinch my eyes closed as I hear the suspicion in his voice. Julian is intuitive and careful with when and how he expresses his thoughts. Mason, on the other hand, is impossibly perceptive and quick to share his suspicions. Why couldn't he have stayed in the pool a moment longer? When I don't turn back to him, he moves closer to me and places his palm on my shoulder. The unexpected touch makes me flinch. "S-sorry," he stammers, removing his palm. "I don't mean to push you or make you uncomfortable. It's just... Emma, you won't even look at me. Did I do something wrong? Is that why you went out today, because you didn't want to be around me?"

"No!" I blurt out. "I went out because..." I may not be able to tell him the truth, but that doesn't mean I have to let him think he's the problem. Although, it would be an easy out. But no. Mason means too much. He's been through too much. We all have. "I went out because I wanted to," I say then. "So much has been taken from me, this city is only the most recent trophy the brotherhood has won. You know what that's like, don't you? I just—I just wanted a moment to myself in the city I love before I have to say goodbye."

"Yeah, I get it." I hear the emotion in Mason's voice. I want to turn around and hug him, listen to him. He's been alone for so long. Before today I would say I can't imagine how he must feel. But now I do. I'm alone, alone in this fight *that I never wanted, this fight that I'm not prepared for, that I don't know if I'll—*

"Mason, I—I'm sorry. I just need to lie down."

Mason means well. So does Julian. If I weren't afraid for their lives *and* unconvinced of their ability to restrain themselves and keep a secret while the three of us come up with a plan to escape the Blood King on top of evading the brotherhood, then I would tell them everything. I don't want to do this alone, whatever this is, but I *am* afraid. I know Alister won't hesitate to order their execution if I betray him. And for what? What do I actually know about him? I know he knows far too much about the brotherhood to be innocent. I know he has guards who carry guns and are skilled in the art of torture. I know he's smart enough to have a decoy desk in his restaurant and no doubt has many scattered across the city. Something tells me he doesn't keep all his skeletons buried in one place. Like the brotherhood, if one element of his operation is exposed, he'll know in enough time to protect the rest. I never figured out what the green sticky note meant. Wherever it led, no doubt Alister and his men have erased any trace that could be linked back to them. Regardless of what I consider a failed mission, I've seen too much for him to let me live. I know he intends to kill me when this game of his is finished.

When I told Alister I didn't expect him to let me live, I was fishing for his intentions. And his response, or lack of, told me everything I need to know. He didn't refute my statement. He didn't even bother giving me false hope. He told me himself he is the Blood Prince. *No.* The Blood King. I don't know what kind of illegal activity he's into. But as much as I know he is evil, I know he has the power to keep his wicked ways secret. He has men in the police force and God only knows where else. How else could he have known about the 911 call I made yesterday? So, yes, he's right. He has scared me into submission, a kind of submission more crippling than anything I've ever felt before. If I reveal this most unspeakable truth, I risk the lives of the people I love. And yet, if I don't, I'm walking into the Devil's den alone with no hope of returning to the land of the living.

As I stare into the mirror before me, assessing the damage of the day, I feel disgusted. Not at my appearance. Not at the minor marks left on my body. I am disgusted because the simple pattern of bruises does nothing to reveal the true torment I've endured today. I thought I was going to die. *No.* I imagined a fate worse than death as I regained consciousness tied to a chair in the dark room of an abandoned warehouse. Only it wasn't abandoned. Even before I spotted the countless guards roaming the property on the screens of Alister's video monitors, I could feel it in my bones. Thinking myself captured by the brotherhood, finally, after all this time, I felt an energy of death and despair dance across my skin as I imagined all the ways they would hurt me, break me, over and over again. And yet, I wasn't prepared for Gio, for the chains, for the torch, for the torture.

I let my hand slip from my neck down to my inner thigh. Of all the times I've imagined what the brotherhood would do to me if they caught me, of all the nightmares that have forced me to live through their attacks, I never imagined something so sinister as a torch between my legs. At the thought, my legs begin to shake and I catch myself against the cool marble vanity before me.

Gio said he underestimated me, that I held out longer than some of his own men. You'd think his words would make me feel strong. And yet, I couldn't feel weaker because I know if I'd known how to answer his questions, I would have. I would have crumbled out of fear for my body and what he planned to do to me. The second he showed me the torch, I melted at his feet. And Alister—I played along, juicing him for every bit of information I could. But not for a second did I believe I'd have the chance to act on it. I was curious, sure. But, most of all, I was desperate for more time, time to wrap my head around my downfall and the fact that I would never get to hold the ones I love again.

 I like to think of myself as a fighter. No matter how badly Beaux hurt me or how terrifying his threats, I didn't back down because the moment Julian walked into my life, I had something to fight for. I had hope. But by the time Alister got me alone in his office, I was defeated. I told him to *just get it over with*. I practically gave him permission to rape me because I knew my time was up. And that is the fate I know waits for me once I'm captured by the brotherhood. It's what I keep running from and yet, in that moment, there was nowhere left to run to and I gave in.

 My lip quivers as tears fill my eyes. In that moment, I was broken, broken by the fear of an unspeakable pain, broken with the realization that I was too weak to continue fighting. Broken. And yet, as I stand here, my reflection does nothing to tell the story of how he and his men shredded my pride and my hope and cast new fears upon me that I will never escape. Alister said it himself, if the brotherhood catches me, what Gio did to me today will be nothing but a fond memory.

 I grab the washcloth from the vanity and shove it in my mouth so that Mason doesn't hear my screams. My efforts to conceal my cries bring tears to my eyes as the pain of this secret, this silent Hell tormenting me from the inside out, rivals the physical pain I endured today. I bring my hands to my stomach as the cries rip through me. I'm not sure which is worse—if Alister is telling the truth or if he isn't.

 If Alister is telling the truth, then I have a dangerous and deadly temporary ally who may have the power to destroy my greatest enemy. The only price I must pay is my life. And if he can destroy the brotherhood, then what hope do I have to survive him? And yet, if he's lying, if he's one of them, then my greatest nightmare is now my reality. Only this reality is far more sinister than I ever could've imagined. And I can't tell anyone. I can't warn the people I love, because, if they knew the truth, it would be their death sentence. And yet, what if they're already dead? What if we all are? We just don't know it yet.

I throw my hands out and use the vanity to hold myself up as my cries drain what little energy I have left. I have no idea what Alister's real plans for me are. I have no way of ensuring he lives up to his end of the bargain to protect the people I love. Yet, if there is a chance that he will, I have to keep my word to him. I have to keep this secret. Because the brotherhood is real and they're coming for me. And I can't stop them. If Alister can, then I'm at his mercy. Which is precisely why he let me go. Because he knows, just as the brotherhood controls me, now, so does he.

I pull the cloth from my mouth as my breaths become shallow. As my eyes return to the mirror before me, fresh blood mixes with my tears, trickling down my rose-red cheeks. It escapes the small cut on my cheek now aggravated from my screaming. I look like something from a horror film and yet, I still don't look like myself, my real self, the self no one but Julian is ever able to see.

It's then that I pull my fist back with all the strength I can muster and slam it into the glass mirror in front of me. Small splinters of glass cut into my knuckles, but despite my force, the mirror barely cracks. So I hit it again and again and again until the pane shatters and shards of glass fall around me. This isn't just about Alister and Gio, or even the brotherhood. The events of the past year, including the pain Beaux and my father put me through, have morphed me into someone I don't recognize. Like me, the mirror takes a few sucker punches before it breaks. Today was the final gut punch, the last bit of pain I could endure before everything in me shattered, and once broken, there's no putting me back together.

When I'm finished, my right hand is a bloody mess. Only a few jagged pieces of glass remain attached to the frame of the mirror. Cracks crawl across their surface like snakes slithering across a smooth, sandy beach. *Finally.* A girl I recognize stares back at me.

"Emma! Emma, what's happening? Are you okay?" The doorknob jiggles as Mason tries to rip the door open from the other side.

"I'm fine," I lie. He won't believe me. Neither will Julian. But it's okay. They know as well as anyone the toll the brotherhood demands. What they don't know, what I pray they never know, is what it feels like to stand over your own grave, waiting for the shadows to shove you in.

CHAPTER 14

Cool air caresses my skin, lulling me from the clutches of my subconscious. I jolt up in bed and am met by the rhythmic sounds of Julian's breathing and waves crashing onto the shore. My chest aches as my heart settles. We've been away from New Orleans for almost three weeks now. Each night, I have the same nightmare that began after Beaux first attacked me. We're in my old room. A small sliver of light streams from the bedroom door as he leaves me, swollen and whimpering on my bed. And then, the light leaves me once again as another man enters. And another. And another. None of them have faces. They have hands, mouths, and every other body part. But no face. And I wake, just like this, covered in sweat and on the verge of a panic attack, because I know it could be anyone. And I won't be sure until it's too late.

At that, I swing my legs off the bed and stand, careful not to wake Julian. It won't be long now and his wound will be healed enough for us to fly to Europe. I don't think I'll sleep more than twenty minutes at a time until there is an ocean between us and the brotherhood. At least, I pray the distance will help. I'm not sure how much longer I can go on like this. And yet something tells me this Hell has only just begun.

Moonlight illuminates the shore beneath us as I make my way out onto the balcony. We've been staying in a beachfront hotel on Tybee Island. It was a careful choice. Nothing too expensive so we don't find ourselves in the same circles as members of the brotherhood. But also nothing too cheap or private. We need to stay safe while Julian recovers, and we need to do it without drawing attention from the locals. I have a feeling this philosophy will guide our decisions abroad too. I bite my lip. The more I feel I may cry, the harder I bite until I taste blood.

I'm not complaining. Complaining would be stupid considering the man I love is alive and resting just mere feet away. My forehead wrinkles as I remember back. Though remember isn't the best word because the visions of that morning never leave me. Every time he removes his shirt. Every time I clean his wound. Every time he winces from lifting something that tears at his stitches. Every time his breath catches when he sleeps. I am transported back to that morning when he lay bleeding in my arms. Tears slip slowly down my face as the images come to me. My skin is damp with the thick humidity and yet, my tears are cold on my cheeks, cold with the realization that I almost lost him. That Beaux almost took him from me. He didn't succeed, but that doesn't mean they won't.

I turn sharply toward the bedroom as the sound of breaking glass travels through the night air. "No! Please! Take me! Take me instead!" I scream the words but no sound crosses my lips. Instead, my legs are heavy as I move toward the balcony door. It's pitch black inside the room. All that is visible is the broken lamp next to Julian's side of the bed and the slash of blood *sprayed across white pressed sheets. And then—there's a cry in the night. But it's not human. It's a familiar sound I know all too well. It's too beautiful to belong here among this despair. And yet, it calls to me. It begs me to close my eyes until—*

I wake as Julian moves his bow across the strings of his violin. He doesn't look at me as he plays. He's lost in his mind as he pulls me from mine. His eyes are closed. His mouth is pressed into a flat line, his body moving back and forth with the fluidity of his song. He knows not to touch me when I'm having a nightmare. It only makes it worse. Instead, he plays for me. He allows his music to find me and bring me back to him. And bring me back he does. Julian finishes, finally allowing his eyes to meet mine. He gives me a pained grin and sets his violin to the side. There's no need for him to ask what my dream was about. He knows. It's the same each time. A dream within a dream. A nightmare that leaves me in shambles unless he can pull me out in time. What he doesn't know is that my waking hours are no longer a reprieve from my nightmare.

I fold back the covers as Julian moves toward me. He slips into the bed easily and immediately pulls me against his chest. My damp hair sprawls across his arm as I rest my bandaged hand over his ribs. The bathroom door is open just past the foot of the bed. I know he's seen the mess I've left. Thankfully, he hasn't cleaned it up. I want it to stay there as a physical representation of the pain I feel inside, the pain of this secret, the pain of this new reality that pursuing Alister has thrust me into.

"What happened?" Julian finally asks, breaking the silence between us. I inhale his calming scent and snuggle tighter against him as he moves his hand up and down my back. "Mason said you seemed a little off when you got back home today and then he heard glass break."

I nod. "Yeah, *off* is a way of putting it."

I open the bathroom door to find Mason sitting on the edge of my and Julian's bed. "Mason, what the Hell! What if I had been naked?" I tug the towel wrapped around my body higher over my chest, thankful for the makeup I used to cover the bruises around my neck.

"Then you would've been stupid to think I would just walk away after hearing what I heard." Mason stands, taking a step toward me.

"And what did you hear?" The words come out with more bite than I intend. He doesn't deserve my anger and yet it still courses through me as present as the blood in my veins.

"I don't know. You tell me. At first, it was something that sounded like a strangled cat and then glass shattering." It's then that he notices the cut on my cheek and the fresh wounds on my knuckles. "Emma, what the Hell?" He brushes my wet hair behind my ear. Makeup doesn't exactly cover broken skin as well as it does bruises. "I take it your hand was your doing," he says, glancing at the mess I've left in the bathroom. "But your cheek. That's another story."

My lips part as my mind scrambles for an explanation. And yet, the more I think, the more I'm forced to remember how I received my wound. Flashes of Alister's office come to me, and then the man, the gun. I froze, just like I feared I would. I could've stopped him. I could've saved myself and I didn't. I move past Mason to sit on the edge of the bed as light-headedness returns to me.

"Emma? Tell me. What happened? What's going on?"

Mason sits next to me as my breaths become rapid. I bring my hand to my chest and close my eyes. Minutes pass before I regain control of my lungs. Finally, I open my eyes. "It was an accident. I...I had glass in my knuckles and somehow I nicked my cheek. It's no big deal."

"No big deal?" I turn to Mason then and pray he buys my story. If he doesn't, what will I do? What can I do? My chest tightens as I imagine Gio lurking outside as we speak just waiting for the right moment to pounce. "Those aren't exactly the words I would use, nor would Julian. And it's more than your cheek, it's—" Mason moves his eyes to the broken glass covering the bathroom floor. Some of it has specks of blood on it. "Were you trying to hurt yourself? Because of the brotherhood, the stress, the fear, the fact that your time in New Orleans is coming to an end?"

As Mason speaks, his voice is soft, gentle, almost fragile. It's like he's afraid to ask me what's on his mind, which would be a first. Though perhaps he's more afraid of my answer.

"No. No, I wasn't trying to hurt myself." I move my eyes to my wrists then, remembering back to a different time, a time when I did resort to such measures. "I just needed to let go, to allow myself to feel my anger. I needed to break something so that maybe I would feel—"

"Less broken," Mason offers. "Or, perhaps just more honest."

I watch Mason as his eyes move from the broken glass to his own hands, hands that have no doubt left a few broken things in their wake. "Something tells me you know the feeling."

"Today kind of got the best of me. Well, maybe it's more than today."

"Talk to me." Julian brings his lips to my hair, kissing me softly. I wrap my arm around him tighter and close my eyes, as if doing so will mean I can live in his arms forever. In his arms, I feel seen, safe. At least, I normally do. But even as I close my eyes, in this moment, I can't shake my fears. I know Gio and his men are watching us. Just thinking about them makes my skin crawl. They would've followed Julian home. They won't leave until they're sure I haven't told him anything about Alister and his request for my help, a request Julian would never let me meet.

I take a deep breath as my head aches with my reality. I inhale Julian's scent once more and do my best to memorize the way his fingers caress the smooth skin of my back. They brush over the silky fabric of my top before trailing up my exposed back to the nape of my neck. This simple moment will give me comfort if I ever find myself bound by the Devil again. Though the thought of Alister, of the brotherhood, of the ropes around my wrists and ankles and the chains gripped around my neck... I push myself to a sitting position then as my throat constricts and oxygen becomes harder to consume.

"Emma?" Julian sits up beside me. Worry contorts his features as he brings his palm to my lower back.

"I'm okay." It's a lie, but I can't have him know otherwise.

"No. You're not. What's going on?"

I bite my lip as I move my eyes from him to my hands resting on my thighs. Alister's balm reduced the redness and swelling of my wrists, leaving no trace of their presence. I suppose I should be grateful. That's one less thing I have to hide from Julian. But instead, it makes me angry and reminds me of why I broke the mirror in the first place. Mason recognized my pain. I imagine he grew accustomed to it as he hid for months in isolation. Silence and secrets are two things that will eat away at you, two things Mason and I know all too well. But Julian? More than my pain, Julian knows me. He knows when I'm upset, when I'm hurting and scared. He can see it all over my face, in my blank eyes, in the worry line above my brow, and in my slumped shoulders. He can't know the truth, but I also can't hide my fears from him. I won't.

"I thought coming back here would connect me with who I used to be, but I just keep getting sucked deeper and deeper into this world of darkness. Julian, I've lost so much of myself to it. I don't even recognize myself anymore."

My brows crinkle and my eyes glaze over as the words leave me. Today isn't the first time I've felt myself slipping away nor is it the first time I've felt the darkness of Alister's world, Beaux's world, *my* world invade my being. It's not that I feel myself becoming a monster, like them, like I was in Paris. Instead, I feel the parts of me that are normal and innocent suffocate within me. Escaping the brotherhood *and* Alister while fighting the consumption of this world, it's more than a physical thing. It's mental, emotional. It's all-consuming. And once the darkness has devoured the light, I'm not sure what will remain, who I will become, or if I'll even have a chance to find out. I blink away fresh tears as my cheeks tighten.

"So much has happened so fast." I look to Julian then. "My life before Beaux and the brotherhood feels so foreign to me. It's almost like it never even happened. It's like this moment, who I am today is who I've always been. It's like nothing before now even matters, because this…this reality of fear and anxiety and pain and exhaustion is all I am. And how can I expect the future to be any different?" *If I have a future.*

"Hey. Come here." Julian rests his back against the headboard and pulls me onto his lap. I wrap my legs around him as he brings his palms to my cheeks. His icy eyes scan every inch of my face. They take in my worry lines and the sliver of broken skin left in the wake of Alister's henchman. I drop his gaze, shielding the rest of me from his view out of fear some of my concealer may have rubbed off my neck. When he brings his finger to my chin, forcing me to look at him once more, I see that it hasn't. Or else I'd be met with a hard look of vicious protectiveness rather than the gentle understanding only he can offer me. "You are not this moment. You are not this pain," he says then.

Julian reaches for my wrist and brings my bandaged knuckles to his lips. I'm thankful for his patience and the gentle way he handles me. My body is still tender from Gio's torment. But mostly, it's my heart that's fragile, that feels as if the parts of me I recognize, the parts of me that Julian loves, are hanging on by a thread. "You are the same girl who loves to dance even if there is no music. You're the girl who appreciates the little things, a game of checkers, a home-cooked meal, a peck on the cheek, a conversation. You find the beauty in the disaster."

"Perhaps I've become the beauty in the disaster," I mumble.

"Well, you are beautiful," Julian says, bringing his hands to my hips. "And I'm not going to lie to you and tell you that our life is perfect, easy, fair." Julian stops himself, presses his lips into a flat line, and shakes his head.

"Hey. What is it?" I ask, brows crinkling.

"Nothing, I just…I want to say the right thing. I want to be there for you and take away your pain. But…I don't think I can."

I nod. He's right. He can't take away my pain. He never could.

"I don't need you to take away my pain," I say then. "I need…" I start but stop myself. I've never needed or wanted Julian to save me. Our relationship has never been about that. There's only one thing I need from Julian, one thing that only he can give me. After what happened today, I'm not sure it's fair of me to even ask it of him. I'm not sure it's even possible.

"What? What do you need, my love?" Julian's eyes search

mine for the answer I'm reluctant to give. There was a time when I wondered what life would be like if I'd met Julian first. If I'd never known Beaux, if he'd never hurt me, if I never knew of the brotherhood. Now, I can't even imagine what that world would be like. Mason warned me. My father warned me that my life would never be the same if I chose to expose the brotherhood, to pursue justice against Beaux. I came into this world with my eyes wide open. I chose to give up normal for the truth. I came into this world with my eyes wide open, yet I made my decision blindly, because I didn't know then what I know now. I didn't know the pain of losing yourself to a world of darkness and sorrow. I didn't know how much I'd crave a normal life and the despair I'd feel knowing that normal is the last thing I'll ever have.

I run my fingers through Julian's hair and adjust myself over him so that we're so close I can feel his heart beat beneath the fabric of his T-shirt. A year ago, I could see the bigger picture. I could see that *my* truth and *my* justice wasn't just about me. It was about all the other women preyed on by Beaux and the brotherhood. But now, after a year on the run and with my life on the line every second of every day, all I can see are the shadows closing in, waiting to consume my body and soul. Perhaps that's why I gave in to Alister. Perhaps that's why I didn't fight back when the man approached me in Alister's office. I'm so exhausted. Maybe there is no fight left in me. Maybe, deep down, I'd rather die than—

"Hope," I say then. "I need you to give me hope."

CHAPTER 15

"Julian, this blindfold is giving me déjà vu in the worst way."

"Little step," he says as he helps me from the car onto a sidewalk. "Steady." Julian releases my hands and positions himself behind me. I told him I didn't think leaving the house was a good idea. But after my request for hope, he insisted. He said he has something he wants to show me, something he worked on for most of the day after a few hours spent planning our upcoming departure. I have no idea what it could be. The blindfold along with knowledge of Alister's men lurking in the shadows only intensifies my anxiety and desire to get whatever this is over with.

"You think you've lost yourself. You think this world is consuming you. Maybe it is changing you, but that doesn't mean you're any less *you*." Despite my anxiety, Julian's words, for a moment, put me at ease and allow me to forget about what hides in the thick New Orleans night. I take a deep breath as Julian removes the blindfold. As I open my eyes, what I find leaves me speechless.

Before us, sprawling across the bright blue exterior of Lucid Records is a painting. No, *the* painting, the one that brought me and Julian together for the first time. Only now the girl isn't some random, unimportant backdrop to a metaphor. She looks like me. She *is* me. I step forward, just out of Julian's grasp. I take in her blond locks flung across the side of the building in dramatic disarray. Instead of charcoal and nondescript, her eyes are green. Her lips are strawberry pink. And the words scattered throughout her hair and the lines of her features reach inside me and squeeze every part of me that's still willing to feel.

Making up the lines of her eyes, lips, and face are the words *Daughter. Sister. Friend. Lover. Writer. Preservationist. Advocate. Truth Teller. Warrior. Survivor.* "Those are the things that you are," Julian whispers, wrapping his arms around me. I snuggle into him. "But you wouldn't be any of them without the sum of your experiences, both the good and the bad." Julian directs my attention to the left side of the painting. Written among the strands of blond hair are the words *Loved. Valued. Respected. Trusted. Worthy. Chosen.* And to the right, in similar fashion, *Hurt. Misunderstood. Shunned. Manipulated. Devalued. Abandoned. Abused. Gaslit. Threatened. Hunted. Attacked.*

As my eyes graze over the final word, I wrap my arms over Julian's. He pulls me tighter against him as if to remind me I'm not alone. "You're not broken, Emma," he says then. "You're experienced. You can't...*we* can't escape the horrors we've endured. They've forever changed us. But they don't make us empty. They are what make us whole." Julian goes quiet then as I allow his words to sink in. He drops his head until his lips press onto my shoulder. His dark locks tangle with mine as a soft summer breeze and the sounds of the French Quarter trumpet players wrap around us. I take note of his use of the words *we* and *us*. This Hell that has become my life is also his. It's also

Mason's. I know that and yet, it's so easy to forget, especially after a day like today.

"I'm sorry," I whisper.

"For what?"

"For dragging you into this, for everything you've had to sacrifice because of your love for me."

"Hey." Julian spins me around, forcing me to face him. "Don't say that. I knew what I was getting into when I decided to leave New Orleans with you. None of what happened last year is your fault and neither is anything that's happening now. You have no reason to apologize to me."

"But how could you have known what you were getting into when I didn't even know?" Julian's eyes scan mine. I see the question resting on his parted lips. I bury my face in his chest before he can ask it. "Everyone warned me of the consequences of going against the brotherhood. I thought I was listening. I thought I could handle it. But...I didn't realize what I was giving up. If I had known then what I know now...I don't know if I would've made the same choice."

My admission riddles me with so much guilt I pinch my eyes closed to keep fresh tears from falling. It's the same pang of guilt I felt when Alister called me out for not continuing my own investigation into the brotherhood after the FBI let it go cold. I never wanted them as an enemy. I never had a personal vendetta against them. Everything I did that led me to them was in pursuit of Beaux's secrets, not theirs. And yet, they are one and the same. Still, I never wanted this fight. I never wanted to be a part of this world, *their* world, which is slowly becoming my own. I thought the FBI would take them down and there would come a time when I'd be safe again, when Julian and I could be normal again. But normalcy requires more than safety, and even safety is in short supply since the brotherhood is free to continue its reign of terror. And now Alister—

"I do," Julian says then, pulling me from my thoughts. He rests his chin on my head as I watch the flame of the gas lantern down the street dance in the wind. "Courage. It's one of the many qualities that I love about you. You do the right thing, no matter how hard it is, no matter the risk it forces you to take. Last year, you did the right thing, Emma. And you'd do it again, even knowing what you know now, because that's who you are. Maybe you don't need hope or the promise that things will get better. Maybe you just need to remember who you are and what you stand for. Because more than anything, that's what you need to cling to. That's what will remind you that this is all worth it."

I bite my lip, allowing his words to course through me as if they are my life source. And, in many ways, they are. "And what reminds you that this is all worth it?" I ask.

Julian brings his finger to my chin and guides my eyes to his. "I'm holding her in my arms." At that, something broken in me begins to heal. My chest is warm with his words, with his love. His faith in me is like a thread working its way through the broken pieces of my heart, knotting it back together again. For my own sanity, I do my best to see myself through his eyes, to remember who I am. Julian brings his lips to mine, and I get lost in his kiss. So lost I don't think about who may be watching or how we'll escape the most dangerous men in New Orleans. At least, I try not to.

"JULIAN, are you sure about this? Maybe we should just get something to go." To say my moment of escape fizzled as quickly as it arose would be an understatement. Julian wraps his arm around me as I take note of every suspicious figure loitering along the dimly lit street.

"No. We made time for date nights while abroad. We can manage a quick meal and a dance or two every now and then. If not, we might as well be dead."

"*Julian!* Don't joke like that!" I scold him by popping my hand against his abs. He only laughs. Despite my wariness, I know he's right. Without moments like tonight, what is the point in being alive? Our life would be nothing but stress and fear and constant running. Without hope for happiness, there is no reason for us to even leave New Orleans. No reason for me to go along with Alister's plan while Julian finds us a safe route out of the city and untraceable new identities. And yet, my decision and renewed sense of hope does nothing to quell the fear inside me.

"Ah!" I gasp. I inch closer to Julian as a hooded figure propels himself from the shadows.

Julian's hand immediately moves to his pocket where I know he keeps his knife while his other wraps around my wrist, ready to shove me behind him at a moment's notice. The man before us keeps walking without sparing us a glance. The asshole probably just wanted to scare us. I take a step forward so I can watch him disappear into the alleyway on the opposite side of the street. He takes only one step into the darkness before it consumes him. The gas lanterns and neon signs lighting up the French Quarter businesses don't offer the best visibility, which only makes the Quarter after dark even more dangerous.

"You're okay," Julian whispers. "I've got you." I nod. Julian takes my hand in his. Our fingers intertwine. Our walk from Lucid to Mimi's brings back memories, both good and bad, just like every other corner of New Orleans. Mimi's is the place I first saw Julian play the violin. It's where we first kissed. It's where he first saved me from Beaux and from the other predators of the night. As fate would have it, it will be our first and last date in New Orleans.

Julian pushes open the antique wooden door of Mimi's. I step inside the brick-walled space and allow the warmth of the room and the memories here to chase away the chill of the night and the monsters who have me in their sights. It hasn't changed a bit.

"Upper or lower?" the hostess asks.

"Upper," I say.

We follow the hostess up the metal staircase as dozens of jiving bodies move on the dance floor beneath us. It's a Monday night. So, you'd think things would be slower paced. Nope. Here, Mondays and Tuesdays are for numbing the pain of the work-week. Wednesdays are for complaining. Thursdays are for praying—praying your boss forgets about that Friday afternoon staff meeting and praying for a weekend without a hangover or an STD. Fridays, well, they're probably the same everywhere. As the hostess seats me and Julian at a highboy table with a perfect view of the stage and dance floor below, a small smile lifts my lips.

"This is the first time since we've been back that New Orleans has felt like home."

Julian's smile matches mine as he offers me his hand across the table. "New Orleans will always be home, no matter where we go." Julian brushes his thumb over my palm then. I nod as his words settle on my heart. He told me just because I've changed, it doesn't mean I am any less me. Maybe the same can be said of the Crescent City. It's been forever since it has felt like home, but that doesn't mean it isn't. It doesn't mean I won't miss it and the good times when we leave.

"So, how was your day? Have you given any thought about where we may go next?" I ask. But just as I do, our waitress approaches, silencing Julian. He looks to me as the waitress puts the menus in front of us.

"Oh, I think we're ready to order," I tell her. Julian nods. "We'll both have the chicken tacos. No sour cream or cheese with his. I'll have a margarita on the rocks, and he will have a glass of Merlot."

I hand the menus back to her as a young musician takes the stage beneath us. He can't be older than fifteen and yet he plays the guitar as if he's got thirty years of experience beneath his belt. He reminds me of Julian, of what he must've been like as a teen. Even more, he reminds me of the life Julian and I hoped to have upon returning to New Orleans. Us running Lucid Records and the speakeasy together while Julian produced records for local artists. No doubt he would've signed the young man strumming away on stage. It's not just New Orleans we're leaving behind. It's our dream.

I bite my lip and pull my eyes from the stage. I do my best to cling to my hope, to the belief that we will find happy moments in the years to come, even though we'll never be happy, truly happy. We'll never put down roots. We'll never have a home that's ours. We'll never have kids. I mean, how could we? Julian tugs on my hand, drawing me back to him. In the dim lighting of the restaurant, his icy green eyes shine as bright as the day I met him, even though everything around us has changed.

"What's on your mind?" he asks.

I take in our surroundings once more. Finally, I say, "This is why we came back. For moments like this." At that, Julian drops my gaze, and an expression of sadness steals his smile. I know he thinks he's letting me down by pushing for us to leave New Orleans. But that couldn't be further from the truth. The brotherhood is reason enough to leave. Now with Alister and Gio watching our every move, if it wasn't for Kat's wedding, I would've had our bags packed the moment Julian got home today. "Hey," I say, squeezing his hand. "It's okay. Even though it won't last, I'm glad we have this moment. I'm glad we have tonight."

"I'm glad we have each other."

I nod. "Me too. And I…I've been thinking about what you said earlier, about us leaving."

"You have?" Julian's eyes meet mine once more.

"Yes." I nod. I lean forward and place my other hand, despite the bandage, over his as well. "I understand why we have to leave. And even though I'm happy to have tonight, I'm ready to leave."

"*You are?*" Julian's brows furrow at my admission.

"After Kat's wedding, yes. You know, you're right. If we stay here, we're asking for trouble." *We're already in trouble.* "I don't know what life will be like on the road. But I'd take a lifetime of stolen moments like tonight than no life with you at all."

Julian's smile returns to his face then. Gently, he lifts my hand without the bandage to his lips and plants a small kiss on each of my knuckles. "I feel the same way."

WITH MOST OF tonight's patrons sweating their worries away on the dance floor, our waitress has our food and drinks to us in no time. My stomach grumbles at the sight. Similar to my first Mimi's date with Julian, I enter unladylike-mode and scarf down my food as if I haven't eaten in days. And aside from the meal Julian prepared last night, I honestly haven't. As the food fills my belly, it eases the jitteriness in my blood and allows the minor ache in my head to subside long enough for me to consider the predicament I now must face.

Once more, my enemy plans to use Julian and all those I love against me to keep me in line. Beaux wanted my silence. Alister wants my voice. Both were, *are* willing to threaten and kill to get what they want. I made a deal with Alister to keep my loved ones safe, but I can't trust that he'll keep his word. And if I don't do exactly as he says, he'll know how to ensure I do. I've revealed my weakness, and Julian will be the first person he goes after if I don't help him with his investigation into the brotherhood.

I look around the space, checking to see if I spot anyone staring. If Alister or his men are here tonight, they know how to blend in, which only amplifies my nerves. They know too much about me and I know too little about them. But there is one thing Alister and his men don't know. Julian and my time in New Orleans is coming to an end. If I can just buy myself two weeks by playing along with Alister's investigation into the brotherhood, then Julian and I can escape the city with new aliases before he even realizes something is amiss.

It seems simple enough. But there are so many ways this could go wrong. Julian told me to remember who I am. The old Emma wouldn't have just played along with Alister's plan. She would've been in the trenches, finding information on her own and seeking justice in a justice-less world. But I have changed. Taking on Alister is one thing. He's one man. Or, at least, I thought he was. Now I know how wrong I was to pursue him. Still, I can only assume the brotherhood is a million times worse.

I'm not sure I can do this. I'm not sure I can put myself in the positions that this investigation will require. My body aches at the thought of being in the same room as Alister, even for two weeks. And I don't even know what his plans for destroying the brotherhood will entail. But I don't have to be here to see it through. I just have to survive long enough to make sure Julian and I can leave New Orleans in one piece. Maybe it isn't the most noble goal. Maybe it isn't the *right* thing to do. But, after a year on the run from a faceless enemy, it's all I can manage. Yet, my role in this ploy of survival is only one of the challenges.

Gio made it clear he has men watching Julian. What if they learn that Julian is making plans for our departure? I know Julian is smart and careful. He's aware that the brotherhood could learn of our location at any time. He'll be sure not to make it seem like we're planning to flee until we're already gone. But still—Alister's men are more than serial rapists. They are trained killers and torturers. I don't like the idea of Julian roaming around the city alone unaware of who may be watching him. But what choice do I have? I have to trust him in this. I have to trust him to outwit Alister and his men, even if he doesn't realize he's doing it.

And yet, there's still the question of how we will stay safe once we're away from New Orleans. I suppose the same way we evaded the brotherhood could work for Alister and his men. We'll stay on the move. It's the only way. And yet, the thought doesn't offer me any reassurance. Alister said he has the power to make sure the brotherhood goes down and stays down and not just the New Orleans operation. I can't imagine what it would take to make that happen, to truly destroy the brotherhood. And yet as much as I'm uncertain about so much Alister shared with me, I believe him when he speaks of his power. There's a sincerity in his voice that is irrefutable.

How can I hope to escape this man, this man who is powerful enough to destroy a national organized crime syndicate that even the FBI couldn't break? I won't roll over and play dead, not again. But truly, what hope can I have? All of this is assuming he's telling the truth about his intentions to destroy the brotherhood. There's still the very real possibility he is just playing me. The brotherhood is known for their psychological torment.

Perhaps this is just some game meant to make me believe I have a chance at destroying them before they destroy me.

The sharp cry of the violin draws my attention then. I turn to find a young man has taken the stage. I look over to Julian. He's engrossed in the performance just as I was enchanted by him. His eyes glaze over as the music fills him, satisfying a hunger that no food ever will. As he watches the young man play, it's as if he is transported back to a time when things were simple, when things were possible. I know what that's like, the longing for something so far gone you almost don't recognize it when you see it.

I want more for him. I want more for myself than a life on the run, a life in which death nips at our heels from city to city. But how can I have it? How can I fight when I feel so weak? Julian turns to me with tears in his eyes. He wipes them away quickly, letting me know he'd hoped I wouldn't see them. He is so strong, too strong. And yet, I see the weight of our world resting heavily on him just as it does me. I don't know how, but I know it in my heart I have to do everything I can to escape Alister, escape the brotherhood, escape this city. If I have to lie, I have to lie. If I have to blackmail, I have to blackmail. If I have to put myself in the Devil's dungeon to protect my angel, I will. It's just…Alister will be more difficult to blackmail than Beaux. Like Beaux, he won't hesitate to kill me when he realizes my plot against him. Unlike Beaux, he also won't hesitate to serve me to the brotherhood on a silver platter. Whichever fate is worse, he will deliver if he learns of my betrayal. But with my and Julian's future at stake, there is only one choice to be made—danger or death. And with those odds, there's really no choice at all.

I won't allow myself to believe I can destroy the brotherhood. Even if Alister does have the capabilities of seeing it through, I don't plan on being in New Orleans long enough to see them fall. There's a part of me that wishes I could see their demise, a part of me that feels obligated to destroy them, but that's a hope I can't bear to have for fear of losing it. Will Alister continue his plan even after I leave? I hope he does. With the brotherhood's destruction, I may still have Alister's army of dangerous men who want me dead, but all the women the brotherhood has taken will be set free. Countless more women will be saved if the brotherhood never has a chance to abduct them.

What if I'm wrong? What if Alister is lying? What if in trying to protect Julian, I'm sentencing him to death? I don't know what Alister's motives are for destroying the brotherhood or if he truly plans to. I'll never forgive myself if— I bite my lip. The tiny ache keeps me focused on the present and not the horrifying yet completely logical reasons why I shouldn't do this. But if there's a chance Alister is telling the truth, that he truly can destroy the brotherhood, I will do everything in my power to help him while gathering every bit of evidence against Alister to earn my freedom from him. He may be more powerful than Beaux, more deadly. But blackmail works all the same. My guess is his secrets are worth a lot. I just hope he values his privacy as much as I value my and Julian's lives.

I take a sip of my margarita and a few last bites of my tacos. Just as I've decided to call it a night, I spot a familiar face in the crowd below. Fiona scurries across the dance floor to the restroom just past the stage. I shift in my seat to make sure my eyes aren't playing tricks on me.

"You okay? You've been really quiet," Julian says then, his brows furrowed.

"Yeah, yeah. I'm okay. I've just been enjoying the music." And running the scenarios of our survival through my head.

"It's pretty great. In all our travels, we never found a better place for live music." He's right. "Would you like to dance?"

"I would love nothing more. Just...let me use the restroom first."

"Of course. I'll pay the bill and meet you down there."

"Thank you," I say, hopping down off my stool. I grab my purse and shove my phone in the pocket of my black leather shorts. Wrapping my arms around Julian's neck, I pull him in for a kiss. Something about being here, where we shared our very first kiss, makes me kiss him with more passion than I would normally allow in a public space. At least, that's what I tell myself while my tongue inches into his mouth. I'd rather believe my body is reacting to our past passions rather than the fear of our uncertain future. If Alister has men watching us, they won't be pleased at my seeking out Fiona. But she was willing to help me, well, Lyla, earlier today. With only two weeks to take down the Blood King, I can't let this opportunity pass me by.

CHAPTER 16

I make my way down the stairs and across the dance floor in no time. I have to get to the restroom before Fiona leaves. As I reach the bathroom door just past the stage entrance, I stop. Fiona knows Lyla, not Emma. How can I get her to open up to a complete stranger? She fears Alister. I could see it in her eyes earlier. If she knows something of value, perhaps Alister made her a similar deal as he did me. Her life depends on her silence. I could pretend to be a reporter for The Hub. Perhaps I could ask her what it's like working for the Amato family. But something tells me I'd only hear lies. The Amatos maintain a privacy no doubt bought with NDAs and fear. So, how can I get her to talk? I exhale and yank the sleeves of my nude top up to my elbows. And then, it occurs to me.

I push the bathroom door open to find Fiona washing her hands. I brush my hair behind my ear, revealing the small cut on my cheek. "Hi," I mumble, averting my eyes.

"Hi," she says hesitantly. She quickly finishes washing her hands and drying them. I feel her watching me as I stand, shaking, at the other sink. I pull my bandaged hand to my chest and speed up my breathing as if I'm having a panic attack. I'm horrible. I know. But she only warned me about Alister after she sensed I was interested in him. And I was, just not in the way she thought. She was trying to protect me from him, keep me from falling for him. What will she do when she discovers my boyfriend, Alister Amato, dumped me after getting violent? "Are you okay?" she finally asks.

At that, I turn to her and shake my head. "No." I don't cry. I do enough of that in real life. I just need to look pitiful enough for her to have empathy for me. "My boyfriend, he...he hurt me. But...this pain is nothing compared to the pain of a broken heart." I cover my face with my hands.

"Hey, if he physically laid hands on you, then you don't want him. Broken hearts are hard, but they heal much quicker than broken bones." I nod.

"You're right. It's just, I had envisioned the life we would have. It was going to be so beautiful. I was going to be Mrs. Alister Amato and now—"

"*Wait!* You were dating Alister Amato?" I meet her gaze. Her eyes widen with surprise.

"Yeah... Do you know him?" She takes a step back and moves her eyes from me to the ground. *Oh no!* Maybe my approach was off. Maybe she'll be worried I will get back together with my imaginary abusive boyfriend and tell him all about the girl who trashed him. *Damn, Emma!*

"Unfortunately, yes," she says then.

She doesn't elaborate, nor do I bother asking her how she knows him, since I know she works for him. Instead, I ask, "Why *unfortunately?*" She bites her lip as if trying to keep the words in. "Did he hurt you too?" Her cheeks blush bright red. She's so young, too young to be a part of this. But I must know what she knows.

"No. Not me." Relief shudders through me.

"But someone you know." It's not a question. She said people around him tend to go missing. Maybe she was friends with someone Alister used to date. Maybe that's who she's referring to. She nods then, lifting her eyes to mine.

"You should stay away from him. Get a restraining order, but don't waste your time going to the police. They won't help you, not when it comes to him." She begins to walk past me, but I stop her.

"Wait. What do you mean the police won't help? Why wouldn't they and how do you know they won't?" I know Alister has connections in the police department. What I don't know is how or why. Maybe Fiona does.

Fiona turns away from me then and paces the length of the restroom. She brings her hands to her forehead as if to ease a headache. I feel an ache in my cheeks, knowing the pain I'm causing her. I know what it's like to be forced to recount horrific events. It's debilitating. I wait a few seconds longer and then cave. "Listen, I'm sorry. I don't mean to push you. I just—"

"No," she says then, turning to face me. "I...I want to tell you, if it means you'll stay away from him, that you'll be safe."

"I will. I just need to understand." She nods and closes the distance between us. When she speaks it's nothing more than a whisper.

"I had a friend who was close to Mr. Amato. They had a fight. She came back to the dorm in tears."

"*Dorm?*" Fiona nods. I don't point out that Alister appears to be in his thirties and therefore has no place befriending or otherwise a teenage girl. But the thought does turn my stomach. Club

Gent may only be part of the brotherhood's operation, but I'd be naive to ignore the coincidence. Alister had something going on with a girl Fiona's age. And when I spotted him at Midnight Moon, he was joining his contact who also had a girl who was far too young for him. Any hope I had that Alister may be telling the truth about wanting to destroy the brotherhood is beginning to fade.

"The next morning, she was gone," Fiona continues.

I nod, expecting there to be more. "Based on the severity of your warning, I take it she never came back," I say. Fiona nods. Her hands begin to shake. "Hey, hey." I take her hands in mine to steady her. "It's okay. You're safe."

She shakes her head. "Not if you tell."

"What?"

"You have to promise me you won't tell Mr. Amato what I've told you." At that, tears stream down her face. I pull her into me, allowing her tears to seep through my shirt. She's smart enough to be afraid, which means she knows more than she's letting on.

"I won't say anything. But from what you've told me, I'm not sure there is anything to say. What makes you think Alister had something to do with her disappearance? And are you sure she's really missing? Maybe she transferred."

I believe Fiona, but I need to make her think I don't. It's the only way she'll give me more information.

"No, no." She takes a step back from me. "She didn't transfer. She was taken or worse. The night before her disappearance Mr. Amato told her he wanted her out of New Orleans. She refused, but she said she was afraid it wouldn't matter and he'd send someone to take her away."

"She said all of this?"

"Yes!" Fiona's abandoned her whisper. Now the words come out quickly and with bite. "The next morning, not only was she missing, but her dorm was also destroyed. Everything was scattered around the room. Her bed was out of place. I don't...I don't know how I didn't hear it, hear her." Fiona lifts her hand to her mouth as the memories flood her. I want to reach out to her, to console her. But I can't. Not yet.

"I stalked her social media just waiting for an update. I tried calling her. I thought to myself, if she'd left of her own free will and gotten out of town like Mr. Amato wanted, she'd eventually return my call. But she never did. Finally, I went to the police to report her missing. I told them everything about the fight she'd had with Mr. Amato and her fears that he would send someone to take her away, against her will. They did nothing."

"What do you mean nothing? They must've questioned Alister. And he's an Amato. If he was questioned by the police regarding the disappearance of a teenage girl, it would've been all over the news."

Fiona nods. "You're right. It would've been. Which is why I don't believe he was ever questioned. And I know for a fact she was never publicly reported missing because I stalked the news outlets for weeks. I even—" She chokes. More tears flow. "I even kept up with the morgue to see if any unidentified girls matching her description turned up. I'm not sure if I should be thankful or not, but no one who looked like her was ever admitted. Her social media hasn't been updated. Her phone number hasn't been disconnected, so it's not like she has a new number. She's just...gone. He took her away from me."

Realization washes over me. She loved this friend of hers, perhaps more than a friend. Of course, that wouldn't matter to a member of the brotherhood, to Alister. They take what and who they want whether their prey wants it or not.

"I know she's not coming back," Fiona says then. "And yet, I can't let her go. I still work at the restaurant we would hang out at just to feel close to her." So that's why she stays at Eve's Garden. "Is that crazy?"

"No. No, it's not crazy. It's sweet. But you should know, you can still feel close to her even if you leave the restaurant. Sometimes the best way to feel close to someone who is gone is to think of what they would do or say in the present moment. If she was here with you, what would she want you to do?"

Fiona's lip quivers as she thinks, though no more tears fall. "She'd want me to be safe. She wouldn't want me sucked into the Amato drama."

I nod. "I think you're right. I think we should both stay away from Alister."

Fiona splashes water on her face, giving me a moment to process all she's said. I feel terrible for her and the poor girl who God only knows how got sucked into this tragic world. And yet, something still doesn't make sense to me. If Alister were a member of the brotherhood, he wouldn't have asked her or warned her to leave New Orleans. He would have gotten rid of her without so much as a word. I know that to be true even more after what I saw today. Alister isn't a man who deals with problems himself unless he wants to. Had he not realized who I was, he would've let Gio finish me off without a glance. So, why was he fighting with this young girl? Why did he let her return to the dorm of her own free will, especially if his plan was always to abduct her? Then again, he let me go—*for now*. But that's because he wants something from me. What could a girl that young offer Alister?

"Why did Alister want your friend to leave New Orleans? Was she…pregnant?" The words fly from me so quick I barely have time to think of how they may make Fiona feel. Her eyes narrow and a tiny wrinkle forms on her forehead.

"No." She shakes her head. "She wasn't pregnant. She was—"

Before Fiona finishes her sentence, three women who smell of booze and cigarettes crash through the bathroom door. I press myself against the vanity as they fill up the small space. Fiona takes my temporary distraction as an opportunity to run. *"No!"* I brush past the woman who thinks her floral-scented perfume will conceal her night of debauchery in pursuit of Fiona. By the time I make it out of the bathroom and past the stage area, she's nowhere in sight.

"Damn it!"

She knows why Alister wanted her friend to leave New Orleans and she was *this* close to telling me. The women barging in gave her fear a chance to reignite. Knowing Alister, he'll kill her if he ever finds out what she's told me. But if she'd told me the reason for their fight, he'd have Gio torture her first. And yet, if Fiona truly did go to the police and accuse Alister, no doubt he knows about it. Why would he allow her to continue working for him? Why hasn't he already killed her? I bring my hand to my hip. I can work with what Fiona shared, but there's still so much I don't understand. How—

"Hello, Emma." His voice sends a shiver down my spine. I turn. Even though I recognize his voice, his presence draws a gasp.

"H-hi," I stammer. Gio stands before me dressed in dark jeans and a navy blue T-shirt. His black hair, which falls just beneath his ears, is slicked back. In the dim lighting of the bar, he reminds me of our time in the warehouse. I gulp and take a step back. He smiles and closes the distance between us. Again, I gasp. "What do you want?" I manage, mentally praying Julian is still tied up with the bill upstairs.

"You asked for protection. I'm here to protect."

"Sure you are." Rage bubbles inside of me at our proximity. Rage and fear. We're so close, he could kill me in seconds, and no one would even notice. But he won't. Alister's plans for me are more complex than a random stabbing at a restaurant. The thought is meant to be comforting, but it's anything but.

"Why were you talking to Fiona?" *No!* If he saw us, then it's possible he heard us. He'll know I'm still looking into Alister, which he won't repay kindly. And Fiona—God only knows what he'll do to her.

"I...I wasn't," I lie. "And I didn't ask for your protection. You're supposed to be watching over my friends, my family, and my boyfriend." Not that I want this man anywhere near the people I love, near Julian.

"Yes, I know. But my first priority is protecting Mr. Amato, and I don't trust your motives for accepting his offer." At that, Gio's eyes scan around the dance floor. His alertness puts me on edge. I'm pretty sure he'd win every fight he's in and yet, there is still a sense of caution in the way he stands. Regardless, I shove my fear aside to state the obvious.

"*You* don't trust *me*? Let me be clear, the feeling is mutual. And the only reason I accepted Alister's offer is because I'm pretty sure I didn't have a choice otherwise." Gio's eyes flit to mine. The tension in his expression softens. I guess he believes me, probably because he knows I'm right. "Now, please hold up Mr. Amato's end of the bargain by protecting the people I love. Do that, and I'll be sure to hold up mine."

I speak quickly and sharply to hide the fear pulsing through me. I'm not sure if the smile spreading across Gio's lips is because I've fooled him or because he's sees straight through me.

"For what it's worth," he says then, "I'm sorry about earlier. That's my least favorite part of my job. Well, almost. If I'd had to kill you, that would've been the worst."

"I thought you said you wouldn't kill me. You'd just make me wish I was dead."

"That's true. But there does come a point in the torture when the person is so used to the pain, death is the only thing that remains."

His words hit me in an unexpected way. My knees grow weak at the thought of being in so much pain, death is the only thing left that can hurt you. And yet… "That's a relief."

"What is?" His dark brows furrow.

I exhale and sling my purse over my shoulder. "To know that it won't last forever." Gio's eyes scan my body. I'm not sure if he's imagining the ways he'd like to hurt me. Or if he thinks letting me live is crueler than taking my life. On some days, he'd be right. But I can't let myself think that. Not when I've just found an ember of fight, of hope left in me.

"Mr. Amato sent this for you," Gio says, handing me a slip of paper. "Read it when you're someplace private. And again, no one can know anything about what we have planned. When you visit the Amato estate it will be under the guise of a maid. You're good at disguises, aren't you?"

I look between Gio and the note. I wasn't expecting us to get started so soon. I may have found a will to fight but thinking about it is a lot different from actually doing it. Gio presses the note into my chest when I hesitate to take it. Every nerve in my body is on high alert at Gio's touch, reminding me of how much more uncomfortable things can get. I take the note and slip it into my purse before anyone sees, before Julian sees.

"I don't understand. Why…why the need for a disguise? I'm sure Alister's properties are impeccably secure. No one in the brotherhood would get close enough to know if I was working with him." *One can only hope.*

"Members of the brotherhood aren't the only ones our plan

must stay protected from. Mr. Amato keeps a tight circle. Even his family doesn't know—" At that, Gio stands tall as his eyes latch on to someone over the top of my head. Within a matter of seconds, the tension in my body eases as Julian pulls me underneath his arm.

"Hey, babe. Is everything okay? Who's your friend?" Julian sizes up Gio as he takes his place next to me. *Shit!*

"Yeah, yeah. Um, this is my friend Gio. We used to work together at The Hub." I'm not sure if I'm convincing. But as Gio crosses his arms over his chest, flexing muscles that rival even Alister's, I pray I am. I'm not saying Julian would lose in a one-on-one battle with the King of Torment, but it's a fight I certainly would not want to witness.

"Oh, wow! It's nice to meet you," Julian says, offering Gio his hand. *Oh, thank God!* Gio cocks an eyebrow, giving me a look of approval as he takes Julian's hand. "I haven't really met any of Emma's old friends except for Kat."

"I guess she likes keeping you hidden away. Anyway, it's nice meeting you too. Perhaps we'll see each other again sometime." *God, I hope not.* "Emma." Gio tips his head, bidding us both farewell before disappearing into the sea of dancers. As he leaves us, my legs give out. I fall into Julian. Though somehow, I make my collapse look like a dance move. The violinist finishes his set, making way for an up-tempo DJ set. Julian wraps his arms around me, holding me up, none the wiser.

"That must've been nice seeing one of your old coworkers," Julian says.

"Yeah," I mumble.

"So, what do you say? Dance off these tacos or head home for a cozy night on the couch?" I raise my brow at Julian's question as I finally regain the feeling in my legs. "Home it is," Julian says.

CHAPTER 17

After a quiet night with Julian back at the house, I spent all morning snooping through Fiona's social media accounts, which I found through a photo she was tagged in at Eve's Garden. I know it's a long shot. If her friend's disappearance wasn't investigated by the police, then there probably isn't much of a paper trail to follow. But there is so much about Alister that doesn't make sense. If I can understand who this girl was and why he wanted her to leave New Orleans, then maybe some of the puzzle pieces will start to fit together. Maybe I'll learn something I can use to negotiate my freedom from Alister before Julian and I leave New Orleans for good. Something like why Fiona's friend was pictured wearing an ornate brooch with the same crest as Alister's ring.

I nearly fell out of my chair when I spotted it. It wasn't in a picture on Fiona's feed, it was on hers, the raven-haired girl known as *@nolaprincessa*. I had to scroll through Fiona's feed over a year before I found her former roommate. Her real name wasn't listed anywhere on the account, which means I'm working off assumptions until I can get Fiona to confirm them. If I'm right about who this raven-haired girl was and about the depth of her and Fiona's relationship, it's possible Fiona knows more about the Amatos than I originally thought. A burst of hope makes me quicken my pace. Fiona said she found her friend's dorm room destroyed the morning she realized she was missing. There's no way her friend could've been nabbed from her dorm if she and Fiona shared a room. And there's only one dormitory on Tulane's campus that has private dorm suites. And so, that's where I'm headed.

The afternoon sun beats down on me as I make my way through the maze of buildings and tree-lined sidewalks that is Tulane University. It wasn't that long ago that I was a student here, and yet, it feels like a lifetime. In many ways, it was. I bite back my emotion in favor of perseverance as I round the corner and walk onto the large lawn fronting Fiona's dormitory. As the building comes into view so do the blue and red flashing lights of police cars and an ambulance. The sight stops me in my tracks. A crowd is gathering. *Please!* Don't let it be her.

I take off running and cross the lawn in under two minutes. Yellow police tape keeps people from entering the building, creating a mix of concern and agitation in the air around us. "Does anyone know what happened?" I ask as I catch my breath. There are some mumbles in the crowd, but no one asserts an answer. It's then that the police escort a small blonde from the building. They've draped a comfort blanket over her shaking body. She looks familiar. Where have I seen—? *Oh no!*

My vision blurs as the stretcher comes into view. A black body bag sits atop. Everyone around me gasps in horror. They all ask, *What happened? Who is it?* But I know.

"Everyone," the sheriff addresses us. "I am sorry to say it appears a resident of Drayton Hall has committed suicide. We cannot release any details until the family has been notified. However, we have no reason to believe there was foul play. The campus is safe. You'll regain access to the building momentarily. Campus officials would like me to remind you there are grief counselors on site for anyone who may wish to seek their guidance."

Students clear out, dividing up into cliques. The ambulance pulls away, revealing a coroner's vehicle on the other side of it. Men in nylon coats load the stretcher into the vehicle and drive away, leaving behind a trail of hushed voices and dust. I put one foot in front of the other, heading down the sidewalk where the small blonde who I know to be Fiona's current roommate sits. She and her grief counselor stare at me as I reach them. For a minute I say nothing. I don't want to know the truth. I don't want to know that Fiona is dead. Because if she is, I know it's because of me. She didn't commit suicide. They killed her, Alister and Gio, because she knew too much. She told me too much.

"Was it Fiona?" I finally ask. My words make the young girl's face contort with sadness. I imagine my insides twisting just the same. She was too young to be involved in this. And yet, aren't they all? All the girls the brotherhood preys on are too young. How many lives are they responsible for destroying? Alister may or may not be one of them, but he is just as evil. And I know he's responsible for Fiona's death.

"Please, miss. She can't reveal anything she knows, not until the family has been notified," her counselor says. The young girl shakes her head.

"Were you her friend?" she asks me. No. No, I wasn't. If I was, I wouldn't have questioned her. I wouldn't have risked her safety by approaching her in a public place, especially when I knew Alister and his men were watching me.

"I...I would've liked to have been. We'd only just met." The girl nods. At some point, she stopped crying. Now she just looks pale.

"Yes. It was Fiona. She...she hanged herself." I take a step back as the words hit me. The poor girl bursts into another fit of tears, resting her head against the counselor's shoulder. The counselor consoles her while using her eyes to direct me to leave. And I do. I race to the nearest bathroom in the nearby student union and cry the tears I shouldn't be allowed to cry. Of course they made it look like she hanged herself. The bruising left behind by a rope is similar to the bruises of strangulation. Gio's go-to method.

ALISTER HAD a maid's uniform left for me at my storage unit across town. It's where I change in and out of disguises. It's also where he sent the town car to pick me up. The drive across the causeway was a quiet one. Thoughts of Fiona refuse to abandon me. They wouldn't have killed her if she didn't know the truth. She didn't tell me everything, but she told me enough. Enough to assume the girl who Alister made disappear wasn't some random college girl. She was his sister. Why else would she have had a brooch of the Amato family crest? And yet, I wonder. Could Alister have truly killed his own sister or is there more to the story, something that may redeem him yet? Or would've redeemed him had he not had Fiona murdered.

As we approach the stoic stucco mansion on the Amato estate, fear and anger bubble inside me. If I had any choice at all, I wouldn't be here. I wouldn't allow myself in the same room as these monsters. But as much as Fiona's death saddens me and makes me fear for my own safety, it also proves how ruthless Alister and his men are. I can't allow us to suffer the same fate. I have to learn Alister's secrets and find a way to use them against him. Or else mine will be the next body he drops. The thought sends a chill up my spine. As the driver moves farther down the gravel drive, the crunch beneath the tires becomes slower and my imagination begins to wander to places I'd rather not visit. I pull myself back to the present by reminding myself of the value of Alister's ruthlessness as he protects the ones I love. That is, if he isn't playing me for the fool I feel myself to be.

As my car comes to a stop in front of the two-hundred-year-old home, I can't help but imagine what may await me on the inside. Even if Alister is telling the truth about wanting my help to destroy the brotherhood, he killed Fiona for knowing something she shouldn't. Why should I expect anything less? There are no neighbors for miles. Exquisitely manicured gardens and thick orchards of oak trees conceal the private lakefront estate from the rest of the world. My screams would be muffled by the limbs of the trees and the flowing lake water just out of sight. If I ran, I'd face the armed guards at the edge of the property or the alligators swimming in the lake. What have I gotten myself into? And yet, I pray my usefulness to Alister will allow his ruthlessness to subside.

The driver dressed in a black suit opens my car door, startling me. I was so consumed by my thoughts I didn't even notice him exit the vehicle. *Okay, Emma. You're here. There's no turning back now. Get a hold of yourself.* I scold myself in proper Anne Marshall fashion and remember Julian's words from the night before. A lot has changed in a year, but there's still some fight left in me yet. I just have to remember it.

At that, I press my knees together and slowly exit the vehicle.

You'd think a maid's uniform would be more sensible. However, the skirt of my gray and white dress hits several inches above the knee. At least my legs are somewhat covered with the sheer black stockings Alister provided. And my shoes are sensible enough. Heavy too. I'll remember that in case I have to kick someone. The driver closes the car door behind me as I move toward the grand steps leading up to the main entrance. I've got one black clunky shoe on them when movement to my right draws my attention.

"Excuse me, ma'am. The help does not enter through the front. Please, allow me to show you through the kitchen."

I turn to find Gio standing next to a bed of immaculately pruned boxwoods several feet away. His presence makes my body ache, forcing me to hide my fear with spite. I purse my lips and make my way from the stairs to where Gio stands. "Seriously? Who is this act for?"

"You are here as a maid. Maids do not enter through the front," Gio says. His pace is quick as he leads me around the front of the house, mansion, castle. Whichever noun best describes the ancient, gorgeous, and creepy building before me.

"Fine by me, just as long as no one expects me to clean anything. That's where I draw the line." *There you go, Emma. Stand your ground.* Gio laughs then. Just like his smile, his laugh is off-putting. "Was something I said funny? Because I'm serious," I assure him. "I have my own house to clean. And even that, I hardly do." I allow my humor to ease my nerves. Or, at least, I try to.

"It's funny you think you have a choice. You're in our world now." All humor leaves Gio as he speaks. I know he's telling me the truth. I've known it all along. And yet his words force my feet to stick to the walking path like glue. Gio closes the distance to the wooden door on the side of the house I'm assuming leads to the kitchen. That is, before he notices I'm no longer beside him. He turns. When his dark eyes graze over me, there is a warning in them that turns my pale skin pink. "Emma. Do not cause a scene. We've got work to do. You made a deal. Remember?"

"I remember. I just…" I look away from Gio to take in my surroundings once more. I don't know what waits for me on the other side of that door and I'm not keen to find out. Gio exhales at my delay and runs his fingers through his dark hair. It isn't slicked back today. It flows freely, which somehow puts me at ease. Perhaps he doesn't plan on partaking in strenuous activity, or rather torture. It's then that I remember Fiona. I take him in from toe to top. He's clean as a whistle. Perhaps his hair isn't gelled because he recently showered, to wash off the remnants of Fiona's life.

Gio snaps his fingers, pulling me from my thoughts.

"Sorry." I regain my composure. "Did you say something?"

His brows furrow. "Mr. Amato is expecting you and he does not respond well to tardiness."

I open my mouth with a million excuses at the ready. But the impatience in Gio's eyes silences me. I take two steps forward, expecting Gio to open the door and escort me inside. Instead, he stands still waiting for me to reach him. The hairs on my arms rise at our proximity. *What is he waiting for?* As if reading my mind, Gio exhales. He's tense, which only amplifies my nerves. What the Hell does *he* have to be tense about? I'm in his world now, right?

"A few things before we enter. When we walk through those doors, you are a maid. That means you act like a maid, and you speak like a maid. Yes, ma'am. No, ma'am. Yes, sir. No, sir."

His comment catches me off guard. "If you knew my mother, you'd know you don't have to explain social graces to me."

"Well, good." Gio nods. "I'll take you straight to Mr. Amato's office. You know why you're here, but no one else does. Not the guards. Not the staff. Not even Ms. Amato."

I furrow my brows. Gio began to tell me last night about how Alister's family doesn't even know what we're up to. Why is that? Is that the reason for my disguise? "Ms. Amato as in Alister's mother?" Not that it matters, but somehow speaking of Alister's family helps ease my nerves. Maybe he is telling the truth about wanting to destroy the brotherhood. If this was all a trap, I doubt he'd go to such measures to sell the lie, especially when he could take me by force if he wanted to.

"No. Ms. Amato as in Sophia, his sister. While we're on the topic, it's best not to bring up his mother or his family in general."

I nod and take a deep breath. I get it. If I was planning a top-secret mission to destroy the most dangerous men in New Orleans, I'd want it kept secret too. Though I can't help but ask. "What about his other sister, Cara? Will I need to avoid her as well?" My mention of Cara is a test, one that Gio fails. Gio is a man of few expressions. And yet, at the mention of Cara, Alister's youngest sister and Fiona's former roommate, there is a new look on his face.

Gio's lip curls in anger. His eyes narrow. Yet he does his best to conceal his emotions. After all, Cara was never reported missing. What is there for him to be so upset about? I expect him to chew my head off. Yet all he says is, "Like I said. Don't mention his family. And don't let anyone find out why you're really here."

Gio's warning settles heavily on me as he pushes through the wooden door into the kitchen. As Gio leads me through the house, I spot several other maids dressed in similar uniforms cleaning from the wooden floors to the crown molding adorning the fifteen-foot ceilings. I suppose it must take a large staff to keep a property of this size in the immaculate condition a man like Alister requires. But maids aren't the only presence I notice. They do their best to stay out of sight, but their shadows betray them. Guards dressed in black suits stand at each end of every hallway. We must've passed six just on our walk from the kitchen up to the second floor. Gio opens a door I expect to be the entrance to Alister's office. Yet, as I step through, I find only another hallway.

"Seriously? This place is a maze." My words are louder than I intend due to the hollowness of the hallway. Gio glares at me, reminding me of my place. I give him a little nod and then we continue. The hallway is dimly lit with lanterns that look original to the house. The wooden panels beneath us are thinner and longer than the ones of the main floor. They creak as we move toward the large door waiting for us at the end of the hall. Now that I think of it, it's the only door in this corridor. I'm surprised there isn't a guard standing in front of it, since no doubt behind it is Alister's office. Yet, something tells me Gio is the only person ever allowed to get this close to the boss, the Blood King.

As we reach the door, Gio stops. I gulp, anticipating the meeting soon to be had.

"Give me your bag," Gio says then.

"*Hmm?*"

"Your bag," Gio repeats. His eyes move to the small purse I have slung over my shoulder.

"Is that really necessary? You have a gun and I'm sure other mechanisms of pain. I have a thirty-dollar bag from Target." Which happens to hold my knife, pepper spray, and cell phone.

Gio's brows rise. "I won't ask a third time."

No. I don't suspect he will. The look in Gio's eyes reminds me of what he did to me when we first met, as if I could ever forget. It's the same thing I suspect will happen if I disobey him or am caught collecting evidence against Alister. I nod and hand him my purse. At that, he pushes the door open, and I enter, knowing the only weapon remaining on my person are the thick, heavy shoes strapped around my ankles.

CHAPTER 18

As I enter Alister's office, I find him seated at a grand desk in the center of the room. He nurses a glass of scotch while seemingly waiting for Gio and me to join him. "Sorry we're late, Mr. Amato. I was giving Emma here the rundown." Alister's eyes do not leave mine nor mine his as Gio explains our tardiness. He wears a white button-down, per usual, with dark slacks. His facial hair has grown out a bit since yesterday. The dark stubble gives him an even more intimidating presence than I remember. After what feels like forever, his eyes move to Gio. Immediately, Gio taps me on the back, motioning for me to take a seat. I jump at his touch but follow his lead and sit in one of the upholstered chairs across from Alister.

"That'll be all, Gio," Alister says then. Gio pauses mid-sit. He seems shocked at Alister's request to meet with me in private. I'm not sure how it makes me feel. If things become dangerous, well, more dangerous than they already are, then I'd prefer my odds one-on-one. Still, I always feel anxious when Gio is caught off guard. At that, Gio collects himself and leaves the wood-paneled room without a word. I take note of how he acts around Alister. Gio isn't a patient man. Something tells me his boss isn't either.

"What happened to your hand?"

"Hmm? Oh!" My eyes graze over the bandage stretched over my knuckles. Perhaps this is his way of breaking the ice. "I got into a fight with a mirror." Out of instinct, my lips twitch into a smile, but thoughts of Fiona and Alister's mercilessness steal it from me as quickly as it comes.

"For the sake of another discussion of metaphors, I assume this encounter was prompted by your time with Gio yesterday." I bite the inside of my cheek and nod. "Are you…okay?" Is he honestly going to pretend he cares? His question confuses and angers me. *No, I'm not okay.* I part my lips ready with my response, though an inkling of self-preservation keeps me from saying everything I want to.

"I appreciate your attempt at making me feel comfortable in your presence. But, like I said yesterday, I don't think that's possible. So, if it's alright with you, I'd like to keep our conversation focused on the brotherhood and whatever intel you have for me to review." That's not true. I'd also like to learn more about Alister and what he's hiding. But that will come only when he feels comfortable with me, not the other way around.

Alister nods. "I understand." He stands and moves to the sofa pressed against the left wall of his office. It's then that I notice a coffee table covered in manila folders and, ironically, green sticky notes. "You won't be of much help if you stay over there. Come. As you can see, there's lots for us to review."

"Yes, I do see." I've never been more relieved to see a stack of papers in my life. I suppose that's one question answered. Alister's plans to destroy the brotherhood are real. Yet, as I take my seat next to Alister on the firm settee, my sense of relief leaves me. Alister is still a threat, an enemy that must be destroyed. But, as I take in the papers upon papers detailing the brotherhood's every move, I'm reminded of the original enemy, the one without a face, the one that can be anywhere, the one that stole a year of my life and so much more. My voice is shaky as I speak. "Why so old-school? Are you worried about the brotherhood hacking your computer?" Alister sets his folder to the side as if sensing my change in demeanor.

"Partly. But mostly because my father was old-school. This information isn't all recent. Some of it dates back decades."

Oh. I'm not sure if that makes me feel better or worse. "Decades? But how…why? I thought you just recently discovered the truth about the brotherhood. How could you have intel on them from so far back? And why is any of that important now?" I can't keep the questions from spewing from me as I grab the nearest folder. I have a feeling this is exactly why Alister wanted my help. *He* wanted *my* help. I'm still wrapping my head around the fact that I'm here to help take down the men who stand to steal everything from me. No. No. I'm here to gather intel on Alister, nothing more. This, this isn't my—

"*I* did only recently discover the truth. And you're not here to question me. You're here to question them and find the patterns that no one else can. But…" Alister hesitates as if thinking through his next words carefully. "You should know, my father died last year. He was the head of our business for thirty years. It was only after he died that I took over and became privy to certain dealings. One of which just so happened to be with the brotherhood."

I narrow my eyes as he speaks. His guard is up or else he wouldn't be so keen to redirect my line of questioning. Yet, he's giving away more than he thinks. The Amatos own half of New Orleans and employ just as much with their many business holdings. Yet, something tells me Alister isn't referring to the dealings plastered all over The Hub's business section. Perhaps I should take a closer look at his family's holdings. It's possible some of them are fronts for backdoor businesses. Like a strip club that supplies sexy cocktail waitresses to work the Club Gent parties. Or worse, provides girls for the brotherhood to drug and abuse. But I'm getting ahead of myself.

"Okay," I say slowly. "Well, I think this would be a lot easier if you'd tell me what kind of dealings you had with the brotherhood. I mean, I've thought about this before. Everything from the waitstaff to the cleaning crew to the drapery company would've needed a point of contact within the brotherhood. Maybe—"

"Yes, I thought the same thing. Which is how I found Hayden Posey." Alister avoids my question by tossing a manila folder in my lap. I set my original folder to the side and open the new one. Inside, I find handwritten scribbles and green sticky notes galore. Clearly, this isn't Alister's first time perusing his findings. "Posey is, *was*, an accountant for the brotherhood."

"*Was?*" I ask. Alister's dark eyes flit to mine.

"He's no longer with us." The way he speaks, I take it Posey isn't the first constituent of the brotherhood he's killed. And if this investigation goes as he plans, he won't be the last. The thought gives me a small sense of comfort, one I quickly shove to the back of my mind.

"Okay. Continue." I flip through the folder as Alister speaks. It's detailed. Everything from the man's full name and home address to the mistress he kept in Key West.

"I interrogated every point of contact I could find for the brotherhood. Somehow Posey always came up. He was a money man. Perhaps *the* money man for the New Orleans operation. It's possible there are more men like him, each in charge of their own city."

"Makes sense," I mumble. It occurs to me then the night Alister bumped into me at Midnight Moon he was meeting a known member who he later described as his contact. Perhaps he's how Alister's father communicated with the brotherhood. Now, he's supposedly providing Alister with intel on how to destroy them. Why? And if Alister's father was in bed with the brotherhood for thirty years, why would Alister suddenly want to end that partnership? "So, why'd you kill him?"

"Excuse me?" Alister looks at me like I've lost my mind. As if it should be clear as day why he'd kill one of the most valuable brotherhood assets.

"I said, why'd you kill him? If he was the money man, no doubt he had transaction records that would've allowed the FBI to know valuable information about the brotherhood, like who they employ, what their holdings are, and—"

"Who they sell." Alister's lips press into a flat line as the words leave him. There's a vulnerability in the way he sits, shoulders slumped, that I haven't noticed before.

"That's how you found out, isn't it? About the sex trafficking? It was through Posey. You...you have his records, don't you?" Alister nods, though he's unable to meet my eyes. "But wait. This doesn't make sense. You said your father worked with them for years and when you took over, you had access to certain records. But if you didn't find out about the sex trafficking until you found Posey, then... Your father didn't know what they were really up to. And you...you had another reason for going after Posey, for wanting to destroy them."

Alister pushes himself off the couch, walks to his desk, and pours himself another glass of scotch. Except, he doesn't drink it. Instead, he crushes the glass in his hand. I jump. *Oh no!* I shouldn't have said all of that out loud. Every muscle in my body is on high alert as I watch Alister stew across the room. Gio warned me not to speak of Alister's family. Yet, I can't help it when his family is so clearly tethered to the brotherhood. Understanding his family's business is the secret I need to earn my and Julian's freedom. But, if I push him too quickly, I'll never learn the truth.

"I...I'm sorry. I didn't mean to get off track. I'm just trying to understand."

"Understand what?" Alister snaps as blood drenches his palm. "How to destroy the brotherhood or me?" My eyes widen as he stalks toward me. He pays no attention to the blood, or the small splinters of glass still stuck in his skin. "After everything you've gone through, after losing an entire year of your life to these bastards, you should want to destroy them as much as I do. And yet all you can do is ask me about *my* family and *my* motive. Isn't it good enough that I'm on your side? Isn't it good enough that I want them to drown in their own blood? Isn't it good enough that I'm willing to risk my men's lives to protect you and the ones you love?"

Alister towers over me as he speaks. The vein in his neck throbs. The arms of his shirt tighten around his flexing muscles. His words tear at the seams of my heart and force me to consider that which I've done my best to ignore. He's right. Isn't he? It should be enough that I have someone on my side, who would rather fight than run, who believes in me and my abilities to destroy these wicked men. So, what's stopping me from seizing this opportunity? Is it truly my fear of Alister? The death sentence he's promised me? The fact that he can erase me from this earth just as easily as he can protect me? Those are all excellent reasons not to trust him or what he's promised me—both protection and the abolition of the brotherhood. But, even still, is there something else holding me back? Some other reason why I'd rather focus on destroying him than the brotherhood?

I look away then to allow him a moment to collect himself as well as myself a moment to think. He doesn't give it to me though. Instead, he drops to his knees before me and takes my shaking hands in his. His blood drenches the white of my bandage, staining it the color of the tapestry of the Amato family crest hanging above us. The Blood King is on his knees before me. Desperation and confusion contort his features, leaving me at a loss.

"Those were not rhetorical questions," he says then. "I expect an answer." Sweat dampens his cheeks. The simple shimmer of his skin reminds me his outburst wasn't a figment of my imagination.

"Can you let go of me? Please." Alister drops his head, gives my hands one last squeeze, and does as I say. He moves across the room and takes a seat in one of the upholstered chairs. I'm thankful for the distance, though it does nothing to help me make sense of what I'm feeling inside.

"I'm waiting," he says, reminding me once more of his impatience.

I nod and smooth the hem of my skirt, covering as much of my thighs as I can. Finally, I say, "In all honesty, I don't trust you."

"Okay. Explain." He seems to have let out most of his built-up frustration and now speaks more calmly.

I allow my eyes to scan over the folders before me. Each one represents some horrid aspect of this vile organization. I've been here less than an hour and I already feel myself memorizing this feeling, this moment. It will haunt me just like all the other moments. I'll never be able to look at another manila folder the same way. And yet, that is not why I'm holding back from this investigation, neither is Alister or my and Julian's upcoming departure from New Orleans.

"When you first propositioned me, I still thought there was a possibility you were a member of the brotherhood, that all of this was a trick. Maybe you wanted to give me hope, hope that I could actually destroy the brotherhood before ripping it away from me and shoving me into a cage of despair for the rest of my life."

Alister's brows furrow as he listens. I'm not sure if I should be so honest, but I can't stop myself.

"So, I didn't allow myself to have hope. I focused on the now. I focused on you. It's been a year, Alister. And the brotherhood hasn't approached me. I don't know why. Maybe they're lying in wait for the perfect moment to strike. Or maybe, just maybe, they've decided they have bigger problems than the chick who accidentally discovered a small facet of their operation. Now that you've shared what their real crime is, Club Gent seems so small. And Beaux is dead. He was the reason I was at that party. He was the reason I got sucked into this life. And now…he's gone. So, why am I still struggling? Why do I have to fight this fight?"

My vision blurs with tears to the point I can no longer see Alister. His figure blends in with the wood and bloodred room surrounding me. It makes it easier for the words to rip through me.

"I don't want to do this. I don't want to be here." My lip quivers. "But I have no choice because I know either you will kill me, or they will. And as much as I'd like to believe they've decided to let me live, I know that's only the lie I tell myself. And that knowledge makes the fact that they haven't come after me even scarier. They've had a year, Alister, a year to decide all the ways they're going to hurt me. So, maybe it's easier to focus on you and the monster you are, rather than the idea of destroying them. Because when I think about them, I have to think about what they're going to do to me and probably to the people I love. And I know you said you would protect them. I know you said you have the power to destroy the brotherhood. But Alister, I have no reason to believe you won't use that same power against me if I step out of line, if I choose to say *no*. And what if we fail? If I allow myself to have hope just for it to be taken away, I just... I can't."

Tears drench my face as the truth rips through me. Running from the brotherhood is the hardest thing I've ever had to do. But running is easier than going up against them and failing. It's like I told Julian, I'd take a lifetime of stolen moments than no life with him at all. If I go up against the brotherhood and fail, I lose everything. I lose Julian. I lose my freedom. I lose my life. It's then that Alister stands from his chair and crosses the room, kneeling before me once more. "No," I choke out, holding up my hands for him to stay back. "No. Don't touch me."

"I'm not. I'm just going to sit," Alister says. His tone is softer than I expected. I allow myself to cry all the tears I can and then wipe the wetness from my skin with the white dust rag that came with the maid's uniform.

"As I look at these folders, I feel like a failure," I admit.

"What? Why?"

"Because—I promised those girls justice. When I was investigating Beaux, I was lucky enough to find a few girls who were willing to tell me their stories. It was because of them that I had a glimmer of hope, hope that I could free myself from Beaux. And I told them, with their help, he'd go to jail. He'd never be able to hurt another woman again."

"Jail or death, either way, he isn't hurting anyone else. You kept your promise."

"Maybe in the technical sense, but...Beaux was only one monster. I knew about the brotherhood, and I ran. Sure, I turned over my evidence to the police, but I didn't stay to make sure they actually did their job. And I know what you're thinking, the same as my boyfriend thinks, I did my part. It's not that the police and FBI were corrupt. The brotherhood was just *that* good. Although, considering your connections in law enforcement maybe I'm wrong about that too." At that, Alister smirks. "But I think most of all, I'm ashamed because even when you told me about the sex trafficking, all I could think about was myself."

I don't tell Alister of my and Julian's plans to leave New Orleans, which haven't changed, despite the guilt I feel for continuing to run away from this fight, this fight that Alister seems ready and willing to win. He's a monster, one that senselessly murdered an innocent girl and no doubt countless others. But he's a monster with the means and mind to do something good, something terrifying, something necessary, something I can't. Despite the horrible things I know he's done and will continue to do, in his presence, I feel like a coward. I understand why Julian and I must leave New Orleans. I no longer view running as giving up, but, after today, I can't help but view it as selfish.

"Emma," he says then, pulling me from my thoughts. "Maybe you didn't think of the victims, but... In the short time I've known you, I know you are anything but selfish. As you said, you didn't trust me when we met. You probably still don't. You thought me one of them. Given your experience with Gio and all the imaginings you've had a year to conjure, you still bargained for the safety of your friends and family rather than your own release. So don't beat yourself up too badly. You're not a bad person. You're just in a bad situation."

I allow his words to settle on me and try to find comfort in them. His golden eyes scan my face, tracing the tendrils of blond hair that have slipped from my ponytail. His gaze makes me feel small, so small I'd like to disappear. Alister isn't a good man, but perhaps he can't be. Perhaps good men can't vanquish monsters. Perhaps good women can't either. That's why I've done my best to keep Julian out of this. It's yet another reason why I can't see this through, why I have to run. The more I'm in the presence of darkness, the more I fear it will consume me.

"I'm sorry about your dad," I say, breaking the silence between us. Alister focuses on me, before propelling himself from his knees to a standing position.

"Thank you," he mumbles. "He was a complicated but good man. He never would've stayed in business with the brotherhood had he known what they were truly up to." I nod, biting back the question on my lips. Alister returns to his desk and pulls a first aid kit from one of his desk drawers. He tends to his cut palm and pours himself another glass of scotch once he's finished. "Would you care for a glass?"

"Sure," I say. I stand and cross the room. My legs feel heavy as I walk, so I sit in one of the chairs across from Alister's desk. He slides the glass of warm alcohol to me and then sits on the opposite side of his desk. Our déjà vu moment is quiet as my insides finish warring against themselves.

It's then that Alister says, "Emma, I don't know where you got the notion that I'm going to kill you when this is over. I agreed to protect your friends and family both during and after our investigation. And I don't even need them. I *need* you. So, consider yourself under my protection as well. Hopefully that will make it easier to sleep at night. I'll need you sharp and wide awake as we continue our investigation."

The thought of continuing this investigation makes me feel exhausted. I can't imagine what horror waits for us in those folders, and something tells me they're just the beginning. I shove one batch of fears to the side in exchange for another.

"As we continue our investigation, sure, you'll protect me. But afterward, that is *if* we actually manage to take down the brotherhood, you won't need me anymore. And you said it yourself, you do unspeakable things to maintain your control, to keep your secrets. I may not know much about you, but I know enough. And you know it too."

"Enough to warrant a visit from Gio? Sure, I agree with you." He's so nonchalant as he speaks. His carelessness reminds me of how easily he could kill and dispose of me, as if I could ever forget. "But I don't repay those who help me with bullets. And if you know *enough*, as you say, then you know you'd be stupid to turn your back on an ally like me." He takes a sip of his scotch then. The amber liquid almost matches the color of his almond-shaped eyes. "Stay loyal to me and I'll stay loyal to you until the day I die. Betray me and, well, you know enough to know what will happen next."

Yes, I do. But Alister's assurances do nothing to change my mission. I can't face the brotherhood, even with him by my side. I can't stay in New Orleans, waiting for them to find me just to put Alister's protection to the test. And I can't leave New Orleans, betraying Alister and earning his wrath, without something worthy of my freedom in my back pocket.

"We should get back to work," I say then.

CHAPTER 19

Hours feel like minutes as Alister and I work our way through the mountain of information he's gathered on the brotherhood. A lot of it appears to be records of business dealings between the Amatos and the brotherhood from years past. From the looks of the papers I saw, it wasn't clear what exactly the Amatos sell. Yet, I know a transaction record when I see one. They're what have my eyes burning. Alister quickly separated out the documents related to his family's business and handed me Posey's records to review. At first, I was annoyed by Alister's efforts to keep his family's secrets, seeing as their discovery is my main reason for being here. But it didn't take long for Posey's transaction records to consume me in the most disturbing way.

The records not only include his dealings with vendors for the Club Gent parties, but also a record of every girl sold, when she was sold, and for how much. It's sick. Of course, Posey doesn't list out anyone's name. He uses their initials followed by a series of numbers for their inventory code. My lip curls just at the thought of this smug man. He didn't even view them as human beings. Now I understand why Alister was so shocked when I questioned him about killing Posey. This monster deserved to die. Or, at a minimum, rot in solitary for the rest of his life.

It took a while to make the connection, to figure out the letters in the inventory codes were actually initials. But, like Alister said, I find the patterns no one else can. I cross-referenced Posey's inventory codes and sell dates with missing persons reports from New Orleans. Alister said the brotherhood trafficked girls from other places to the Club Gent parties for entertainment. Once the brothers are done with them, they are sold on the black market. But it turns out, it's not just girls from other places who are trafficked and sold. There aren't many compared to the register of codes, but there are enough to determine a pattern if you look back far enough. Some of the girls sold are from New Orleans. At least, that's what it looks like.

Avery Adams was reported missing in New Orleans on March 7, 2019. According to the report, she and her friends went out one night in the French Quarter. They were dancing at a bar. One minute she was there. The next, she wasn't. Her friends waited until the next evening to report her missing, thinking she'd met a hot stranger and decided to hook up. Avery was taken that night, most likely drugged so she'd be easy to handle. Five days after, Posey lists a transaction for AA11305F. She was sold for $250,000. My house costs more than that, more than a human life according to these animals. This pattern repeats for years on end. Except, it did end.

Once the brotherhood was exposed, Posey's eerily routine transaction records ceased. I'm not sure if that's because Alister found him and killed him or if his change in record keeping marked a bigger change in the brotherhood's operation before Alister discovered him. Something tells me it's a little bit of both.

The information in Posey's records is exactly what the FBI would need to hunt and destroy the brotherhood. At least, the New Orleans operation. But they gave up on the investigation months ago. And, if Alister has the ability to source this information without a badge, maybe he does have the power to destroy the brotherhood. And after what I've seen today, I not only *have* to help him, I *want* to help him. I just don't know what this will mean for me and Julian. I quickly shove the thought from my head, grab a green sticky note, and write down the codes of girls I suspect were taken from New Orleans.

As much as I feel we're making progress, there's still so much that doesn't make sense. Like where these sales take place and how the brotherhood keeps the girls from escaping in between their capture and the auction. I've scanned Posey's records for things like apartment buildings, warehouses, shipping containers, anything that could be used to keep the girls hidden. Nothing. Nothing but auto drafts to cleaning and catering companies, the hiring agency that helps place the cocktail waitresses at their parties, and rent payments to the location I know to be the former Club Gent. All of which stopped the moment news broke about the brotherhood.

"What are you thinking?" Alister asks, peering at me from his end of the couch.

I shake my head.

"I'm not sure. I have so many questions, it's hard to pick one to focus on." I look at the green sticky note once more. "At least two girls a year for the five years predating the brotherhood's exposure were taken from New Orleans. I don't know what the numbers in these inventory codes mean. Maybe that's how many girls they've sold. Maybe it's completely random. It's the letters that I think are important." I scoot closer to Alister and hand him the sticky note. He leans in.

"Do you see how every code ends in an *F*?" Alister nods. "Look at this." I hand him a page from Posey's register. It includes twenty inventory codes, all representing girls sold in a single month two years back. "Each code ends with a series of letters. I've scanned Posey's records five years back. There are only four ways the codes end. Every girl who was taken from New Orleans has a code that ends in *F*. But they aren't the only ones. All the codes either end with *KW*, *F*, *HMC*, or *N*. Do you think—" I stop myself. No, it's too far-fetched.

"What? What are you thinking?" Alister's brows crinkle as he searches my face for the truth. I move my eyes to the register once more. I bite my lip. This is the last thing I wanted, to be sucked in so deep I not only can't escape but I don't want to. And yet, here I am, once again discovering truths I'd rather not know, discovering truths I *have* to know.

"I just… I think it's really strange that in five years, every code ends one of four ways. Something about these letters is important. And then there are the dates. If you look at it, every girl who I've identified as possibly from New Orleans is sold within four to five days of being reported missing. At first, I thought maybe the codes had something to do with the buyers, or maybe labels to identify something specific about the girls. But, if that were the case, I feel like there would be more than four possibilities. So, then I noticed the dates. All of these sales happen within a day of each other, always within a single week in a single month over the same six months out of the year."

"Emma, this is why I need your help. I'm not following you." I look between the paper and Alister. Assuming I'm right about the first two letters in each code being the initials of the girl sold, paired with the date of sale listed, the last letters in each code must mean something, something Posey and his anal self would need to keep up with. *Think, Emma.* These deals are only successful because all parties are keen on privacy. It's unlikely Posey would keep detailed records of his buyers, even in code form. He's a merchant. And though he doesn't have a government agency looking over his shoulder, he does have to answer to someone or perhaps multiple someones. If these girls are the way they make their money, whoever is in charge would want to know when and where they are— *That's it!* My idea wasn't so far-fetched after all.

I turn to Alister, my eyes wide with the thrill of a lead. "Do you think it's possible these letters have something to do with *where* the girls are sold?"

"You mean like abbreviations for cities or countries?" Alister asks. I nod. He takes the paper from me then, stands, and paces the room while examining it. "There's something about these letters that seems familiar."

"Let's pretend for a second that I'm right, that these letters represent the locations of the auctions. Each auction is within one day of each other, which means they can't be far apart. Maybe different buildings in the same city. Or different cities close together. And, considering New Orleans is a hub for the brotherhood and some girls have been taken from here, wherever they are being sold is within travel distance."

"That doesn't exactly narrow things down," Alister notes. "New Orleans is home to an international airport with flights to South America, the Caribbean, Canada, and Europe. Not to mention the cruise ports and the interstate that takes you across the entire gulf coast. You can get almost anywhere from New Orleans within the amount of the time between these girls being taken and being sold."

"You're right," I say, bringing my hands to my hips. "But we know that New Orleans is only one of the brotherhood's locations. Take Los Angeles for example. If the brotherhood is trafficking girls in and out of LA, they'd more than likely come from Mexico, Canada, possibly even Asia. But New Orleans? It's less likely the girls are from Asia and more likely they're from South America, possibly Europe. We need to think local and what routes would be easy for the brotherhood to take operating in and out of New Orleans." Alister nods. I stand and begin pacing like him.

"Traveling along the interstate would be too risky," Alister says. "It's heavily populated, sometimes backed up with accidents. It would be too easy for a driver in another car to see something suspicious. Not to mention, the brotherhood has the means for private travel, even a private plane. And, with the prices they're selling these girls, they have rich clientele, which means…"

"Rich destinations," I mumble. Alister nods again.

I look away then. It's weird talking with him like this. But, even more so, it turns my stomach to talk about the girls who are being sold and how the brotherhood has been pulling it off for years. A sense of hopelessness inches its way into my heart. All these years and no one has been able to stop them. What makes us think we can? And yet, I know those thoughts and feelings have no place in my mind, not if I want to crack this case. And I do. It scares the Hell out of me, and I have no idea how I'll explain it to Julian, but I do. I want to see these bastards fall.

"I'll check Posey's register for anything that looks like a means of travel, private plane or boat. Why don't you think on the letters? See if you can come up with some possibilities for the locations."

"You got it," Alister says, moving from the center of the room to his desk. He flips open a laptop and begins his research. I didn't think the Blood King took orders from anyone. His eagerness reminds me I still don't know why he's so invested in destroying the brotherhood. Yet, in this moment, I don't care about his why. I'm simply thankful for his help, thankful he's willing to take on this fight and remind me of what I'm fighting for.

I return to my place on the couch and scroll through Posey's register once more. If the brotherhood had a private plane, they would've had to pay for a hangar and a fee to keep a pilot on standby. There would also be flight records tracking their movements. And yet, I find nothing resembling what I'm looking for. Just as I begin to second-guess my theory, Alister rises from his desk. His bottom lip falls open as he stares blankly ahead.

"Alister? What is it?" I set my folder to the side and watch him as he leans against his desk, almost as if he can no longer hold himself upright. "Alister? What do the letters mean?" He looks at me then as I rise from my place on the couch.

"I know why these letters are so familiar." Alister moves from his desk to the opposite side of the office. Similar to his office at his warehouse, there is a wall of cabinets home to God only knows what. He opens one and quickly pulls out a large roll of white paper. It looks like some kind of blueprint. Alister returns to his desk and spreads the papers wide. Before us is a detailed drawing of a ship. I furrow my brows. Just as I'm about to ask him what we're looking at, he flips the page and again and again until we are staring at a map. That's when I realize—*KW* for Key West. *F* for Freeport. *HMC* for Half Moon Cay. *N* for Nassau.

"They're not just cities. They're ports," I whisper.

"Cruise ports." Alister's expression darkens as realization seems to wash over him. "My company is planning to start a cruise line next year. These ports are all part of a cruise route regularly taken from New Orleans to the Caribbean and back. That's where I recognized the letters from." I nod. I remember seeing something in The Hub's business pages about the Amatos' plans to start a cruise line. Though it isn't worth mentioning to him now.

"It makes sense, doesn't it?" He leans against his desk once more. "New Orleans is one of the few ports that offers transport through the Caribbean. Everything is so tourist centered nowadays, the islands are used to having an influx of unfamiliar faces. It would take a large vessel like a cruise ship to navigate the waters safely, especially during hurricane season, especially with that many people aboard. And law enforcement wouldn't look twice at a cruise ship."

"That's how you think they're doing it? A cruise ship operated by a third party filled with tourists?"

Alister nods. "Keeps them from having to supply their own transportation, which would stick out like a sore thumb both in the Port of New Orleans and at the islands, which may not be the isles of luxury themselves, but are close to luxurious Turks and Caicos. Maybe they have a side deal with someone at the port or someone who works on the ship. Maybe they keep the girls in cargo storage where the water pressure would muffle their screams. When they reach the islands, all the attention is on keeping the tourists safe and happy. No one's paying attention to the crew or what's happening below deck."

There's a bite of anger in Alister's voice as he relays his theory, his knuckles whitening as he grips his desk. I stand still, mindful of the sharp objects within his reach. He's already broken one glass today, and he looks close to breaking something else.

"How could I not see it?" He looks to me then. "The man's mistress lived in Key West. Why did I not look into that further?" He tilts his head to the side, clenching his jaw. He points to the map and draws his finger from New Orleans to Key West, and down through the Caribbean. "You said all of the girls taken from New Orleans had a code ending in *F*. They were sold in Freeport, the first Bahamian island on the cruise route."

"Officially no longer in the United States. That's why they didn't sell the American girls in Key West. Because then whoever bought them would have to find a way to get them out of the US, which would be next to impossible to do once they've been reported missing."

At that, Alister balls the paper up in his palms and throws the lump clear across the room. It doesn't make a loud noise or shatter into pieces as it falls softly to the floor, but the impact is all the same. He doesn't have to say it, but I think I know why Alister is so desperate to destroy the brotherhood—why the deeper we get into this investigation the more pain radiates through him rather than hope. The thought first occurred to me this morning. It was the thing I needed Fiona to confirm. And yet, a second look at Posey's records is almost all the confirmation I need.

May 24, 2020 is the date of the last human trafficking sale recorded in Posey's register. The transaction script reads CA40567F for $1,000,000. Back-date for transport time from New Orleans to Freeport and we find ourselves roughly two weeks before the brotherhood was exposed by my father, two weeks before their entire operation changed, and members scattered. This is also around the time when Fiona's friend, the one who wore a brooch of the Amato family crest, disappeared. Fiona said Alister and her friend got into an argument the night before she disappeared. The girl told Fiona she was worried Alister would send someone to take her away, even though she didn't want to leave New Orleans. So of course Fiona thought Alister was the one who took her friend. But I think there is more to the story. I think—

"*Alister!*" I turn as a brunette woman dressed in an ivory pantsuit storms through the wooden door of the office. Alister clears his throat, drawing my attention. His eyes move to the duster at my hip. I grab hold of it and make my way across the room to dust the various shelves lining the walls of his office.

"Sophia, is everything alright?" Alister asks.

His sister.

"No. Everything is not alright. I was just at a luncheon for the St. Clarice Society and had to field yet another slew of questions about Cara's societal debut. We put it off two years ago because of Mom's illness and last year because of Dad's passing *and* her sudden international studies trip. Alister, I am tired. Every time I go out, I'm asked about Cara. I've tried calling her. I've emailed. I even got a stupid Snapchat just to try to talk to my own sister. When the Hell is she coming home?"

I steal a peek at Alister as his sister finishes her rant. Alister's plans against the brotherhood aren't the only thing she's unaware of. She doesn't even realize her sister, Fiona's roommate, the girl with the initials CA, was taken. Perhaps Alister hopes to find her and bring her home without telling Sophia. The thought makes me feel something for Alister I'm not ready or willing to feel.

"I...I don't know," Alister says then, slumping into his chair. His eyes move back to the map in front of him. That's why he was so upset, so desperate for my help, desperate for us to discover the brotherhood's patterns.

"If she doesn't come home soon, the chatter will shift from *When is she coming home?* to *Is she ever coming home?* And then people will start asking more questions, questions that you and I both know won't lead anywhere good. Call her. You're her big brother. She'll listen to you."

"Yeah, right," Alister mumbles.

Sophia faces me then. I quickly turn back to the bookshelf

and continue my dusting. Sophia moves closer to Alister then and whispers something I can't hear. He nods and she leaves much quieter than she when entered.

With Sophia gone, I bring my duster down to my hip and return to my seat across from Alister's desk. When he doesn't say anything, I do. "Alister—" At least, I try to.

"Emma. Thank you for your help today," Alister says, cutting me off. His voice is strained as he speaks. "I'd love to continue, but I just remembered there is something I must take care of this evening. Gio will make sure you get home safely. I'll send for you again once I return."

"*Return?* Return from where?"

Alister's eyes lock on mine as he rolls his sleeves up to his elbows. There's something dark in them. His usual golden gleam has been replaced with something wicked, something bloodthirsty that makes me weak at the knees.

"Freeport."

CHAPTER 20

It's been four days since I last saw Alister. And to be honest, the more time that passes without hearing from him, the more anxious I become. I never asked Alister specifically about his sister Cara. But I can only assume his sudden trip to Freeport has something to do with her. CA40567F. CA meaning Cara Amato. Ever since I spotted the raven-haired girl on Instagram wearing a brooch of the Amato family crest, I've suspected she was related to Alister. Hearing Sophia confront her brother about their sister accompanied with Posey's records lets me know I'm right. Furthermore, it explains why Alister would argue with someone, a teenage girl no less. I may not know Alister well, but I know enough to know he doesn't argue. He demands. He orders. He tells. He threatens. But he doesn't argue.

She was his sister. The brotherhood abducted his sister. I'm not sure why or if they even knew that they were crossing a devil as dangerous as Alister. What I do know is that Alister will stop at nothing to get his sister back. And I can't blame him, but I do fear him, even more than before. Alister went to Freeport in the hopes of finding his sister. My throat aches with emotion at the thought. I could be wrong. The hollow feeling inside of me tells me I wish I was wrong because, if I'm right, then the pain he must feel is unimaginable. No matter what he's done. No matter how devious and dangerous he can be, *is*, the pain of losing someone you love to men as monstrous as those of the brotherhood is not a pain I would wish on anyone. They will torture, defile, and kill every part of the person you used to know, making them unrecognizable. That's if they survive at all. And the pain of their loss makes *you* unrecognizable. It's what Julian fears will happen to me. It's what I fear will happen to me. And so, I fear what Alister will do, what he will become if his trip to Freeport results in nothing more than more bloodshed.

The loss will destroy him, and he will destroy me because, one year ago, it was *my* actions that led to the brotherhood's exposure. When they scattered, it made them harder, if not impossible, to track. Which means any chance Alister had at saving his sister last year was ruined because of me. Maybe he did want my help. Maybe he believed I was the only one who could help him get Cara back. And maybe, just maybe, I'll be the only one left to blame if he doesn't find her, if his trip to the Bahamas shatters the last ember of hope he held.

I do my best to shove the thought from my mind and focus on filling the cardboard box before me. Julian has gotten in touch with the FBI agent who helped us disappear the first time. We haven't received our new identities yet, but they should come in any day now. And not a day too soon. I'm not sure what Alister's trip to the Bahamas will mean for our plan against the brotherhood. If he finds his sister alive, he may not want to provoke further retaliation by the brotherhood. Would he pull his protection? Would he abandon our efforts? How would that make me feel? I've just found a renewed sense of fight within me. I don't want to let it go. I don't want to run anymore. Would I go after them alone? And yet, if Alister does not return with his sister, then my choice may be made for me. And instead of running from one group of men, I'll run from two.

I shake my head as I open the last drawer of the secretary next to Julian's piano. I still haven't told Julian about Alister and our plans against the brotherhood. And, considering how uncertain those plans are, I think it's for the best. So, I pack as if this is our last week in the city that's been my home for nine years. For all I know, it is. We won't be able to take much with us when we leave. Most of these boxes will be donated to local charities for auctions. Mason handles the heavy items. Julian sorts through the kitchen. And my task is all things sentimental—books, records, knickknacks. The kinds of things you want to keep but, in this situation, can't.

I shove a bundle of books into a box, only to find Alister's face staring back at me. I gasp. I pop my head up to see if Mason or Julian heard. Thankfully, they're both otherwise occupied. I pull the sketch pad from the drawer and examine it as Grey nuzzles beside me. "Thanks, girl," I whisper. It's unsettling, not only to see him here, inside my home, but to know that when I drew him, I knew absolutely nothing about him. I didn't know if he was following me or why. Nor could I ever have imagined how complicated things would become. The man I thought would be the death of me is now my safety net. And yet, with all the uncertainty centered around his trip to Freeport, I'm not sure how much longer his protection will last.

At that, I flip through my sketch pad, taking in the faces that haunt me. Looking at them makes my head hurt. Until I find him, the one man I drew not because he scared me, but because I knew he was innocent. His face is covered with fine lines that represent his wisdom. His eyes are an icy blue and yet they aren't cold. They are filled with life, life that Julian and I almost stole.

"Hey, babe. You doing okay in here?" Julian asks, coming up behind me.

"Yeah." He sits down beside me and plants a soft kiss on my cheek. His touch fills me with warmth I desperately need. "You're in a good mood."

Julian's lips draw up into a smile. "I found a Le Creuset shoved to the back of the cabinet."

"Is that supposed to mean something to me?"

"To you? No. To me? It's one of the best cookware pieces you'll ever own. My mom used to have one."

"Well, then we are definitely keeping it," I say. I bring my hand to his knee as his eyes shift to the sketch pad in my lap.

"What about that?" he asks. "Are we keeping that?" I return my gaze to the sketch pad, to the man from Paris. For so long, I thought my sketches were valuable pieces of evidence, a key to a door I hadn't encountered yet. But meeting Alister has proven to me how wrong I was. These sketches are nothing more than a reminder of my fear, of the brotherhood's control. I don't know if I'll ever be free of them, but I do know these sketches won't be the key to my freedom or even my survival.

"Only one," I say. I tug on the paper, ripping the sketch of the Parisian man free from the rest. "He reminds me not every man is out to get me. Just like you." At that, I toss the sketch pad in the trash bag, along with Alister's image, and redirect my attention to Julian.

"That's a big step," Julian says. I bring my hand to his hair and run my fingers through his soft, tousled locks.

"Maybe. But it doesn't make things any easier. The sketches were never going to protect me, to save me. I'm not sure...I'm not sure anything or anyone can." Julian nods and, without a word, stands. He reaches down, offering me his hand. I take it. Julian leads me to the piano bench, the place we come when we need to get lost in another world because our own is too much. He plays a few notes before turning to me.

"I found something while I was at Lucid the other day, something that belongs to you." I frown, unsure of what it could be. That's when Julian pulls a crumpled piece of notebook paper from his pocket. "I found it beneath the cash register." I take the paper as a small ache tickles my throat.

"I...I thought I'd lost it. Well, I guess I did."

"It found its way back to you, maybe when you need it the most."

I unfold the paper as Julian brings his fingers back to the keys. I look over the words as he plays a melody he wrote just for me, a melody to accompany my own words, the words I need to hear.

Maybe she was right.
Maybe I can't do this.
Maybe I should go home.
Home.
Where is home?

Not the place where whispers burn my ears.
Not the place where screams bring me tears.
But that doesn't mean home is here.

The place where dust itches my skin.
The place where static shields me from sin.
The place without my kin.

Family.

I've lost them.
If that's true, then were they ever mine to lose?
My comforts now are worn records and booze.
But that isn't true.

The girl who laughs.
The man who protects.
We're a family without blood connection but with honest intent.

Maybe there's more to life than other people's expectations.
Maybe there's more to family than blood.
Maybe there's more to me than the whispers that burn my ears.
More to me than the tears I cry.
More to me than sleepless nights.
More to me than I will ever write.

There's more to me. More to this life.
I don't need a savior without a soul.
I don't need a house that isn't a home.
I don't need a family who'd rather disown.

I need me and honest intentions.
I need me and a warrior's spirit.

As Julian finishes his song, he turns to me. "I told you I wanted to say the right thing, but I couldn't because you'd already said it. Emma, I will protect you until my last breath. But it won't be me who saves you or anyone else. Because you're going to save yourself. You always have and you always will."

I nod. I want to tell him *Thank you*, but all I can do is hug him. I set the paper to the side and throw my arms around him. He pulls me into him, burying his face in the crook of my neck. I wrote that poem while working a night shift at Lucid. Mr. Turnip had just gotten me the job so I wouldn't have to go back home to my parents, to a place that was never truly home. Compared to what I've been through since, the spat between me and my mom and dad seems so small. But, back then, it was huge. Standing up to them and making a life for myself in New Orleans was the first time I had to rely on myself to survive. I had help in Kat and Mr. Turnip. Just like I have help now in Julian and Mason. But Julian's right. I saved myself back then. Maybe I can save myself again. That is, if I get the chance to try.

"Thank you," I finally whisper. "I needed that. You have no idea how much."

"Might I suggest putting that Le Creuset to good use?" Mason says, interrupting our moment. I turn to scold him, but I'm silenced by the look on his face, a look of longing I haven't seen before. "We should take advantage of the time we have left."

The time we have left. Who knows how much or little it will be? And, once we do leave, will we all still be together? Is Mason planning on coming with us? If we go to war against the brotherhood, will he fight beside us? Who am I kidding? He'll lead the charge. At least, I think.

"Mason's right," I say, turning back to Julian. "Why don't you take a break from packing and whip us up something good for dinner? I'll start on the upstairs."

SMELLS of Julian's cooking waft through the house as I pack up the small items in our bedroom. That is, until something catches my eye in the stack of manila folders Alister sent me home with before his departure. I move to the bedroom door and close it before making my way out onto the balcony for additional privacy. As I move, my arms weigh heavily with the truth splashed across the pages of the folder I'm not meant to have. I sit and run my fingers along the edge of the red-trimmed folder, the folder different from all the others. Finally, I open it to find it's just as I thought. It isn't one of Posey's records at all. It's one of Alister's. Or rather, his father's. It's from before the Amatos ceased working with the brotherhood, which means in it lies the evidence I've been looking for—the smoking gun I need to earn my freedom from Alister. If he does come back from the Bahamas with my death warrant clasped in his bloodstained hand, then perhaps it'll be enough to stop him in his tracks.

Just like the document I got a brief peek at in Alister's office, this one is a list of transactions. Only Alister, or rather, his dad, keeps track of his inventory differently from Posey. The entire sheet is a record of transactions to one buyer named Leo Ricci. I haven't seen this name before, but something tells me I have seen the man it belongs to. I grab my phone and search all platforms—social media, news outlets, the New Orleans society pages. Within a matter of minutes, staring back at me is the man Alister met at Midnight Moon, the same man who approached me when I infiltrated Club Gent a year ago. No surprise. Alister said he was his contact. Clearly, the Amatos were supplying the brotherhood with something, and he was the man receiving the product on the brotherhood's behalf. The question is, what?

I frown, brows crinkling. Posey's records, though written in code, were relatively straightforward to interpret. Item, price, date of sale. In contrast, the Amatos use the alphabet. The letter *A* represents a specific product sold and so on. If it weren't for the measurements listed next to each entry, I'd have no way of knowing what products the Amatos deal in. Alas, at the sight of ten ounces and twenty grams, the truth of Alister's family business dawns on me. I feel stupid for not thinking of it sooner. He's a drug dealer. Or, rather, he's a drug kingpin, a mafia crime boss. The money he makes illegally must fund his legitimate businesses, including the new cruise line he plans to launch next year. Hell, for all I know he plans to use the cruise line much like the brotherhood did, to transport illegal goods in and out of the US. And yet, that thought isn't the most disturbing of all. Rather the fact that his family undoubtedly supplied the drugs the brotherhood used to subdue and rape the women they brought to the Club Gent parties. Those same drugs would have been used in the brotherhood's trafficking scheme.

Maybe this is why Alister cut ties with the brotherhood and why he said his father never would've done business with them had he known the truth. Though I'm not sure what else they could've expected. Illegal drugs are harmful even when taken with the best intentions. And in the wrong hands, they are a weapon of bodily destruction and a deliverance of death. I suppose selling drugs is better than selling human beings. But, however unintentional, his family has made it possible for the brotherhood to subdue, abduct, and assault women for generations. And that's just the consequences of working with the brotherhood. No doubt he has other present-day clients responsible for the destruction of lives just like the brotherhood. He's a different kind of monster, just like he said. But he's still a monster.

I set the folder to the side and allow the truth to wash over me. Is this why Cara was taken? Is this why Alister couldn't report her missing? Because doing so would link back to the real way he makes his money? Even more so, reporting her disappearance would lead back to the brotherhood, who are no doubt the ones Alister warned Cara of the night before she disappeared. When Sophia told Alister that Cara would listen to him, he scoffed because she hadn't. When it mattered, she hadn't listened. She didn't leave New Orleans and they took her. Perhaps because Alister cut them off. Perhaps because of something else.

I shake my head as I battle frustration and sympathy inside me. I feel Alister's pain. I feel his wrath and desire for justice, because I know if I lost someone to the brotherhood—

I lean forward, allowing the soft smell of moss and tree bark to calm me. I can't go there. I can't imagine that pain. It's debilitating.

This crusade began with me trying to destroy Alister before he could destroy me. I didn't know what I was looking for at first. Now that I have the smoking gun I need, I'm not sure what to do with it or what to think of Alister. But Alister isn't the one I run from, is he? At least, not yet. Alister may be a monster, but he is also my ally, at least until he proves otherwise. I know things may change when he gets back from the Bahamas. But, for now, he's willing to fight in the war I can no longer ignore.

If the brotherhood is daring enough to abduct the sister of the Blood King, then they are daring enough to do just about anything. What's worse? They've gotten away with it. For a year, they've gotten away with it. If I can end their reign of terror, I have to try. And so, what I once thought would be my saving grace is now nothing more than another piece of the elaborate puzzle depicting the brotherhood's actions. Because they are the target now, not Alister. After everything I've learned over the past week, I can't lose sight of who the real enemy is, not again. I just pray Alister remains an ally. Without him, I don't know if I can do this. I don't know if I'll survive.

I stand with resolve. Though my attention is quickly drawn to my cell phone as my text chime dings. It's from an unknown number.

There's a gift for you in your garage.

What the...?

This is Alister, by the way.

As realization dawns, the familiar rev of an engine makes its way from the street to me. The burgundy sports car from last week zooms by. It's him. He's the stalker. Well, I guess I already knew that. What I don't know and what I'm not sure I want to know is what this so-called gift is.

CHAPTER 21

"That's your second glass of champagne in thirty minutes. Is everything okay?" Julian asks.

"Yeah, just nervous, I guess. We haven't been around this many people in what seems like forever, especially this many of the New Orleans elite."

My eyes gaze past Julian's worried features to take in the crowd. Everyone is dressed immaculately in formal gowns, tuxedos, and intricate masks. The garments Alister left for me and Julian in our garage are no exception. Julian wears a black tux, the coat of which is velvet. He's classically dashing. And my dress looks like something that belongs on the carpet of the Met Gala. It's bloodred adorned with burgundy lace floral appliqués. The bodice is tight and low cut. It shows off my figure before the waist flares out with chiffon and more and more layers of lace florals that cascade down to the floor. Burgundy beads connect across my exposed back. My skin feels like ice as the beads dance across my flesh. With the weight of the dress, it's a wonder they are strong enough to hold it up, considering the sleeves are for nothing more than appearance's sake. Soft, lacy sleeves fall off my shoulders, allowing the pale skin of my chest to glow beneath the lights of the chandeliers hanging above us.

Despite the extraordinary beauty of my gown, Julian and I seem to fit right in among the crowd. Still, I'm on edge, waiting for someone to recognize me, someone like the Thomases or an unidentified member of the brotherhood. Even more, Alister has yet to make his appearance or explain why he requested both my and Julian's presence at tonight's ball. Is he planning on bringing Julian into the fold? Or does he plan to begin his revenge against me by killing him? My eyes dart around the space in search of him or Gio. Nothing. Nothing but ball gowns and masks surround me. God only knows where he is or what he's up to.

"Hey, where's the Emma that insisted we take your friend Gio up on the invitation?"

I give Julian an apologetic look while letting a waiter take away my second empty glass of the evening. Despite my fear, I couldn't resist attending tonight's festivities. I'm not sure what would've happened if I had. I have to know if Alister is now my enemy. And if he isn't, I need to know what happened in the Bahamas and what to expect next. With my and Julian's departure quickly approaching, Julian needs to know the truth. But first, I do. So, I told him Gio was covering the event for The Hub, much like I used to cover events, and he had a few extra tickets.

We've been looking for ways to spend more time together and make what he believes are our last days in New Orleans memorable. It didn't take much convincing to get Julian to tag along, considering it's a masquerade ball and I've got on far too much makeup. With the masks and makeup, no one unsavory *should* recognize me. Still, the one hundred people filling the grand ballroom of the Amato mansion are just the types to know of or be involved in the brotherhood. And with Alister nowhere to be found, I'm beginning to wonder if that's his plan. Lead me into a den of wolves and see if I make it out.

"I know. I know. I thought it would be fun and we need fun. It's just being here... What if someone recognizes me? Someone as in a select group of people we've been doing our best to avoid for over a year now." I look around once more, noting the only exit nearby. It's then that Julian places his hand on my back and leans in. His breath is hot against my neck, giving rise to a set of emotions I crave.

"That's why you're wearing a mask, my love." With that, he leaves a slew of soft kisses behind my ear, trailing into my sloppily pinned updo. "Tonight is about letting go and living in the freedom of disguise." He takes a step back then. His raven hair blends perfectly with the black etchings of his mask. As he stands before me, he's too perfect to be human. "My love, may I have this dance?" Julian extends his hand and I blush.

"Of course you may." I take his hand as he leads us toward the center of the room where couples of all ages dance. I welcome the distraction from my anxiety. And yet, I can't help but note the dance floor is the perfect vantage point to locate Alister's guards and anyone else in attendance I should avoid.

Julian swoops me into his arms as the deep chords of a piano blend with the rich bellow of a cello. Even with the addition of the vocals, the song is soft and slow. I give in to Julian's embrace, my body melding with his. I allow my straining eyes a moment of reprieve and close them, losing myself in the song, in this moment with Julian.

"I can't believe I'm saying this, but the Biebs is speaking to my soul." Julian's voice pulls my eyes open as the sweet song comes to an end.

"*Biebs?* I cannot believe you just said that.*" Something that sounds like a laugh and a scoff all at once escapes me. Julian's lips draw up into a half smile before he brushes a clump of blond curls from where they cover my face.

"Old and gray, when you're slipping away, I'll still want to know everything about you. The good, the bad. There's nothing you can say or do that will make me stop loving you. It's a blessing and a curse to be loved by you, Emma Marshall. Calling you mine is the greatest honor of my life. And yet, I know we'll never have enough time. Even eternity with you isn't enough."

There are a million things I want to say, to assure him of my love for him, to confess my secrets to him. And yet, I can't help but wonder, would he be saying the same things if he knew I've been lying to him after I promised him I never would? I have my reasons. And they're damn good ones. But will he see it that way?

My lips part. I swallow the words that beg to escape and allow my lips against his to reveal every feeling I have for him. He's the one. The one I love with every fiber of my being. The one I know I can count on, even though I don't want to. The one I can trust. The one I want to protect. And, in my darkest moments, he's the one who brings me back to life. He's my foothold in this world, even when there are so many forces that seek to pull me into the next. Which is why I've had to keep him as far away from Alister, as far away from the darkness of this world for as long as I could. But tonight, I feel that darkness swirling around us. It tickles my skin, letting me know my time is up. Our time is up.

"Emma, are you...are you okay?" Julian's words pull me from my thoughts to the present, though I can barely make out his features through the tears filling my eyes. I quickly blot them away, taking note of the couples dancing around us with more pep than before.

"Yes, I, um... What you said was so beautiful it brought tears to my eyes, literally."

"Are you sure that's all?" Julian's icy green eyes shine brightly against the dark contrast of his suit and mask. It feels as if they see inside my soul, taking note of all the cracks that slither through my essence, the cracks left in the wake of Beaux, the brotherhood, Gio, Alister, and this world that is theirs.

"I...um..." I shake my head. Not here. I can't tell him here. But Alister is nowhere to be found, and the longer I stand here, the more I feel this is a trap meant for more than just me. "Julian, I think we should—"

It's then that I feel my phone vibrate in one of the discreet pockets sewn into my dress. It's late, too late for my mother or Eva to call. If it was Mason, he'd call Julian. That only leaves Kat and—

I glance over the text from Alister requesting my presence in the parlor on the other side of the grand spiral staircase.

"Is everything okay?" Julian asks, taking in my pale expression. I press my lips into a flat line and shove my phone back into my pocket. *Decision time, Emma.* I know I need to get Julian out of here and tell him everything. But I also know I won't sleep until I know what Alister discovered in the Bahamas *and* if that discovery, or lack of, means he now wants me dead. There are plenty of people here. If Alister tries anything, I'm sure I could fight him off long enough to—

I shake my head, dislodging all unwelcome thoughts from my mind. What's the point? If I walk out that door now, I walk away from Alister's protection *and* any chance I have at destroying the brotherhood. And I can't do that, not when we're so close. I can't let my fear keep me from this opportunity.

"Yeah, um, just Kat. I'm going to go to the restroom, freshen up, and call her. There may be a line so I'll probably be a minute."

"Okay. Do you want me to walk with you?"

"No," I say a bit too quickly. "No, I'll be fine. I have my mask. There are a lot of really cool paintings on the walls. You may want to check some of those out. Just don't...don't stray from the crowd. In a place like this, I'm sure it's easy to get lost."

"Famous last words," Julian says with a grin.

I smile and give him a soft peck on the cheek. *I sure hope not.*

"I love you," I whisper into his ear.

Julian holds on to me a moment longer. His eyes study me, as if to make sure I'm telling the truth. I don't make a habit of lying to him, which only makes this one sting more. "I love you too," he finally says.

As I walk through the crowd, people seem to move out of my way as if they are scared to get too close, as if they know I'm a dead girl walking or, perhaps, just cursed. I'm sure it's my overactive imagination on steroids. And yet, the air becomes eerily still as I round the staircase and spot the door to the parlor. It's hidden from the rest of the party by a passageway framed in marble. The clank of my heels echoes through the space, reminding me that I'm alone. And, convenient for Alister, we're far enough from the party that no one will hear my screams, not even the man I love, who is far too close to the Devil for my comfort.

This was a bad idea. I should've left when I had the chance. Or, better yet, I never should've come. Now I've dragged Julian, unsuspectingly, into this. I'll never forgive myself if something happens to him. I—

I turn only to be met by Gio, who I somehow didn't hear following behind me. "Going somewhere?" he asks.

"Just the bathroom," I say. "I'm not sure what Alister wants to talk about or how long it will take. My two glasses of champagne have caught up with me." I try to move past Gio, but he sidesteps in front of me. "Gio?"

"Mr. Amato is ready for you now." He doesn't say anything more than that. I know him well enough to know he won't keep Alister waiting, and, therefore, the only way I'm making it past him is... Well, even then, I doubt I'd get far. I turn and close the distance between me and the ominous wooden door, doing my best to keep my nerves in check. "Aren't you forgetting something?" Gio's words pull me back to him just as my fingers reach the doorknob.

"What am I forgetting?" The words nearly catch in my throat as they leave me.

"You may not carry a purse, but I've been doing this long enough to know dresses like these often have hidden pockets, especially ones made for the Amato women."

"This dress was made for—?"

"Cara," Gio says then. Her name lands heavily at my feet as a chill nips at my skin. Why would Alister give me a dress meant for his sister? He wouldn't. Not if he'd found her alive. But if he didn't find her at all, or worse?

"You know the rules, Emma. All personal items must be turned over before meeting with Mr. Amato."

"No. No, Gio. I can't." I do my best to get past him, but my dress slows me down. Gio wraps his arm around my waist and slams me into the wooden door. "Ah!" I cry. My heartbeat quickens as my limbs shake. "Gio, no. Please! I know you don't want to do this. Please!"

Gio's hand rummages through the fabric of my dress while he uses his other to hold me still. He doesn't stop until he finds my Chapstick and cell phone. His eyes meet mine then, filled with warning or perhaps just death. Whatever it is, the hairs on my arms rise. I try to find adrenaline resting in my muscles, but instead they feel heavy, heavy with the truth. This *was* a mistake, a huge one. Whatever happens on the other side of that door, it's my fault. I walked into this trap. I put my trust in a man—no, monster—who never deserved it. And now—

"You're right," Gio says. "I don't want to do this. Neither does he." *What?* Neither does he? What does that even mean? "But it's the only way." At that, Gio pulls me into him and opens the door. My throat aches with screams I can't bring myself to release. Julian. I can't let him hear me. I can't let him try to save me. I have to save myself. I must survive, if only to ensure Julian makes it out of here alive. Gio shoves me through the doorway just as my knees give out.

I fall into the wall, catching myself with my arms. Gio's words course through me as I take in my surroundings. Where I expected to find Alister, he is nowhere to be seen. Instead, ten men all wearing masks fill the room. At the sight of me, their laughter and conversation fades. The silence is deafening. Or, at least, it would be if my inner self weren't screaming at the top of her lungs for me to run. They look me up and down with lustful eyes that make my legs heavy. Before my body goes into shock, I turn and reach for the door as it swings slowly closed. As my fingers graze the rough wood, the door clicks, latching in place. The sound of it being locked from the other side sends shooting pains through my head. *No!* This can't be happening. Alister wouldn't. He wouldn't. He needs me. He…

"Gio!" I cry. "No, please! Please help me!" I scream and pound my fists against the door I know will never give. He knew. He knew what was waiting for me and still he let me walk right into Hell. What else should I have expected? From him or Alister? I've gotten too comfortable being in the presence of monsters. I forgot who they were, what they are truly capable of. And now, I will pay the price for my stupidity with my body.

CHAPTER 22

The sound of my rapidly beating heart fills my ears, while the intoxicating aroma of freshly smoked cigars invades my nostrils, drowning out all my other senses except one—the sense to run. As the large slab of wood before me stands tightly closed, I know running is not an option, which only adds to the anxiety riddling my bones. The air shifts as I sense the men move closer. My skin becomes hot as cigar smoke dances against it.

"Take off your mask," says the man I refuse to face. I pinch my eyes closed as thoughts of what will happen next plague me. What has Alister done? What have I done? I know things will be worse for me if I don't obey. Yet, my body is so numb with fear I'm unable to move a muscle, much less comply with his request.

"I said, take off your mask!"

I scream as the masked man pulls me from the corner where I cower and throws me into the middle of the group. I stumble, falling into the leather sofa that anchors the room.

My ears ring so loudly with fear I can't hear the words as they cross my lips. "What do you want?" I choke out. I look around the room, trying to take in identifying details like I've done for over a year now. But I can't. My vision is blurry with how quickly my eyes move, unable to focus on a single man. There are so many of them. Too many of them.

"We want you to take off your mask. And if you can't oblige, then we'll do it for you. And your mask won't be the only thing we remove." The sadistic lust in his tone is undeniable. It makes me sick to my stomach. Yet, I find the strength to do as he says. I reach behind my head and pull loose the red satin ribbon keeping my mask attached to my face. I'm not sure why he wants me to take it off, but it's better than him asking me to remove my dress. Knowing that that's still an option, I stand tall and force my fear to settle. I need to be strong, strong enough to survive this. Whatever this is.

I pull the mask to my side and find a place on the wall to focus on while the men inch closer, studying me. They mumble things I don't understand. Some of them chuckle. If I weren't so focused on the wall in front of me, I'm sure I'd find them smiling. And yet, my focus is stolen as a man wearing a navy blue tuxedo moves in front of me, forcing my eyes from the wall to him. Or rather, his chin, considering our height difference. My lips part as I dare to lift my eyes to his. They are blue. If he wasn't staring at me like something he wants to devour, I'd say they are beautifully blue. But circumstance makes me think of more negative adjectives, like *dastardly*.

"Such a shame. If you weren't the most wanted woman in our world, I'd take you right here, right now. We all would. Though, a woman of your exquisite beauty, I might not be so inclined to share." The man in the blue tux brings his knuckles to my cheek. I gasp, though his caress is unexpectedly delicate.

"You're...you're one of them, aren't you?" I'm surprised I'm able to speak considering his proximity constricts everything inside me. His response does not come in the form of words. Rather, he moves his thumb to my painted-red lips and tugs down, exposing my teeth. The cigar smoke lingering around us seeps inside me through my parted lips. It scratches my throat, though not as much as the emotion I fight to keep inside.

"Such a shame," he repeats. At that, the man in the blue tux moves to the edge of the room. He is replaced by another and another until finally I'm met by the oldest of the bunch, the asshole who shoved me and demanded I remove my mask. He isn't tall enough to tower over me, which only makes our encounter more nauseating. I can't avoid his gray gaze or the wicked twitch of his lips as his weathered eyes linger on my cleavage.

"Emma Marshall, we've been looking for you for quite some time. But, of course, you know that, don't you? You know our organization doesn't allow for loose ends." I gulp. Every nerve in my body is on fire under his gaze. My body shakes with the realization of the truth. Alister has made a deal with the brotherhood, one I suspect is meant to earn him back the sister he lost. Was this his plan all along? Earn my trust and serve me on a silver platter to the brotherhood?

"You know too much," the old man continues. "But something you may not realize is how much money you've cost us over the past year. Once the feds caught on, our entire operation went dark. Couldn't risk being tracked. That is why you're going to die the slowest of deaths, the kind that breaks your body and your soul. When there is nothing left of you but the skin that hangs on your bones, then and only then will you be given the sweet mercy of death."

The old man's words cut the deepest parts of me, because I know he speaks the truth. I've always known the brotherhood would take their time with me if they ever found me. And yet, his words aren't what hurt the most in this moment. What hurts are the tears spewing down my cheeks. They give him pleasure. They let him know he's hurt me even without touching me. They let him know he's won. His lips draw into the wickedest of grins and—

"That's enough," Alister says. He storms into the room through a secret entrance with Gio by his side. "You see she is who I say she is. Now, do we have a deal?" As Alister, the man I never fully trusted and yet believed would protect me, bargains away my life, I lose all strength in my lower body and collapse onto the couch behind me.

What will happen to Julian? What will he think happened to me? Will they take me tonight? Is this it? Is this my last moment of freedom? And yet, even in this moment, I am not free.

"We'll reach out to the superiors and call a meeting where the girl may be presented in exchange for the information you seek regarding CA40567F," says the old man. Just as I suspected. Alister wants information on who purchased his sister. This entire thing has been about him getting her back. He's been lying to me from the start.

"Good. Until then, the girl is under my protection. Anyone who comes near her prior to the exchange dies. And since she is promised the slowest of deaths, I'll make you the same promise." There's a tinge of protectiveness in Alister's voice. The sheer thought makes me want to laugh. He sees me as nothing more than leverage, a bargaining chip in a war I never wanted any part of.

"Emma. Emma?" Alister waves his hand in front of my face, bringing me back to the present. The men are gone. I don't know for how long. All I know is I'm done. I rear back and slap Alister across the face with every ounce of strength I can muster. "Let me explain," he says, recovering far too quickly. So, I slap him again and again. My rage chases away the numbness long enough for my legs to wake. I stand, towering over him. I shove him, forcing him to lie on his back. It isn't lost on me that he could have me pinned to the ground in seconds. He's letting me win. Perhaps he feels guilty for betraying the one person who was stupid enough to believe his lies.

I sense Gio moving toward me, but I can't take my eyes off Alister, the man who will truly be the death of me. It's then that Alister waves Gio off, sending him from the room. It's only us now, which does nothing but make me feel more guarded. Every time we've been alone together, he's found a way to make me bend to his will, to make me believe in what he says. It was all a lie. Anything he says now will only be the same brand of deceit.

"*Explain?*" The word cuts through me like a blade made of ice. "You want to explain how you lied to me? How you played me like the fool I am for ever trusting a man like you? You want to explain how you plan to trade me for the name of the man who bought your sister? Yeah, I know about Cara. Just like I know you had Fiona killed for knowing too much about her disappearance, for telling me too much. Why couldn't I see it? You had a nineteen-year-old girl murdered and I…I actually felt sorry for you. What the Hell does that say about me?" I bite my lip and fight the urge to kick him. It would be the only good use for these painful monstrosities strapped around my ankles.

"Emma, it's not what it seems." Alister pushes himself up from the ground, adjusting the coat of his burgundy tux. "I didn't lie to you, and I did not have Fiona killed. She was like a little sister to me."

"Bullshit. You're a liar. After the stunt you just pulled, there is nothing you can do or say that will ever make me trust you. This entire time we've been working together you've used my past to motivate me. But if you really understood my pain, the sheer fear I've lived with every day for the past year, you never would've put me through that. I don't care what your reasons are. I don't care if this is the only way to get your sister back, you… you wouldn't have done it."

"This isn't about getting my sister back, Emma." Alister looks away then. Emotion tightens his features. I do my best to ignore it. Whatever pain he feels, he deserves. "Emma, my sister Cara is dead." Alister turns his back on me then, wiping away his emotion. "She was taken by the brotherhood a year ago when I took over the family business from my father and stopped supplying the brotherhood with drugs. I spent so many months trying to find her. When I found out she was dead, in a way, I was relieved. The more time that passed, the more it tore me apart thinking of what she must be going through, what *they* must be doing to her."

Alister turns back to me then. "The brotherhood doesn't know that I know the truth of what happened to my sister. Hell, my own family doesn't know the truth because I couldn't risk it getting out. Pretending like I didn't know was the only way to keep my family safe while trying to figure out a way to crush the brothers like the cockroaches they are. If I let on that I knew, they'd know I was coming for blood. Their guard would be up, and I'd never have an opportunity like I do now."

"You mean the opportunity to have a sit-down meeting with the leaders of the brotherhood, a meeting in which you will trade me for information you don't even need."

"It's not about the information, Emma. It's about getting the leaders of the brotherhood in the same place at the same time. It's the only way to destroy them. So, yes, I used you. I *am* using you to get this meeting. You were the only one who could bring them together. But I never lied to you. The streets of New Orleans will run red with their blood. And once it's done, you will be safe to live your life the way you've always wanted."

"That is, unless you fail, or you decide something else or someone else is more valuable than my life. Just like your secrets and reputation were more important than Fiona's life." I shake my head. Now it's my turn to turn my back on him. My hand stings from the beating I gave him. Yet, I welcome the sensation. My physical pain chases away my emotional torment. I blink away the last of my tears and exhale, doing my best to forget the men whose ghosts still linger.

"For the last time, I did not kill Fiona. She knew about my family, yes. But don't you think if I was going to kill her, I would've done it a year ago?"

Maybe. But if he didn't kill her that means she actually— I shake my head, dislodging the thought from my mind.

"Why did you even go to the Bahamas then?" I ask. I'm both curious and in desperate need of a distraction. I turn back to him. "When we discovered the brotherhood's means of transporting and selling the girls, you were so surprised, angry even. And you took off for days. I assumed you were going to find your sister or at least the man who bought her. But it sounds like you've known about her death for a while now? So, why go? And don't lie to me! Not again."

"I went for blood, for the heads of anyone I could find that worked with the brotherhood."

"But doesn't that defeat the entire purpose of this grand master plan? If you killed members of the brotherhood while in the Bahamas, they'll know about it, and they won't let you get within one hundred yards of them regardless of what or *who* you've promised them." Alister nods as anger roils through me once more.

"I realized that after I'd already left. I didn't kill anyone while away, Emma. I lost sight of our end goal for a moment. But I see the end clearly now. We *can* destroy them, together." Alister moves toward me far quicker than I expected of him. He takes my hands in his, which I quickly rip away.

"*We?* There is no *we*, Alister. Not after what you just did. You…you betrayed me. And they… God, you don't even know what they just did to me!"

"I was watching from outside. This room is under video surveillance. I was never going to let them—"

"Not physically, Alister." I take a step back from him. "Mentally. I am plagued with nightmares of the brotherhood, of what they'll do me if they ever catch me, of what they'll do to the people I love. During the day, I live in constant fear. Anxiety shakes me to my core. I draw the faces of men I encounter, most of whom are probably innocent, but could very well be the death of me. And tonight, you locked me in a room with those men, those men whose faces I still didn't see. Who, even if they weren't wearing masks, I wouldn't be able to identify because I was too afraid to look at them. I could hardly keep myself upright in their presence."

I bring my hand to my stomach. I feel as if I may vomit. I had just found the will to fight, the will to face them. And he took that from me. No. *They* took that from me. They proved to me I am as weak as I've always felt myself to be. I hate them for that. I hate him for that. I hate myself for allowing myself into this world, this fight, and for allowing myself to have hope, actual hope that we could, that *I* could destroy them.

"They promised the death sentence I've felt hovering over my head for the past year. I've always known they would torture me, rape me, kill me. But coming face-to-face with the reality I fear is much different than the Hell waiting for me behind closed eyes. *You* did that. *You* brought me face-to-face with those monsters. Now there is nothing stopping them from coming after me, from discovering where I live, from obliterating the terms of your so-called deal and—"

"I won't let that happen." Alister speaks with a certainty that I want to believe in, that I want to trust. But I can't. Not anymore. I shake my head, doing my best to press my quivering lips into a flat line. I have to get out of here. I can't let him see me break. I won't.

Though I have no intention of playing any further part in his plan, I can't let him know that. He'll lock me up like the prisoner he's made me out to be, or he'll pull his protection, whatever it's worth, when I need it most. I must play along just enough to escape the pit he's thrown me into.

"You better not." At that, I leave through the door I entered, the one Gio unlocked during my and Alister's quarrel. I can't run fast enough as I make it through the marble passageway and past the spiral staircase in search of Julian. God, please let me find him before those masked monsters do.

"Julian!" I yell. I don't care that I'm a sobbing, shaking mess committing the most heinous of party fouls. I have to find him. And while normally I'd be able to pick him out of any crowd, tonight everyone is in disguise. Most of the men wear dark suits and masks. They all blend together behind the tears threatening my vision.

"Emma? Emma Marshall, is that you?"

My lips part as a voice from my past makes this night even

more unbearable. *No!* I can't let her see me. Damn it! With no mask to hide behind, I barrel through the crowd surrounding the dance floor, pretending as if I don't hear her calling my name. Her being the woman who introduced me to New Orleans high society, who made feel a part of a family I never belonged in, who now, undoubtedly, wants my head on a stake for the so-called murder of her son—Penelope Thomas.

As I approach the exit, I dare a peek over my shoulder to see if she's still following me. She isn't. Wouldn't want to be associated with the crazy girl crying at the ball. But she is watching me. Dressed in a velvet purple number, she is to die for. Okay, poor choice of words. It's then that I feel him. Even before I turn my head, I know it's him by the warm gooey feeling inside that lets me know I'm safe.

"Emma, I heard you calling. What's wrong?" As I turn to face Julian, he sees the tears staining my cheeks and the swipe of red lipstick coating my chin, a reminder of my time with the man in the navy blue tux. "Emma, what happened?" There is a fierceness in his voice that says he's ready for a fight. And yet, that's the last thing I need tonight.

I shake my head. "We have to go. Now!" I take hold of his arm and pull him from the party and through the back entrance of the Amato mansion.

CHAPTER 23

Julian pulls the car inside our garage and closes the overhead door behind us. He cuts the engine and it's quiet, just like the drive from the Amato estate to home. I watch him as he stares blankly forward, his jaw clenched in anticipation of what I will say. I told him I'd tell him everything once we made it safely home. We had to get away from there, from Alister, from the brotherhood, from Mrs. Thomas. Yet now that we're home, the truth rests heavily on my chest. So much has happened, so much I have to tell him. Tonight was too close of a call and only the precursor to what Hell waits for me, for *us*. Still, I don't know where to begin.

He looks at me. His green eyes scan my tearstained face. He brings his thumb to my lip, touching me in the same spot the man in the blue tux did. He pulls my lip down, dragging more lipstick onto my face. It's as if he's envisioning the encounter that will surely infuriate him. That's another reason why I've waited until we made it home to tell him the truth. He's safer here, safer from doing something stupid. Yet…

I lean forward and take the keys from where they bite into his hand. His eyes follow them from his palm to mine. "Emma, tell me. Tell me what happened." There's an edge in his voice that lets me know he's scared and angry, that his insides have coiled like a snake ready to lurch. And he is ready to lurch, to take down any man who has threatened me. But I can't let him.

My lips part. "Promise me you'll forgive me. I won't ask that you're not angry. I won't ask that you aren't hurt. Just…just promise me you'll forgive me, that you won't let my mistake ruin us."

Confusion washes over Julian. His brows furrow. His eyes move from mine to the smeared lipstick on my face and back again. "Emma, did…did you…?"

"No," I say before he can finish his sentence. "I would never. But…I have been keeping something from you." Julian's eyes narrow. I take a deep breath and tell him about Alister, about how he's been following me for weeks, about how he approached me shortly before Julian arrived back from LA, about him asking for my help to take down the brotherhood.

"When we decided to leave New Orleans, he had already made his presence known. At first, I thought he was a member of the brotherhood. I thought he would out us to them, assuming they didn't already know of our location. I couldn't take that chance. I couldn't have him following us once we left, because then it would've been for nothing."

"But why didn't you tell me, Emma? You went after this lunatic all on your own. Do you have any idea of what could've happened to you? If he had been a member of the brotherhood, he could've raped you or worse. Even still, he could have. Or did he? And that's why you're telling me now, that's why your lipstick is smeared all over your face."

"Julian, no!" I stop him. "No, he didn't rape me. Just…just

let me finish." I take Julian's hands in mine, doing my best to pull strength from him. Alas, he doesn't feel as if he has much to give, with every bit spent doing his best to remain calm. "I...I soon learned that Alister wasn't a member of the brotherhood. I wasn't sure what he was or why he wanted to take down the brotherhood, but when he asked for my help in destroying them, I couldn't say no."

"Couldn't? Or wouldn't?" Julian asks. His lips press into a flat line and his eyes blaze with hurt. It kills me to know I've caused him this pain. I can't imagine the thoughts he must have. *Does she not trust me? Does she think I'm weak?* He's already admitted to feeling like he's failed me.

"I *couldn't* say no. By the time Alister made his proposal, I already knew too much. He would've killed me had I not complied. And I knew that if there was a one percent chance he was telling the truth, I...I had to take him up on his offer."

"Why?"

"Because, Julian, he has the power to protect us from the brotherhood. I never intended to see his plan through to the end, to be a part of the brotherhood's destruction. I never wanted that. I've wanted nothing but to forget they exist and move on with my life. You know that."

"But that isn't possible." Realization brings life to Julian's cheeks. I feel his body relax within my grasp.

"No," I admit. I take a deep breath, relieved the tension between us is easing. "So, I bargained for his protection. Not just for me, but for you, for Kat, for my mom and sister. Because I've always known the brotherhood would come for us one day and we'd have no way of defeating them. That isn't to say we're weak or that you are. It's just to say you are one man. We are one couple. We can't stand in front of an army of men and win. We need our own army. That's what Alister offered me. In exchange for my help in his investigation, he will protect us, and he will destroy our greatest enemy. It seemed like an okay deal, a necessary deal. All the while, I investigated him. I knew he was hiding something, some criminal activity. I thought I could find something blackmail worthy, so that when we took our leave, we could buy our freedom from him and leave him and his army of goons to take on the brotherhood by themselves. But…" I look away from him then, pulling my hands from his into my lap.

"*But?*" Julian watches me closely. I haven't yet told him of the findings of my and Alister's investigation against the brotherhood, or my discovery that Alister is New Orleans' very own kingpin, or the fact that everything Alister sold me on was a lie. He may be telling the truth about his sister's death, I may finally know his motive, his plan, but I can't trust him. And if he's willing to put me in the position he did tonight, then he doesn't care to or know how to protect me. Not really. The only thing he cares about is his revenge.

"Julian, the information Alister has on the brotherhood, it's… it's heartbreaking. They are more dangerous, more sadistic than we ever could've imagined." I turn to him. I feel cold despite the muggy summer air filling the car we still sit in. "Club Gent is only part of their operation. Their main activity is sex trafficking." I go on to tell Julian of the brotherhood's trafficking routes through the Bahamas and Alister's connection to them and his motive for revenge, the abduction of his sister.

Julian is silent and still as the news hits him. I'm not sure what he's thinking. Finally, he says, "Could Mason have known the truth? Could he have been involved?"

"I don't think so." I shake my head. "From what Alister says, only certain members are privy to the true nature of the organization. It's an oligarchy, not a democracy." Julian nods and sighs in relief. I bring my hand to his shoulder and massage his neck. He closes his eyes and relaxes into my touch. "When I learned the truth, the extent of their horrific reign of terror, I...I decided I would see the investigation through."

"*What?* Emma, no." Julian's eyes blaze with warning. "There is no way you're going within one hundred yards of that man ever again!"

"No, no. I agree. I'm done with him," I tell him. "After tonight—"

"Wait," Julian stops me. "What do you mean *after tonight*?"

I shake my head, fighting back my emotion. I grip the keys tightly in my palm, ready to fight him off should he try to retrieve them.

"Tonight, I learned how he plans to destroy the brotherhood. It involves using me as bait to lure the leaders to New Orleans. Get them in one place and kill them all. I didn't give him a chance to go into details. I was too furious and shaken after being inspected by his contacts, members of the brotherhood he invited to the ball in the hopes of persuading them to call a meeting of the brothers." I shiver. Just mentioning the encounter brings me back to the wood-paneled room riddled with cigar smoke, pride, and predatory lust. It's then that Julian brings his hand to my chin, forcing our eyes to meet.

"You were in the same room as members of the brotherhood tonight? That's why you were crying, why your lipstick is smeared, why you made us leave in such a panic?" There's a look in Julian's eyes I've only ever seen twice before. It scares me, not because of what he will do to me, but because of what he'll try to do to Alister and to any member of the brotherhood he can get his hands on. Just like the night he rescued me outside of Mimi's, he will face down any enemy, no matter if he is outnumbered. His brazen protectiveness will get him killed.

Unable to speak, I simply nod. Finally, he knows everything.

I would be relieved if not for the dark expression contorting every one of his features. He pushes the sleeves of his dress shirt up to his elbows, revealing his tattoos. His jaw clenches as he stares blankly over the dash of the car. It's as if he's imagining all the ways in which he will make Alister pay.

"Julian." I reach out to him.

"Are you okay?" he asks. "Who the Hell am I kidding? Of course you're not. *That bastard!*" Julian slams his fist into the dash. I jump. "Give me my keys," he says. His voice is low and haunting.

I pull my hand back. "No."

He turns to me then. The veins in his neck throb. "Emma, give me my keys."

"No," I whisper. Julian nods, removes his seat belt, and storms out of the car, slamming the door behind him. I jump again, watching him from inside the vehicle. He brings his hands behind his head as he paces the length of the garage. I drop my eyes to the keys, which have left an imprint in my palm from my tight grip. I've protected him this long from outside enemies by keeping him from the truth, and now that he knows everything, I have to find a way to protect him from himself.

I put the keys in the glove box and exit the car. Julian has slowed his pace. At the sight of me, he drops to his knees, finding a place on the ground where he can lean against the car. I join him, despite the powder puff of a dress I still wear. No matter. It'll never see the light of day again. Too many painful memories are now attached to it.

"This is why I didn't tell you about Alister and his proposition. I knew you'd want to kill him, and I couldn't let you do that. For so many reasons, I couldn't. I won't let you become a monster like every other man I know, nor could I let you be harmed by one."

At that, Julian wraps his arm around me and pulls me against him. I rest my head softly on his shoulder. "Emma, I have the utmost faith in you. I need you to have that same faith in me. Just like I respect your choices, even your choice to keep this from me, I need you to respect *my* choices, even if I choose to die for you."

"Julian, I—"

"And protecting the woman you love doesn't make you a monster, Emma, even if it means taking a life to protect the one who gives you life."

"Julian, I do have faith in you. I trust you more than anyone else I've ever known. Which is why I can't lose you, neither physically nor mentally. Once you take one life, it's a slippery slope to becoming someone you no longer recognize, someone who justifies their behavior with sentiments of self-defense and righteous cause. Alister put me at risk tonight in the name of avenging his sister. Beaux thought he was justified in raping and beating me and for killing Mr. Turnip when he found out I had an abortion. Everyone has their reasons. None of them are good enough."

"Emma, I am not Beaux, and I am not Alister. I could never be like them."

"I know." I nod. "But Beaux wasn't always a monster either. At least, he wasn't born a monster. This life turned him into one. I won't let it destroy you, destroy us, like it destroyed him."

Julian is quiet for a moment as he moves his palm up and down my arm. He hasn't said he forgives me, but the way he touches me lets me know he has. It's then that he breaks the silence between us with the question I'm sure he's fought hard not to ask.

"Did they hurt you?"

I pinch my eyes closed as the words invade every part of me.

"No," I breathe. "Not physically."

Julian's body collapses beneath mine. I hadn't even noticed how tense he was until he let the weight of worry leave him. He leans forward and brings his lips to my forehead, planting a soft kiss on my hot skin.

Julian stands then and offers me his hand to pull me from my place on my ground. I take it, nearly stumbling under the weight of my gown as I rise. Julian holds me steady, not releasing my hands even as I stand before him. It seems as if he wants to tell me something, yet the words do not cross his lips as he takes in my features and the loose tendrils of blond hair now fallen around my face.

"Julian?"

"Emma, I…I understand why you didn't tell me about Alister, about all of it. I know you only had good intentions. I understand your past has embedded certain fears inside of you, including the fear that I will become someone you don't recognize. I understand. But I'm not Beaux, and I'm not your father. Nor is every man you know a monster like them. Mr. Turnip wasn't a monster. Mr. Edgar isn't a monster. Mason is…flawed, but not a monster. I am not, nor will I ever be, a man who will hurt you, nor will I hurt anyone else without good reason. So, you have to start trusting me, not just to love you and remain loyal to you, but to protect you."

"I do trust you to protect me, Julian. I'm just… I'm scared of what that may entail."

"Well, too bad," Julian says. He closes the distance between us and releases my hands only to bring his to my cheeks. "Because just as fiercely as you want to protect me, I want to protect you. I *will* protect you. I won't be kept in the dark anymore, Emma. If we're going to work, I must know the burdens you carry, so that I can help with the load. That's what partners do. That's what a husband and wife do."

My lips part in surprise. I move my eyes from his to his mouth and back again, making sure I didn't imagine that last part. As Julian leans forward and brings his lips to mine, I know I didn't imagine it. He actually said... It's then that Julian drops to one knee before me and from his pocket pulls out a tiny box that can only enclose one thing.

"Oh my God!" I gasp. "Is this...? Is this happening?" I cover my mouth with my palm in complete shock. All this talk of Beaux couldn't have come at a more perfect time. It's true. There's a part of me that has worried that Julian will become like him. Not in the sense of becoming a sex trafficking rapist, but as in someone who justifies murder and other heinous actions in the name of self-preservation. Hell, maybe I worry about myself too and what this life will do to me. It's already done some permanent damage. But Julian? As he kneels before me with that boyish grin of his and his sparking green eyes, I see the difference between him and Beaux more clearly than I ever have before.

When Beaux proposed to me, he spoke of what he could give me, not what I gave him, not why I was the one for him. He told a tale of the perfect life he wanted for himself. Looking back, anyone could've fit the bill. Anyone could've been the trophy wife he wanted. The proposal wasn't personal. It was all about the image he wanted to portray, the fairy tale he wanted to believe possible despite everything he was hiding from me. But Julian?

"Emma, since the very first time we met, I knew you were special. I could see your intelligence and intuitiveness as you examined my painting. I could sense the depths of your heart as you spoke of the internal battles we face every day to be good, to withstand the natural darkness that resides in all of us. As you spoke of Mr. Turnip, your compassion reached inside of me and made me feel something good, something wholesome in what was the first time in a long time. And when you interviewed me that day at Lucid, I saw your protectiveness both over Mr. Edgar and his legacy, a legacy that honors tradition and kindness and artistic expression. I can't say I've always been what you would call a romantic. I was young when my parents died. I hadn't had much time to love before I knew pain. And after they passed, especially given the broken state of their marriage at the time of their deaths, I wasn't exactly a believer in the fairy-tale ending. Knowing you changed everything for me."

Julian drops my gaze to keep his emotion from breaking through. I wipe away my own tears as his words wrap around every broken part of me and sew me back together.

"I once told you that you taught me what it means to love, and it's true. The love I have for you is so all-consuming, it makes me want everything with you—the big house with the pool, mundane suburban chores, children that make us feel older than we are, adventures that remind us of who we really are, and every good and bad thing in between."

"I want everything with you too," I whisper. At that, tears fill Julian's eyes. I wipe them away as they trickle down his cheeks. And finally, he opens the box that his captivating words forced me to forget. I gasp. "Oh my." I'm speechless. From the ring box, Julian plucks a cushion-cut pear-shaped dazzling diamond attached to two diamond-encrusted bands. I suppose one band wasn't enough to support the sparkler.

"There are one hundred candles and ten dozen white roses waiting for you inside. I've been wanting to ask you this for so long, Emma. When you mentioned the ball, I put Mason to work to create what I thought would be the perfect proposal. But nothing in our life is perfect. Nothing in anyone's life is perfect. And so, in this dusty garage that smells of motor oil rather than roses, I humbly ask you, Emma Kathleen Marshall, to marry me and live the rest of your days with me as my partner, as my friend, as my confidante, as the mother of my children, and the protector of my heart. All these things I ask of you. All these things I give to you."

"Yes! Yes! I will." The biggest of smiles spreads across both my and Julian's faces as, without hesitation, I agree to be his wife, his partner, his best friend, the person he will live and die with. Julian places the ring on my finger with ease and stands, pulling me into the tightest of embraces. The threat of the brotherhood hangs over us. Alister's men no doubt linger in the shadows outside, both as protectors and predators. Thoughts of them remind me of how fleeting this moment truly is. And so, I cling to Julian and close my eyes even tighter. "I want everything with you," I whisper against Julian's neck. "Everything." And for a moment, I'll let myself believe I can have it.

CHAPTER 24

The warmth of Julian's body next to mine chases away any of the chill left by my encounter with Alister and the men he paraded me in front of. I trace his abs with my fingers, working my way up to his newest tattoo written across his ribs.

Where there is you, there is light. Where there is you, there is hope. Where there is you, there is love.

He had it done once we made it overseas and his gunshot wound was fully healed. He told me that it didn't matter where life took us. As long as we were together, we would be okay. The tattoo was meant to remind us of that. It was a sweet sentiment, one I'm not sure I fully believed until now. There are one hundred enemies lurking outside our doors, and I don't know how we will face them. But, one thing is certain, we will face them together.

"I've been thinking," Julian says, drawing my attention from his exquisite core to his warm eyes.

"About going for round three?" I ask. I'm only stalling. There's an edge of seriousness to his voice I'm not ready to embrace. He laughs.

"Not quite. I still need a little recuperation time." I blush as he trails his fingers up my arm.

"What is it?" I ask, nestling my head into the crook of his neck. Julian's caress ceases.

"I've been thinking about how you said we'd need an army to face off with the brotherhood." His words bring unwanted tension to my bones. I push myself up so I can face him. "That could be arranged. If you still want to destroy them, only without Alister's help."

"Julian, I…I don't know what you have in mind, but I…I just don't think I can pursue this anymore. Just being in their presence tonight, it practically brought me to my knees. I can't face them, no matter how much I want to."

"But that's just it, you wouldn't have to." At that, Julian sits upright. Confusion washes over me. *What is he thinking?* "You know I've been in touch with Agent Clark with the FBI. He's the one who has been helping me prepare for our New Orleans departure, yet again. You said you have evidence against Alister *and* the brotherhood. We could tell him of Alister's plan. The FBI could infiltrate whatever meeting Alister is planning to have with the brotherhood leadership and boom. Both of our problems will be taken care of in one fell swoop."

"Do you really think the FBI would help?"

"I think it's worth mentioning that the leaders of the largest sex trafficking syndicate in North America will be hosting the kingpin of New Orleans. How could they not want to help?"

Hope shines bright in Julian's cheeks all the way down his chest. He's right. Bringing in the FBI would flip the script.

Instead of relying on Alister for protection and the destruction of the brotherhood, we could side with the good guys, the ones we don't have to bargain with to earn our safety. But what if Alister finds out? This will be the ultimate betrayal, the kind he will repay with a visit from Gio and a bullet to the head. Maybe we should just run while we still can. Sure, Alister and the brotherhood will chase us to the ends of the earth, but we were already planning to run. Now, we'd just be leaving New Orleans with two enemies instead of one. But if there is a chance we could see this through without me having to come face-to-face with the brotherhood, isn't it worth the risk?

"If we fail with the FBI's help, no one will be able to save us from Alister *or* the brotherhood," I say.

"And if we fail *with* Alister, no one will have a chance to save us from the brotherhood," Julian counters. "So, the choice is leave New Orleans like we planned with two enemies nipping at our heels, or stay and fight, knowing we may still lose and fall to the same two enemies."

I exhale. "Why do we have to talk about this now?"

"Because." Julian looks away from me then. "We've waited too long to act like the partners we were always meant to be. This war with the brotherhood and now Alister has been weighing on you for far too long. I want to help you with this, Emma, for you, for us, for the life we hope to have together."

I nod. "I hear you. And you're right. We should decide soon. I led Alister to believe I would still work with him so he'd continue to have his men protect us. It's more important now than ever since the brothers have seen my face and know I'm in New Orleans. But his plan to use me as bait is not something I can get behind. Not only do I not trust him after what he did tonight, I just…physically, I can't let him use me that way."

"I won't let that happen," Julian says, caressing my cheek with his knuckles. I close my eyes and savor his touch. I'm surprised by him. All this time I thought he'd be the one bolting from the battle, not me. But now he's the one willing to stay and fight, and I'm the one ready to flee. I'm not sure how it makes me feel. Maybe he's just offering because he truly wants us to be partners. He doesn't want to impose his desire on me, especially considering how fiercely I've fought to see this investigation through. But, after tonight, I just…I'm not sure I can do this anymore, with or without Alister.

"I'm…I'm thirsty."

"I'll get you some water."

"No. No, I'll go," I say, moving to the edge of the bed. "You need to recuperate." Julian smiles, yet I can still see the worry marked in the wrinkles on his forehead.

"Emma, just think about what I said. I'll do whatever you want. Just promise me you'll be honest with me about what you decide."

I nod again. "I will. I'll be back." I push myself from the bed, drape my silky robe over my bare skin, and make my way down the rose-petal-laden stairs toward the kitchen.

Never did I imagine I'd spend the night of my engagement plotting the destruction of two criminal organizations. But after what happened tonight, it's even more imperative we make a decision. I don't know how long it will take the brothers to set their meeting. A day? A week? A month? In addition to that, what will Alister expect of me in the meantime?

As long as I'm in New Orleans, I have to play along with his plan, so he'll continue to protect me and Julian. Even if we decide to bring the FBI in, it won't be wise to make an enemy of Alister, especially not when there are already enough men in New Orleans who want me dead. The FBI won't be able to handle them all. Nor can they be seen meeting with or protecting me and Julian. If Alister catches us in communication with the FBI, our alliance will be shattered. He'll kidnap me and chain me up in his warehouse until the meeting with the brotherhood. After which, he'll kill me along with Julian. If the brothers see the FBI snooping around, they'll cancel the entire meeting and our chance at finally destroying them will be lost.

Alister was wrong, so wrong for how he handled tonight. I will never forgive him for what he did. But he was right about one thing. We will never get a shot at the brotherhood like this again. The question is, which side will be the winning side? Because as much as I don't want to run for the rest of my life, I would rather run with Julian than fight with him and lose him.

As I reach the bottom of the stairs, I take in the intoxicating scent of rose and vanilla. When Julian and I entered through the sunroom, Mason was nowhere to be found. But his handiwork covered every inch of our main floor, including Julian's piano from which he serenaded me and made love to me for the first time tonight. My eyes drift to it from where I stand. I can't help but smile. Nor can I ignore the soft blue light of the television shining in from the living room.

Instead of heading right toward the kitchen, I turn left and make my way around to where Mason sits on the sofa. He pets Grey with one hand and shoves popcorn into his mouth with the other.

"There she is! The future Mrs. Cole," Mason coos from his place on the couch.

"That is to be determined." His brows furrow. "I may hyphenate."

"Oh, that's cool too." I sit next to him and am tempted to pull Grey from her cozy spot next to Mason's thigh but decide against it. She is in full purr mode. I knew she'd warm up to him. Just like I did. "Emma?"

"Hmm?" I ask. Mason's words pull my attention back to him. "Hmm?"

"What are you doing? Shouldn't you be upstairs with Julian?" Mason asks.

"Yeah, I just came to get a glass of water," I say, returning my attention to Grey. It's then that her purring becomes louder. My forehead crinkles. I lean forward trying to see if she's okay until I realize Mason muted the television. "You didn't have to stop your program. I'm just—"

"Getting a glass of water? Emma, what's wrong?" Mason's brown eyes peer into mine. *God!* What is it with these intuitive Cole men? My father was a self-centered log and Beaux was too consumed with work to notice anything. With Julian and Mason, I can't pet my own cat without them assuming my world is crumbling. The sad thing is, they're always right. I don't have it in me to tell Mason everything. Julian and I will fill him in tomorrow after we've slept and have a better understanding of how we're going to move forward. But perhaps Mason can help me make sense of this mess in my head, especially since he is plagued by the same demons.

"I guess getting engaged puts things in perspective. It makes you think about life and where you see yours going. Julian and I have been committed to each other ever since we left New Orleans together a year ago. But this…this ring, this vow, it makes everything so much more real."

"Yeah, I get that," Mason says, taking in the sparkler.

"It makes me think about the brotherhood." At that, Mason's eyes return to mine. "You know as well as I do the toll it takes living under their watchful eye. The constant running. The constant fear. And yet, the fear of facing them, it's even greater."

"Facing them? Emma, where is this going?" Mason shifts in his seat, turning his body toward mine. Grey moans and flings herself from between us. It's as if she knows this conversation isn't one she cares to hear.

"Mason, if you had the chance to take down the brotherhood, like scorched-earth destroy them, even if it meant you could die, the people you love could die, would you take it?"

I'm not sure I want his answer. Still, I ask. Aside from Julian, he's the only other person I know with as much to lose. There's Alister, but he's not exactly in the same position as us. He has an army of men that will never let anything happen to him. And, as far as loss goes, he's already lost his sister in the most horrible way. I imagine he's not operating off fear, like I am in this moment, but from a place of anger and hatred. And, most of all, he's acting off the pain of heartbreak while I'm trying to avoid that pain.

"Emma, are we talking hypotheticals here or…?"

"Just answer the question," I snap. "Knowing the risk, what would you do?"

Mason's lips press into a flat line as he sees straight through me. He knows this isn't a hypothetical situation. He knows there's more than I'm letting on. Thankfully, he doesn't push me to tell him. Instead, he asks, "What are the odds of success?"

My lips part. In all this time, I haven't even thought about the odds. I've thought about the risks. The risks have haunted me. But the odds? "I'm not sure," I admit.

Mason nods. He's quiet for a moment, as if thinking his answer through. Good, he can think for the both of us because my brain is fried, literally fried over this bullshit. It's then that I notice my fists are balled in my lap, clenched around the silky fabric of my robe. I release them just as Mason says, "You know, I've thought a lot about what I'll do once we all leave New

Orleans. You and Julian aren't going to want a houseguest forever, especially not once you're married."

"You'll always be welcome wherever we are. You're family," I say, bringing my hand to his. He smiles then and returns the gesture with a squeeze.

"Yes, but, one day, you and Julian will have a family of your own. At least, I assume you will. Regardless, things are going to change for all of us once we leave this place. I'll still be wanted by the brotherhood. We all will be. I wouldn't feel comfortable bringing someone into my life while I have a bounty on my head."

"So, you'd be alone forever?" I ask.

"*Forever*," Mason says, as if it's a foreign concept to him. "I can't even wrap my head around *forever*. For some reason, I can't see my life past a few more years, and even those are fuzzy." He pauses then, moving his eyes from me to the popcorn bowl in his lap. "You know, when I realized the brotherhood suspected I had something to do with Beaux's death, I knew I had to cut and run. It was instinct. But, when I finally got settled off the grid, I looked around my hotel room and, for the first time, I asked myself why. Why am I running? I'm…alone. I have no one to protect, no one to live for. I mean, yeah, there's Julian, but… I knew just as you two did that our relationship was never going to be the same with the brotherhood involved. And he has you, so—"

"But he still needs his brother," I say. "Mason, Julian missed you every day that we were away. We never stopped thinking about you. And he was so relieved when the two of you finally got together in LA. More than that, he was heartbroken that he had to say goodbye."

"*Goodbye*," Mason says then. His eyes move to mine. "I don't want to have to say goodbye to someone I love. And with the brotherhood after me, after *us*, there's always going to be the threat of goodbye." He shakes his head. "I guess what I'm trying to say is, with the threat of the brotherhood's retaliation hanging over my head, I may be alive, but I wouldn't have much of a life. Not with you. Not with Julian. Not with someone special. So… yes, I would risk everything to have a chance at a full life. I would risk everything to try to destroy the brotherhood."

I nod, taking in his words. Hearing of Mason's lonely moments breaks my heart. And he's right. With Julian and I engaged, there would come a time when this arrangement would no longer be feasible. Of course, who am I kidding? With the brotherhood after us, it's not like Julian and I would have a normal set of newlywed years. There would always be the threat of goodbye, the threat of losing Julian or someone else important to me. As realization dawns on me, I ask Mason one last question, the question I'm too afraid to ask myself.

"If Julian were to die because of your choice, would you still make it?"

Mason drops my gaze, seemingly fighting the urge to ask me the questions racing through his mind. Perhaps he doesn't want to be put in a position to lie to Julian if, by chance, Julian doesn't yet know the truth. Finally, he says, "If I knew my choice would result in Julian's death, then no. I would gladly live a life on the run than cause my brother's death. But, Emma, we can't know the future. We can't know who will live and who will die."

He leans forward then, so close I feel his breath on my cheek. His next words are so soft I barely hear them. "When Julian was shot, I told you to take care of him and you have. You have kept him alive, happy, and honest for more than a year. But you can't protect him forever. You can't sacrifice yourself for the sake of others forever. If you know something I don't, if you know a way we can destroy the brotherhood, then we have to try."

"I know. I know you're right, Mason. It's just… I don't know if I can take the risk. I'm not strong enough to face them. And before you say I am, I'm not. But most of all, I'm not strong enough to survive losing Julian. And if I fail, if *we* fail, he'll be the one they take from me. Because losing him would be worse than losing myself."

CHAPTER 25

My skin turns to ice as the grand Amato estate comes into view. It's been three days since the horrific masquerade ball and one since Julian and I met with our contact in the FBI. Agent Clark was thrilled to hear of the intel I've gathered on Alister and the brotherhood. Even more so, he was eager to assist with the destruction of both criminal organizations plaguing his city. Unfortunately, he also agrees with Alister's plan to use me as bait to lure the brotherhood leadership to the same place at the same time. We went to the FBI, risking the wrath of Alister, so that I wouldn't have to come face-to-face with the brothers. Even with the FBI's assistance, that's exactly what I'll have to do if I want the brotherhood destroyed. And after talking with Mason, there is no doubt in my mind that I do. I'm just nauseated with the idea of being in the same room as those monsters. So, Julian and I came up with a counteroffer, one that rides solely on our ability to manipulate the Blood King.

I look to Julian where he sits behind the steering wheel. He hasn't smiled all day. His muscles are tense beneath the fabric of his white dress shirt. I know he's furious with Alister for the stunt he pulled at the ball and for propositioning me in the first place. Part of me worries today's meeting will drum up some unresolved anger he feels toward me for lying about working with Alister. But it isn't like him to let things fester. Which, on a day like today, is both a comforting and disarming thought. He may have said his piece to me. But Alister? I'm sure there are many words he'd like to throw his way, perhaps more than words. His honesty may get the best of him, but for the love of all that is holy, I pray it doesn't.

Assuming Alister doesn't already know of our secret meeting with Agent Clark, we'll both have to remain calm if we expect Alister to believe we're interested in working with him to execute his plan against the brotherhood. Without information that only Alister has, the FBI won't be able to do much considering they stopped gathering their own intel months ago. That's what today is about. We have to get Alister to tell us how he expects to destroy the brotherhood, and not just the New Orleans group. If we can get Alister to reveal the key to wiping the brotherhood from the face of the earth, then the FBI has agreed to step in without using me as bait. If Alister won't open up, then, in a way, this was all for nothing. We should've just run when we had the chance.

Julian pulls the car to a stop in the crescent moon drive directly in front of the main entrance of Laroux House. While normally I'd have to sneak in under the guise of a maid, Alister made an exception once he heard Julian was coming. Our visit will be disguised as an apology lunch for leaving Saturday's ball in such a fuss. I didn't have it in me to ask Gio of Alister's reaction when he learned I'd told Julian everything. With the way Gio treated me at the ball, I wanted to keep our conversation brief. And, after Saturday night, Alister had to have known this day was coming. He must've known I couldn't explain away the tears drenching my cheeks. Instead of being angry, he should be surprised I contacted him at all. I know I am.

Julian turns to me then just as goosebumps cover my arms. "It's going to be okay," he says. Taking my hand in his, he presses a soft kiss to my knuckles.

"I can't tell if you believe that."

His lips draw up into a half grin. "You know I'd never lie to you."

I blush. I kept my investigation with Alister a secret because I didn't want to put Julian in danger. And now? We're about to walk hand in hand into the Devil's den. This is exactly what I've tried to avoid. And now an Alister and Julian confrontation is unavoidable. What's worse, I have no idea what Julian will do if Alister refuses to give us the information we so desperately need. While the guilt of my deceit has subsided, the gut-twisting nausea of the truth has overtaken me.

"We'll get the information, and we'll get out," I say then. "No extra drinks or small talk. We'll be pleasant enough to make him think we're on his side and—"

"Well, if we're shooting for realistic, then I'd say a little less pleasant is more believable. He has been following my fiancée for weeks now, threatening her behind my back, and he locked her in a room with known rapists, probably murderers. So, yeah, I think a little anger is just what the doctor ordered."

My lips part as I search Julian's eyes for the depths of his anger. Maybe this wasn't a good idea. Maybe I should've come alone. Would Julian have even allowed that? *Allowed?* Who am I?

"Hey," Julian says, drawing my attention once more. "You don't need to worry about me. This isn't the first time I've been forced to play nice with a cocky, controlling asshole. You may have been raised by Anne Marshall as the daughter of the mayor in the precious town of Presley, but I was raised by John Cole as the heir to one of the largest recording labels in Los Angeles. I can handle myself."

"You never talk about your father."

Julian nods, pulling his eyes from me to assess our surroundings. "Only when the conversation warrants it. Giving you the assurance that I know a thing or two about handling men like Alister Amato seems like an appropriate time."

At that, I smile. Maybe he's right. Julian lived an entirely different life before his move to New Orleans, one completely different and yet eerily like my own upbringing. And while I'm not sure there are any other men like Alister, our time on the run has proven to me that Julian can handle himself. Perhaps I should worry less about him and more about me and the fact that I can't think of Alister's face without envisioning myself barreling into it with my fist. To say I'm still upset about Saturday night is an understatement.

"Um, Emma." Julian motions toward Gio who now stands on the front stoop, dressed in a black suit much like Julian's, with his hair slicked back. I can already imagine the lecture he'll give us for keeping Alister waiting. And yet, the sight of him makes me sit firmly in my seat for a moment more. I can tell by his attire that Alister will be approaching today's lunch with the sternness of business rather than the relaxed nature of a social visit. That means his guard will be up and he'll be watching us like a hawk. *Great.* As if we didn't already have our work cut out for us.

"Mr. Amato will be in shortly. Please, help yourselves to the hors d'oeuvres." Gio motions to the spread of scrumptious-smelling delectables on the wooden table before us. "Would either of you care for a cocktail?" It's then that Gio moves to the bar cart in the corner of the dining room. I can't help but wonder what else his job description includes. And, though I'm not sure how it slipped my mind, I'm grateful I didn't tell Julian of my torture session with Gio. Perhaps my psyche has done its best to overwrite the encounter. Though, as Gio moves around the space, it isn't lost on me that no other guards or waitstaff seem to be present. Is that because Alister is still keeping his plans secret from his staff and family? Or because it's easier to get away with murder when there are no witnesses?

"No, thank you. None for me," Julian says then. I don't blame him. For all we know, Gio has been instructed to poison the Merlot.

"Me either," I mumble. I take a seat with my back to the large window that overlooks the crescent drive. Our car is still parked just outside. If things turn to trouble, I'll fling the canapés server through the window for a quick although painful escape.

"Very well," Gio says, a bit too cheerfully for my comfort. "I'll leave you to it then." Gio exits the room as Julian takes a seat next to me. I made sure there was one seat between me and the head of the table so that Alister and I wouldn't be too close. Now that Julian has chosen that seat, I regret my decision.

"You don't want to—" Just as I'm about to convince Julian to change seats, the air in the room thickens as Alister enters with Gio on his heels. Julian's jaw clenches as he rises to his feet to greet the two men. I do the same, wrapping my arm around Julian's to both restrain myself and him.

"Ah, you must be Julian. We meet at last," Alister says with a grin as wide as Texas. He makes his way around the table to where we stand and offers Julian his hand. I feel the muscles in Julian's biceps flex as he takes Alister's hand. The two of them lock eyes. It feels as if they are magnets that only a firm hand can separate once they've got each other in their sights.

"And you must be the man sneaking around with my fiancée behind my back." Alister's smile widens as Julian tightens his grip. "I would say it's nice to meet you, but we both know that would be a lie."

Alister nods. As he lets go of Julian's hand, his eyes meet mine. "Well, it seems congratulations are in order," he says. Before I can make a snarky remark, he takes a step back and motions for Gio to close the French doors through which they entered. Once they are closed, Alister takes his seat. Julian and I do the same while Gio stands with his back against the door. His eyes don't leave Julian.

"So, let's cut the bullshit. You clearly don't like me," Alister says to Julian. "Understandably so. If I found out my girl trusted another man to protect her more than me, I'd be upset too." Julian's cheeks blaze red. Once more, his biceps clench. Though he doesn't bite back at Alister, which I'm thankful for. "And you, Emma. The last time we spoke you made it violently clear you never wanted to see me again. So, why are you here?"

Talk about getting to the point. Alister's golden eyes bore into mine as he waits for my response. My lips part as my throat tightens. *It's okay, Emma. You can do this.* Just as Julian opens his mouth to speak for us, I force the words from my lips. The less he interacts with Alister the better. "To be clear," I begin. "I never *wanted* to see you."

"Could've fooled me," Alister taunts. At that, he motions for Gio to pour him a glass of scotch, his signature drink.

"Stop with the immature remarks. You're beyond that. At least, I thought you were. But given our last encounter, I'm not so sure I know you at all." Alister's lip twitches as I scold him. Julian turns to me, just as surprised as I am by my behavior. "Nevertheless, I've had some time to think on what we discussed the night of the ball. And, while I'm still outraged and traumatized by being locked in a room with those animals…" I pause to collect myself. Julian squeezes my hand for support. I give him a squeeze back. "I know that, now more than ever, the brotherhood needs to be destroyed. And your plan to use me to infiltrate a meeting of the brotherhood superiors may be the only way to do that." Alister nods as he sips his scotch.

"We don't want to run anymore, Alister. We don't want to live in fear. We're engaged and we want to start our married life together without the horrors of the past lingering over our heads. So…" I look to Julian for one last dose of strength. I don't want to do this. I don't want to work with Alister. I don't want to put myself in his bloodstained hands. But making him believe that I'm willing to work with him is the only way he'll give me the information I need to have the FBI fight this battle in my stead. Please, God, let Alister tell us of his plan because just pretending to align myself with him makes me want to vomit. I can't imagine actually— "So, what I'm saying is, I'll go along with your plan. We both will if it means we get to—"

"Live happily ever after," Alister interjects, brow raised. I purse my lips.

"As happily as this life allows."

At that, Alister stands, pushing his chair in behind him. "And how do you play into this?" Alister asks Julian.

"I'm here for Emma. After she told me of your threats and the stunt you pulled at the ball, there's no way in Hell I was letting her meet with you again alone. You can understand that, right?" Julian asks, throwing Alister's dig back at him.

Alister smiles. "Of course I understand. What I don't understand is how you could agree to let her be used as bait to lure out some of the most dangerous men in the world. I mean, scantily clad, paraded around a room of men who all want to do vile, horrific things to her. I don't care how much you want your happily ever after, a man truly in love, no matter how progressive the relationship, would never let his bride take all the risk."

"You're right," Julian says, pushing himself to a standing position. Alister cocks his chin in response.

"Julian," I warn, standing next to him. He looks to me with nothing but anger blazing in his eyes. I rub his arm, silently begging him not to out us. It's then that he bites back his anger, at least as well as he can.

"You're right. I don't plan on letting Emma take all the risk. Which is why you'll have to find a way to work me into your plan for the night of the attack."

"Julian, we didn't discuss that," I say, drawing his attention once more from Alister. Julian looks at me with a softness I haven't seen since we stepped foot in this house. He brings his hand to my cheek and caresses me with his palm.

"That's because there is nothing to discuss on the matter." His voice is just as soft as his touch. My lips part. I'm not sure if he's being serious or if he's just trying to sell our story to Alister. Regardless, if Alister doesn't share his plan for brotherhood annihilation, we'll have no choice but to follow through on his dangerous scheme. And now that Julian has promised his involvement, it's even more important we discover the truth. I may have agreed to this fight, but my greatest fear remains.

I offer Julian a gentle nod of approval, despite the fear coursing through my veins. Julian plants a small kiss on my forehead, as if to let me know everything will be alright. But as I steal a peek at Alister, I can't say that I'm as confident. He watches Julian with disdain, the kind that makes me wonder if he was ever truly protecting him, the kind that makes me worried for how Alister will work Julian into his plan.

"Fine," I say then, turning my attention to Alister. "But if we're doing this, then we have to know everything you know. You blindsided me once, Alister. I won't let you do it again, especially now that the stakes are so high."

Alister pulls his eyes from Julian to focus on me. He reads the worry in my features. Finally, he nods and motions for Gio to open the doors. "We'll continue this in my study."

CHAPTER 26

I sit at the walnut-stained vanity as I apply false lashes to my eyelids and sparkling earrings to my ears. My painted reflection stares back at me threefold in the mirrors of the vanity that must date back to the 1920s, much like everything else in this Tiffany-blue room. I've been anticipating this day for weeks now. No, not the day I must face off with the animalistic men of the brotherhood. And yet, a day of almost equal importance. Today is the day my best friend gets married. And I could not be happier for her, both for her impending union and for her to leave New Orleans and never return.

Alister refused to tell me and Julian of how he plans to destroy the brotherhood. He told us the basics—when and where the meeting would take place and how his men have infiltrated the brotherhood's guards and will serve as our protection once we're on the inside. But…the key piece of information we needed to get the FBI to step in in my place, he kept to himself. Part of me wonders if he did it on purpose. Then again, I don't think I'd be gearing up to walk the aisle of Kat's wedding if he knew the truth of my arrangement with the FBI, my arrangement which includes turning him in for drug trafficking and distribution.

I exhale and stand, smoothing my low-cut powder-blue dress over my hips. I've done my best to pretend like everything is fine. After all, what kind of maid of honor would I be if I let my problems ruin Kat's big day? But that's not why I've kept my investigation into the brotherhood and my looming attack against them from Kat. She can't know the truth, because if she knew, she wouldn't leave. And then she'd be yet another person I love in the brotherhood's crosshairs. I still don't know how Alister intends to work Julian into his plan. If the thought of Julian in the brotherhood's grasp didn't turn my stomach enough, the look on Alister's face when he saw Julian kiss me makes me worried he'll deliberately put Julian in danger. I'm not sure I'd use the word *jealous* considering I'm nothing more to Alister than a bargaining chip. But there was something dark in the way he looked at Julian, something that made, and still makes, my skin crawl.

"Ah, Emma, you look beautiful."

"*Mom?*"

Anne Marshall dressed in a sleeveless sundress adorned with blue and green florals stands in the doorway of the bridal suite. "Well, don't just stand there. Give your mama a hug," she says, opening her arms wide.

I can't help but smile as I cross the room and wrap my arms around her. She's warm and not in the *it's ninety-eight degrees and humid* warm. Just warm, comfortable, home. A year ago, I never would've thought of my mother like this. But we've come a long way. And so has she to attend Kat and Demetri's nuptials even though I—

"Mom, I'm glad to see you. But I told you not to come." I

give her a look of warning and then pull her out onto the balcony while the other bridesmaids use the suite to get ready.

"I know, but I really wanted to see you and *that ring*!" My mom pulls my hand into hers as she inspects the stunning diamond Julian used to pledge his love and life to me. "Well, I always knew Julian had good taste." I raise an eyebrow then. If I remember correctly, they didn't have the best of first impressions. "For choosing you, of course. But this? This is timeless, classic, and yet fun and modern. It's so you."

"Thanks, Mom." I know I don't need her approval, but it's always nice when she gives it. Still, she can't be here. Not when I'm set to meet the brotherhood tomorrow night. I say *meet* because it's easier to wrap my head around than what is actually going to happen. "But really, you shouldn't have come. Julian and I were actually thinking of making a trip to Presley soon."

"Well, that would be wonderful. Your sister is due any week now. Maybe you could come in for the birth. Regardless, I'm here now. So, let's make the best of it. Shall we?" My mom, more chipper than usual, smiles and begins to enter the bridal suite when I grab hold of her arm and pull her back to me. "*Emma?*" She looks between me and where my hand wraps around her.

"Mom," I say, my voice deadly. "It's not safe for you in New Orleans. It's not safe for any of us. You have to leave before—" I jump as squeals of joy and laughter echo from inside.

"Oh, Kat, you look beautiful!"

"Emma, come quick!"

I pinch my eyes closed and exhale. "Mom, I have to go see Kat. Just promise me you'll leave."

Worry contorts my mom's features, making her look more her age than her Botox and airbrush makeup typically allows.

"Emma, what's going on? Is there someone after you? The brotherhood?"

"Emma, come on! We have to take the pictures."

"Mom, I can't explain now. Just please, leave. I'll call you after the ceremony."

I enter the bridal suite, leaving my mom on the balcony before she can demand an explanation. I move in a hurry, but I'm not prepared for what waits for me inside. Kat, in all her bridal glory, stands before me. Her red hair is pulled back into a loose updo with soft curls hanging on the sides of her face. Despite her usual glam, she keeps her jewelry simple with a pair of emerald-cut diamond earrings and her engagement ring, of course. I suppose she doesn't need the extra bling when her dress is such a standout.

Soft chiffon cascades in pleats from her waist, filling the entire room with a cloud of white. A simple slit shows off her tanned leg and sky-high heel. And yet, as beautiful as her chiffon train is, it is the top of her dress that is the most eye-catching. A sheer square-shaped bodice is adorned with white lace flowers that delicately cover her chest, while a deep cutout from her neck to upper abdomen elongates her otherwise short frame and offers a touch of sexiness a Kat and Demetri wedding wouldn't be without.

"Kat, you... You're an angel, a fairy flower princess angel," I say with a laugh. "That dress was made for you." Tears of joy well in my eyes. I quickly dab them away as Kat sashays toward me.

"Let's give the bride and her maid of honor a moment, shall we?" Kat's mom directs the rest of the bridesmaids out of the room, which I'm thankful for as Kat pulls me in for an embrace.

"This dress was, in fact, made for me." At that, we both laugh. "Thank you for standing by me today. It wouldn't have been right without you," she says. The emotion in her voice only makes me hug her tighter.

"I wouldn't have missed it," I say. And it's true. Come Hell or high water, nothing could've kept me from being here today. And yet, as I spot my mom leaving the bridal suite, I wish something would've kept her away.

AFTER AN HOUR of taking photos in the summer heat, I couldn't be more thrilled when the violinist begins playing and the girls before me, dressed in matching powder-blue dresses, begin their march down the stone walkway lit with the setting sun and string lights. Kat opted for a courtyard wedding with a reception to follow in the historic Degas House. It's on the front porch of Degas House where we stand now.

"Just the two of us now," Kat says. I give her a big smile. Even though her mom is an attendance, she decided to walk herself down the aisle, which I thought couldn't be more appropriate.

"Kat," I say, closing the distance between us. "Thank you."

"For what?"

"For being my best friend, for supporting me through the most difficult time in my life, for not allowing me to hide the truth from myself, for…for not letting me give up on myself and a shot at love that I didn't even realize how badly I needed."

"Gosh, Emma." Kat blushes. "You sound as if you're saying goodbye."

Depending on how tomorrow goes, I might be. But I can't think like that. At least not until I've successfully completed my duties as maid of honor.

"Not goodbye," I say. "Just thank you. Today, you begin a

new chapter in your life. You become Mrs. Demetri Belov. And I just want to take a moment to pay homage to Kat Collier, the girl who saved my life without even realizing it."

"Oh, Emma." Kat pulls me in for one last hug as the violinist signals me for the third time. "Frederick is going to kill you if you don't start walking soon."

"Let him try." We both laugh. I bend to fluff Kat's train once more and then make my way down the side steps of the porch onto the stone walkway leading to the ceremony. Lush greenery and white roses frame the walkway. It's going to be a beautiful serv—

"Hey, Emma," Kat calls.

"Yeah?" I turn back to her.

"Kat Collier Belov is just as thankful for you as you are for her."

I nod. "I'm glad to hear you're keeping your name."

"Today isn't a day of loss, Emma. It's a day of celebration, of love, of embracing the new without letting go of the past."

"I'll remember that." At that, I take off down the aisle, walking faster than I should given the look of exhaustion on Frederick the violinist's face. By the time I reach my marker and the guests and altar come into view, the sun has nearly sunken beneath the clouds. String lights illuminate the altar, which is denoted by nothing more than a pastor dressed in a black suit. There is no need for fancy floral arrangements when the branches of a grand oak tree droop through the courtyard, giving the otherwise ordinary space a touch of grandeur.

The photographer takes my photo and then gives me the thumbs-up to continue walking. And yet as soon as she gives me the cue I see Mason, dressed in a T-shirt and sweatpants, in deep conversation with Julian just a few steps from Demetri. Mason, who isn't allowed to leave the house and was no doubt spotted by Alister or the brotherhood or both on his way over. And Julian, who serves as one of Demetri's groomsmen and would have to have a damn good, or perhaps completely horrifying, reason for disrupting the ceremony in such a way. No sooner do I see the letter in Julian's hands, etched with gold calligraphy, do I hear the gunshots.

Panic erupts in the small space as everyone screams and ducks for cover. I should do the same, but I'm frozen in shock, unable to process what I know to be true. The brotherhood is here. They left a warning at the house, which Mason must've found and then attempted to warn Julian of their looming attack. He was too late. We were all too late. We should've destroyed the brotherhood weeks ago, months ago. And now?

"Emma?" Kat's shallow voice finds its way to me from where she stands at the opposite end of the walkway. I force myself to move at the sound. I'm not sure which direction the gunshots came from, or if the shooter is still active, but something dark and inky in my heart warns me of what I will see as Kat comes into view. My wide eyes lock with hers just as blood stains her white dress red and she collapses to the ground in a pool of chiffon and roses.

"*No!*" I take off running toward Kat, screaming for someone to call 911. Julian's voice melds with mine as he tells me to stop, to take cover. I don't listen. I throw my bouquet to the ground and block him from my mind as I reach Kat's crumpled body. "No, no, Kat, stay with me." I drop to my knees and immediately begin ripping fabric from my dress to pack her wounds with. "Shh, shh, shh. It's going to be okay. We're going to get you help."

My eyes are wild as I take in her wounds. She took three bullets. One to the shoulder. One through her back. Another somewhere in her thigh. It's only a matter of seconds until Julian,

Demetri, and Mason reach me. And they couldn't reach me a moment sooner as I feel myself start to break.

"Emma, it's not safe." Julian shields me from the road, scanning the streets and roofs of surrounding homes for possible threats.

"I'm not leaving her," I snap. "Help me pack her wounds." Julian slaps the sobs out of Demetri and the three of us pack Kat's wounds as best as we can. It takes everything I have not to let my own emotion overcome me. But I know if I do, she'll… she'll… God, I can't even let myself think it. "Has anyone called an ambulance?"

"I have." A middle-aged woman with her teenage daughter approach. "We were out for our evening walk when we saw it happen. A car slowed down right when it reached where your friend was standing. Then the gunshots came. As soon as we dropped to the ground I heard an engine rev. I looked up and saw a dark-colored car bolting down the street. Another car followed it. It was red or maroon, a sports car."

That was Alister. Lord help me if Kat dies, I will kill him for letting this happen to her. He was supposed to be protecting her and Julian. That bastard has me risking my life for him on the promise that he can destroy the brotherhood. How can I believe him if he can't protect one girl on her wedding day?

Mason thanks the woman just as the siren of the ambulance sounds. It feels so far away, just like Kat. It's then that I notice fresh blood making its way onto my hands through her packings and the fabric of her dress. "No, Kat." I pick her head up and try to shake life back into her. She doesn't move. Her eyelids don't flutter. "No! Kat, wake up! Kat, come back to me!" Demetri bursts into tears once more, pulling Kat's lifeless body into his arms as Julian pulls me into his. "No, I can't. I can't leave her," I say as Julian pulls me from the ground.

"You're not. You're not going anywhere," he whispers. "We're just going to stand right here." Julian turns my head away from Kat, burying my face in his shoulder. I try to fight him, but he holds me tight. "Just breathe, Emma. Just breathe."

"I can't. I can't because she isn't, Julian. She isn't breathing," I choke out. He squeezes me tighter as I hear the ambulance pull up.

"Don't look," he says then. "Just focus on me." Julian's words pull my eyes from the black fabric of his tux to his icy green glare. I'm not sure why he doesn't want me to look, but considering I can't see through my tear-filled vision, I listen and only focus on him. That is, I try to. But the squeak of the gurney pulls me back to the present as they lift Kat onto the plastic device and haul her into the ambulance. I don't know if she's alive. If she is, she's barely hanging on and the ambulance is a good ten to fifteen minutes away from the nearest hospital.

"I can't lose her, Julian," I whisper. Julian nods. As he brings his thumb to my chin, I notice it is stained red. The ambulance pulls away, my best friend and her husband-to-be inside. Once I'm sure the ambulance is out of view, I turn around, taking in the bloody mess left behind.

Julian and I are both covered in blood as are the stone pavers on top of which Kat laid. Kat's bouquet is the only thing left of hers in the slender alleyway. Petals coated in blood blow in the soft breeze. The same breeze tickles my skin to remind me I'm alive. But I don't feel like I am. I feel numb. No, empty. And yet, as I turn, finding my mom consoling Kat's mother just a few feet away, I feel something more than emptiness. I feel anger, guilt, and fear. Because as much as I have lost, I still have so much left to lose, and when I do, it will be all my fault. It will be the end of me.

CHAPTER 27

I sit in a cold, stark white room filled with people still as logs. Everyone is afraid to move, both the people whose names I'll never know and the ones I love who are still in shock. It's as if the more still they remain, the quieter the room, the easier it is to get lost inside themselves, to find a place to disappear to where everything is fine, normal, happy. I find myself wishing and hoping for the same thing, the ability to leave this place and this moment without leaving Kat. But the more I think of her, of the good times, of Wednesday-night checkers with Mr. Turnip, of Sunday brunches at Bessy's, of *Gilmore Girls* marathons, of every time she picked up my broken pieces and glued me back together, I think of the very real reality that I may never have another moment like that again.

We arrived at the hospital over an hour ago. Maybe it's closer to two hours now. Just like the people surrounding me, time seems to stand still in this stale hall of death. When we arrived, Demetri was all alone, covered in the blood of his wife-to-be. Kat had been taken into emergency surgery. Which, I suppose, is a good thing. It means she was still alive when they reached the hospital. But hope is the last thing exuding from Demetri.

I pull my eyes from the sparkling white floor to take him in. Kat's mom has one hand wrapped tightly around his while she fills out the hospital paperwork with the other. I'd offer to help, but the truth is, I don't think I can. It would make it all too real, the fact that my best friend was shot at the brotherhood's hand, and the fact that she may not make it. I may lose her.

I jump as Julian places his coat over my bare arms. I forgot he'd stepped away to get Kat's mom, Demetri, and me each a cup of hot tea. He's an angel. And yet the sight of him tugs at the strings of my heart in an unexpectedly unpleasant way. The last time I was at this hospital, it was because he'd been shot. He'd taken one bullet and almost didn't make it. Kat took three. My lip quivers at the thought, at the images of her lying bloody and broken on the very aisle that was meant to take her into the next phase of her life. What if that never happens for her? What if she dies before she and Demetri can truly have a life together? All this time, I've worried Julian and I would never get that chance. But what if it's Kat who doesn't? What if I took that from her? At that, I break, using Julian's coat to hide my blubbering. I should be stronger. I should be there for Kat's mom and Demetri, like Kat would be for my mom and Julian. But I can't. I just can't!

"Come with me," Julian whispers. He wraps his arm around my body and helps pull me from my seat. I force my legs to move with him, not wanting to make things harder for Kat's mom and Demetri. After we've walked a ways, and I can no longer hear the background noise of the television in our waiting room, I let Julian's coat fall to my shoulders once more. A few people pass us by with wide eyes. One little girl drops the candy bar she's just plucked from the vending machine. It's then that I remember the blood that stains Julian's and my clothes and our skin. We look like a train wreck. Or, perhaps, like the survivors of one.

"Let's sit here." Julian motions toward a row of just three cushioned chairs near the elevators. Mason sits in one, staring at the letter that replaces my grief with raging-hot anger.

"Let me see it," I say, holding out my hand to Mason.

"Emma, I don't think—" Julian begins. Before Julian can stop me, I rip the paper from Mason's hands, refusing to take my seat. Both brothers sigh in response, knowing the contents of the letter now gripped in my bloodstained hands will upset me. But I'm already upset. I'm broken. What more can a simple piece of paper do to me, take from me? And yet, as quickly as the thought comes to me, so do the faces of my mom, Eva, Julian, and Mason. I bite my lip, letting my eyes linger on the gold seal now broken. "Emma, just come here," Julian says, taking my arm and pulling me into the chair between him and Mason.

I exhale and move my eyes from the letter to his. "It can't make things worse, Julian. Kat was shot because of me. We're all at risk because of me. You, Mason, my mom." I shake my head.

"Emma, none of this is your fault," Mason says. "We always knew this day would come. Not because you asked for it. But because the brotherhood would seek us out. They were never going to let the events of last year go."

"But what if I did ask for it, Mason? I mean, I allowed myself to get sucked into this investigation all over again. I'm the one who made a deal with the Devil to destroy them."

"But the brothers were out for revenge long before you ever started working with Alister," Julian says, drawing my attention back to him. "According to what you said the night of the ball, they told you themselves they'd been looking for you. So, Mason is right. They were always going to come for us. That's why we left New Orleans a year ago. That's why we were planning to leave again."

"You never should've come back." It's then Julian, Mason, and I are pulled from our conversation to Demetri. He stands just a few feet away. Kat's blood stains his white dress shirt and his palms. His dark eyes are empty, void of any emotion. Yet, the vein in his neck throbs in anger. "Before the three of you returned to New Orleans, everything was fine. We went on the run for a while, like you suggested. Took some time to visit my family in New York and visited Kat's mom in Alabama. But then we stopped running. We came back to New Orleans, and everything was fine, normal," he bites out. He shakes his head then.

"Do you want to know why we came back? It's because we both knew that the brotherhood was never after us. They were after you. And as long as you stayed away, we'd be fine. They couldn't use us against you if you were nowhere to be found."

My throat aches with fresh emotion as Demetri's words rip through me. It's then that he takes a step forward, and another, and another, until Julian and Mason are forced to stop him before he reaches me.

"Settle down, man," Julian says as he and Mason push Demetri back a few steps. "We understand this situation is heartbreaking—"

"You understand?" Demetri asks. "You understand nothing. Kat explained the mess you'd gotten yourselves into. And yet, through it all, you've always made it out unscathed. Even now, you stand here with your girl by your side. Emma with her two protectors. All while the people around you suffer, because of your actions!" Demetri yells.

"Hey!" Mason barks. "Emma didn't ask to be raped. She didn't ask to be in this world, to be targeted by one of the most dangerous criminal organizations."

"Maybe not," Demetri concedes. "But, from what I just heard, it's not just the brotherhood who couldn't let things go. You're still investigating them, aren't you?" Demetri asks. I don't answer. I can't. I can't argue with him. "I knew something like this would happen. And, from the sound of it, so did you. You put us all at risk by coming back here, Emma. And for what? For a chance at a normal life now robbed from me and Kat? For justice?" Demetri scoffs. "Justice is like the American dream. Everyone thinks it's so attainable. And then, you wake up one day and you realize you've spent your entire life trying to build something that cost you everything and everyone. Was it worth it? I would say, *You tell me*. But something tells me you'll never be able to."

"Demetri, I will only ask once more. Calm down. This isn't Emma's fault, and you know it. Kat knows it. We're all friends here. It's time you remember that and stop looking at my fiancée like she's the enemy or I'll treat you like you are," Julian warns. Mason moves closer to Julian, blocking any path Demetri may have to me.

Julian and Mason may be offended by Demetri's outburst, but I'm not. No, I didn't ask for any of this. I didn't ask to be raped. I didn't ask the brotherhood to shoot my best friend. I didn't ask to lose a year of my life to fear and anxiety. And no, I can't let it go. Because the brotherhood will only continue to take and take and torture and torture until they're destroyed. But Demetri is right about one thing. This never would've happened if I had stayed away. If the brotherhood had never found me, they wouldn't have been able to use my friends and family to cause me pain. That's why they haven't gone after them until now. And while Demetri may blame me, rightfully so, I have someone else in mind I'd like to impose my anger on.

It's then that I shove the unread letter in the pocket of Julian's coat still draped over my shoulders and dart toward the elevator before it closes. Demetri's eyes follow me as I move, but Julian and Mason don't notice. They're too focused on the threat before them to worry about the one I'm going to confront.

THE GRAVEL OF THE AMATOS' crescent drive crunches beneath my silver heels. Alister left my name with his guards at the gate so I'm able to get inside at any time. Yet, I didn't give him the courtesy of a heads-up. Not when this visit is anything but social. The flickering flames of the gas lanterns illuminating the main entrance glint off the black metal of the gun I found stashed in the console of Julian's car. After what happened that first day in Alister's office at Eve's Garden, I scheduled and took a gun safety course on the down low. I can't say I know everything about guns. But I know enough to point, shoot, and cause pain, which is exactly what I want to do right now.

When I reach the front door of Alister's house, it swings open before I can even grasp the knob. Alister stands before me dressed in jeans and a dark T-shirt. His normally golden eyes have a dark hue to them in the dim lighting of the entryway. They, accompanied with the facial hair darkening his cheeks, make him look dangerous and devious. So much so, I should turn on my heel and run in the opposite direction. But, instead, I lift my weapon of choice and point it at his chest.

"This is all your fault," I choke out.

"*Emma.*" Alister lifts his hands in surrender and takes a step back. I enter the grand Amato mansion and slam the massive door closed behind me without removing my eyes from Alister. "Emma, stop. You don't want to do this."

"You're right. I don't," I admit. "I don't want to be the girl responsible for her best friend's death. I don't want to put the people I love in danger. I don't want to be this monster. I don't want to be just as bad as them, gunning down innocent people for no good reason. But you're not innocent, are you?" I continue moving toward Alister and he continues his retreat. It's then that I'm reminded of his line of business and that this probably isn't the first time he's been held at gunpoint. He probably has a weapon stashed somewhere in this room or perhaps a panic button. "*Stop!*" I say then. "Stay right where you are. No more moving."

"Okay, okay," Alister says, resting his hands on the back of a chair he's now positioned himself behind. "Emma, listen, my men—"

"Failed, Alister! My best friend, the person I care most about in this world, aside from Julian, was shot! Gunned down in her wedding dress. How could you let that happen? How could *I* let that happen?"

"Emma, I am so sorry. I never thought—"

"You never thought they'd kick-start their revenge party a day early? You never thought of how they would get off on ripping my world apart before they rip me apart?" I shake my head and lower the gun to my side as the weight of it becomes too much to bear. I sense Alister's muscles relax with the gun no longer pointed at him. But he has no reason to think he's in the clear. "If it wasn't for you and your ill-thought-out quest for revenge, the brotherhood never would've found me."

"You don't know that."

"Maybe not," I admit. "But I do know that Julian and I had a plan. The second we found out the brotherhood was investigating Beaux's death we planned to leave New Orleans. We were going to leave the day after Kat's wedding, as in tomorrow. If you had never exposed me at the ball—"

"Maybe they wouldn't have found you before tomorrow. Maybe they would've. Regardless, I know you, Emma," Alister says, moving from his place behind the chair toward me.

"No, you don't. You know nothing about me. Now, stay where you are," I say, pointing the gun at him once more. Alister lifts his hands in surrender, but he doesn't stop moving toward me, slowly but surely.

"I know you, Emma. I know there is no way that a life on the run is what you wanted. I know that as much as you didn't want to fight the brotherhood, you wanted them exposed, destroyed, and not just so you wouldn't have to live in fear, but because you wanted justice for their victims and safety for the ones they would eventually go after."

Alister stops then as the barrel of my handgun presses into his chest. He's a mere two feet away, yet he makes no moves to disarm me. The way he looks at me, it's as if he believes I'm strong enough to disarm myself, to choose to be better, to choose to spare him even when he doesn't deserve it. But…does he deserve to die?

"I know you," he says once more. "Just like I know that you're going to put the gun down, because you're not a monster. You're not like those men. You may think they've broken you, that they've crushed everything good inside you. But as long as you rise above, as long as you don't let yourself become like them, then you're not broken. You're still you."

"Yeah?" I ask. My voice is raspy with emotion. "And what's so good about being Emma Marshall? The best part of me is Julian and…and…"

It's then that I break. I fall to my knees as my emotion overcomes me. Alister moves with me. He reaches for the gun still clasped tightly in my hand. I let him have it. Even if this was all an act and he chooses to kill me for simply threatening him, I'll welcome it. I've ruined enough people's lives. Instead, Alister unloads the clip and the single bullet located in the chamber that was meant for him. He sets the weapon to the side and then, to my complete surprise, he sits beside me on the floor and pulls me into his body.

"What are you doing?" I ask, pulling away from him.

"Just trying to be normal for a change."

I search Alister's golden eyes, not sure of what I expect to see. In them, I find sadness. Perhaps because he knows the pain I feel all too well, the pain of losing, or potentially losing, someone you love to the brotherhood. My greatest fear, even before learning of the brotherhood, has been losing the people I love to the wrath and whims of dangerous men. First, it was Beaux. Then, it became the brotherhood. Julian and Kat have always been the source of my strength and my two greatest weaknesses. Now, because of my actions and Alister's, my best friend is lying on a cold, steel operating table with a slim chance of survival. Who will the brotherhood go after next? My mom? Eva? Mason? Julian? According to the letter left by the brotherhood, it could be anyone.

Her blood is on your hands. By the time the Blood King releases you to us, there will be no one left to remember you, to search for you. There will be no safe place left in your mind to disappear to. We will take everyone and everything from you. This is only the beginning.

"I don't need your comfort, Alister. I need your protection. And, this time, I need you not to fail. Or, so help me God, I will kill you, even if it means I have to give up every last bit of good inside of me to do it."

Alister nods, registering the severity in my tone. I mean

every word I say. I didn't want to kill Alister when I walked through that door. I wanted to make him suffer because I do blame him. Even though I know no one person, not even myself, is responsible for what happened today, I need someone to direct my anger toward. Because if I don't, it will eat me from the inside out. He is that person for me. And if Kat dies... I bite my lip to keep it from quivering.

All this time, I've thought about how I'm not strong enough to survive losing Julian. And now, I'm staring upon the horizon of a life without Kat. Losing her, especially in this way, would be to lose myself. Everything good in me would die. And so would any chance of me sparing Alister or anyone else I deem responsible for Kat's death. I will become the monster I felt myself becoming in Paris, the monster I've fought to keep Julian from becoming. Unrecognizable and filled with darkness, I don't know what I'd be capable of, and I hope I never have to find out.

"Emma," Alister says, pulling me from my mental Hell. "Most of my men have already infiltrated the brotherhood's compound. That's why...that's why the protection detail on your friends and family was stretched thin tonight." My cheeks blaze red with anger at his admission. "I have two guards at the hospital now, protecting your loved ones in case the brotherhood attacks again. But it would be easier for me to protect everyone if they stayed here."

"*Here?*"

"Yes. Under one roof, I can rally what men I have left. In addition to the gated entry, security cameras, and weapons I have stashed, there is no safer place in New Orleans for you and your friends and family tonight."

"But what about Kat? She's in surgery. No one is going to leave until we know if she's going to..."

"Make it?" Alister asks. "Your friend made it out of surgery just as you arrived to kill me. My men overheard the doctor giving your friend's husband the news. They aren't sure when or, *if*, she'll wake up, but the bullets have been retrieved and she is stable."

"But…but how can she be stable, and they not be sure if she's going to wake up?" Confusion washes over me as my heartbeat quickens. Alister hesitates, looking away from me.

"You know, I'm not a doctor. Maybe you should—"

"No," I say. Moving my hand to his neck, I force him to look at me. Surprise shudders through him at my abrupt touch. "I want to know now. What did your men overhear?"

Alister's lips part. Our proximity isn't comfortable for either of us, but I won't release him, not until he tells me what he knows.

Alister clears his throat and says,

"The doctors say when she was shot, she fell to the ground hitting her head. There was swelling on her brain in addition to the gunshot wounds. She's…she's in a coma, Emma."

"But what does that mean? I mean, I know what a coma is, but what's the prognosis?" I search Alister's eyes for the truth. He tries to look away from me once more, but I don't let him. My fingernail digs into the thick flesh of his neck, keeping him in place.

Finally, Alister says, "If she doesn't wake up on her own in a few days, then, the chances of her waking up are…not good."

I let my hand fall from his neck to the floor between us as his words hit me. There is no roar of anguish or loud shatter as my heart rips open. Instead, silent pain slithers through me, sharp as a knife and cold as death.

"Emma," Alister begins, but I shake my head. My body begs him to remain quiet even though I'm unable to voice my plea. If Alister knows me as well as he claims to, I shouldn't have to.

And yet, just as fresh tears work their way out of my eyes, Alister brings his finger to my chin. This time, he forces me to look at him, and to my surprise, I let him.

"I know that nothing I say now will take away the pain you feel. But there is one more thing you should know."

"What? What could possibly matter?" I choke out. It's then that Alister's lips press into a flat line and his eyes go dark with the same vicious expression from when I arrived.

"Gio and I caught the men who shot your friend. I was planning to reach out to see what you wanted to do with them."

"They're still alive?" I ask.

Alister nods. "Waiting for your sentencing." I part my lips, unsure of how Alister's admission makes me feel. It's good that Alister showed restraint. Yet so much of me wishes he hadn't. I wish those bastards were dead and rotting in the ground, like…

I shake my head, trying to regain control of myself so I can process what he's said. He has them waiting for me. If I sentence them to death, they'll die. If I sentence them to punishment, they'll bleed. I know it's not healthy. None of this is. But somehow Alister has shifted my rage and blame from him to the two people who truly deserve it. And now, I'm not sure what I want to do with it.

"Killing them won't make you a monster, Emma," Alister says then. "Killing them would be justice."

CHAPTER 28

I've shoved Alister's words and the gnawing reality that the men responsible for Kat's condition are located somewhere on this massive property to the back of my head. As Julian, Mason, Demetri and Kat's and my moms make their way inside Laroux House, it's all I can do to stay focused and show everyone to their rooms. Alister may be generous, letting us use his home, but he isn't exactly the calm and gentle host everyone's frazzled nerves need right now. And with the influx of unexpected house-guests, he has his own family matters to attend to. Over a year after his youngest sister's disappearance, he is finally telling his sister, Sophia, the truth of what happened to Cara. While wrangling Julian and the others has been more difficult than I expected, I don't envy Alister or the pain Sophia is sure to feel, the pain I will feel if Kat doesn't wake up.

It took some convincing to get everyone to leave the hospital. Julian and Mason, who know the truth of our enemy's strength, refused on the grounds of not being able to trust Alister. Need I remind you that Julian is the level-headed, quick-to-forgive brother, and even he can't stomach Alister? Mason, who's never met Alister, snaps his neck back and forth, looking to pick a fight as we make our way down the grand hall of the second floor. I nudge him in the back as his room comes into sight. As much of a challenge as the two brothers have been, no one was more against the idea than Kat's mom.

It seems Kat and Demetri never told Ms. Collier of the brotherhood or the reason why they took an abrupt four-month-long vacation last year. To add to Demetri's stress, heartbreak, and growing disdain for me, he had to explain to his mother-in-law-to-be why her daughter was shot and why, though he detests the idea, staying with me and Alister is the best thing for them. Demetri may hate me for what happened to Kat, and I don't blame him, but he isn't too proud to accept help. And so, on one condition, he and Ms. Collier agreed to join us at Laroux House.

"Okay, Mason. You're all set. I suggest you stay put tonight. Tension is high as it is," I say as I pull a pair of men's pajamas from the armoire to lay on his bed.

"Stay put? Yeah, right," Mason scoffs. "Not only am I not letting you out of my sight, but I also haven't eaten. And considering we're at war, I need nourishment."

I roll my eyes. "Okay, there is no need for this brazen protectiveness. Or, perhaps a more appropriate term would be *possessiveness*," I say, giving Mason a pointed look. At which, his shoulders slump in defeat. "We're here because this is the safest place for us." It's then that my eyes drop to the hardwood floor. The brunt of our reality hits me for the first time.

"Emma? What is it?" Julian asks, bringing his hand to my back.

"I just...I just realized that this isn't only the safest place for us. It's the *only* place for us. The brotherhood left that note taped to our front door. They know where we live. We can never go back."

I'm not sure if Julian and Mason had come to the same conclusion and that's why they finally agreed to stay at Alister's, but the looks of silent sadness on their faces lets me know the truth is just as painful for them as it is me. For so long, I bashed my new home, my neighbors, my life. Now, I'd give almost anything to have it back.

"Hey, we can't go back now," Julian says. "But, if tomorrow goes as planned, we won't have to live in fear anymore. We can reclaim the life we lost or start a new one. The choice will be ours." Mason nods. I know they're right. All hope isn't lost. And yet, after what happened to Kat, I know my world will never be the same. The more I lose, the less there is to reclaim, the less there is to hope for.

"Yeah. You're right," I say, pulling myself from my thoughts. "And so is Mason. We could all use a meal before tomorrow. I would go check out the kitchen, but something tells me we're not going to find cereal and chips in this house. And I—"

"Want to see Kat," Julian says, pulling me into him. The sight of his wrinkled dress shirt reminds me we all need to shower and change. "You've done enough, my love. You go see your friend. I'll handle the cooking."

"Thank you," I say, planting a soft kiss on his cheek. "Thank you both."

"Of course," they say in unison. Taking that as my cue to leave, I turn on my heel, quite literally, and head in the direction of the room next door. I've worn Kat's blood long enough. And yet, just as I reach the large wooden door concealing my and Julian's quarters, hushed voices stop me in my tracks. I take a step back, just out of Julian's and Mason's sight, but within earshot.

"I'm worried, Jules," Mason says. "She's running around playing house with the literal Devil. She thinks this is the answer, that *he's* the answer, that there *is* an answer."

"What are you saying?" Julian asks.

"I'm saying that the brotherhood won't be easy to destroy, if it's even possible. What happens if we fail? What happens if we succeed, and Kat doesn't make it?"

"You're the one who told her it was worth the risk!" I hear Julian sigh in frustration. "Are you telling me you don't think it's possible? That we're walking to our deaths tomorrow?"

"I'm not sure. Which is why I also told her there is no way to know the future—whether we will succeed or fail. It's all fun and games when you're talking hypothetical. But, right now, we're losing, Julian. And it's real and it's bloody and it's scary. I see it in her eyes. She knows it too. And she's doing everything she can to hold on to hope. But no matter what happens tomorrow, if Kat dies, Emma will lose her hope and we will lose Emma. So, yes, I am worried we are walking to our deaths. But I'm also worried about her and what surviving could do to her."

Julian is quiet for a moment. Finally, he says, "So, maybe we can't win. Maybe we lose everything. Maybe I lose her." It's then that Julian's voice cracks. "But we're not dead yet. Kat is still breathing and so are we. Emma is a fighter. There's no way she's backing down from this fight and so neither am I. If I lose her, no matter the context, I will fight to bring her back. If she loses her hope, I'll have enough for the both of us, because that's what partners do. That's what I've vowed to do."

I SIT, freshly showered, dressed in Sophia's silky pajamas as Kat lies before me in the hospital-grade suite located on the third floor of Laroux House. It's quiet save for the chirp of Kat's heart monitor and the subtle whoosh of the oxygen tank. This was Demetri's condition, that Alister use his connections to get Kat relocated to the mansion. I'm thankful for his quick thinking. Though, seeing her like this, it makes the truth of Mason's words all too real.

Tomorrow we go after the brotherhood, one of the most dangerous criminal syndicates in North America, and we may lose. But, even if we win, what will a world without Kat look like? A world where I must live with the blood of my best friend forever staining my soul. And who is to say she'll be the only one I lose? The brotherhood may have started with Kat, but there is no doubt in my mind that they've got Julian in their sights. I bring my fingers to my lips, forcing them closed as my emotions threaten to escape.

I want so badly to believe tomorrow is the end of this torment. And maybe it will be. But Mason is right. As much as Julian is my hope, so is Kat. If I lose her… Julian says he'll bring me back, he'll find a way to make me whole again. But what if that's not possible? What if I lose him too? I shake my head and bury my face in my hands. It's scary when the thought of dying becomes more comforting than the thought of living. And yet, if I let myself go there, if I let myself imagine a world without the people I love, then I'm already lost. And I can't…I can't lose myself when I still have something left to fight for. But… What if I am fighting a losing battle? What if Demetri was right and before the war is done, I will have either lost everyone or I will have lost myself?

"Emma." I jump in my chair and turn to find Demetri looming over me.

"Demetri." I stand, keeping the chair between us as I do. Before today, I had no reason to feel threatened by Demetri. But now I'm not so sure. He's tall, almost as built as Alister, and trained in Russian martial arts. I stand strong as he inches closer. Sensing the tension in my body, he stops a few feet away. His dark eyes drift from me to Kat. The sadness on his face eases the stiffness of my muscles. "Demetri, I—" He raises his hand then, silencing me.

"Let me go first," he says. His tone is softer than I expected. "Emma, I...I'm sorry for how I acted earlier. I needed someone to blame, to lash out at. You were an easy target."

"I was an easy target because it's true. In many ways, I am responsible for this."

"No. You're not." Demetri shakes his head. "What's true is that I've been angry at you ever since Kat told me of the brotherhood. For so long, I could only see things from a surface level. Her friendship with you put her at risk. It's why we came back to New Orleans, of all places. Because I knew, or at least I assumed, that it was the one place you and Julian would never visit. And when you came back, it was my idea for us to move closer to Kat's mom. Because all I've ever wanted is to love her and protect her."

"I know that."

"Thank you. But I was shortsighted, and Kat deserves better than that. The woman she trusts, loves, and respects enough to be her best friend deserves better than that. What happened to you wasn't your fault. What happened today wasn't your fault." Demetri shakes his head then. "And it was wrong of me to judge you for seeking justice, for not giving up on this fight. Because this feeling of helplessness that rages through me at the sight of Kat unconscious and unable to breathe on her own, it lets me know I'd do anything to make sure this never happens again. That is, if she doesn't... If I don't..."

"Hey," I say, pulling Demetri off the edge. "It's easy to give up, to let our minds dig graves that haven't been claimed yet. I've been struggling with the same thoughts." I take a step forward. Closing the distance between us, I place my hand over his. "Death is silent, cold. Life is loud and warm." I guide Demetri's hand to Kat's. "Do you feel that?" A single tear drips down my cheek as the warmth of Kat's skin breathes life back into me. "Do you hear that?" Demetri's lips quiver as he listens to the oxygen machine and watches as Kat's chest rises and falls in response. "As long as oxygen pumps through Kat's lungs and blood through her veins, we have something to fight for, to live for."

Demetri nods and I take a step back, giving him a moment. My throat is raw with emotion, but I fight through it, focusing on the words of encouragement I somehow managed to give him. Perhaps it's because Julian fights for me that I can fight for Kat, that I can be there for Demetri in the way that the fiancé of my best friend deserves. It's then that Demetri turns to me. Emotion contorts his face and yet in his eyes it's no longer sadness I find. It's hope.

"Thank you," he whispers. I bite my lip.

"You're welcome, but sometimes words aren't enough. Sometimes the only thing that quells the pain is revenge disguised as justice. But you have to know, I won't let you fight, Demetri. As long as there is a chance that Kat survives, you have to stay safe because she's going to need you when she wakes up."

"Emma, you can't expect me to sit on the sidelines while the rest of you go off and avenge my fiancée."

"That's exactly what I expect you to do," I say. "But that doesn't mean you can't have your revenge." Demetri's brows crinkle. "I have a gift for you. Well, they were given to me by

Alister to do with what I please, but I'm willing to share if you're willing to play by my rules."

I spare Kat one last look and say a silent prayer that she may return to us. Until she does, those responsible will suffer just as we do.

"What kind of gift?" Demetri asks as I move toward the door. I stop and take my phone out of my pants pocket. I pull up my latest chat with Alister and let him know Demetri will be joining me in the dungeon. Yes, I do mean *dungeon*. "Emma?"

I turn back to him and say, "The kind that bleeds."

WITH GIO'S attention on securing the perimeter of the estate, Alister escorts Demetri and me to the dungeon beneath the house. We've been walking these corridors for well over ten minutes and there is still no end in sight. I suppose that's the point. Much like Alister's office, the dungeon isn't a place a drunken party guest could accidentally stumble upon. To say it's a creepy trek would be an understatement. After traveling down more flights of poorly lit stairs than I can count, stone walls and floors blur together, creating a tunnel-like atmosphere. According to Alister, the tunnels date back to the 1800s. While the entire house is ancient, most of it is additions built from the 1920s to 1940s. The labyrinth of passageways beneath the home are eerily original.

"I can't imagine what these tunnels were used for back then," I mutter.

"Yes, you can. I'm sure it wasn't much different from what we use them for today," Alister says. It's a grim thought. As interesting as these old houses are, they are filled with hidden horrors. Given tonight's circumstances, the horror continues. "We're here."

Alister comes to a stop before me and shoves a key larger than my palm into an ancient wooden door. You'd think in two hundred years, someone would've upgraded the security. But like I said, this isn't someplace you find by accident.

The latch clicks. As Alister pushes the door open, a small gust of wind dances across my skin. I take a step back. "You ready?" Alister asks.

I shake my head. "No." Alister's brows crinkle. I take another step back until Demetri now stands between us. I cross my arms over my chest. Maybe this was a mistake. I'm not sure what waits for me behind that door. Two men beaten within an inch of their life and a gun ready for me to finish the job? Two men without blemish, no trace of the blood they've spilled today? Whatever I find, I'm not sure what it will do to me. Or what I'll do to them. And what will that make me? Alister said killing them wouldn't make me a monster. But I'm not sure I buy into his logic. This is revenge, not justice, just like I told Demetri. But… Can it be both?

"Emma, you don't have to do anything you don't want to. They're not going anywhere. You still have time to decide," Alister says.

"But what about me?" Demetri asks. "You promised me, Emma."

Alister looks between the two of us, unaware of the deal we made. Finally, I nod. "I'm ready." Alister hesitates, but finally he turns and leads us into his torture chamber. As we enter the space, which is far larger than I expected, we are met by empty cells that look every bit as old as they are supposed to be. The space is dark, moist, and smells of things I'm sure I'm not meant to breathe. I stick close to Alister so as not to lose him as he continues moving forward.

"For crimes such as this, I find a blank canvas is best," Alister says, drawing my attention.

"Canvas? What does that—?"

I trip into Alister's hard frame as he stops and flips on a switch he knows the location of far too well. Alister extends his arm, steadying me. It's then that the men responsible for Kat's condition come into view. They're half-naked and restrained to metal chairs much like the one Gio tied me to in Alister's warehouse.

"A blank canvas means there isn't a scratch on them to start. It makes the result much more satisfying."

Before I can even process what Alister has said, Demetri lunges for the one with the eagle tattoo on his chest. Alister stops him before he can lay a finger on the man. "What the Hell?" Demetri shrugs out of Alister's grasp.

"Emma decides what happens next," Alister warns. Then his attention shifts to me, waiting for my command. This is exactly what I wasn't ready for. I thought I could do this. I thought I could hurt them the way they've hurt me. A part of me wants to. But there is another part that knows if I accept this gift, a life for a life, then I'm crossing a line into Alister's world, into Beaux's world, that I may not come back from.

Much like how Alister took Posey's life for orchestrating the deal that got his sister killed, this offering is normal to Alister. It's the way things are done in his world, the one I told him I feared would consume me. If I do this, it will do just that, consume every bit of the old Emma, and replace her with the new Emma I've felt clawing at my insides ever since Kat was shot, perhaps even before that. She is dark, ruthless, and bloodthirsty. She is everything I've fought to keep from becoming.

And yet, the power I feel as I stand over these men, these monsters, only makes my choice harder. They stand to take everything from me. Why do I feel so guilty for wanting to take it all back?

Alister's dungeon is set up much like the interrogation room at his warehouse. I remember the fear I felt being tied to a chair and tortured beneath a spotlight. The fact that I know what these men feel in this very moment quenches the rage inside me. I can relish their fear without ever touching them, without crossing a line that would rob me of my humanity. I part my lips, ready to deliver my judgment, one that will disappoint Demetri but one I can live with. That is, until one of the bastards opens their mouth.

"Emma? Emma Marshall?"

CHAPTER 29

"Oh dear," the man coos. "You've gotten yourself into a mess, haven't you?" He laughs then. Is he on drugs? Last I checked, he's the one strapped to a chair, not me. While this should be a comforting thought, it only makes his taunts more disturbing. "First Beaux, now Alister. You just don't know how to stay away from dangerous men. I suppose your father is to blame. Aren't they always? Poor little Emma. You thought you were being raised by a knight in shining armor. All the while, he was conditioning you to love the monster. Even when you've got a beacon of light like Julian at your side, you still find your way into the darkness."

"Stop it," I say.

"I suppose I should be saying poor Julian. You know he's next, right? And if you think keeping us here is going to stop what the brothers have planned, you're wrong." A wicked grin spreads across his face. "There are more of us than you will ever know."

I take a step forward and with every bit of force I can muster,

I bring my palm to his cheek. The slap may have hurt me more than I hurt him, but at least I made my point.

"Is that all you've got? Come on, Emma. If you think holding back now will earn you mercy tomorrow, you're wrong."

"Last I checked, you're the one at *my* mercy. If I were you, I'd shut my mouth. But if you insist on speaking, tell me what the brotherhood has planned for Julian. You lie, you die," I warn, turning my back on him. I'm not sure if the fear I feel inside registers on my face or not, and the last thing I need is to show weakness. Yet, as Alister's eyes meet mine, I gather that's the last thing he sees. Still, our prisoner doesn't seem so convinced. His laughter bounces off the damp stone walls of the dungeon. My cheeks blush as I feel his voice dance across my skin. I press my lips together to keep them from betraying me. Whirling around, I slap the man again. My movement silences him, but only for a second.

It's then that he returns his dark gaze to me. His voice is low as he speaks, so low I find myself leaning in just to hear. "I know you, Emma. I know everything about you. We all do. Which is how I know you don't have the guts to issue the death sentence you're threatening. But if you must know, I'll tell you what the brothers have planned for your beloved. It'll give you something to ruminate on while you consider how your punishment will be one hundred times worse."

"Emma, a word?" Alister brings his hand to my arm, pulling me away from the man before he can tell me of the brothers' plans for Julian.

"Alister, what are you doing?" I ask as he drags me away. The farther we get from the men and the spotlight they sit under, the darker it becomes. As Alister shields me from the prisoners' view, it's so dark I can hardly make out the features of his face. Yet, I see enough to note the worry etched into his brow.

"Emma, if you want information on the brothers' plans for Julian, it's best you let me or Gio handle the interrogation."

"Of course I want to know. And no, I don't have time to waste," I say, pushing past him.

"This isn't a negotiation," Alister says, pulling me back to him. This time, he keeps his hand wrapped firmly around my arm to hold me in place.

"What do you mean this isn't a negotiation? You caught these men for me to do with as I please." As I speak, my insides twist, warning me of the line I'm about to cross.

"Yes, as in let your anger out. Hell, kill them for all I care. Whether you do it or I do, they aren't leaving Laroux House. They know too much not only about you, but about me. But, interrogating them is off the table because it will hurt you more than it will them."

It takes a moment for Alister's words to make sense. I don't have to kill them for them to die. The thought eases some of the tension inside me. Yet, the relief I feel knowing they will die doesn't exactly make me feel better about myself. And yet, something else Alister said occupies my mind more than my self-deprecating thoughts. He doesn't want me to question them, because they would either take pleasure in seeing their answers hurt me, or I would have to result to Gio-like measures to get the truth out of them. Either way, the truth would destroy me. And he doesn't want that because he…he cares? What? No. That's insane.

"They'll start by carving his tattoos from his body," the man yells. My lips part in horror as nausea swirls inside me. Alister was right. The truth is too much to bear, especially hearing it from their wicked lips.

"This is what I was afraid of," Alister says. In one swift

movement, he caresses my cheek and then he spins, rushing toward the prisoner with a taste for a slow death.

As Alister reaches the man, he lays into him with his fist. The man's head snaps to the side and blood instantly pours from his mouth. The sheer swiftness of Alister's movement is terrifying, yet I can't stop myself from moving closer. Alister pulls the man back to him by his hair and lays into him again and again. Blood covers the man's pale skin and the stone pavers beneath him. The sight makes me think of Kat and the real reason why we're here, why they're here.

I want to know the brotherhood's plans for Julian. But we have two prisoners, not just one. Maybe I'm just in denial, unwilling to accept the Hell the brothers want to unleash on the man I love, but something tells me not to trust a word that comes out of the bloody mouth of the man Alister pummels. He just wants to hurt me, to cause the most pain before Alister takes his life. Demetri can have his way with him while Alister gathers the information we need from the other. By the time the spotlight illuminates my figure, I've made the decision I ventured down here to make. Yet, my choice weighs heavily on me the moment I make it.

I look to my right and find Demetri with his fists balled. Every muscle in his body is on high alert. Sweat dots his forehead in anticipation. He will kill them if given the chance. Of course, so will Alister. And if I let that happen, no matter how much I want it to, I might as well have pulled the trigger myself.

"Stop," I say then. To my surprise, Alister stops midpunch, wipes his bloody knuckles on his jeans, and returns to my side. I allow myself to focus on him and the gray fabric of his T-shirt rather than the smushed, bloody face of the man before us.

Just as I've made up my mind once more to leave this place and never return, the idiot, through gargled blood, speaks once again. "The Blood King takes orders from a prisoner? I sure thought that would be a cold day in Hell."

"Keep talking and your day in Hell will be here a lot sooner," Alister bites out, drawing an unexpected laugh from the bloody pulp of a man.

"Careful, Amato. I don't know what kind of back-door deal the two of you have clearly made, but you can't protect her, just like you couldn't protect Cara. Tomorrow, you'll lose a second woman to the brotherhood. The pain of survival will be unspeakable. But the pain of death? That will be unbearable, because then there will be no one left to protect sweet Sophia. You will fall, Blood King, and so will everyone around you."

The golden hue of Alister's eyes shifts to the dark and inky look of the Devil I've seen only a few times before. If I don't stop him, he'll kill him right here, right now. And though I doubt Alister's conscience would bear the weight of the life lost the same as mine, I have to stop him. I have to show him there is another way. Just as Alister lunges for the man once more, I step in front of him. My arms wrap around Alister's waist as his fist slings past my cheek. His body goes rigid beneath my grasp.

"Emma, move."

"No. We're leaving," I whisper.

"Like Hell," Alister grunts.

"Don't let him win. Don't let him see how he's hurt you more than you could ever hurt him." It's then that Alister takes a step back. His golden eyes are filled with uncertainty and gut-twisting emotion as they examine me. Giving the man one last look, he begins to back away. For which I'm grateful. Alister continues down the center walkway of the tunnel, never removing his eyes from mine. The sound of his footsteps stops where the light ends, letting me know he's here even if he cannot be seen.

I turn to Demetri, who watches me with inquisition.

"Demetri, I thought I could do this, but I can't. There is a darkness in me dying to take over. I can't let it. As long as Kat and Julian breathe, I have to cling to the old me, the part of me that's good. Because that's the Emma they know and love. That's the Emma who belongs in their world. I don't want to become the Emma who belongs in this one." I reach out and rest my palm on his arm. "It was wrong of me to bring you here, to put you in the position to choose. But what happens next is your choice. As Kat's husband, it should've been yours all along."

Demetri nods and pulls me in for a hug. I pray he walks out of here with me, but I can feel it in the way he hugs me—he's saying goodbye, goodbye to the old him. As I step away, there's a look in his eyes I've never seen before. It's the look I imagine drawn across Julian's face should the brotherhood overpower us and take what's left of my body and soul. It's the look of a man who has lost everything, who has no intentions of allowing the men who shot his wife to live another day. He doesn't say anything, but I nod as if he has.

"Leave one conscious enough for questioning." At that, I take a step forward, and another, and another. The closer I get to the darkness, the louder the screams of the men Demetri tortures become. I don't turn around. Because if I do, I'll see someone I don't recognize, someone I'm not ready to accept I created.

ALISTER CLOSES the door to the dungeon behind us, drowning out the screams Demetri draws from the man with the eagle tattoo. Light-headed and numb, I rest my back against the wall of the passageway and slide down it to sit on my bottom. I feel light-headed because being in the presence of monsters is exhausting. I am numb because I wish I was stronger. I'm just not sure if I wish I was strong enough to hurt them the way they've hurt me, to accept that revenge can also be justice. Or, strong enough to stop Demetri from becoming the monster I fear myself becoming. Thankfully, the wooden door keeps me from hearing what occurs on the other side of it. But my mind is still flooded with images I'd rather not see. I close my eyes tightly, doing my best to force the memories of Demetri's handiwork from my mind. Even though I walked out, it doesn't mean it was easy. In fact, it was hard. Too hard. And I'm not sure how that makes me feel.

"What's going on in that head of yours?" Alister asks, sitting next to me.

"I could ask you the same question."

"But I asked you first."

I open my eyes to find Alister watching me. There's still a tinge of the emotion I spotted before etched in his features, but the rage he once had has now dissipated.

"When we first met, I told you I was afraid this world would consume me. But now I'm starting to question if I'm more a part of it than it is of me."

"What do you mean?" I look away from him then, unsure of my own thoughts. "Hey, I know I'm not Julian. But you can talk to me."

"Can I?" It's a strange idea, to confide in the man who stalked, manipulated, tricked, and threatened me. But something has changed between us. Maybe it was how he talked me off the ledge of committing murder, despite the fact that it was in an effort of self-preservation. Or maybe it's how he's proven to me he truly does want to stand by his word to protect the people I love. But I think, more than that, it's because I finally see him for who he really is.

He's a man born into a world I only stumbled into. He has crossed lines, even at my expense, that don't exactly make him a good man. But everything he's done has been to avenge his sister. If I didn't know anything different, I would've crossed that line tonight to avenge Kat. Who is to say I won't if something, God forbid, happens to Julian? But Alister has never known anything different. It isn't an excuse. It doesn't make the things he does okay. It just makes it his normal. And I feel sorry for him. Because just like I didn't ask to be a part of this world, neither did he. And just as I fear it will take everything from me, it has taken everything from him.

"I'm sorry," I say.

"For what?"

"For what happened to Cara, for your loss. I don't think I ever offered you my condolences." Alister looks away from me then. His sadness is undeniable.

"And why do you offer them now? Because of what that pathetic excuse for a man said?"

The hairs on my arms rise as I sense the anger returning to Alister. "Yes," I admit. "But it's more than that. I...I finally see you."

"You see me?" Alister turns back to me. "And what do you see?"

I take a deep breath. "I see a man who lives an impossible life, who would do anything to protect the people he loves, and who has compassion and integrity, despite the darkness swirling inside him. I get why you sought me out, why you brought me into your investigation, why you killed Posey, why you went to the Bahamas, why you tricked me into meeting with the brotherhood."

I take a moment to compose myself as fresh emotion builds inside me. "Today, my best friend was shot. She may die. And tomorrow, God only knows what the brotherhood has planned for Julian, planned for me. Everything you've done, just like everything I've done and will do, is to protect the people you love and to avenge those you've lost."

"Emma, I—"

"It's okay," I stop him. "I forgive you. I never thought I would. As you can imagine, the past two weeks have been filled with things I never thought I'd do."

Alister's forehead wrinkles as my words hit him. To be honest, they are just as surprising to me as they are him. And yet, I think I see him more clearly now, because when I look at him, I'm looking at a mirror. Though I find compassion for him, I don't like my reflection. I don't like the person I feel his world turning me into. Yet, I'm beginning to wonder, was the darkness always inside me, something infused in me by the very first monster I encountered?

"I never thought I'd pull a gun on someone. I never thought I'd want to make someone bleed. I never thought I'd justify revenge or at least try to. I never thought I'd have the thoughts that I do in this very moment."

"What thoughts are those?" Alister asks. A mix of confusion and worry contorts his features. I bite my lip as I look down at the floor.

"There was a part of me that wanted to cause them pain. As much as their screams turn my stomach, in this very moment, there is a part of me that wishes I was responsible for one of those screams. There is this anger inside of me that I just want to let out, that I had every intention of releasing upon them. I thought I first felt it when Beaux… But what if it's been inside me even before him? What if the reason I found myself in this world of darkness and torment is because my father somehow made me crave it? I mean, of all the men in New Orleans, I found myself with Beaux, a man who shared my father's wicked secrets. And, when I could no longer bear the thought of running anymore, I chose to come back here, to New Orleans where, deep down, I had to have known we wouldn't be safe. And when you came into my life, I fought you, but not hard enough. If I really wanted out, I never would've come back here."

"Emma, don't let that asshole get to you. That's what they do. They manipulate and control. Just because you've gotten comfortable with the darkness doesn't mean it's where you belong."

"Maybe." I nod and bring my eyes to his once more. "But what if there is truth to it? What if I was always meant for this world? Because, if I'm being honest, I didn't walk out of that room because I have some moral superiority. I walked out because I know that Julian doesn't belong in this world, and he could never love someone who does. And without him, I…I have no reason to walk away, to hope, to rise above. I have nothing."

"That's not true. You have…" Alister thinks for a moment but finds himself at a loss. "Please don't let my lack of answer support the lies you tell yourself."

"They aren't lies, Alister. My best friend was shot, and, somehow, I'm still standing. Well, I'm sitting, but what's important is I'm…I'm surviving. The only reason I'm still me, or, at least, the part of me that I'd like to be, is because I still have Julian. Julian believes in me. He loves me. But… They're coming for him, Alister, like really coming for him. And there's nothing I can do to stop them. There's nothing I can do to save him. And it's all my fault."

At that, I finally release the tears I've been holding in and bury my face in my hands as my emotion rips through me.

"Hey, come here," Alister says. Before I can stop him, he's got his arm around me, pulling me into his side. The warmth of his body chases away the chill of death creeping up my spine.

Yet his touch does nothing to ease the worry racing through my mind.

"I can't. I can't lose him," I blubber. "Because I'm not good. I'm broken. I'm filled with pain and anger. Julian gives me life in ways he doesn't even know. And now, his life is being threatened by men who will stop at nothing to destroy me. And they're right. Destroying Julian would destroy me."

"You don't have to save him, Emma," Alister says then. His words take me aback. I lift my watery eyes to his. What the...? "You don't have to save him because I'm going to save you. And since he's what tethers you to your humanity, then his safety just moved to the top of my priority list, right behind yours."

"Alister—"

"I know what it's like, Emma, to lose your humanity." He looks away from me then, releasing me from his grasp. The vein in his neck throbs as he debates his next words. "I wasn't always this way. Yes, I was born into this life of crime. But when I graduated high school, I left New Orleans. I knew my day would come. I never allowed myself to believe I would be free of the responsibilities left behind by my father. But for those few years that I had a choice, I chose to leave, to live like a normal person. When my father passed and the family business became mine, I had every intention of going legit, of getting out of the drug business. But then my sister was taken, and I...I found myself not only broken and vulnerable, but desperate. Desperate to find her, to save her, to protect the rest of my family from the truth and from falling victim to the same men, to protect my reputation and standing by keeping Cara's disappearance a secret. So, I became who I needed to become to maintain order. I became the Blood King, the monster who keeps all the other monsters in line so the people I care about can remain safe. Because without me, there is no telling who would step in, what morals or lack thereof they'd have. But...in maintaining my power, I lost myself."

He looks to me then. "I lost myself so long ago, I forgot what it's like to...to be normal, human, to have hopes and dreams. Being around you and seeing your determination to remain in the light, to have a life beyond this pit of despair, it's reminded me of what I've lost, what I could never truly have." He drops my gaze and nods to himself. "It was wrong of me to bring you here, to make you choose between the light and dark." He returns my gaze, this time with an expression spread across his face I don't recognize. "The last thing I want is to see you lose yourself to the darkness. After everything I've been through, it's all that's left of me. I wouldn't wish that on anyone, especially you."

Alister's words take me aback. Though Mason's worries of Alister's abilities still linger in my mind, Alister's words do give me comfort. I don't know our odds of success. I don't know who will live and who will die when we meet the brotherhood face-to-face. But there's something about Alister, the way he speaks, the way he sits—I believe him when he says he will save me. Or at least, I believe that he will do everything in his power to save me. Just like I've risked myself to keep Julian safe, to keep him from being consumed by the darkness surrounding us, Alister will do the same to protect my soul from consumption.

He is my mirror. He reflects the parts of me I don't like, the parts of me I pray never take over. But, if that's true, then am I also his mirror? Do I reflect the parts of him he's lost? The dreams he was never allowed to have?

"There isn't only darkness in you, Alister. The fact that you care enough to save me, or at least try to, means there is something in you that's still human." Alister turns to me then. I bring my hand to his. His lips part at my touch. Alister's golden eyes scan mine and drift down to my lips. This look I do recognize.

Though, my body processes it quicker than my mind can. Just as I go to pull my hand back, Alister moves his atop of mine, hanging on to me for a moment longer.

"Thank you for believing there's something good in me, even if I don't believe it myself."

I nod, moving my eyes from his to where his hand wraps around mine. "I believe in you like Julian believes in me."

CHAPTER 30

All around the dining room table, everyone shovels eggs into their mouths in silence. From the looks of their drawn faces, I'm not the only one who couldn't sleep. Even my mother, to my right, didn't bother to brush her hair for this morning's war council. That lets me know she's more shaken by the events of last night than I thought. I can't imagine how she'll take it when she learns of Alister's plan, the one in which I will be handed over to the brotherhood with a shiny red bow splayed across my chest. Well, in actuality, it's a shiny red dress that barely covers my ass. The sheer thought turns my stomach, forcing me to lower my fork.

Julian sits next to me then. The warmth from his freshly served plate is comforting. Yet, he makes no moves to eat. Instead, he slings his arm over my shoulders. I scoot next to him, resting my body against his. He doesn't say what's on his mind. Neither do I. We both had lain awake, my hand wrapped tightly around his, staring at the ceiling until sunrise. We're both avoiding the conversation we know we must have, the one that makes this real. But as we sit here, in deafening silence, waiting for Alister and Gio to walk us through tonight's invasion, I'm not sure how it could become more real.

Kat still hasn't woken. The doctor stopped by this morning and noted no change. Demetri's knuckles are split open, reminding me of the night I wish I could forget. And yet my thoughts of last night are nothing compared to my thoughts of what today will bring. Today will be the end of one life and the beginning of a new one. The question is, will tomorrow bring a life of pain and torment or of hope and happiness?

"Julian, we should—" My words are cut off as Alister enters the dining room with Gio. Julian's eyes instantly move from mine to Alister. He sits up taller as Alister takes his place at the head of the table. I do the same. Everyone else places their forks down and waits patiently for what will happen next. The seconds that tick as Alister collects himself are almost unbearable. The second he opens his mouth, that's it. This allusion of normalcy is shattered. My lips part in anticipation. Beneath the table, I move my hand from my lap to where Julian's hand rests on his. I intertwine my fingers with his, wanting to hold on to him for as long as I can. Because I know, just as he does, there is a chance today is our last day together.

Alister turns toward me. As he speaks, it's as if I'm the only one he addresses. Which, for a moment, allows me to tune out everyone else and the fact that today will change all our lives, not just mine.

"I wish there was something I could say to make this easier. But the truth is, today is going to be hard. Most of all, it will be hard on you." Alister pauses then. Julian tightens his grip around me. Finally, Alister asks, "Are you ready?"

Those three words steal the oxygen from my lungs quicker than anything I've ever experienced. I've been anticipating this day, both in the hypothetical and technical sense, for over a year now. And no, I'm not ready in the slightest. I'm not ready to face the brotherhood, to risk a life of suffering for a life of freedom, to risk the safety of everyone I care about for a life free of fear. But their safety has already been jeopardized. Our lives have already been threatened. Julian was right when he said there was no way I would back down from this fight. After what happened to Kat, I can't. I can't allow anyone else to be hurt by these men. I can't let the brotherhood's control destroy me, and it will if I don't take this chance. Finally, I say, "I'm ready for it to be over. I'm ready for my life, *our life…*" I look to Julian. "To finally be ours."

"Me too," Julian whispers. He leans forward, planting a soft kiss on my forehead. He lingers longer than he normally would in public. The simple gesture makes my throat ache with the emotion we both feel. Everything is about to change. And I pray to God it's for the better. And yet, as Julian releases me and the doors of Laroux House are stormed, I know my prayer has not been answered.

"What the…?" Alister pushes himself from his chair and immediately pulls a gun from behind his back.

"Get down," Julian says, shoving me under the table.

"Not without you." I pull Julian down with me as my mom huddles with us. I watch from my place on the floor as Alister and Gio exit the room with their guns drawn. Mason stands beside the door, ready to tackle anyone who enters.

"Emma—"

"Shh. Keep quiet, Mom."

I do my best to give my mom a comforting look as we hide beneath the large wooden table, but I know I don't succeed. Her eyes shine bright with fear. This is it. If Alister got any information out of our friend in the dungeon he hasn't had a chance to share it with me. But it doesn't matter. The brotherhood has come for us. No, they've come for Julian. And while my ears are peeled for sounds of gunshots, my eyes search for a safe exit. With no options, other than my original plan of tossing the canapés server through the window, I begin to look for weapons, something that will cause a little more pain than a butter knife. And yet, as the sounds of heavy footsteps echo against the hardwood, I know my time is up. Our time is up.

"Julian, Mason, I'm sorry. I couldn't stop them," Alister says as he reenters the room.

What? Julian moves first, peeking his head over the edge of the table. I follow him as his cheeks go pale and his hand, wrapped tightly around mine, turns to ice.

"Julian Cole, Mason Cole, you have the right to remain silent. Anything you say can and will be used against you in a court of law..."

"Wait, wait, what's happening?" I ask. I spot the police officer just as he places cuffs around Mason's wrists. "No! They didn't do anything. What is this about?"

Julian tries to hold me back, but I move around him, placing myself between him and the officer rounding the table to cuff him.

"Emma, don't," Julian says. He spins me around so we are face-to-face. "I don't know what this is, but it's okay. Mason and I have done nothing wrong. We'll make bail. We'll be back in time for— We'll be back in time for tonight."

"No, Julian. It's not safe. The second you step foot outside those gates—" Julian silences me with a kiss he hopes will wipe the worry away. This is it. The goodbye kiss we always knew we'd have to have just in case things didn't go as planned. It's the kiss I've been avoiding, the reality I've been avoiding. And now it's crashed through my front door.

"No," I breathe. I pull back as I feel the officer hovering behind me. I take in Julian's icy green eyes and his jet-black hair. His square jaw and the tattoos painted across his skin. I do my best to memorize everything about him. And yet, the sheer thought of never being able to see him again brings me to my knees. Or, at least, it would if Julian wasn't still holding me up.

"I love you, Emma Marshall. I'll always love you," he chokes out. The police officer moves around me, pulling Julian's arms behind his back.

"No," I cry as his hold on me breaks. The emotion in his voice lets me know he knows what waits for him on the other side of the Amato gates, just as I do. "Don't say goodbye to me, Julian Cole. Don't. This isn't goodbye."

"Of course it isn't," he says, tears filling his eyes and falling softly down his cheeks. He leans forward, tugging on the officer's grasp to give me one last kiss. "I'll never say goodbye to you."

"Walk," the officer commands. The single word steals any strength left inside me.

"Please," I beg. "Please, don't take him."

"I love you," Julian says once more.

At that, emotion rips through me. My eyes are so blurry with tears I can hardly see. My throat aches with every tear I cry. Knowing our time is up, I finally bring myself to say the words that may not mean goodbye but feel just the same. "I love you with everything that I am."

As the words cross my lips, the officer forces Julian past me and out of the room where Mason waits. My mom reaches for me, but I shrug out of her grasp and take off running out of the room. By the time I make it to the formal entry, Julian and Mason have already been removed from the premises. Yet, I am not alone. No. Standing in the room with Alister, Gio, and me is none other than Penelope Thomas, the mother of the Devil incarnate.

I half run, half stumble until the regal woman is within arm's reach. Alister and Gio move with me. Though I'm not sure if they flank me for my protection or for hers. "Are you responsible for this? Why? What did Mason or Julian ever do to you?" Mrs. Thomas looks me up and down as if I am nothing to her.

"Oh, come now, Emma. You didn't think I'd let the men responsible for my son's death live without consequence, did you? Especially once I found out that one of them is your new boyfriend. Or should I say fiancé?" She spots the ring on my finger. I move it behind my back to hide it from her evil glare. "It's a bit of a coincidence, no? My son, your ex, was murdered in the very business your new beau owns. Pun intended."

I'm not sure if it's the lack of sleep or the fact that my heart was just ripped out of my chest, but her words aren't making any sense. The Thomases were the ones to conceal Beaux's crimes, burying the original police report Julian and I filed detailing why Beaux was at Lucid the morning of his death. He was there to kill me. Mason killed him to protect me, but even that wasn't in the report we filed. I took the blame to protect Mason. Which Mrs. Thomas would know if she'd seen the report, which leads me to believe she hasn't. But if she didn't bury the police report, who did? *Ah!* This is too much right now.

"Mrs. Thomas, Beaux was killed in a robbery gone wrong. Yes, Julian and Mason own Lucid Records, but how does that make them responsible for Beaux's death?" Since it isn't clear whether Mrs. Thomas knows the truth of her son's death or not, I stick with the publicly known and accepted story. As far as her insinuation that Julian killed Beaux for me or because of me, that's not even worth diving in to.

"Yes, my son was beaten down like a rabid animal," Mrs. Thomas bites out. "All because of your boyfriend's negligence."

"*Negligence?* What the Hell are you talking about?" I yell.

"Emma?"

"It's okay, Mom. I've got this." It's a lie. I most certainly do not *got* this. I'm about two seconds from losing it.

"It's called negligent homicide. Look it up. There was a party at the record shop the night before, was there not?" The speakeasy grand opening party, but I don't admit that to her. "Per the police report, the robbery occurred after the store was supposed to be open for the day. However, there was no one else there, except my Beaux. My son went to that store. God only knows why. Probably to see you." She jabs her finger into my chest.

"Hey, now. Penelope, let's calm down," Alister says.

"Calm down? You want me to calm down? My son is dead! If that man had updated the store hours online for the morning after the party or, at minimum, had a security system, then my son wouldn't have walked in on the robbery that morning. He would still be here."

"Yeah? Well, thank God he isn't, because he was a monster! And you're crazy if you think that psycho logic of yours will stand in a court of law."

"You bitch!" Her tiny hand stings as she slams it into my cheek. I stumble backward.

"*Hey!*" my mom yells, stepping in front of me. "Don't you touch my daughter, you beast. Or so help me God, I will bring the fury of a scorned mother down upon you. You know a thing or two about that, don't you?" Mrs. Thomas stands tall but not as tall as Anne Marshall as she towers over her. Penelope purses her lips. If she weren't the reason the love of my life was ripped from his place of protection, then I'd feel sorry for her. As it is, I feel nothing for her but a brewing hatred. "I think it's time for you to leave."

"Fine. I'll leave. But this isn't over," Mrs. Thomas warns. She turns on her heel and walks toward the door. I take a step forward, unable to keep the words from crossing my lips.

"This whole negligent homicide thing, did you come up with that on your own?" Mrs. Thomas hesitates as she reaches the front door. For a moment, she looks as if she's going to say something. Instead, she keeps walking. Her silence is all the answer I need. As she closes the door to Laroux House behind her, I do the only thing I can now that the life has been sucked out of me. I fall to the floor, giving way to the weight of this horror.

The brotherhood somehow manipulated Penelope Thomas into having Julian and Mason arrested on some bogus claim, ripping them from their safe place behind the Amato estate gates. I don't have proof. I likely never will. But I feel it in my bones. The brotherhood has Mason and Julian. And now, they'll be tortured, just like the man with the eagle tattoo said they would.

My mom drops to her knees beside me and wraps her slender arms around me. I'm thankful for her touch, but it does nothing to comfort me. Nor do Alister's promises. He still hasn't figured it out yet. "Emma, I have connections at the police department. I'll call and make sure Julian and Mason are kept in their own holding cell until we can get them out on bail. Negligent homicide isn't a violent offense. We should have no problem getting them released."

My eyes flick to his. The old Emma would be grateful for his solution. But the old Emma is gone. She left with Julian, and she won't return until he is by her side once more. And if he doesn't return, then...neither will she.

"You do that," I whisper, pushing myself from my place on the ground. My mom moves with me.

"Emma, I am so sorry. They had a warrant. I couldn't stop them," Alister explains.

I nod. "I know. None of us could. Now we have to get them back, no matter what it takes." Alister's eyes narrow as he registers the emotion in my voice or, more precisely, the lack thereof. I'm all out of tears. I'm out of self-pity. The only thing left in me is that which I've done my best to suppress—anger, darkness. But no more.

"Emma, why don't you go lie down. Alister will handle this," my mom says. She's crazy if she thinks I'm sitting this one out, but it's best for her if she thinks I am. She won't be able to stomach what I do next.

"Good idea, Mom. I'll let Alister handle it."

At that, I turn on my heel and make my way upstairs to sell my mom on my slumber. Then, I take the secret passageway Alister showed me the night before to the dungeon. It's the place I will bury every last bit of good inside me and embrace the monster I've feared I would become. As I reach the door to the dungeon, I don't hesitate. I rip my boot off my foot and slam the heel against the knob of the ancient door until it jiggles loose. Sweat beads on my forehead in the tight space. It stings as it slips into my eyes, but the feeling is nothing compared to the wrath I'm about to unleash.

Finally, the knob loosens. I slip back into my boot and finish prying the heavy door open. Unlike the night before, there is no gust of wind that meets my skin. What waits for me is stale darkness and a foul aroma I can't quite put my finger on. I move forward through the pitch-black dungeon of death with an unexpected ease, much like Alister did the night before.

Alister said just because I've gotten comfortable with the

darkness doesn't mean I belong in it. Last night, I wanted to believe in his words. A part of me did. But that part of me is dead. The bloodthirsty darkness I feel pulsing through my veins has always been inside me. It took breaking me in half to free it from its hiding spot. Now, there is no guilt. There is no second-guessing. There is only the truth. And the truth is, there are no angels in Hell. If I want to survive it, if I want to save the man I love, then I'll become the monster I must. I will get the information I need from the man I told Demetri to leave alive, even if I must torture it out of him. And then, I will kill him. His kind has taken enough from me. He will take no more, not even a single breath.

As I reach the end of the last wrought-iron cell, I know I've made it to the opening where the two men wait for me. I move my hands along the wall in search of the light switch. By the time I find it, my fingers are covered in dirt and dust and God only knows what else. I flip the switch and light illuminates the space. It's then that I find the source of the foul aroma burning my nostrils—rotting corpses, not one but two. "No," I whisper. I take a step forward. "*No!*" I scream.

I move toward the bloody figures still tied to the metal chairs. The one with the eagle tattoo is too disfigured to know the cause of death, but dead he certainly is. The other... I take his limp head in my hands.

"Open your eyes. Open your eyes!"

Dried blood crumbles underneath my fingernails as I hold on to the lifeless man meant to be the key to saving Julian. "No, please don't be dead." At that, my voice cracks as fresh emotion works its way through me. "No." I let the man go, taking a step back. His head falls limply to his chest. The only thing holding him up are the ropes still tied around his wrists, ankles, and waist.

"I'm not going to cry. Not anymore."

"Emma." I bite my lip as Alister makes his presence known. "I thought I'd find you down here." His shadow fills the space next to me, yet he does not reach for me.

"Did you do this? Did you kill him?" I ask.

"Yes." I pinch my eyes closed at his admission. My cheeks ache as I hold in the tears threatening to fall.

"Did he tell you of the brothers' plans? Do you know where Julian is? And please, don't tell me the police station because you and I both know Penelope Thomas didn't come up with that bogus charge on her own."

"You're right," Alister says. He brings his hand to my arm and gently pulls me to him. I allow it, only because I want the truth. I *need* the truth. As I open my eyes, I take in Alister, the wrinkle on his forehead, the downward turn of his wide lips, and I know.

"Just tell me," I whisper.

His jaw clenches. "I called my contacts in the police force. The officers who arrested Julian and Mason aren't employed by the state of Louisiana or any state, for that matter. And Mason and Julian were never booked into any jail in the city." I knew it. Still, having it confirmed only makes my blood boil hotter.

"What else?" I ask.

"Our friend here didn't know the details of the brotherhood's plan—"

"Wait. You killed him without getting any information from him?" I narrow my eyes as Alister's words hit me. "How do you know he wasn't lying to you? How do *I* know *you* aren't lying to me?" I turn away from him then, my eyes grazing over the bloody corpse before me.

"Emma, why would I lie to you? I want nothing but to protect you and give you a shot at a life I could never have."

"You don't think I see the way you look at me?" I ask, spinning around once more. "You care about me. You…you *want* me. And with Julian out of the way, I am just as bloodthirsty and vengeful as you. We're a perfect pair in this pit of despair. Is this what you wanted?" I move closer to him, so close I can practically taste him. "All along, is this what you wanted?" I scream.

"*No!*"

I don't flinch as Alister raises his voice. Instead, I stand firm. Our lips only inches apart, I dare him to show me his true self. He brings his hands to my cheeks. I'm not sure if he intends to kiss me or only hold me still, but the desire in his golden eyes is undeniable.

"I *do* want you," he admits. "But I could never let myself have you, even if there was no Julian, even if *you* wanted me." He releases me then. Taking a few steps back, he presses his back into the wrought iron of the cell across from me. I mimic his actions, standing across from him. After a moment of silence, he says, "I've been where you are. When I lost my sister, I lost myself. So, I'm glad I killed him because if you had found him alive—"

"I would've tortured him," I admit.

"And you would've lost yourself. And that would've been a shame, because as much as you think you belong in this world, you don't. As much as you blame yourself for every bad thing that happens, it's not your fault."

"Alister, stop. Just stop trying to save me or talk me off some invisible ledge." I push myself off the wrought iron.

"*Fine.*" Alister mimics my movements and meets me in the middle of the walkway. "I will when you stop trying to save everyone around you—Kat, Julian, Beaux, *me*. You can't help it. You can't help but see the good in people. You can't help but try to turn monsters back into men." Alister towers over me with his golden glare.

"Maybe because I've always known how easy it is to become one." I lift my chin in defiance. "Maybe because I've always known that *I* could—"

"Maybe. But now, you need someone to remind you of the good in you." I roll my eyes, but Alister forces me to look at him by bringing his palm to my cheek. There it is—the look I've been ignoring for far too long. "Until we get Julian back, I'll be that person. And Emma, we *will* get Julian back."

I bite my lip. My heart softens at the thought of Julian in my arms once more. But it'll take more than a sweet sentiment to shove dark Emma back into her coffin.

"In how many pieces?" I ask.

CHAPTER 31

I begged Alister to let us go after the brotherhood sooner. The men who shot Kat may not have been aware of my and Alister's deal, but the brotherhood knew enough to send fake police officers to Alister's house to collect Julian and Mason. They must've been watching us last night as we shuttled everyone to the Amato estate. If they didn't know this morning that Alister and I are working together and that he has no intentions of handing me over to them, they do now. The brotherhood members who nabbed Julian and Mason saw not only my family here, but Kat's mom and Demetri. Alister wouldn't have offered them asylum if he didn't care about me. And if that isn't enough, they heard Julian say he'd be out in time for tonight, which means they've no doubt spent the day torturing our plan of attack out of him. I squeeze my eyes shut at the thought. All this time waiting has allowed my fear to overcome my anger, so much so I can barely stand straight as I look upon what could be my last sunset.

Waiting—that's what I've been doing. Waiting to save the love of my life. Waiting to exact my revenge. Waiting to earn my freedom. After thinking through every possible plan of attack, we always came back to the same one, the one we've been planning all along. Alister says it isn't enough to have the superiors in the same venue. He needs them in the same room. I'm still not sure why. But the only way to make that happen is if we pretend we don't know that the brotherhood is onto us. As the sun begins to set, casting an orange glow atop the trees surrounding the Amato estate, I've never been happier to walk into a trap.

I turn from my second-floor window and slip into a pair of black strappy heels. Alister's sister, Sophia, laces me into the scrap of material meant to be a strapless dress. I couldn't ask my mom for help. For one, because she'd die if she saw me in the red number with crisscrossed spaghetti straps for a back. And two, because after Julian and Mason were taken, she overheard my and Alister's scheming. And, as only Anne Marshall can, she vehemently opposed our plan. So vehemently, I had to slip a few Xanax into her lunchtime tea.

"Ah!" I wince as Sophia tugs on the last strap.

"Sorry," she says. "I wouldn't want your boobs spilling out while you're fighting for your life. All done."

"It's okay. Thanks."

I move to the mirror propped in the corner of the room Julian and I share. The dress is Amato red. The last time I wore something this color Alister betrayed me. The very next day, I made a plan to betray him. And though I've forgiven him for his betrayal, I still haven't told him I've been working with the FBI behind his back, nor have I ceased working with them. It isn't lost on me that Alister still hasn't told me all the details of tonight's attack. I don't believe he'd betray me again. I truly don't. But it's a risk I can't take, especially now that Julian and Mason are at the brotherhood's nonexistent mercy. I need all the help I can get getting them out of there alive. And yet, as I imagine the lines I'm willing to cross, the bridges I'm willing to burn to save the ones I love, I spot Sophia in the mirror.

She sits on the edge of the four-poster bed, staring quietly at a small glittering object. Her long, raven hair drapes over the shoulder of her cream-colored sweater. It's over eighty degrees outside and the air circulation of Laroux House is musty at best given the age of the place. Still, I imagine she *is* cold with the chill of death, a chill brought on by news of her sister's passing and the threat of losing her brother.

I'd be lying if I said I don't feel guilty. Everything Alister has done has been to protect her from suffering the same fate as Cara. Not only does he not deserve to lose his freedom over the lines he's crossed, Sophia doesn't deserve to lose her brother, her protector. Though I'd like to think, after tonight, she won't have to worry about her brother's enemies coming after her, I know enough to know the brotherhood isn't the only threat Alister faces. And Alister will never forgive me if something happens to his sister because I took away his ability to protect her. I shake my head. I can't think about that now. Julian and Mason must be my top priority, my *only* priority.

"I wish Alister hadn't insisted on the heels. It'll be harder to run in them. But maybe that's the point. I can't go in there dressed in athletic wear ready to kick ass or they'll know something is up." I realize I'm rambling, but I'm not sure what else to say. *Sorry your sister was abducted, raped, and killed because your brother stopped supplying animalistic men with drugs they used to subdue and rape women with?*

"You're right," Sophia says. "You have to play the part, but only for a little bit. Tonight isn't about running. It's about standing your ground. What better to stand your ground in than four-inch stilettos?" Her words bring a small smile to my lips. I see the pain on her face and still she tries to make light of this terrifying situation. "Do you know why we wear the color red, Emma?" Sophia asks me then.

"No." I turn to her and she stands. Her eyes drift past me, as if lost in thought.

"When my family first immigrated from Sicily, over one hundred years ago now, they were shunned because they were different, much like immigrants are today. Only, back then, instead of blasting hate speech over the internet, those who were different were met with the barrel of a gun or worse. I suppose that still happens too."

Sophia blinks the haziness from her eyes, focusing on me. "March 14, 1891 is the day my grandmother always told me, Alister too, to never forget. It's the day this city stormed the jailhouse and spilled the blood of eleven Italian men after they'd been acquitted of a crime they likely didn't commit. In truth, I can't speak to the men's innocence. I can only speak to the hate they were met with and the fate they were dealt. And so, from that day forward, the Amato family claimed the color red, the color of blood. We wear it with pride, in remembrance of those we've lost and as a warning to those who threaten us. The streets of New Orleans will no longer run red with Italian blood, rather, the blood of our enemies."

As she speaks of her family's history, her cheeks shine bright as her strength returns to her. It's good to see her standing tall. Though, hearing of the meaning of Amato red, I'm confused as to why Alister would grant me the honor, not once but twice, of wearing a color with such meaning.

"With this dress, Alister has bestowed a shield of protection around you. The brotherhood won't know our history or our customs. But, now that you do, I hope it makes you feel a little stronger, a little safer. He or she who wears the color of our ancestors will always have our protection and loyalty." Sophia takes a step toward me then and pulls my curls to one side, draping them over my chest. "After what happened to Cara, I'm not sure if the Amato family has the luck it once did. But just in case there is some magic left in this metal..." Sophia pins a glittering brooch to my chest. Like the one Cara wore in the photo I first spotted her in, it's of the Amato family crest. "Now you're ready."

My cheeks burn bright with embarrassment while my insides coil with regret. Both Alister and Sophia have welcomed me into their home and protected me. Now that Sophia has shared some of her family's history, Alister's protection means even more to me. This dress, this brooch, everything he's given me, even Sophia's silent sense of safety, means more. And yet...

"Sophia, would you give me a moment? I may be ready, but I'm not *ready*."

THE MOON GLINTS off the flowing waters of Lake Pontchartrain as Gio drives the Range Rover across the causeway. Alister sits next to me in the back seat. He is eerily calm as he stares out the car window. I, on the other hand, am freaking out. Tonight is a night I never thought would come and yet, a night I've been anticipating ever since I learned of the brotherhood. I knew they would come for me. I just never thought I'd meet them halfway. But what choice do I have?

I was warned by Beaux, by my father, and by Mason that the brotherhood wouldn't stop with me. They'd come after everyone I love. While my sister, Eva, is safe in a bunker with her husband, Bill, and my mom is secure behind the Amato gates, Kat still hasn't woken from the coma the brotherhood put her in. The more time that passes, the less likely she is to wake. And as much as my mind is on her, I am consumed by thoughts of Julian and, by extension, Mason.

They've been in the brotherhood's grasp for hours now. In the few minutes of torture I experienced at Gio's hand, I felt every piece of me break. I can't imagine the damage the brotherhood could've inflicted in the time they've had Julian. Though that's what's most disturbing. I've experienced my fair share of Hell. Examining the bodies left in Demetri and Alister's wake gives me an idea of the kind of pain that can be inflicted. And yet, just as Alister warned, the brotherhood will make my past experiences seem like fond memories. The fact that I can't imagine the things they are capable of scares me.

I feel the hairs on my arms rise as my legs begin to shake. While I'm seated, my dress barely reaches past my upper thigh, giving the back seat air vent the perfect angle to make me have to pee. At least, I'm choosing to blame it on the air vent and not the fact that my insides are convulsing. I've already peed on myself in front of Gio and Alister once. I'd rather not do it again. As if they'd care. But like Sophia said, tonight isn't about running. I should face the brotherhood with dignity and strength, though strong is the last thing I feel. I—

"Hey, what's on your mind?" Alister asks. Reaching over, he places his hand on mine. He's surprisingly warm, warm like life. Which is ironic, considering we very well could be driving to our deaths.

"You first," I say. "You've been anticipating this night just as much as I have." Alister looks away from me then. His eyes go to Gio. Perhaps he doesn't care to talk about his feelings in front of him. Though I'd very much appreciate a distraction from my own and the fact that I may never see my mom again. I may never know if Kat wakes up. If she doesn't, I may prefer it that way. But then that would mean I'm dead or worse, a captive of the brotherhood. And if that's true, then Julian and Mason are dead, tortured in front of me to inflict the most pain and then killed. I shake my head. "Alister, please. I need to focus on something other than my own thoughts."

Alister turns to me. As he does, gone is the strong and stoic man with the steady heart. What I find isn't even the loud and boastful version of him he becomes when he's angry. Instead, I find someone I've never seen before. Someone who is sad, heartbroken, and scared. Though there's something about the hollowness of his cheeks and his flat gaze that makes me think he isn't scared to die. He's scared to fail.

"I'm not sure what to say," he admits. I take it he isn't used to talking about his feelings. As the leader of the Amato family, which I'm coming to think is much larger than his blood relatives, he must always remain strong. It's then that I think back to the article written after his father's death. The article praised him for putting everyone who relies on the Amatos for employment at ease. He was worried about being strong for others when he should've been allowed to grieve.

"You can say anything. Just be honest with me."

His lips lift into a small smile. "There aren't many people I can be honest with. I suppose you can be one of them." At that, I return his smile. "I've been thinking about my father and how he never would've let what happened to my sister occur under his rule." He turns away from me then. "I blame myself," he admits. "I know you're no stranger to that. But, in my case, it's…it's truly my fault. My little sister," he chokes out, "was ripped from her bed in the middle of the night, raped, and sold to the highest bidder. Because she wasn't a virgin, there was no need for her to remain *untouched* before the sale. A fact the brotherhood was sure to share once they were certain I couldn't track them." Alister brings his hand to his face. He doesn't cry, though I can tell the tension in his body is begging to be released. Instead, he covers his face in shame.

"Hey," I say, pulling his hand back to me. "Don't hide from me."

"Why not? I hide from everyone else."

"I know." I nod. "That's why I'm asking you not to hide from *me*, especially now, when—"

"When this might be our last conversation." The chill I'm all too familiar with returns to me as Alister's armor finally cracks. All this time, he's been so confident, so sure we'd win. Though I never allowed myself to believe it would be easy, I trusted him enough to believe defeating the brotherhood is possible. And yet, what if Mason was right? What if I placed too much of my faith in Alister? "Don't worry, Emma. If this is the last time we speak, it won't be because you're dead. It'll be because I am."

His voice changes as he grants me my reassurance and I instantly feel guilty for forcing him back into his role of Mr. Amato, the Blood King. He showed one moment of vulnerability, and I doubted him. "Um, no. No, don't say that."

"It's what you need to hear, isn't it?" he asks. I pull away from him then and lean my head against the headrest.

"Maybe. I'm sorry. I just don't really know what I need right now. I don't know how to do this, how to feel strong." I take a deep breath. "I believe in you. I believe you will do everything you can to protect me." I turn to him then. "I believe you when you say we can win. But, then I…I think about—"

"You think about Cara. You think, how can I put my faith in a man who couldn't even keep his own sister safe?"

"Alister—"

"It's okay. I get it. If that isn't enough, you think of all the times I've failed you in the short time we've known each other. Tricking you into meeting with the brotherhood face-to-face, allowing Kat to be shot, and not thinking twice about the men who walked right through my front door for Julian and Mason. You know what scares the shit out of me? That stupid little scheme that got them Julian and Mason could've been a million times worse. They could do it again. They could come after us at any time."

"Now you sound like me."

"*That's a comforting thought.*" At that, we both laugh. Yet, it's short-lived as Gio makes his way into the French Quarter. It won't be long now.

My cheeks grow tight with emotion as the French Quarter nightlife rages just mere feet away. Neon signs and flickering streetlights, drunken pedestrians dancing and singing, the barefoot violinist playing on the street corner—there's so much life surrounding me. It only makes me realize how dead I feel without Julian, without Kat. Their safety, my safety isn't guaranteed. The only thing that's certain is I'm about to come face-to-face with my worst nightmare. I have no idea how I'm supposed to face them. And what if they've already—

"I…I didn't say goodbye," I admit. "To my mom, to Kat, even to Julian, I…I couldn't bring myself to have the conversation, to say the word."

"Maybe it's a good thing you didn't say it," Alister says then. "It means you believe we will survive."

"Don't you?" I ask.

Alister nods. "Of course." His short answer isn't very encouraging, though my mind is more focused on what he pulls out of the pocket of his cargo pants. Yes, he's dressed for war in the most casual sense. I'm sure the brotherhood will search us before we enter. I suppose that's the one benefit to wearing this scrap. There's no hiding anything. Which means they shouldn't have to…

"Alister."

"Yes?" He turns to me. In his hand, he holds a pair of black brass knuckles. The knuckles have spikes on them the size of bullets. Maybe they are bullets.

"First, what the Hell is that? And second…" My throat feels tight as the next words come to me. The thought of being captured by the brotherhood was debilitating enough. On top of that, worrying about Julian's safety and Kat's recovery was all-consuming. I've done my best not to focus on myself and what waits for me once I'm in the brotherhood's grasp. And yet now that we're minutes away from coming face-to-face with them, I can no longer hold my breath. I can no longer hide from what waits for me the moment I step foot out of this vehicle. "Are they going to touch me? Are they going to—"

"No." Alister is quick to answer. "I won't—" He stops himself. Perhaps thoughts of Cara make him realize he can't promise me nothing will happen to me. He can't promise me they won't touch me, that they won't do things to me. It's then that he says, "I will do everything in my power to keep you safe, which is why I'm giving you these." He hands me the knuckles. Up close, I see that the spikes are simply sharpened metal rather than bullets. But they are long like bullets, about an inch. I press my finger to the tip.

"Ah!" I wince. A small drop of blood bubbles on my finger-tip. "I barely touched it."

"Think of the damage they'll do when you actually throw a punch." The thought is comforting, until it isn't.

"*Wait!* Me throw a punch? Alister, what exactly am I walking into? And how do you expect me to sneak these in? If you haven't noticed, this dress barely conceals me let alone a weapon."

Alister smiles then. "Starting with the simple question—the

knuckles are made of a special material. They're rock solid like metal, but it won't set off a metal detector. As far as concealing them, that dress was made for my sister. Sophia, not Cara. She is, *was*, too young for something so revealing. Anyway, there's a pocket sewn into the inside of the dress. It's the perfect size for something like this and the fabric of the dress is thick enough to conceal the jagged edges." His eyes drift down to where the dress meets my thighs. "You'll have to feel for it. It's somewhere in that general area." He points toward my crotch.

"Got it." I blush. "But first, the not-so-simple question. Alister, why do I need these? I thought you only needed me as bait. Once we're inside, you and your men will capture the brothers and we'll rescue Julian and Mason." I hold up the pointy knuckles once more. Alister turns away from me then as if choosing his words carefully.

"Five minutes," Gio says from behind the wheel. Alister nods and pulls out his phone.

"Got to send that last tweet?" I taunt.

Alister places his phone in the door cubby rather than back into his pants pocket. He *is* expecting the brotherhood to search us, or he wouldn't go in without his only means to call for help. Then again, with all his men already inside the brotherhood compound, I'm not sure who he would call.

"Alister."

He turns back to me, only this time, the Alister that opened up about feeling inferior to his father and like a failure to me is gone. The lines of his jaw are hard. The muscles of his arms and shoulders are tense. His skintight black T-shirt reveals every indention. But his bulldozer-like body isn't what makes me queasy. It's the sharp glint of his golden eyes. He's ready for war, for blood, for revenge. And he isn't leaving without it.

"Now that the brotherhood has Julian and Mason we're

walking into an unpredictable situation. I said I would do everything in my power to protect you. But if I can't, you need to be able to protect yourself. I failed one woman I cared for by protecting her innocence rather than preparing her for the reality of this world, this world that, after tonight, I pray you never find yourself in again." As Alister speaks, a flush of red brightens his cheeks. "Emma, it's you or it's them. Don't let it be you."

"But…but I don't know how to fight. I'm not trained. The last time I had to fight for my life, I—"

"You don't have to be trained," Alister says, inspecting the gun he pulled out of another secret Amato pocket. "You just have to want to live more than they want to kill you. It shouldn't be that hard, considering they don't want to kill you. They—" He stops himself. As focused as he is on his self-defense pep talk, he's aware enough to realize when he's being insensitive. Yet, it's true.

"They don't want to kill me. They want to make me suffer."

Alister turns to me then. There's a slight softness in his eyes that wasn't there before. "Which means they won't go for the easy shots. If things go south and they try to take you down, it'll be up close and personal. That's when you go for their throat or eyes. Hit them in the right place and they'll bleed out."

"Sixty seconds," Gio says.

"*No!* No, I can't do this."

"Emma, look at me," Alister says. Alister brings his hand to the back of my neck and before I know it, his lips press into mine, hard and fast. His facial hair tickles my skin as his lips move against mine.

"What the Hell was that?" I shove him off me.

"Are you angry?"

"*Yes!* I love Julian and I'm not a cheater!"

"Good. Anger makes you dangerous. Fear makes you weak."

He returns his attention to his phone while I stew in the seat next to him. *How dare he?* "Find the place for the knuckles," he orders. I do as he says, locating the hidden pocket as Gio brings the Range Rover to a stop. As the vehicle slows, my heartbeat quickens. I move my eyes to the window, taking in our surroundings.

"*Wait.* This isn't the right place. Alister—"

"Get angry, Emma. These men have taken everything from you—your sense of safety, your home, your best friend, and the love of your life. If that isn't enough to keep you focused through your fear, then embrace your fear. Only don't be afraid of what happens next. Be afraid of death. Be afraid of a life without Julian. Fight like Hell to make sure you survive this, to make sure you survive your greatest fears."

Alister opens the door then and steps out into the New Orleans night. A cool breeze wafts off the river, lifting my curls and kissing my skin. His words ignite something inside me I haven't felt in a very long time, something that reminds me that this *is* my fight. I may not want it. I've avoided it, run from it. But no more. Alister is fighting for his family and so am I. What's more? I'm fighting for my freedom, for the second chance at life and love Julian made me believe I could have. And yet, my burst of determination and the anger I feel toward both the brotherhood and now Alister does nothing to change the fact that I *am* afraid. Afraid because not only am I about to face the brotherhood, I'm facing them alone. Instead of the downtown warehouse I told the FBI they could find us, we're at the docks, waiting to board a moving chamber of torture the FBI will have no way of tracking.

CHAPTER 32

Outside the vehicle, I wince as Alister ties my hands behind my back to further the illusion that I'm his prisoner. I never knew red silk could be so binding. Alister's movements are rough and quick as he restrains me. There's something different about him, something vicious and desperate. He's desperate for this to work, just as I am. His fingers tremble as he ties the last knot. I turn my head to the side to take him in. I can't see his face, only the tension in his arms. The fear I sense in him only intensifies my fear—the fear that's become such a fixture in my heart, I've forgotten what a life without it feels like.

Mason warned me of the consequences of crossing the brotherhood. *Emma, I know firsthand how far and wide the brotherhood's connections run. If you do this, you'll be running for the rest of your life.* So did my father. He assured me that one person would not punish the crimes of the many. And Beaux, he tried to kill me when he learned of my plans to expose the brotherhood. He was going to kill me because he knew the brotherhood would kill him for leading me to them. They are ruthless, merciless, manipulative, and unforgiving. And I have no idea how I, how *we* are going to survive this.

"Alister—"

"You do not address me," Alister bites out. He draws a gasp from me as he tugs on my arms to hold me in place. It's then that he shoves me forward. I nearly fall as I round the Range Rover.

"You don't have to be so rough," I say, though I'm too shocked to say it above a whisper.

"Yes, I do. Now walk." Alister shoves me once more, forcing me to walk ahead of him and Gio. I get that this is all part of his plan. Even though we know the brotherhood is aware we're working together, we can't let them know that. Not until we're inside and Alister has the brotherhood's superiors in his sights. Though, the way Alister speaks to me and forces me toward the ship, he is a stranger. He is the Blood King, a monster just like the men I'm about to face. I suppose it should give me comfort that he's my monster, but it doesn't. The change in him only makes me feel even more alone.

I've seen a side of him that is angry, loud, menacing, and violent. Yet, I've never seen the side that I've always known was there, the side that earns the respect and loyalty of men like Gio, the side that will see nothing but red the moment he comes face-to-face with the men responsible for his sister's death. It'll be up to me to save Julian and Mason. I can feel it in my bones. And yet, as I step onto the boarding ramp, the weight of Mason's and Julian's lives resting on my shoulders isn't the only thing I feel.

Two dark, looming figures appear on the deck at the end of the ramp. Despite the warm light illuminating the deck of the shiny white sea vessel, there isn't much I can identify of the men before me, the men who will no doubt put their hands on me. Every nerve in my body pinches inside me. Sharp pain dances beneath my skin, reminding me of what I fear most, reminding me of the worst night of my life, the night I've fought to forget, the night I know will be nothing but a fond memory if we fail and the brotherhood sets sail with what's left of my soul.

> *Blood pools in my mouth to the point where I feel I may drown in it. There is a reprieve in his assault as Beaux removes his pants. I gasp and spit the blood on my white duvet. The sight of him over me ignites my body in fear, and with fear stronger than my adrenaline, the pain of my wounds overcomes me, as does the pain of him entering my body.*
>
> *Beaux moves his hands from my shoulders to my throat. He squeezes and with more and more pressure, my mind goes numb, and my insides burn as he moves in and out. I flounder and try to push him off, but my efforts are in vain. He is too strong.*
>
> *I stare at the ceiling until the room starts to fade. "Look at me," Beaux grunts. He pulls me by my hair and forces me to look at him. As it becomes harder to remain conscious, blurred edges inch closer and closer to his face, yet I still see him, over me, choking me, violating me. Until I see nothing at all.*

I gasp as a rough hand wraps around the back of my neck. The foreign touch pulls me into the present. Steel blue eyes meet mine as one of the brotherhood's guards yanks me from the ramp and forces me face-first against the side of the ship. I scream and close my eyes as my face smushes into the wall. My entire body shakes in anticipation as I sense the large man move closer to me.

"Christmas came early, Blood King. You've got her wrapped up like the gift she is. The superiors will be pleased."

"I'm glad to hear it. Though I'd imagine they'd prefer to

receive their gift in the pristine condition that I've delivered her in."

I open my eyes at the sound of Alister's voice. He sounds calm, which somehow allows my beating heart to slow. *Breathe, Emma. This is for Julian. This is for love. This is for freedom.* Just as I manage to stop my legs from shaking, Alister and Gio are pressed against the ship's side next to me. The guards kick their feet, nudging them to spread their legs wider. They oblige. I watch, frozen as the two guards work their hands up and down their legs and around their abs. Then, they repeat the process with a metal detecting wand. My lips part and my eyes widen as Alister's hidden weapons go undetected, just as he said they would. "Clear," the guards say in unison. I should be relieved, though I am anything but as the guard's attention shifts to me.

Silver metal glints beneath the warm light of the deck as one of the guards pulls a gun from his holster, a warning to Alister and Gio should they try to stop what happens next. The sight is almost enough to distract me from the other man's shadow, which now bleeds into mine. The wood planks squeak beneath his weight as he kneels behind me. I gasp as his breath tickles the exposed skin of my upper hamstring. He starts by bringing his hand to my ankle. Slowly, he moves up. I flinch at his touch.

"She's clean," Alister says. "If we don't have any weapons, do you honestly think she does?"

"No," the guard admits. "But you can never be too careful. Now, hold still, sweetheart." Using his free hand, he presses into my lower back, forcing me harder against the ship's side. With my hands still tied, I can't move. I can't stop him when he—

Alister lunges for the man but is quickly subdued by the guard with the gun. He presses the metal into Alister's skull, his finger hovering over the trigger.

"Please, don't," I beg, both for my safety and Alister's.

I'm surprised I have it in me to speak. I'm surprised I'm still conscious. Though I instantly wish I wasn't as my plea goes disrespected. The guard moves his thick fingers past the hem of my dress all the way up until they brush against the lacy fabric of my underwear. I pinch my eyes closed as he cups me.

"Got to make sure you aren't hiding anything in there." He grunts as he slips his fingers inside my—

"No. No, please!" I bite my lip until it bleeds in the hopes the sensation will override the pain ripping through my lower half. It doesn't.

"She is to remain untouched," Alister yells. I jump as the air moves next to me once more. I'm forced to open my eyes. I find Alister closer to me than he was before. He reaches toward me, but the guard presses his arm into the wall, refusing to let him reach me. I can taste the words *you promised* on my tongue. But I don't say them. If I do, the pain of this invasion will be for nothing.

"What? Like your sister?" I gasp as the man behind me pulls out of me and stands, redirecting his attention to Alister. As he moves closer to him, I take a step back. Giving way to the ache inside me and my vanishing strength, I fall to my knees. "You know she was so tight, I could only fit—" Alister's lip curls as the man holds up his hand.

At that, Alister forces his body off the wall of the ship, knocking the guard with the gun to the ground. His gun falls free. Alister pops up in mere seconds and rushes the guard who violated me, who violated his sister. He tackles him. They land just inches from me as Alister lays into the guard with his fist. I know I should move away, but I can't. My legs prick with numbness. Instead, I watch the men in horror as blood spews from the blue-eyed guard's face. The second guard struggles to pull

Alister off the other. But once he has him, it is Alister who struggles.

The guard pins him against the wall while the other collects himself. Then, using the same hand he put inside me, the blue-eyed guard buries his fist into Alister's stomach. And again. And again. Gio doesn't step in and, for a moment, I wonder why. Then I realize. If they wanted Alister dead, he'd be dead. If Gio steps in, it'll mean war. It'll mean death. Alister hunches over as I hear something crack. Our eyes meet only for a moment before he closes his in anguish. His breaths are short and labored as his rib breaks. The sight of him, *my* monster, *my* protector, outmaneuvered by two low-level greeter guards makes my insides burn even more. This is a fight we can't lose and yet, we are losing. And it's real and it's bloody and it's scary, just like Mason said. Tears fill my eyes as reality sets in. We should've run when we had the chance. What's more? We never should've come back.

The blue-eyed guard pulls Alister upright by the back of his T-shirt. "If you're done playing hero, the superiors will see you now."

AS THE GUARDS lead us through the ship, it's quiet. No footsteps. No chatter. Not even a chime of a cell phone. With the blindfold the guards placed over my eyes, I can't see a thing. But I feel everything—the bite of the ribbon that binds my wrists, the pressure of the guard's palm against my bare back as he forces me forward. Not to mention every nerve in my body is on high alert, ready to rupture if one more person touches me. I jump as the sudden sound of doors opening lets me know we're here. Wherever *here* is, I know it won't be good. The guard nudges me in the back once more and I slowly move forward as new noises fill my ears. The low hum of chatter, the clank of shoes against tile. Most of all, I hear him.

"Emma," Julian whispers.

"Julian." My voice is hoarse as his name slips across my lips, as is his. Without thinking, I move out of the guard's grasp and run in the direction of Julian's voice.

"Emma, no!" Alister yells before bursting into a fit of coughing brought on by his broken rib. I hear him scuffle with the guard once more, but I don't stop. I run full force toward—

"Ah!" I stumble backward, or I would if foreign arms didn't wrap around my torso. It isn't Julian I find in the darkness. It's—

"Well, that was easy." At that, the man with cigar breath removes the blindfold from my eyes. What I see makes me wish he'd left it on. I stand in the center of a grand ballroom painted in shades of white and gold. The perimeter of the room is lined with armed guards just like the ones who greeted us while six men of varying ages surround me. They are all in addition to the gray-haired man who pulls me tightly against him. He has the same gray gaze that stared back at me the night of Alister's ball and the same wicked smirk.

"You."

"Me." His smile grows as realization dawns on me. All this time, he was part of the brotherhood's secret council of superiors. Despite his age, his grip on me is fiercely tight. And without the use of my arms, I can't wriggle free of him. I can't get to— That's when I spot Julian and who I believe to be Mason over the gray-haired man's shoulder.

"Julian," I whisper once more. It's then that the old man shoves me into the arms of another superior wearing a suit. This one is younger and stronger. He wraps his hand around my neck and forces me to walk.

Julian and Mason are restrained, half-naked, in chairs side by side like the ones Alister uses for torture, except these chairs don't have a back. Metal poles form the shape of a cross, allowing their arms to be outstretched and their bodies to be accessible to torture from all angles. Their legs are out turned, exposing their inner thighs and groin. If they were women, no doubt the brotherhood would've removed their underwear.

I fall to my knees as the superior shoves me down at their feet. Julian looks at me with bloodshot eyes wide with fear. His cheeks are damp with tears. His chest is damp with sweat. Aside from a few bruises on his cheeks and a busted lip, he appears untouched, which means the brothers plan to torture him in front of me just as they have Mason in front of him. His lips part as if he wants to say something, but he doesn't. Instead, he drops his eyes, doing his best not to look at me as I turn to Mason. As I do, I pray for tears to keep me from seeing the horror before me. But, for once, they do not come.

Mason's brown hair, drenched in sweat, looks almost as black as Julian's. His head hangs with his chin pressed against his chest. His posture hides much of the damage done to his face. Still, his light skin is painted with blood, his blood. Cuts of different shapes and sizes cover his body from his head to his feet. The faint burnt smell in the air accompanied with the crisp clumps of blood on his chest let me know his wounds have been cauterized. No doubt to prolong his suffering. The farther down my eyes drift, the more my heart breaks. Burns shaped like the butt of a cigar cover his inner thighs. As my eyes reach his feet, I find two bloody toenails cast aside on the floor. If it weren't for the faint sound of his ragged breath, I wouldn't know whether he is alive or dead. I'm thankful for the sound, thankful he's still alive. And yet, seeing the torment he's endured, I almost wish he wasn't. At that, I break.

Screams of agony roar through me. My face contorts as rage

and sorrow fill me. My eyes feel as if they may burst from their sockets as they refuse to leave Mason, the man who taught me what it is to forgive, the man who showed me redemption is possible, the man I call *brother*. The air is sucked from my lungs as Mason struggles to lift his head. I go silent as his bloodshot eyes meet mine. Physically, he is unrecognizable. But there's something about the way he tilts his head, the way his eyes peer into mine, that allows our souls to connect. I see him inside Club Gent as he helped me escape the club of horrors. I see him in my old bedroom, begging me to find a way to forgive Beaux. I see him at Lucid, saving me and saying goodbye to his brother. Goodbye. *I love you, little brother. Take care of yourself.* Please, God! Don't let this be goodbye. Don't let this be real.

"You shouldn't have come," he says then. "They know everything." No sooner do the words leave his swollen lips do bullets fly. The deafening sound of gunfire in close quarters pulls a shrill scream from me as my ears ring. I lean forward, lowering myself to the ground as much as I can. My mind goes to Julian. I feel the need to shield him with my body, but before I can move an inch, the shooting stops.

All around the perimeter of the room, men fall to their knees as blood spews from their bodies. I take a deep breath and force myself upright. Is this it? Is it over? Please, God! Let it be over. As my eyes find Alister and Gio, still on their knees with guns to the backs of their heads, I know this Hell has only just begun. Alister's men didn't kill the brotherhood's guards. The brotherhood's guards killed Alister's men. And now, truly, all hope is lost.

CHAPTER 33

"Well, now that our unwanted guests have been dealt with and our guest of honor has arrived, this party can truly begin," the gray-haired man says. "Grab her."

Two of the superiors yank me up from the ground while the others move another torture chair directly across from Mason and Julian. My chest aches with screams that rip through me, but I don't hear them. Instead, I hear Julian and Alister as they beg for my release and struggle against their bindings. Every muscle in Julian's body is taut as he pulls against his bindings. He tries to stand and rush the man holding me while still attached to his chair. But the metal pole, somehow anchored to the ship's floor, holds him in place. The brothers cut the red silk ribbon from my hands as they prepare to bind me to their liking. For a moment, my arms find relief as they fall to my sides.

I flick my eyes to Julian as adrenaline overcomes me, numbing my fear. I tilt my chin up in defiance as the brothers force me down into the chair. Julian's lip curls as he knows what will happen next. What they plan to do to him, to me. And the fact that I will die before I let them harm either of us. Before the brothers have a chance to bind my arms, I reach for the secret pocket beneath the hem of my dress and slip my fingers through the brass knuckles with razor-sharp spikes. As I pull my hand back, I look to the man to my right, the one who's too busy taking in my cleavage to think of me as a threat. I've had to fight for my life before and I lost. I'm alive because others have stepped in. First Julian, then Mason. In a way, so has Alister. But now, it's up to me to save them and I won't fail. I won't choke. My enemies will on their own blood.

With the weight of Julian's, Mason's, and Alister's lives empowering my punch, I bring my fist to the brother's neck, severing his carotid artery. Just like Alister said, blood shoots from his neck as he falls dead to the ground. His blood sprays across my face, but I don't care. Like the color of my dress, I wear my enemy's blood with pride as I face off with the man to my left. He wraps his hand around my throat as I crash my knuckles into his ribs. He cries out, stumbling backward as the spikes sink into him. I stand. Moving toward him, I uppercut him between his legs. His dick may not be the vital organ Alister told me to go for, but it sure as Hell feels good to take away his pride and joy. His mouth opens in silent agony as his eyes roll back in his head from the shooting pain. I pull my knuckles from between his legs with the same force and disregard as the blue-eyed guard used with me.

I turn and find Alister and Gio now with guns in their hands. The two guards who held them lie in pools of blood on the floor, including the one who assaulted me. If I weren't so focused on making it out of here alive, I'd be pissed. His death should be at my hand. To Hell with guilt. To Hell with morality. This is life and death. This is revenge *and* justice. It's me or them. And by the grace of God, I won't let it be me.

Alister and Gio hold the superiors at gunpoint. Yet, they too risk taking a bullet as the brotherhood's guards surround us. I move slowly toward Mason and Julian, positioning myself between them. I don't know what will happen next, who will fire first. If I have to, I will take every bullet these guns have to offer before I let a single one hit my family. Yet, it requires only one to take a life. And, deep down, I know there is no way I can protect Julian and Mason both. As my adrenaline begins to wane, I ball my fists tighter, refusing to let my fear cripple me. The room is thick with quiet tension as the brothers look between Alister and me. And yet, despite our resourcefulness, they only laugh and clap. Even the death of their own is entertaining to them. *Sick psychos.*

"Well, I can honestly say I didn't see that coming," the gray-haired man remarks. What is he? Their leader? "Nevertheless, you're outnumbered, Blood King. Or should I be addressing the Blood Queen?" The old man turns to me then. He takes a step toward me. Alister cocks his pistol.

"One more step and I shoot," Alister warns.

The old man holds his hands up in surrender, though his carefree quip lets me know the last thing he'll do is yield. "And you'll die shortly thereafter." The man turns back to Alister. "It's obvious you have an affection for Ms. Marshall. She's wearing your family's crest after all. But she isn't family, is she?" The old man's tone becomes more serious as Alister's brow twitches. "She isn't blood. Like Sophia. Like Cara." Alister's lip curls in anger at the mention of his sisters. "You've already failed one sister, dear Alister. Would you truly leave another defenseless and at our mercy? If you haven't noticed, we don't have any." The old man gestures to Mason, whose head still slumps against his chest. I move my hand beneath his nose to check to see if he's still breathing. The soft tickle of his breath calms the tension inside me and reignites my determination to survive this.

I look to Alister and see him weighing the options in his head. If the brotherhood wanted him dead, he'd be dead. They've known about our plan this entire time and yet, they let him walk me into their den of sin. And, even still, as he holds them at gunpoint, they don't shoot. I don't know how quick Alister is with a trigger, but there are three guns pointed at him while he has only one. I don't know what the brothers have planned for him, but it's obvious they want him alive for a reason. Perhaps they believe they can make a deal with him to honor the contract his father made and supply them with drugs in exchange for Sophia's safety. If so, it's a deal I can't imagine him walking away from.

They're right. I'm not family. I'm not blood. I can't expect Alister to protect me at the risk of losing his sister. And, if he refuses them, I'm not sure what odds any of us have in surviving this. The brotherhood's guards close in. I look back and forth as I prepare to dart in front of Julian or Mason, whomever they target first.

It's then that Alister says, "You're wrong." His words draw my attention back to him. "Emma *is* family. She's worth every sacrifice. But I don't have to choose between her and Sophia. Because they are both more than capable of taking care of themselves."

At that, the double doors through which we entered fling open. Gunfire ensues as Sophia walks in with a flock of muscled men. Their arms are almost as big as their guns. Alister and Gio keep the superiors in the center of the room as Sophia and her men take out the guards around the perimeter. As bullets penetrate their skin, they squeal like the pigs they are. And I can't help but smile as my enemies, *our* enemies fall. That is, until one slick silver one charges me. As the man with gray eyes throws his body into mine, I fall to the ground.

"Emma!" Julian shouts.

My brass knuckles slip from my fingers upon impact. Before I even have time to scream, my chest aches as the man's titanium grip constricts my airway. "I promised you the slowest of deaths, but it looks like I'll just have to settle for watching the life fade from your eyes."

I shove my fist into his throat, but it doesn't have the same impact without the razor-sharp help of the brass knuckles. Julian struggles in his bindings just inches from me as I continue to fight the man. And yet, as my eyes meet Julian's, I am reminded of the moment that brought us together, the same moment that plummeted my life from one path to a life of wicked darkness that's led me here.

I flounder and try to push him off, but my efforts are in vain. My arms are paralyzed in fear as Beaux rips the life from my lungs.

As my vision fades and numbness begins to take over, I find Julian's icy green eyes once more.

"Emma, fight!"

I press my lips together, holding what little oxygen I have left inside. I won't be the victim, not again. I spot the brass knuckles to my right. Gray Eyes sees them too, but he can't reach them without removing one hand from my throat. Either way, I won't let him win. I'm a survivor, a fighter. No. Tonight, I'm a predator and he is my prey. At that, I reach for the brass knuckles just as he does. I slip my fingers through them just as Alister pulls the old man off me. Still, I don't stop. I ball my fist and punch through the man's throat, ripping his esophagus to shreds. Now it is he who will gasp for air. It is he whose life will fade from his eyes.

"*No!*" Alister shouts. Blood drips down the man's neck, staining his white button-down shirt crimson. "No. *No!*" Alister lays the man on his back as confusion washes over me. I suck in air, refilling my lungs. It's then that I notice the stillness in the room. Sophia and her men have slaughtered all the brotherhood's forces. They and Gio now hold the superiors hostage. Why they aren't dead, swimming in their excrement, dumbfounds me. Yet, nothing is more confusing than the look of horror plastered on Sophia's face and Alister's response to me killing the man who taunted and threatened me, who tried to kill me, and no doubt had a hand in Mason's torture.

I stand, slowly, taking in the fact that we've won. We're safe! No more bullets. No more blood. Well, at least not ours. "Am I missing something?" I ask.

Alister looks to me then. "I needed him alive. I need them all alive, all seven." Alister stands then as the life truly does fade from the man's gray gaze. "*Fuck!*"

"Alister! What the Hell is the problem? We won! They're all dead. At least, they will be. With Sophia and—"

"Emma," Alister bites out, turning back to me. As I spot Sophia's eyes fall to the floor behind him, dread inches its way back into my bones. "This was just the first step of the plan. You know as well as I do this organization is bigger than the men in this room. If we want to destroy them, to truly take down the brotherhood as a whole, I needed the superiors alive, including the man you just killed."

Realization digs its sharp claws into me, just like I dug my spikes into my only chance at freedom. "No," I gasp. "No, no." I shake my head, letting my brass knuckles fall into the puddle of blood pooling around me. "How was I supposed to know that? You never told me the whole plan. You never—"

"Yeah, well, I had my reasons." Alister brings his hand to his side, reminding me of his broken rib.

"Like what? What happened to all that talk of we're family, we're a team?"

"*We are.*" Alister's golden eyes peer into mine as words left unspoken float in the air between us. "I'm not the one who needs reminding of that. I kept the truth from you, but only because you kept things from me. Because nothing and no one, not even the FBI, is going to stand in my way of getting justice for my sister and ensuring the safety of the family I have left."

As realization dawns, Alister turns away from me. He knew I was working with the FBI behind his back, and he still chose to work with me. I suppose because, like he said, no one would stand in the way of his revenge, not even me. And yet, isn't that what I just did? Unknowingly, I…I killed our only chance of justice, freedom, revenge, *his* chance. He crosses the room to Sophia then. She brings her hand to his chest, sensing the brokenness just beneath the surface. "The brotherhood operates off a server," he says.

I take a deep breath. I'm glad he isn't returning the favor I dealt Gray Eyes. "The one I gained access to last year," I mumble.

"Yes." Alister nods. "That server is the key to everything—the brotherhood's club locations, their member logs, their trafficking routes and contacts, and sale records. It's everything we need to destroy them. But it can only be accessed with a series of codes, codes that only the brotherhood superiors have. One individualized code for each member that even the others don't know."

How does he know this? And yet, as his words hit me, *how*

isn't important. "That's why you needed me. That's why you needed them all in the same room at the same time." I move to Julian as my fight leaves me. All this time, I've fought the darkness inside me. I've fought the monster I felt myself becoming. The moment I gave in, the moment I felt my acts of vengeance justified, I killed my only chance at freedom. I killed my and Julian's chance at the life we've always wanted and finally had the chance of attaining. I drop to my knees then and rest my head against Julian's knee.

"Please, unbind them," I mumble. It's all I can think in this moment. All I can feel is my desperate need to hold Julian, to hold on to him and never let him go. I need him to remind me of who I am. I need him to find a way to bring hope back into my life. Because if what Alister says is true, if we just lost our only chance at destroying the brotherhood, all hope for a life of freedom, for a normal life, truly is lost.

Alister motions for his men to help Julian and Mason, though he refuses to look at me. I thought I would feel better in this moment. After all this, all this worry, all this fear, all the fighting and bloodshed, after worrying I'd never see Julian again, after thinking I wouldn't make it out of here alive, I am walking out of here with Julian, with Mason. And though the thought of my entry onto the boat still makes me sick to my stomach, I am relatively untouched compared to what could've happened, what would've happened had I not fought for my life like Alister and Julian told me to. And yet, I am not overwhelmed with the relief I'd hoped for. Because after all this, I am not free. Even if Alister tortures the codes out of the six men who are left, which I'm assuming was his plan all along, it won't matter because I killed the seventh.

Julian moans next to me as Alister's men free him from his shackles. He is slow to move as his muscles adjust to their normal positions. I push myself onto my knees so he doesn't have to move much to kiss me. I bring my lips to his without a word. For a moment, I forget where we are, that we're surrounded by death and despair, that even though we won the battle, we lost the war.

Julian brings his hands to my back. His touch is gentle, just enough to let me know he's here. His gentleness suddenly makes me aware of the soreness working its way through my arms. Though my pain is nothing compared to what Mason endured. I pull away from him then, taking in the bruises dotted along his cheekbones. He brings his hand to my neck, assessing the damage left behind by the man now lying at our feet.

"You fought," he says then. I nod, though the sentiment doesn't offer me the comfort it should.

"We lost," I whisper, dropping my eyes to his chest. He brings his fingers to my chin, forcing me to look at him with the same empowered gaze I gave him just before I broke free of the brother's grasp.

"Maybe we lost tomorrow. But today, today we won." At that, Julian brings his lips to mine once more. That is, until Alister's men remove the shackles binding Mason and he tumbles from his chair to the floor.

"Mason!" Julian and I move in unison toward him. We drop to our knees on either side of him, slipping in the blood that I now see isn't just the blood of the man with the gray gaze. It's Mason's too.

"No, no. All of his wounds were cauterized, but there's fresh blood on his chest."

"Mason, look at me. Mason, wake up. Come on, man. I can't...I can't do this without you," Julian cries out in desperation as he holds Mason's limp head in his hands.

"Where is this blood coming from?" I press my palms gently

to Mason's torso in search of the fresh wound. But it isn't the bullet holes in his chest, hidden from the naked eye beneath the brotherhood's handiwork, that let me know we've lost him. It's the ice-cold touch of his skin, his skin, which I now see is a uncharacteristically white in the few spots not covered with blood. "No!" I choke out. I move my hands from his body to my mouth to muffle my cries, but it's no use. They rip through me just as they do Julian as he rests his head against his brother's chest.

"Mason! Mason!" I scream as if my cries will bring him back to life, as if they'll make his spirit linger here in this room with us before ascending to the great beyond. But deep down, I know. He's already gone, in body, in mind, and in spirit. Like I told Demetri, life is warm and loud. Death is silent and cold. Mason is too cold. He's too cold. He passed away silently. Who knows at what moment? Did it happen instantly when Sophia barged in, triggering the shoot-out that led to his death? Or was he still with us while I fought the man with gray eyes? Did he slip away right before I killed him or after? Does he think we defeated the brotherhood, or does he know I killed our only chance at freedom? Was he still with us when Julian and I kissed? Were we too caught up in ourselves to realize he was dying? Did he try to reach out to us, to say something, to say goodbye? We'll never get to say goodbye.

Another cry rips through me as I move across the bloody floor, making my way to Julian, who still rests against Mason's cold flesh. I wrap my arms around him, giving him my warmth without pulling him from his brother. If I were him, I'd stay beside Mason forever. Because the second he lifts his head, the second his eyes meet mine is the moment his life without Mason begins. As long as he holds on, as long as *we* hold on, we can feel his presence, even if it's not the same. My body shakes as

Julian shakes beneath me. Finally, I'm forced to pinch my eyes closed, unable to look at Mason in this way. I don't want to remember this. This isn't him. This isn't the loud, goofy, over-protective man who walked into my life and heart a year ago. This isn't the brother Julian found himself reunited with just to lose again. *Again!* How much more will the brotherhood take from us?

I open my eyes then to find Alister standing over me. "Emma, Julian, I'm sorry, so incredibly sorry." It's then that Julian's body ceases shaking beneath mine. His breath catches and I release my hold on him, feeling him begin to move. He takes in Mason's body one last time. Fists balled, he looks straight ahead and forces himself to a standing position. I follow suit.

"Sorry? You're sorry?" There's an edge to Julian's voice I haven't heard before. He looks at Alister as if he wants to kill him. With Mason gone, he just might. Just the thought of losing Julian made me murderous. Now Mason is actually— I flinch as a new unspeakable reality haunts me. "How many more people have to die before they do?" Julian yells. "My brother is dead. Your sister is dead. Who else, Alister? *Emma?* Does she have to die for you to finally make good on your promise?" Julian shoves Alister, forcing him several steps back. "For you to finally live up to the hype?" He pushes him again. Alister winces as Julian's fingers jab into his ribs. "You said it yourself. You needed all seven of them alive. Now that there's no chance in Hell we get into the server, there's no reason they be allowed to take another breath when they've stolen so many."

Alister meets Julian's hard glare. I can't see Julian's face from where I stand, but I can imagine his eyes shine with murderous lust like mine did only a few hours before. Alister looks to me then. It's as if he asks for my permission. He knows as well as I do that once that line is crossed, there is no going back. Today, I killed three people. And yet, as tormented as I am, I'm not a monster for killing them. I may look like one with their blood painted across my skin, but I acted in self-defense. Even in the end when Alister plucked Gray Eyes from atop me, I couldn't be sure if he'd break free, if he'd try to kill me again. At least, that's what I tell myself. That's what I'll continue to tell myself as we rip into what's left of the brotherhood leadership, because they *will* kill again. They will continue their reign of terror and torment until someone stops them. Today, that someone is me. That someone is Julian. That someone is the Blood King and his army. My father was right. One person won't punish the crimes of the many. But the many *will* punish the crimes of monsters.

At that, I nod, giving Alister the go-ahead. As my eyes drift to the men kneeling before us, I move to Julian's side and extend my hand, offering it to him, but I don't force him to take it. For all I know, he blames me for his brother's death. The thought takes the fragile pieces of my heart and crushes them once more. That is, until Julian intertwines his fingers with mine. Warm and strong, his touch breathes life into me as death and despair surround us.

"This is going to be slow. This is going to be excruciating. This is going to be inhumane, because you are not human," Alister says, extending his hand to one of his men. From his cargo pants, a guard removes a pair of pliers and hands them to Alister. The sight of them makes me jump. I squeeze Julian's hand tighter, though I make no moves of protest, seeing as I'm sure that's exactly what the brothers used to remove Mason's toenails. The thought births fresh rage, and I can feel my cheeks burn from the inside out. And yet just as quickly as the heat of vengeance ignites, it fizzles as the Devil himself waltzes through the double doors of the grand ballroom.

He wears a gray suit, pressed, and tailored to perfection. His blond hair is slicked back. His cheeks clean-shaven. He looks too pristine to belong in this war zone and yet, here he is. There are a few ghosts I'd welcome. His is not one of them. Though, ghost, he is not. He is flesh and bone. He is ripe with life. He is Beaux Thomas.

CHAPTER 34

It's been three weeks since we confronted the brotherhood, three weeks since Mason died, and three weeks since we discovered Beaux is alive. The events of that tragic night still don't seem real. It turns out, one year ago, as the ambulance raced to the hospital with a half-dead Julian in the back, Beaux came to from a momentary loss of consciousness. Mason didn't kill him, though we thought he had. Contrary to my belief, the Thomases, Beaux's mother, had no idea her son had survived. She couldn't. No one could know the truth if Beaux was to have his second shot at life, free from the brotherhood's control. So, he sought out his old friend Alister, the only person he could trust with his unspeakable truth. Why? Because he knew of Alister's unspeakable truth. He knew of the Amato family's dealings with the brotherhood.

Alister wasn't keen on helping Beaux escape the brotherhood, considering his sister had just been abducted by them. But, in true brotherhood fashion, Beaux had blackmail that could destroy what was left of Alister's family. So, Alister had no choice but to oblige. He was the one who buried the police report I filed revealing Beaux's involvement in the brotherhood, why he was at Lucid that morning, and all his crimes leading up to the moment he came to kill me. That's how Alister knew the truth about me, my past, and my track record for investigation. He was telling the truth when he first sought me out. He wanted my help in destroying the brotherhood, because even though he helped Beaux fake his death, Beaux wasn't keen on helping him. Well, at least not on the ground level.

Beaux got Alister started on his quest for revenge, pointing him in the direction of certain people who would know enough to get Alister the answers he sought. That's how he found his contacts. That's how he found Posey. But Beaux knew Alister would never succeed at destroying the brotherhood. No one would, unless they had something or someone the brotherhood found worthy of a formal meeting—someone like me.

Beaux had been keeping tabs on New Orleans, enough to know that his mother was safe. That's how he discovered I'd returned. And that's when he convinced Alister to parade me in front of the brothers. That's when he told Alister how we could truly destroy the brotherhood once and for all, something he was now invested in, seeing as the brotherhood never bought the story of his death. That's why they sought out Mason in LA all those months back. Beaux's fresh start was made difficult by the brotherhood's unwillingness to accept his passing. And why might that be? Why would the men of the brotherhood, the superiors no less, care so much about the death of one man?

"Oh, please, don't stop on my account," Beaux says as Alister lowers his pliers to his side. His voice dances across my skin like the sharp edge of a knife. It lets me know he's real. He isn't a figment of my imagination. He isn't a ghost that haunts me

during the day or a demon in my dreams at night. He's, he's— His blue eyes meet mine. I feel my fingers loosen their grip around Julian as my body begins to sway. Julian wraps his arm around me, pulling me into his chest to hold me steady.

"What the Hell are you doing here? Alister, what is this?" Julian asks. Beaux looks to Julian with his brow slightly raised. No, please! I've already lost Mason. Kat is on her death bed. Please, don't take Julian from me too.

Beaux's eyes drift back to mine and finally he says, "This is your second chance. This is your freedom." My lips part as realization dawns on me. After everything that's happened, I thought I'd sooner die than find hope from Beaux Thomas, especially considering he himself is dead, was dead, should've — "You didn't kill the seventh man, Emma. I am the seventh man, and I am very much alive."

When I exposed the brotherhood last year, or rather, when my father exposed them in my stead, the brotherhood was forced to shut down their server to protect themselves from prosecution. It worked. But they never intended the shutdown to be permanent. But without the codes of the seven superiors, that's exactly what it was. When Alister tricked me into facing off with the brothers the night of his ball, Gray Eyes told me I had no idea how much money I'd cost them. I didn't know what he meant then, but I do now. Without access to their server, access that only Beaux could grant, they couldn't conduct business, at least not in the way they had been. And so, the brothers searched far and wide for Beaux Thomas, the man whose death sparked too many unanswered questions.

The old man who taunted me, threatened me, and tried to kill me was nothing more than a decoy. Very few people in the organization know the truth. That it's a sex trafficking syndicate controlled by a council of seven superiors. Even fewer people know who the superiors are. Which is how even Alister was fooled into thinking the old man was one of them. While we risked our lives to capture the superiors, Beaux snuck into the command room on the ship. He was standing by, waiting to enter the codes as Alister collected them by whatever means necessary. After all the codes had been entered, Beaux planned to enter his own, not revealing his presence until the very last moment when he could be sure the brotherhood would fall. Had he not shown up when he did, we would've killed the superiors thinking all hope was lost of destroying the brotherhood. But, with Beaux's help, destroy them we did, both in body and organization.

As I walk along the gravel walkway of Lafayette No. 1, the air feels lighter, the breeze cooler. The soft scent of magnolias and moss carried by the wind is sweeter. It's been three weeks and, after convincing the FBI to look the other way on Alister's behalf in exchange for the information gathered from the brotherhood's server, hundreds of arrests have been made. Low-level brotherhood members like my father to high-up orchestrators like Posey are all behind bars. But what helps me sleep better at night isn't their capture. No. It's the thousands of girls who've been rescued from their captors.

Alister was right. The server was the key to everything. Not only does law enforcement have access to all of the brotherhood's records, they have access to their records on their contacts and competitors both in North America and overseas. The takedown is ongoing, but it's underway with no chance of stopping.

After all this time, after every sacrifice, every loss, the world now knows the unspeakable truth that's haunted me for over a year. Well, they know everything except…

I turn to Julian then as the white blossoms of the crape

myrtles surrounding the Thomas family mausoleum dance in the midsummer breeze. "This is something I need to do on my own."

"Are you sure?" he asks. His bloodshot eyes meet mine as he moves his hand to my shoulder. Since Mason's passing, the tiny red veins etched across the whites of his eyes have become permanent. I nod. Julian pulls me into him, allowing me to collect what strength he has to give. "I'll be right outside." He brings his lips to my hair then. I close my eyes, relishing his touch and his minty scent.

"So will I," Alister says then, reminding me of his presence. I open my eyes and watch as Alister leans against the stone resting place where we had our first conversation. It seems so long ago. It's sad to know that it wasn't. In just a month Alister has become a permanent presence in my life while Mason... I pull away from Julian then, ready to get this over with.

"I'll be fine," I say. Though I'm not sure whether the sentiment is for Julian and Alister or myself.

As I move toward the angel-guarded entry of the Thomas mausoleum, I am reminded of Mason's words said over a year ago now.

What if he could stop hurting people? What if he could be better? When given the chance to change, when shown true empathy, even the most vile and cruel can change for the better.

I didn't want to hear Mason then. I wasn't ready to hear him. Only a month ago, I couldn't imagine granting Beaux my forgiveness.

By the time I reach the Thomases' mausoleum, I'm angry. Which, I suppose, is better than panicked. But the sight of the two stone angels guarding the entrance in quiet honor makes me take a deep breath and push my anger somewhere deep inside me. I remember the first time I saw them. I thought them so beautiful, so humble as their expressions share in the pain of the families who've suffered a loss. One holds a Bible. The other holds an olive branch. They remind me of the last conversation Beaux and I had. Fittingly, it was about forgiveness. I never gave him mine. He didn't earn it. Could he have? I haven't been to church in a while. Still, I know enough about forgiveness to know that it isn't earned. It's given freely, without condition. I told myself he had to take responsibility for what he'd done. He had to change. He never did. Now that he's gone, he never will. Is that what's holding me back? Is that why visions of him still haunt me? Because even in death, he is a monster? Or is it the realization that me forgiving him has nothing to do with him and everything to do with me? If forgiveness is what it will take to rid myself of Beaux Thomas, I worry I'll never be free of him or, rather, his ghost.

"I wasn't sure you'd come," Beaux says then. He stands with his back toward me as he examines the copper placard on which his name is engraved.

"I almost didn't." I'm thankful when Beaux doesn't turn around. Being in the same room as him is hard enough. I take a step forward and light one of the candles located on the table between us. Perhaps I do it to distract myself from the fact that I'm mere feet from the man who's beaten and raped me on multiple occasions. Perhaps I hope my prayer will grant me the strength I need to face him and to finally, after all this time, forgive him. I owe it to myself. I owe it to Mason to no longer carry this burden, this pain. I will never be free of Beaux or the world he lured me into. I know that now. Julian, Mason, Alister,

Beaux, and I are bound together by a horror that has forever stitched itself into the fabric of our souls. It's a truth I can no longer run from. But this fear, this anger, this darkness inside me is not something I will succumb to, not again.

"Why did you come? My mother extended her apologies for the charges against Julian and Mason and requested we meet two weeks ago. When I didn't hear from you, I assumed you had no intention of seeing me."

I nod, though he cannot see the gesture. After we gathered the information we needed from the brotherhood, Beaux made a deal with the FBI. In exchange for his cooperation in their investigation, his reputation is preserved as he lives the rest of his life as a free man under their watchful eye. Which means, after a year, he and his mother were reunited. His sudden reappearance required an explanation, one he reluctantly gave to the only woman whose heart he never broke. Though I suppose the truth may have. Yet, New Orleans high society, ready and willing to welcome him back with open arms, is left none the wiser. This is the part of the truth, *his truth*, that will remain hidden, hidden within the hearts of the unlucky few who know the real Beaux Thomas. Or at least, the version of him that was a monster, a rapist, a murderer, a manipulator, a liar, a cheater. It's the version of him I pray truly did die on May 31, 2020. It's the version of him I've come to forgive and to say goodbye to.

"Beaux Thomas has been dead for over a year, as far as I'm concerned. But…in all that, I never made my peace with him." I step forward then, bringing myself to stand beside Beaux. I feel him look at me, but I do not look at him. Instead, I stare blankly ahead at the copper placard, the one I sought out upon my return to New Orleans, the one I needed to see to remind me he's dead and I'm not. Today, I look upon the same placard and I say my goodbyes to the man who in many ways lives on and yet in many ways, I pray, does not.

"There was a version of Beaux Thomas I saw a life with, a version of him I loved. I think, in his own way, he loved me too. But the man I knew then, or thought I knew, was only half the man. The other half wasn't a man at all. The other half of him was a monster." My breath catches as I watch Beaux out of the corner of my eye. If my memory serves correctly, and it usually does, he doesn't respond well to his secrets and sins being exposed. When he makes no sudden movements, I continue.

"The night I said goodbye to the man I thought I knew, I met the man I never wanted to. He raped me. He hurt me," I choke out. "Even though I didn't want it to be true, even though I tried everything I could to escape my past, to escape the pain he put me through, he forever changed me. I can never go back." I bring my hand to my cheek then, wiping away a single tear as it falls. Perhaps today I mourn the death of the old me as much as I do the death of the monster who forever changed me.

"I used to think I needed the world to know my story, that I needed him to pay for what he did to me and to so many others. And if he wouldn't pay for his crimes, then I thought maybe if he could change, then I could…I could forgive him, and I could finally move on. But the truth is, I can't control what happens next, what he does, or even if my story is told. All I can control is myself. And so today I say goodbye to the monster known as Beaux Thomas. And I forgive him. Not for him. But for me. Because I deserve the second chance at life and love that I've been blessed with. I deserve to be happy. I owe it to myself to let him and all the pain he's caused go."

At that, I take the single red rose pinched between my fingers and place it in the vase attached to Beaux's grave. As I do, there is a release inside me I know I've needed, but never thought I'd manage to have. I don't know what Beaux will do now that he's resurrected from the ashes of exile. I don't know what he did during his year off the grid. What I know is that I will no longer live in fear of him, because, like Alister said, I am more than capable of taking care of myself. And what I know is that he is no longer my responsibility. If the FBI want to grant him his freedom, knowing the crimes he's committed, then they can bear the weight of any future crimes he may commit. Though, as I turn to him, sparing him only one look, I see the tears that drip from his bright blue eyes, staining his cheeks. They give me hope, hope that Mason was right. *Even the most cruel and vile, when shown empathy, can change for the better.*

"May he rest in peace," Beaux says then.

I nod. "May he rest in peace."

CHAPTER 35

As our two-story Garden District home comes into view, so does the giant U-Haul parked in front of it. I grab hold of Julian's hand then and kiss his shoulder. "It reminds me of when we first met. Remember?"

"How could I forget?" he asks. "That was the day I met my soulmate." He looks at me then just in time to see me blush. "You weren't ready for me, but I knew. There was something special about you, Emma Marshall, something I would never give up on. There still is." At that, I stand on my tiptoes to bring my lips to his.

"I'm happy for you two," Alister says then. "New Orleans is an exquisite city, but it's also a dark and dangerous one."

"Yeah, and we've had about all the dark and dangerous we can take," I say as we come to a stop beneath the oak. "When I graduated high school, I couldn't wait to get out of Presley and come somewhere new, eclectic, artsy, and diverse. New Orleans quickly became my home. I fought to stay here. I fought my mom and dad. I fought Beaux and the brotherhood. But, after everything that's happened, it's just not home anymore. At least, it's no longer the place I want to call home." I look around then, taking in the beautiful historic townhomes, the oak-lined street, the St. Charles streetcar in the distance. "I said I wanted to leave New Orleans on my terms and that's what I'm doing, that's what *we're* doing." I look to Julian. "New Orleans was never meant to be a permanent move for either of us."

Julian squints as the sun breaks through the moss-covered branches of the oak. "It looks like the movers are almost done. I'll go make sure they haven't forgotten anything and give you two a minute to say your goodbyes."

I watch Julian as he bids Alister farewell. I know him checking on the movers is just an excuse to be alone. Kat, as queen supervisor, would never let them forget anything. Though maybe she would so we'd have an excuse to spend a little more time in the Crescent City with her and Demetri before they make their official move to Alabama. She woke from her coma a few days after our night with the brotherhood. Her recovery was the burst of joy we all needed after losing Mason. But even her bright smile and bouncing strawberry curls aren't enough to quell the ache inside me, inside Julian.

"He'll be okay."

"*Hmm?*" I turn to Alister then as Julian's frame disappears inside our home. Alister looks at me with those golden eyes I'll never forget, reading the worry in the lines on my face.

"He'll be okay," he says once more. "The pain of losing his brother will never go away. The first year is the hardest. Hell, I'm going on year two without Cara and there's still a hole in my heart. I feel it every second of every day. But I think one day it'll be easier. The pain of losing her won't be as frequent. When it comes, it'll remind me of her and the love she brought into my life, the love I had for her. I'll always think of her. I'll think of what she would say, do, think. I'll wonder what she would want for her birthday, what she would've been when she—" Alister stops himself then. I hear the raw emotion in his voice as he speaks of Cara. It's the same rawness Julian and I feel every time we think of Mason.

"But maybe thinking about her, about Mason, is a good thing," he says. "Maybe, in some way, it allows them to still be a part of our lives. And maybe the fact that we aren't a part of theirs isn't the worst thing in the world. If you haven't noticed, we're kind of screwed up."

At that, we both laugh. It's been so long since I have, I've almost forgotten what it feels like. The moment of calm doesn't last long as my lip begins to quiver. "You're right. It's just... We never got to say goodbye. And the way he died, the torture he endured—" I bring my hand to my mouth to conceal the cry threatening to come out. I've done my best to be strong for Julian. I don't allow myself to cry or talk about Mason unless he does first. With him away for a moment, it gives me a chance to feel the emotions I've been bottling. Mason was, *is*, my brother. Not in the biological sense, but in every other sense he was my family.

"Come here," Alister says. He opens his arms, allowing me to rest my head over his heart. Since this is a goodbye I get to have, I take him up on the offer. He locks his arms around me, squeezing me so tight I can hear his heartbeat beneath his T-shirt. "The whole goodbye thing, it's overrated. Words are only one way of letting someone know how you feel. A lot of times they're misused or misinterpreted. But actions? Actions are the truest form of love. And you loved Mason. Julian loved Mason. He knew that. And even though he told you you shouldn't have come, I can guarantee you, deep down, he was glad you did. You showed up for him, for Julian. You put yourself at risk to save them. What greater act of love could you have given him?"

Alister brings his lips to my hair then just as Julian did a few moments before. I know Alister has feelings for me. I also know he would never act on those feelings. Nor would I allow him to. But for this moment, this final moment, I allow him to show me how he feels. Fresh tears fall from my eyes as I bottle up his affection for me and hide it somewhere deep inside me. Alister is the monster I never knew I needed, a mirror that reflects the worst parts of me. And yet, maybe he reflects more than the darkness. The way he protects his family and honors his word, the way he holds me in this very moment as if I'm the only good thing he's ever known, lets me know there is light in him too. There is light inside of me.

"I'm sorry I failed you," he whispers then.

Though he's reluctant to let me go, I pull away from him as his words work their way into my heart. "You didn't fail me, Alister."

I'd be lying if I said the very thought hadn't crossed my mind. For so long, I thought of him as invincible. And yet, he couldn't keep the blue-eyed guard from violating me. He couldn't protect Julian and Mason. Mason is dead because I had faith in Alister and his plan, a plan that Mason himself didn't even believe in. I shake my head. But…the truth is, it's not that he *couldn't* protect me or save Mason. It's that he couldn't protect me and save Mason without crushing our chances of freedom.

Mason told me if he knew Julian would die because of his choice to go after the brotherhood, he'd gladly settle for a life on the run. Now that Mason is gone, I can say the same thing. I would run for the rest of my life if he could be by my and Julian's side. But Mason also said we can't know the future, and if there's a chance we could destroy the brotherhood then we have to try. Something tells me, even if he knew he wouldn't make it out alive, he still would've wanted us to take the risk, to fight. Because that was who Mason was.

He put himself at risk to save me from Club Gent. And again, when he rescued me and Julian from Beaux. And yet again when he left the safety of our home to warn us that the brotherhood was coming after Kat. He always sacrificed himself. That was how he showed us he loved us. And no matter the sacrifice he had to make, he wouldn't have wanted us to lose our chance at freedom.

"With or without you, the brotherhood would've come for me, for Julian, for Kat, for Mason. You gave me the one thing I could never give myself, that no one else could. You gave me a shot at freedom. And for that, I thank you, truly."

Alister nods. Though neither of us say the word *goodbye*, we both feel it in our bones that this is it. This is the last time I will look upon his golden eyes. Though I'll never fully shake the bonds of this world, this world that is his, that is Beaux's, that was my father's, I know it's not where I want to belong. And Alister would never allow himself to be the reason why I find myself sucked into it yet again. We are bound by the unspeakable, by secrets, sins, and sorrow. But, most of all, we are bound by love, love of family and love of freedom, a freedom that neither he nor I am willing to jeopardize. At that, I take a step back, as does he, though our eyes remain locked.

"I don't want to know where you end up," he says then. "It's better that way." I nod and take another step back. "But you'll know where to find me, if you ever need me." Again, I nod. "For the love of God, Emma, don't need me." I laugh once more. Smiling, that's how I want him to remember me. That's how I want to remember him. So, with a smile on my face, I turn, leaving him beneath the oak as a soft summer breeze dances away with any remaining memories for us to make.

THE MOVERS WALK PAST ME, carrying the last of the boxes labeled *Kitchen*. I take a deep breath. Wanting to remember this moment, this last moment in the home that never truly became mine, I— "Emma! Emma, dear. *Wait!*" *You've got to be kidding me.* I turn, my big emotional moment shattered, as Mrs. DeClairmont races down the sidewalk from her home to mine. I swear, if she thinks today is a good day to complain, she's got another think coming. "Emma, so glad I caught you before you left."

"Mrs. DeClairmont, I really don't have time to talk," I say, stepping onto my first porch step.

"No, no. I don't want to bother you. I was *surprised* to hear of your moving so soon after you moved in, but I get it. This neighborhood probably isn't as hip and young as you and your fiancé would like."

"Yeah, that's it," I mumble.

"Well, anyway, I won't keep you, but I came across this as I was cleaning today, and I just wanted to make sure you had it before you leave."

I furrow my brows as Mrs. DeClairmont hands me a folded slip of notebook paper. From what I see, the edge is jagged as if it was torn with haste.

"We overheard you and Julian speaking in the courtyard the other night. We didn't mean to eavesdrop. I swear." She raises her hands in surrender, though I don't buy her innocent plea for a second. "We heard that Julian's brother passed away, the one who left sweet little Grey with us for those few days you were away. Anyone who has lost someone knows the value of the little things." She motions for me to open the paper.

Hi, my name is Grey. I eat two times a day, at nine a.m. and five p.m. Wet food only. Don't try to play with me. I prefer to sleep. If I sit next to you, you may pet me but don't move me. My mom and dad will be back for me soon. Please take care of me until then. When you see them, tell them Uncle Mason loves them. If he can't tell them himself, he'd want them to know.

I bite my lip to hold in the ache begging to be released. Yet, I cannot keep the tears from pouring from my eyes. He knew. Maybe he didn't know how or why. But he knew there was a chance he wouldn't make it. And he knew he'd do everything in his power to make sure Julian and I did. I drop to my bottom, sitting on my porch step. To my surprise, Mrs. DeClairmont sits with me, wrapping her arm around my shoulders.

"I am so sorry for your loss."

I nod. "Thank you."

"Emma? Emma, what's going on?" Kat asks as she makes her way onto the front porch.

"It's just this letter," I say, handing her the slip of paper. She takes it. Her forehead wrinkles with understanding.

"I didn't mean to upset you. I just—"

"No," I say, stopping Mrs. DeClairmont. "Thank you for bringing it. I know Julian— We're both very happy to have it." At that, Mrs. DeClairmont stands, leaving me with Kat. Kat takes Mrs. DeClairmont's spot next to me, wrapping her arm around me. I lean into her and rest my head on her shoulder.

"You're the one who was shot on her wedding day and in a coma for nearly a week and somehow you're still the one wiping away my tears."

Kat smiles then and hands me back the letter. "Well, it's like I said. You're never going to lose me."

I look to her then. "But I almost did."

She nods and says, "But you didn't."

WITH THE MOVERS on their way to Los Angeles and Kat recently departed, the bare home is quiet. There is no dining room table to my left. No piano to my right. All the antiques and expensive rugs are on their way to owners who will appreciate rather than loathe them. And the pantry that Anne Marshall would've been proud of is now as empty as our bank accounts. Rather than force Mr. Edgar to give up his retirement money to buy back Lucid Records, we've decided to retain ownership while bringing Mr. Edgar back on to run things. He agreed, seeing as we, as in Julian, won't be around to look over his shoulder. It'll feel like his place again, as it always should've been. Between maintaining the upkeep of Lucid Records, purchasing a new home in LA, and starting a new record label in the heart of recording country, we're a little skint. Or we will be once all the paperwork has been processed. And yet, though I have lost far more than money, I feel rich, rich with love, rich with life, rich with the possibilities that freedom offers.

I make my way up the stairs in search of Julian, not bothering to skip over the squeaky parts. In fact, I'm sure to step on each one. There's something honest about the way the stairs whine. They've seen a hundred lives. I wonder how the next one will compare to mine.

As I reach the landing, I see the door to Mason's room open. Inside, I find Julian. He sits with his back against the wall, his arms slouched over his bent knees. I take a seat next to him and pull his hand into my lap. At my touch, he breaks. "It's okay," I whisper as he rests his head on my lap. "Let it out."

I brush my fingers through his soft, tousled hair as his tears drench my bare skin. There was a time when he found me in a similar position. We hardly knew each other then. And yet, he held me. He danced with me. He allowed his presence to chase away my tears, my pain. I'd like to say that was the moment I started falling for him. But the truth is, like him, I knew there was something special about him the very first moment we met, something I could never give up on. And I won't.

"Dance with me," I say. Julian wipes his tears from his cheeks and stands, pulling me up with him. Just as we did the night he found me crying on the floor at Lucid Records, we dance to no music at all. The silence isn't deafening as the warmth of life burns between us. Though it's impossible to feel our warmth without thinking of the chill of death that slithered from Mason to us the moment we realized we'd lost him.

Julian pulls me tighter against him, burying his face in the crook of my neck. His lips tickle my skin as he speaks. "When I came to New Orleans it was to get away from Mason. My life in LA was nothing but a broken mess after my parents passed. And Mason, he…he blamed me for what happened."

"But you two worked through that," I say. "He didn't blame you in the end." I know guilt. It's a heavy burden I don't want him carrying.

"I know," Julian says. "But now that we're leaving, it just…" Julian lifts his head, allowing his eyes to meet mine. We stop our dance, though we don't let go of one another. We never will. "It feels like I'm leaving him behind. This was the last place he was alive and once we leave—" He looks away from me.

"Hey." I pull him back to me. "We don't have to go. I can call the movers and have them back in an hour."

"No. That's not what I want, I just—"

"You want your brother."

Julian's icy green eyes shine even brighter as tears blur his vision. He nods as a single tear falls, leaving a damp streak down the center of his cheek. "I don't know how I'm supposed to do this without him. He's always been there, you know? Even when I ran away, he chased after me. Maybe he'd still be alive if he hadn't."

"Guilt and regret are wicked tools of torment. Please don't blame yourself for what happened. Mason made his own choices. We both know that. And one thing is certain, he always chose you. He always chose family." It's then that I hand Julian the note given to me by Mrs. DeClairmont.

"Mason may not have known how his story would end. But, from the sound of things, it seems like he knew he may not make it. And what's clear is that he would've done anything, no matter the risk, to make sure you did." I bring my hands to Julian's face, wiping away the fresh tears that fall. "It's like you said, he's always been here. And he always will be. No matter where we go or what happens, his spirit will live on in us, in you. And as far as this thing called life goes, we'll do it together, because that's what partners do. That's what husbands and wives do."

CHAPTER 36

One Year Later

My pear-shaped engagement ring weighs heavily on my finger as my mom zips me into my wedding dress. I lift my eyes to the floor-length mirror before me, taking in the reflection of a woman I finally recognize. I've been engaged before. I've tried on more wedding dresses than I can remember. I didn't know then why the dresses never fit right or looked right, why they never made me feel the way I do now. I know now things didn't work out in my past not only because I wasn't with the right man, but also because I wasn't ready. I was too young to know myself let alone know what I wanted in a man. I wasn't prepared to demand the respect I deserved or even to notice when I wasn't receiving the bare minimum.

When Julian walked into my life, I wasn't ready for him. I wasn't ready for love. Yet, he made me believe in it again. In a way, he made me believe in it for the first time. He loves me in the way I deserve to be loved, with respect, honor, loyalty, with a forgiving and understanding heart, with an open mind, with a shoulder for me to cry on and a hand ready and willing to pull me out of the darkness. But more than love, Julian makes me believe in myself. He gives me a reason to hope, to fight, to live. He's never given up on me and he's never allowed me to give up on myself. How do I know it's right? How do I know he is the man meant to be mine? I know, because in my darkest times he brings me peace, not more pain. He is the light that chases away the darkness, the angel who saved me from my demons.

I used to worry I'd destroy him, that my darkness and my demons would consume him like they consumed me. But the past year has shown me Julian needed me as much as I needed him. I am his strength just as he is mine. And so, today I stand, dressed in white lace and chiffon, finally at home in my own skin and at peace in my own life. My blond curls flow freely, with a touch more hairspray and teasing than I'm used to, but still. There is no need for fuss. No insane amount of makeup on my face or bobby pins in my hair. No painful shoes strapped around my feet. Instead, I wear a pair of single diamond earrings passed down to me from my mother and the most gorgeous dress I've ever seen.

The bodice of my dress is sheer as are the long sleeves covering my arms. Like Julian's tattoos cover his skin, flowers made of white lace dot up and down my arms and over my chest. The haphazard lace pattern continues onto the shorts hitting at my upper thigh. My mom almost coughed up a lung when she realized my wedding dress was hardly a dress at all. To be honest, I didn't wear the skirt at our first fitting just to mess with her. But today, pinched around my waist is a flowing chiffon skirt with slits that reveal the lace of the shorts as I move. It's sexy, comfortable, and light enough to blow in the Malibu breeze as I marry my best friend at a vineyard in the Santa Monica Mountains.

"There was a time when I thought this day would never

come. Now that it's here, I certainly never expected it to look like this," my mom says, taking me in.

"Me either. But it's right, Mom. It's really, truly, completely right." I offer her my hand. She takes it, giving me a squeeze.

"I'm going to take my seat. Are you sure you're okay to walk alone?" she asks me.

I move my eyes from her to the mirror once more. Secrets and scars rest quietly beneath the surface of my skin. They remind me of what I've been through. Like the painting that first brought me and Julian together, like the mural Julian splayed across the concrete wall of Lucid Records, my past proves to me we have both good and evil inside us. We are both human and inhumane. Man, and monster. Without each piece of us, even the most tragic pieces, we wouldn't be us. I wouldn't be me. And who I am today is a woman who *can* walk alone, who is no longer afraid of her broken parts or the darkness swirling inside her, but ready and willing to tap into them should the world bring another war to her door.

"Yes, I'm okay, Mom." My mom leaves me with a smile. I grab my bouquet and ready myself to walk the stone path to where Julian waits. For now, I'm done fighting, done hiding, done running. It's time for me to live. As I walk through the wooden doors of the vineyard house, down the stone steps, and out onto the veranda, I think back to the vision of Julian and my wedding that came to me as Beaux fired his gun at my head two years before. In my vision, as Julian raced down the aisle and took my hand, I didn't know if I was alive or if the altar before us would open wide, transporting me into the next realm. Still, I walked with him toward the unknown. I walked hand in hand with Julian because I knew no matter where I was headed, I wanted him by my side.

Today, as I take Julian Christopher Cole to be my lawfully

wedded husband and the father of the children I hope to one day have, I take that same simple vow, to walk with him hand in hand through any and all of life's storms and sanctuaries. He is mine and I am his. And, for the very first time, the life I've always wanted is mine to have. What's more? I believe I *can* have it, because I know I will do anything to protect and preserve it.

Julian

IF YOU WOULD'VE TOLD me two years ago that I'd both lose my life and find it in the mysterious, music-filled city of New Orleans, I would've told you you're crazy. I left Los Angeles when I lost my family and disappointed the bit I had left. I wanted to hide from myself, not find myself. What I found in that two-bedroom cottage once owned by the grandfather I never knew, in the dusty French Quarter record shop, and in the girl next door was more than I bargained for, more than I could've ever asked for. And yet, everything I needed. Now, I'm back in LA with all blood ties to this city severed. But I'm not alone. I'm more alive and at home than I've ever been.

My angel walks toward me now, the one whose brokenness mirrored my own, the one whose strength has built us a home. I smile as the same breeze rushing through my hair sends her dress flying behind her. She laughs. *God.* That's a sight I'll never grow tired of. She's a woman, a soul, I'll never let go of.

Emma stands before me now in front of the only people we care about and God as the setting sun sets the grand Santa Monica Mountains aglow. In all the natural beauty surrounding us, the mountains, the grapevines, the sliver of ocean in the distance, she is the most beautiful thing I see, the only thing I see as my life, my future plays out in her warm eyes. Pastor Tom motions for Emma to begin her vows. She blushes as Kat hands her a folded piece of notebook paper. I brace myself. Though I know nothing she says now will compare to the love she's already given me.

It's then that she says, "I used to wonder what life would be like if I'd met you first. But, as I stand here today, I couldn't be more thankful that I met you last."

ABOUT THE AUTHOR

Emily A. Myers is an author of romantic suspense and mystery, thriller, and suspense titles. Emily enjoys writing complex characters in the midst of intense conflict. When not writing, Emily enjoys bingeing the latest Netflix series, traveling, and spending time with her friends and family. Readers can connect with Emily on social media @emilymyersauthor or via her website www.emilyamyers.com

CPSIA information can be obtained
at www.ICGtesting.com
Printed in the USA
LVHW090605090322
712468LV00008BA/6

9 798985 028218